The sidewalks of Steel Canyon shook. Streetlamps swayed. A large window in a storefront facing Blyde Square shattered, and screams of panic rang out.

"It's not an earthquake," Maiden Justice said. "This rumble is the sound of automatons on the move."

She pointed to the Southern United Building, half a block away. The pavement in front of the skyscraper was crumbling. Huge chunks of earth and cement burst outward from a widening pit. The road collapsed as a huge claw ripped open the street from one side to the other. Burst mains spewed water high into the air.

Immense forms appeared in the water and dust rising from the pit. The robots' metallic shells were twenty feet in diameter and edged with a rotating blade. These hulking brutes stood a little more than four feet off the ground and balanced on six black metallic legs that marched in perfect synchronization. A dozen metal stalks rose above each machine's inner rim. Four held mechanical eyes, shielded with armor and shatterproof glass, while the rest carried weapons. In the first trio of automatons, these were flame throwers.

"I think Nemesis has opened his bag of tricks," Statesman said grimly.

"City of Heroes flies high above the competition, thanks to its staggering character-customization options, its immersive setting, and hands-down the most creative use of source material we've ever seen in this type of game."

— *Computer Gaming World*

CITY OF HEROES

THE WEB OF ARACHNOS

ROBERT WEINBERG

CDS BOOKS

NEW YORK

ACKNOWLEDGMENTS

First and foremost, I'd like to thank Jack Emmert for letting me play with his signature creation, Statesman. Thanks also to Sean Michael Fish, creator of Lord Recluse, for all of the time he spent with me on the phone and the hundreds and hundreds of pages of documents he sent to me. Without question, I'd like to thank everyone at Cryptic Studios, NC Soft, and CDS for their support and encouragement during the writing of this novel.

Special thanks must be given to James Lowder, my editor for this book and the person who got me involved in the project in the first place. Jim's extremely helpful suggestions and concept brought order to chaos and made this book a joy to write.

Thanks to George Pérez, one of the giants of comic book art, for his fabulous cover for this book.

Thanks to Angeline Hawkes-Craig, who served as first reader for the book and who caught some of my more glaring errors of logic. Way to go, Angeline!

Thanks, of course, to my wife, Phyllis, who let me describe in great detail how much fun I was having writing this book. And to my son, Matt, who helped me explore some of the more dangerous areas of Paragon City.

Thanks to the Moody Blues, Las Ketchup, George Harrison, Vanessa-Mae, Billy Joel, Kylie Minogue, the Buggles, Pink, Bruce Springsteen, Twelve Girls Band, and especially to Robin Luke for "Susie Darlin." All sources of constant musical inspiration.

And, most of all, thanks to the many players of *City of Heroes,* who made this novel possible.

This book is dedicated to Murphy Anderson, Jim Steranko, Reed Crandall, Wally Wood, Gardner Fox, Julius Schwartz, Stan Lee, Roy Thomas, Chris Claremont, Will Eisner, and Roy Krenkel, who made superheroes so much fun!

Robert Weinberg
Oak Forest, Illinois
February 18, 2005

CHAPTER ONE

Fog—deep, dark, and dank—gripped tight the streets of London as Big Ben tolled eight o'clock. It was the evening of the first of December, 1929. As if summoned by the clock's mournful sound, eight sturdy men, all clad in the heavy brown tweed topcoats of the Metropolitan Police, materialized like ghosts from the mist. One by one, they gathered beneath the dim glow of the solitary streetlamp illuminating the rear entrance of the famed British Museum. Three of the octet wore caps, while the rest went without. A steely-eyed bunch, they carried themselves like soldiers, which many of them had been during the Great War, fought little more than a decade earlier.

Their leader, for there was no question to his identity, was a trim, sinewy man standing slightly over six feet tall, with thick muttonchop whiskers and penetrating eyes. He went by the name of James Lancaster and he exuded a toughness that went beyond skin deep. Here was a man who had experienced all the hardness of the world and refused to back down. There was no surrender in Inspector James Lancaster of the Criminal Investigation Division.

Standing to Lancaster's right and a step behind was his assistant and comrade-in-arms, "Tiny" Timothy Benton. Towering six foot six, Benton possessed the chest and shoulders of a great African jungle gorilla. His arms were massed with muscle. Huge hands like shovels ended in long fingers that could envelope a billiard ball and crush it to powder. A quiet, even-tempered man, Benton was said to have grown up in the same rough neighborhood of London as his friend Lancaster. Whatever the truth—and no one knew for sure—the two men were very close.

The rest of the bunch, six in all, were as rough and tumble a group of constables as had ever been seen in the Metropolitan Police. Hard men, they were grizzled veterans of the street who could take a pounding or dish it out. This was Lancaster's team, assembled over the past two years, trained and thrashed and bullied into becoming the roughest, meanest, most decorated band of "coppers" ever to walk the dark streets of London. The scourge of the British underworld, they were a law unto themselves. Yet, for all their successes and their commander's relentless strategies, there was a single annoying blot on their record.

One criminal mastermind had managed to elude them for the past twenty-four months. He was a faceless, unseen genius, an American soldier of fortune who only stole the rarest of antiques and the most spectacular of curiosities. His name, according to the taunting letters he sent to the newspapers, was Marcus Cole. James Lancaster had sworn that the mystery man's criminal career would end tonight, no matter the price.

Scowling, Lancaster gave his team their final once-over. His thick brows furrowed in concentration as his penetrating gaze surveyed the officers man by man, weighing them, judging them. It wasn't until the huge clock drummed its last note that he finally nodded his satisfaction. His features broke into the slightest of smiles. "This is the finish," he declared, stating it as an indisputable truth. "The end for—"

Lancaster coughed, breaking his sentence. It was a deep, wracking hack that shook his whole body, a cough that came up howling from his lungs and turned his face white with pain. "Sorry," he muttered, wiping a bead of sweat from his brow. "My apologies."

All of the inspector's men knew about his bad lungs. He was one of many unfortunates who had fought in the Second Battle of the Marne and inhaled a whiff of the Boche's deadly mustard gas. He'd been one of the lucky ones who survived, but there was no cure for the unholy poison, which had been sapping his strength and stamina for years. Time was running out for James Lancaster.

Which was why the Marcus Cole case had to come to an end that night—or remain a mystery forever. The master criminal had made it clear in letters posted to the *Times* that when James Lancaster retired, so would Marcus Cole.

"Watch ho," called a voice from the landing at the top of the sixteen marble steps leading from the street to the museum. A solitary man dressed in a black tuxedo, white dress shirt, and white tie, and wearing a silk top hat, held a gas lantern high up in the air. The beams of radiant light seemed to freeze the patrol in place. "Is that you, Inspector Lancaster?" asked the man. He was an elderly gentleman with white hair, thick white beard, and ruddy red cheeks. A crimson rose was pinned to his left lapel. He possessed the voice of a foghorn. "Come on up, if it's you."

Up the steps, in two lines, went the police officials, side by side in quarter time. Lancaster and Tiny Tim were last to arrive. As they did, the old man pulled out a large gold watch from an inner pocket and stared at its face. "Five minutes past the hour. Prompt by police time, I expect, though I prefer my ship run on a tighter schedule."

"My apologies, Sir Bertram," replied Lancaster with the slightest of bows.

Sir Bertram Whiteside, the museum's director, hadn't been on a ship in fifty years, but he still liked to pretend he was a master sailor. From what accounts of the director's exploits Lancaster had been able to obtain, Whiteside would be wise to keep his past a closed book. But Lancaster knew better than to criticize his betters. Especially since the director was one of the biggest contributors to the police pension funds.

"Tut, tut, not a serious breach of discipline," said Sir Bertram after a moment. "Though I would like it better if your commander would make his appearance. The exhibit opens promptly at eight-thirty, which gives us just enough time for your men to station themselves throughout the hall."

The director sucked in a lungful of fog, clearing the space around his face for an instant. A trace of apprehension haunted his eyes. "You're sure that this man Cole will make a try for the scroll tonight? This isn't some wild goose chase that will cost the museum thousands and only result in bad publicity?"

"While nothing in this universe is certain, Sir Bertram,"

said Lancaster, "I think it's a safe gamble to assume Cole and his gang will be among tonight's crowd. As you well know, he tends to strike on the first evening of an important exhibition."

"That's because the opening night is when the rarest of the rare are displayed," said Sir Bertram. "It's standard practice, done to impress a museum's wealthiest benefactors. Our best must be served."

"Of course," replied Lancaster. "Cole knows that, as well. He also knows that within a day or two after an exhibit opens, the curators will often lock away the most precious gems and the most rare curios, making them all but impossible to steal. Since Cole only wants the best, he invariably strikes on the show's first night."

"Quite logical," said Bertram. "I knew Cole favored opening nights, but never gave much thought as to why. Obviously, you did, Inspector. You know Cole like a brother."

"Closer," said Lancaster. "Cole's string of robberies started shortly after my transfer from Berkshire to London. He was my first case and my only failure. I've spent my every spare moment for the past three years studying his crimes, analyzing his methods. If it's the last thing I do, I'll bring Marcus Cole's reign of terror to an end."

"Tonight will be the night," declared a deep, loud voice chopping through the dense fog like a machete. The speaker stepped into the light. Bald, with a curled moustache and bright blue eyes, he stood nearly as tall as Lancaster but weighed twice as much. A big, solid man, he wore a starched white shirt so tight the pearl buttons looked ready to explode. His black tie barely encircled his huge neck. His fingers, encased in white gloves, looked like sausages. One of the most famous men of his time, here stood Lieutenant Colonel Sir Hugh Turnbull, chief inspector of Scotland Yard, nicknamed "the Walrus," for obvious reasons, by the Sunday *Post*.

"Tonight will be the night, my dear boy," repeated Colonel Turnbull, slapping Lancaster on the back with a ham-sized hand. He chuckled, as if laughing at some joke only he had heard. "Tonight, Inspector, the amazing truth will finally be revealed!"

"Well, come on then," said Sir Bertram, beckoning impatiently. "Into the hall, gentlemen. The doors for the public will be opening shortly. We have no time to spare."

A service hallway took them to a doorway at the rear of the exhibit hall. Hurriedly, the police officers filed into the huge room. It was a magnificent hall, with gilded white marble columns, elaborately carved and lacquered wood floors, and an intricately painted roof some fifty feet up in the air. Gigantic glass chandeliers hung from the bright white ceiling. There were no windows and the only access to the hall was through a massive pair of doors connected to the museum's main concourse.

Each exhibit consisted of two huge glass display cases resting on a specially designed table four feet wide by twelve feet long. Surrounding the exhibit were eight gold poles connected into a large rectangle by a thick velvet rope. In all, there were six stations in the hall. The number was no coincidence.

Without prompting, each constable took up a position between and behind two of the glass cases. His duty was clear. No one, under any circumstances, was to open a display. Inside each transparent box rested one or more of the museum's fabled pieces from the Lost Treasures of the

Library of Alexandria collection. It was, without doubt, the finest collection of Greek and Roman papyrus scrolls ever assembled in one place.

"Ten minutes until the opening," said Whiteside, checking his gold watch once again. "Everything appears to be in place. I suspect that a robbery, Inspector, will be quite impossible."

"Cole considers the impossible a challenge," noted Lancaster.

"Indeed he does," said Colonel Turnbull. "Over the years, Scotland Yard's compiled quite a dossier on the man. I can't help but admire his fortitude, if not his actions. He was born in the slums of Paragon City, the largest metropolis in the United States, in 1898. His mother died giving birth to him and his father drank himself to death. Yet Cole managed to rise above his beginnings and organized the dock workers union when he was only sixteen."

"A labor agitator?" said Whiteside, frowning. "Was he a Socialist?"

"Perhaps," said Turnbull. "Cole and his older brother, Ezra, were raised by a family friend, an Austrian immigrant named Rudolf Richter. The man's politics were questionable, to say the least. He was a leftist for sure. Had a son, Stefan, who became Cole's closest friend. Still, they didn't lack for patriotism. When war was declared, they both enlisted in the army. Our last records place the pair in France in 1918."

"A possible Socialist who turned into a thief," said Lord Whiteside. "How fascinating. Does he rob from the rich and donate his loot to the poor?"

"Not according to our records," said Turnbull. "There's no record of him giving anything away. The war changed

Cole. It hardened the man, made him bitter. Afterward, he became a soldier of fortune and a master criminal. A good man gone wrong. What a waste."

"You sound sympathetic, Colonel," said Lord Whiteside. "Perhaps you and Cole are brothers under the skin. After all, you, too, served in the Great War. As did Inspector Lancaster."

"A good point, my lord," said Turnbull. "But there's one difference between us and the rogue. We're not criminals."

"Enough about Mr. Cole," said Lancaster. The inspector had moved so that he now stood in front of the lead exhibit, the glass case closest to the door. His shadow, Tiny Benton watched from two steps back.

"What, if I may ask, is the most important scroll in this collection?" asked Lancaster. "What piece is worth the most?"

"You're standing right next to it," said Lord Whiteside. He walked over to the front case. "Here's our treasure. We acquired the manuscript five years ago in Egypt for a hefty sum. It's the earliest known transcription of the *Histories* by Herodotus."

"Herodotus," repeated Lancaster. "Seems I remember his name from my school days. Some Greek explorer or such?"

"The father of history," said Whiteside. "We owe much of our knowledge of the ancient world to his histories, which described his travels."

"Greek or not, you can bet that's Cole's target," said Lancaster. "I might not know history, but I know my criminals. I'd stake my career on it."

"The scroll?" said Lord Whiteside. "Why on earth would this Cole fellow want our *Histories*?"

"Ransom," said Turnbull, walking over to the men. He stared at the rolls of papyrus. "He'd sell it back to the museum."

Lancaster shook his head. "That's not Cole's style. He only steals rarities for a purpose. What he takes, he keeps."

"Knowledge, then," said Whiteside. "Herodotus delivered his *Histories* as a series of lectures throughout ancient Greece. Over the course of his life, he changed the text, added and discarded information. This extremely early transcription might contain some information not available in other, later versions."

"You mean like the whereabouts of a treasure?" asked Turnbull. He laughed. "Still undiscovered after three thousand years? My word, how ridiculous!"

"Perhaps not," said Lancaster. "Who knows what Cole thinks. What is the time, my lord?"

"Five minutes to go," said Whiteside, glancing down at his watch. He sniffed at the rose pinned to his collar. "Time for me to step outside and welcome the crowd."

"I think not," said Lancaster. He reached into the inner pocket of his overcoat and pulled out an army pistol. Without wasting a motion, he placed the cold steel of the gun barrel against the startled director's cheek. "The time for masquerades, I'm pleased to announce after three long years, is over."

Without a whisper of sound, all the constables pulled firearms from beneath their tweed overcoats. Tiny Benton held a huge shotgun that looked powerful enough to knock down an elephant.

"My dear Inspector Lancaster, can it really be true that you are the notorious Marcus Cole?" Chief Inspector

Turnbull did not sound the least bit surprised to be asking the question. "No wonder he was the one crook you could never apprehend. After all, it's difficult for one half of a man to catch the other half. These other officers are your gang, I assume, and this giant must be the notorious Stefan Richter."

"One and the same," said the big man. "You're less emotional about all this than I thought you'd be, Colonel. I bet Marcus that when we finally revealed our true identities, you'd have a fit."

"A fit?" The colonel seemed genuinely amused. He glanced over at Lord Whiteside, who looked as if his precious scrolls had just been lit on fire. "Please try to calm down, Sir Bertram. There's nothing to worry about. Your treasures are safe. Besides, these men are honorable thieves. They hunt only for booty, not violence or revenge. No one will die tonight, unless we force the issue."

"Force the issue?" said Marcus Cole, looking up from the glass case that held the scroll of Herodotus. "No chance of that happening. We're already in control of the papyrus. Within a few minutes, when the doors open, we'll announce a robbery has taken place and go dashing off after the criminals. Sooner or later, you two gentlemen will be found tied up in the rear closet. Meanwhile, my crew and I will be on our way to a lavish holiday in Switzerland, spending the spoils we've collected during our three years of working both sides of the law."

"A brilliant plan," said the chief inspector. "Except for one fatal flaw. Carefully, very carefully, stick your nose out the front door, Mr. Richter, and tell me what you see."

Richter looked at Marcus. Marcus nodded; he was

starting to feel a tingle of apprehension. Turnbull was accepting things far too calmly.

Inching the front door open a crack, Richter peered into the museum's main hall. "It's packed with cops," he reported. "All the rich and famous in the city are milling out there, but there's also at least thirty policemen barring the doors. Maybe more."

"If you check the rear entrance," said the chief inspector, "you'll discover the situation is the same, minus the civilians. I brought in several dozen of my best men from outside the city to handle your arrest. You and your gang are completely surrounded."

"Magnificent! Caught red-handed at the scene of the crime." Marcus nodded his approval as he etched the top of the glass case with a diamond-tipped cutting blade. "I'm impressed with your deductive powers, Sir Hugh. How did you ever connect Inspector James Lancaster with the notorious Marcus Cole? I prided myself on immersing my personality in the character I was playing. Some days, I never once thought of Marcus Cole. And all of my men did equally well. For three years, we were the best squad of constables working for the Metropolitan."

"That you were," said Colonel Turnbull, still smiling. "You solved the numerous small crimes assigned to you, even as you committed larger capers under your Cole alias. It was a grand scheme. You might have succeeded tonight if one of your old army buddies, a chap named Blair, hadn't come to me several weeks ago and revealed the deception. Gave me just enough time for me to arrange this trap."

"Betrayed by an old friend," said Marcus. He lifted out the piece of cut glass, reached into the case, and pulled out the Herodotus scroll. "What a cruel jest. Tonight was our last scheduled job. Both Inspector Lancaster and Marcus Cole were scheduled to disappear this evening, leaving a puzzle for the police to ponder for years to come."

"That puzzle is solved," said Turnbull. He held out a hand. "Surrender your weapons this moment and I'll make certain that none of you are hurt."

"A fair offer," said Marcus, "but not to my liking."

He pointed at the chief inspector and the museum director. "Tie them up securely and leave them in the rear closet. Then, let's prepare for the show."

"The show?" said Turnbull, sounding puzzled, just before he was gagged and bound and tossed along with Sir Bertram in the cloakroom. No one bothered to answer his question. They were all too busy.

Off came the heavy brown tweed topcoats and caps. Next the men tugged off their pants and shirts. If he had still been watching, Chief Inspector Turnbull would have gasped in surprise. Beneath their uniforms, the men were wearing tuxedo pants, dress shirts, and ties. With a quick rip, out came the linings of their topcoats, revealing tuxedo jackets and dress shoes. After weeks and weeks of practice, it took the entire crew less than a minute to transform from policemen into gentlemen.

Several of the gang had even packed folding top hats that they opened and then put on. Two of the men, approximately the same size as Sir Bertram Whiteside, attached phony white beards to their chins and pinned bright red roses to their collars. The pair barely resembled the museum's director, but in a rush, barely was more than enough.

"Everyone remember his part?" asked Marcus, knowing

the question was unnecessary. These men—*his* men—were a well-trained unit, and had functioned as such since their army days. "Hobart, you're at the lights. Gleason and Sawyer are the phony directors. Remember, split-second timing makes this deception work."

"See you all ten days from tonight," said Stefan Richter. "You know the place—across the street from the Eiffel Tower."

Marcus grimaced. Sometimes Stefan spoke without thinking. He should never have mentioned their rendezvous point with Colonel Turnbull so close at hand, even if he was trussed up in the closet. Plans would have to be changed.

Marcus coughed, a flicker of bright red blood crossing his lips. No time to inform the others now about the new rendezvous point. He'd contact them later, when things were settled. Angrily, he wiped the blood from his mouth with a tuxedo sleeve. He hated revising plans at the last minute. He pushed the thought from his mind. It was time to begin.

"All ready?" he asked. "Then, on my mark, begin to count back from sixty. Begin: Sixty . . . fifty-nine . . . fifty-eight . . ."

Moving at a deliberate, unhurried pace, the eight men scattered. They all had their jobs and knew exactly what was expected of them. Gleason headed for the rear entrance, Sawyer for the main doors.

"Forty-eight . . . forty-seven . . ."

Hobart located the light switches for the hall. The rest of the crew took their positions next to the glass cases.

"Thirty-five . . . thirty-four . . ."

The two men disguised as Sir Bertram Whiteside were

just pulling open the doors to the front and rear entrances of the hall when the countdown came to an end.

"Three . . . two . . . one!"

"Help! Help!" shouted a false director at the exhibit hall's front doors. He rushed out into the crowd of policemen. "The crooks are already inside and stealing the treasure!"

"Help! Help!" bellowed a false director at the museum's back entrance. "The crooks are disguised as police and have gained access to the hall. They're stealing everything!"

In a mad rush, the forty constables stationed in the front of the museum dashed into the exhibit hall. At the same instant, the twenty constables stationed at the rear also swarmed into the room. The officers at the front doors, spotting the policemen at the back, immediately assumed *they* were the criminals. The constables in the rear, seeing the mass of officers at the front, instantly jumped to the conclusion that *they* were the lawbreakers. Almost in unison, men from both groups shouted at the top of their lungs, "Halt, you're under arrest!"

The confusion might have been straightened out in a few seconds, except that, as planned, the lights in the exhibit hall went dark.

Glass crashed as the barrels of five guns smashed into the display cases. A shotgun roared, its charges aimed harmlessly into the floor. Someone screamed, "Thieves, thieves!" Then a second cry went up, and a third. The museum guards joined the fray, and the chaos spread to the crowd milling outside the exhibit hall. Several matronly women fainted. An elderly gentlemen adorned with a chest full of medals collapsed, gasping for air.

"Don't panic!" yelled an unseen man in the crowd, so, of course, everyone panicked. The museum guards, not trained for such a crisis, rushed about doing nothing. Constables searched through the dark for other officers they recognized, but since all of them came from outside London, no one was familiar with anyone else. A few constables trained in crowd control tried to control the crowd, but the guests, being composed primarily of the British upper crust, weren't in the habit of obeying orders. What had begun as an exercise in disorder soon turned into a full-scale riot, and no one caught up in the mayhem noticed eight men in tuxedos leaving the premises. Exactly as Marcus Cole had planned.

"That worked well," said Stefan Richter, sitting next to Marcus Cole in the back seat of a taxi speeding them to the railway station some twenty minutes later. The big man loosened the white dress tie around his neck. "One of your best schemes."

"I thought so, too," said Marcus. He looked out the rear window for the tenth time since leaving the museum for pursuit. "I'll have to send the colonel a note of thanks. He arranged everything exactly as I'd hoped he would."

"Do you think he'll ever realize that Blair was working for us all along?" asked Stefan.

"Anything's possible," said Marcus, laughing. "Though in regards to Scotland Yard ever figuring out precisely what happened tonight, I have my doubts."

CHAPTER TWO

He deserved more credit. Plus a bigger share of the loot. But as long as Marcus was in charge of their gang, Stefan knew he'd get neither.

With the wave of a hand, he summoned the waiter. "Another," he said, pointing to his empty wineglass. "This time, leave the bottle."

"Don't overdo it," said Marcus in a soft voice that couldn't be heard beyond their table. Stefan expected no less. Marcus was no saint, but he didn't like anyone drinking on the job. Marcus believed in rules, too many rules for Stefan's liking. Still, there was no arguing with the man's success. For the money Cole made, Stefan was willing to put up with Marcus's silly rules. Just not forever.

"We need a bottle," said Stefan, slowly turning his head to take in all the tables of the outdoor café. Dozens of small tables stretched out a half-block, covering the wide sidewalk from the storefront to the cobblestone street. Though the opera had let out an hour earlier, the café was still packed with theatergoers and cast members.

"The wine serves as protective camouflage. With a bottle on the table, we're merely two French businessmen out for a late supper. No drinks would mark us as outsiders, tourists, Americans. You know the French, Marcus. Even the peasants raise a glass or two with dinner."

"You're right, of course," said Marcus. He coughed, raising his handkerchief to his mouth. That terrible hacking cough had grown more and more common the past few months. Stefan had a bad feeling about that cough. Too often, the white handkerchief came away from Marcus's mouth stained with blood. Neither of them talked about the coughing but Stefan knew the sickness was growing worse. Marcus was dying. It was a terrible death and Stefan understood his friend was doomed. Unless the information in the stolen *Histories* saved him.

"I wish you'd kept your mouth shut at the museum last week," said Marcus. "Meeting at an outdoor café is not my idea of a sane rendezvous."

"Relax," said Stefan. "Turnbull is still scouring London looking for us. We're safe in Paris."

"I hope so," said Marcus. "Nothing much we can do anyway till the others arrive. Pour me a glass of wine, too. No reason for me to save my money. Better spent on myself than donated to the Widows and Orphans Fund."

"Ain't that the truth?" said Stefan. He filled Marcus's glass and his own. "A toast, then. To loot!"

"To Herodotus," said Marcus, draining his glass to the last drops.

Ten days had changed both their appearances. Gone were all traces of Inspector Lancaster and his assistant, Tiny Tim Benton. Marcus was clean-shaven, though his cheeks and chin were still bleached white from three years' lack of sun. He had a noble chin, a firm jaw, and a slightly flattened nose, the result of a dock fight fifteen years earlier. He possessed the air of a born leader, mixed with the subtle confidence of a sophisticate, a man who was never at a loss for the right thing to say or the right thing to do.

Stefan was all-American. Gone were any indications of the Irish cop he had played to perfection for three long years. There was no changing his massive chest and powerful arms, but there was a pronounced difference in the way he walked, the way he talked. The hint of a scowl darkened his features, and his hands, always in front of his body, constantly clenched and unclenched. As Tiny Tim Benton, he'd been imposing, big but slow. As Stefan Richter, he looked like a dynamite charge ready to explode. The distinction was small but significant.

They sat in the open patio of the Café de la Paix, perhaps not the most famous restaurant in Paris, but definitely the most notorious. It was located on the wide sidewalk across the street from the Paris Opera. For decades, it had served as the premier destination for the rich and sophisticated of the Parisian nightlife. Sitting at a table at the Café de la Paix, one would sooner or later see all the important people in the world. It was here that Marcus Cole had told his gang to assemble once the hue and cry of the museum robbery died down. Stefan still thought that they could have met at the bistro directly across from the Eiffel Tower, but Cole insisted on playing things safe. Stefan didn't bother arguing. The others always supported Marcus.

"You've written a will, I suppose?" asked Stefan, pouring them both another glass of red wine. "If nothing comes of this crazy dream of yours and you go down, I'd hate to think of all the money you earned as a bandit and adventurer ending up in the government's coffers."

"That won't happen," said Marcus. "Though you might be surprised who will inherit. Not my brother, the one honest police officer in Paragon City, that's for sure. He'd never accept a dime from me."

"Yeah, Ezra's on the straight and narrow," said Stefan. "Always was, even when we were kids on the street. I always knew he'd end up being a cop."

"So, having no other close relatives or friends—other than you," said Marcus. "And knowing your spend-thrift ways all too well, I've willed my entire fortune to your sister."

Stefan thought his friend had lost the ability to catch him by surprise. He should have known better. Marcus Cole was the most unpredictable man alive. "The last time you saw Monica she was seven years old and we were leaving for France."

"Agreed," replied Marcus, taking a sip from his wine-glass. "But she's written me faithfully once a month since then. That's twelve years of letters, telling me news of Paragon City, of your father, of her life. Letters she's sent without fail, though I've not answered them anywhere near as often as I should have. Surely her determination deserves a reward."

"You're a sentimental fool," said Stefan, meaning every word he said and knowing Marcus didn't care. "For a soldier of fortune, you have no shame."

"Your cynicism touches me deeply," said Marcus. He checked his watch. "It's nearly ten. The others should be here soon. Keep your eyes open for the police. Perhaps Turnbull is in London. That doesn't mean he didn't alert his French brethren to be on the lookout for a pair like us. I swear I'm being watched."

"That you are," said Alan Gleason, sliding into an open chair at the round table on Cole's right. Tall and slender, he still possessed the sharp eyes and ears he'd developed as a scout in No Man's Land during the Great War. "Check out the three gendarmes, across the street, near the opera's front entrance. Plus there be two others hiding in the stage door entrance fifty feet farther along. They've been staring at you gents for the past twenty minutes."

"Not to mention the two prefecture of police officers inside the café," said Greg Hobart, dropping into a chair on Stefan's left.

Whereas Marcus was cautious, Greg was brash and outgoing. He'd never encountered a problem he didn't think could be solved by sheer force. Greg was a good man to have in a fight, but a bad man to lead a band of thieves.

Reaching out, Greg took the wine bottle from the table. Pouring the water out of a nearby goblet onto the ground, he filled the glass with wine and drank it down. "Expensive stuff. I assume this was paid for from our profits from the heist?"

"Would you care for a hot pigeon truffle pie?" asked Marcus Cole, smiling. "They're famous for it here. Are you sure all these police are watching us?"

"Most certainly," said Sid Sawyer, settling into a chair at the same table as Alan Gleason.

Short and plain, Sid had brown hair, brown eyes, and pale skin. He looked very much the mild-mannered office worker—completely forgettable—which came in quite handy when he wanted to disappear in a crowd. Sid was also much more dangerous than he seemed.

"The whole area is crawling with officers," Sid noted. "At least three of them are carrying sketches of you with those ugly muttonchop whiskers. If you hadn't shaved them off, you'd be sitting in the gaol already."

"More likely the Bastille," said Greg. "Word on the street says that Lieutenant Colonel Turnbull has offered a ten-thousand-pound reward for your arrest. For these officers, that's probably double what they earn in a year."

"More likely triple," said Alan. "If you hadn't saved my life in the war, Marcus, I'd probably turn you in myself. Easy money. I could live like a king—for a month or so, at least."

"All right, I made a mistake," Stefan snarled, revealing his teeth in a wolfish smile. He hated apologizing, or even admitting he was wrong. "I learned a lesson: never talk out of turn. Won't happen again."

"The past is past," said Marcus. His mind had already shifted to new worries. Quick to anger, he was equally quick to forgive. "Just remember never to underestimate your opponent. It's a dangerous weakness. Where's the rest of our merry bunch?"

"Somewhere in the neighborhood, stealing cars," said Greg. "If all goes well, they should be pulling up across the street in a few minutes in two vehicles."

"Just enough time for a round of drinks," said Sid Sawyer. He was a man of unshakable calm. According to battlefield legend, Sid had once been attacked by a German commando during breakfast. After being shot point-blank in the shoulder and sidestepping a bayonet thrust, Sid had killed the man with his fork. Then he'd finished drinking his coffee before reporting to the medic for bandaging.

"I'm parched," said Sid, tossing down a glass of wine.

Stefan sighed and signaled the waiter to bring another bottle. "Your best," he told the server. "And ring up my tab. I'll be leaving shortly. Mention that fact to anyone, and I'll return someday and break all your ribs."

White faced, the waiter did what he was told. Stefan paid him double the amount of the check. "I'd take a break about now," he said softly. "A word to the wise is a gift best not ignored."

The waiter nodded and scurried into the restaurant. Stefan poured them all drinks. "To the Cole gang—the best of the best," he declared.

"I'll drink to that," said Greg, downing the entire glass with a flick of the wrist. Greg liked expensive wine and cheap women. It sometimes made for a dangerous situation. "Any clues from the scroll, boss? You got any idea where we're heading?"

"The Greek isles," said Marcus. "As I suspected, halfway through this scroll, Herodotus described a brief stopover on an island to take on fresh water. He called the place the Isle of Vengeance; there's a temple on its cliffs named the Well of the Furies. He said its priests guarded a treasure so valuable he dared not reveal what it was. Evidently, those priests exerted enough pressure on Herodotus that he completely dropped any mention of his visit to the isle in all later versions of the *Histories*."

"You're certain this island is filled with treasure?" asked Sid Sawyer.

"All sorts of treasures," said Marcus.

Stefan restrained a smile. Only he and Marcus knew the real secret of the lost island. And they weren't prepared to share that knowledge with anyone yet, not even their closest friends.

"But," continued Marcus, "it's going to take me months to figure out an approximate location for the island. Even in this scroll, Herodotus is extremely vague."

"Fascinating stuff, gents," said Alan Gleason, gulping down the rest of his drink, "but the time for talk is over. See those two yellow and black taxicabs pulling up in front of the opera house? I believe our transportation has arrived. Besides, the police are getting restless. I think they've finally decided you're the man they want. We be needing to get a move on."

"Taxis?" muttered Stefan. "They stole taxis?"

"Don't get distracted," said Marcus. He paused again and coughed. His handkerchief was wet with blood. His features were white. But there was no surrender in his eyes. "We need to concentrate on escaping. Use no guns. The police won't use them in a crowd and we can't afford an accidental shooting. Thieves are thrown in jail in France. Murderers have a date with the guillotine."

"Agreed, then. No guns," said Stefan, rising to his feet. He reached down, helped Marcus stand. "Stay close and don't try anything heroic. This is my type of game."

His huge fingers clamped down on the table's edge. All around them, undercover policemen and gendarmes were moving, approaching the five criminals with a certain wariness, well deserved. With a jerk of his wrist, Stefan wrenched the table into the air and hurled it at the nearest adversaries. "At them!" he cried and waded into the crowd of suddenly faltering policemen. The officers were anxious to make an arrest, but not certain they were willing to sacrifice their bodies to accomplish it. They hesitated with good reason.

In close, hand-to-hand, was Stefan's type of fight. No

weapons, just flesh against flesh, man against man. His arms thrust like pistons. His massive fists pounded like hammers into anyone foolish enough to stand in his way. Blood spattered across his shirt as he bludgeoned his way through the mob of policemen trying in vain to prevent his escape. Marcus, following instructions for a change, stayed close behind. "Stop him! Stop him!" screamed an officer from the back of the crowd. "Pull the man down!"

If it had been Stefan alone in the fight, the gendarmes would sooner or later have succeeded in halting his progress. Even he was only capable of carrying so many men draped across his back and dangling from his arms and legs. A dozen of them would have finished the job. Except they never had the chance. While most of the attention focused on the big man, three other battle-hardened veterans of the Great War charged into action. It would have taken more men than belonged to the Paris police force to bring them down.

The Cole gang fought with the economy and precision of men who had learned their craft in the trenches and battlefields of the Great War. Every blow counted and every blow connected. Sid Sawyer jabbed with sharp lefts and rights. Greg Hobart was a brawler who aimed for the face, but wasn't too proud to kick and scratch and even bite when necessary. He fought with an all-consuming fury that overwhelmed his opponents.

Alan Gleason was Black Irish and, before the war, had sparred in Boston with Sam Langford, considered by many to be a better boxer than the world champion, Jack Sullivan. A slender man when compared to his comrades, Gleason had whipcord-lean muscles and fists made of steel. Like Stefan Richter, he was a man who enjoyed fighting. For every two steps forward, he took one back. Weaving and shuffling, he picked his targets carefully. When his fists connected, his target went down and stayed down for the count.

"Form a V!" cried Stefan. He'd learned the finer points of close-quarters gang fighting on the streets of Paragon City. He and the rest of the gang had used the same tactics during the worst days of the war. Gleason joined him on the left, while Sawyer and Hobart took the right. At the center of their phalanx, protected from assault, was Marcus. Arms linked in a human chain, they pushed forward through the crowd, smashing anyone in their path. Years ago, Marcus Cole would have spearheaded the attack, taking the point position, but those times were long past. Stefan provided the muscle and brute determination that guided their effort today. His old friend was a sick man, a dying man, desperately pinning his hopes on a legend that offered one last gamble to save his life.

"Stop them! Stop them!" screamed the police detective at the side of the café, but the Cole gang was a gale force wind, a compact hurricane that cut across the crowded street. With an almost audible crash, they smacked into the black and yellow Citroën taxi parked on the far side of the boulevard. Stefan shoved Marcus into the front seat. Sawyer tumbled into the back, leaving room for one more. "You three in the second taxi," roared Stefan to the others. "Move, before we get stuck in the crowd."

Stefan whirled around in a circle, bellowing at the top of his lungs, clearing the policemen from the side of the car. His savage features glowed as red as the Devil's. "Get the hell out of way!" he shouted at the crowd, "or I'll smash you flat!"

For an instant, Stefan was free. The Frenchmen pulled back, stunned by the ferocity of his threat. Snarling, he leapt into the rear seat and slammed the door shut. "Take off!" he yelled to the driver. "Now!"

Billy "the Bean," one-time battlefield ambulance driver, shifted and slammed a foot down hard on the gas. Growling, the taxi surged forward, scattering policemen and onlookers. In an instant they were clear of Opera Boulevard and streaking like a meteor down the narrow back streets of Paris, the second taxi close behind. Within moments, the wail of sirens filled the night air. The French police weren't giving up so easily.

"Who's driving the second Citroën?" asked Marcus. His features were still pasty white. Bloodstains blotched his white shirt. "What are our chances of a clean getaway?"

"Ricks is at the wheel of the other taxi, Captain," answered Billy. Like many of the gang members, he still addressed Marcus by his military rank; it was a practice that made Stefan grit his teeth in annoyance. "He knows these streets like the back of his hand, sir."

"Where's Shaw?" asked Stefan, inquiring about the final member of their gang. "I thought he was going to steal a car, as well?"

"Not just any car," said Billy. "Riley guessed there might be some difficulties making a getaway, so he planned a little surprise for the gendarmes. Just hold on tight, gents, and be prepared for anything."

Riley Shaw was the joker of the gang. He had tricked his way into the army at sixteen and even the horrors of the Great War hadn't dented his bizarre sense of humor. When he wasn't masquerading as a police officer or participating in bandit raids, he spent his free time writing jokes for numerous vaudeville comedians at the magnificent rate of ten cents a joke. Riley's crimes had a certain flair that even Marcus couldn't match.

Shifting gears, pounding on the gas and brake, Billy the Bean wove the taxi through the side streets and alleys of Paris at maximum speed. Ten times it looked as if they were going to crash into a building or a crowd of pedestrians, and ten times they did not. Billy had learned to drive in the back streets of Boston, perhaps the narrowest byways ever designed for automobile passage, and had perfected his art on the battlefields of France during the war. There were few men who could drive a car any better. None of the gang members knew Billy's real last name and he refused to use it, so they called him Billy the Bean in honor of his hometown.

"On your left, gents, if you're interested," said Billy, "is the Le Marais district, famous for its grand mansions and outdoor market. Coming up in a few minutes will be la Place de la Bastille, the site of the prison where the French Revolution began. . . ."

"Wonderful," said Stefan. "Enough with the sightseeing. Those sirens are getting closer. I thought you jokers had a plan."

"Patience," replied Billy. Coming up fast was the Bastille plaza, with the July Column at its center. "Everyone get ready to change cars when I come to a stop."

Brakes squealed and the taxi screeched to a halt. Hurriedly, they all piled out of the Citroën and into the open doors of a huge silver and black limousine. As they scrambled inside, a taxi driver jumped into the front seat of the car they had abandoned and, with a shriek of rubber, was gone.

"Sit down, sit down," yelled Riley Shaw from the driver's station at the front of the limo. To no one's great surprise, he wore the fancy uniform and hat of an employee of the Paris Ritz. "Here come the others."

Repeating what they had done less than a minute before, the rest of their gang piled onto the luxurious red leather seats of the limousine. The second Citroën was off an instant later. Immediately, the limo's doors closed and locked, shades were drawn, and the magnificent silver and black 1929 Dodge touring car pulled onto the wide boulevard paralleling the Seine. Police cruisers, their horns blaring, zoomed past. The officers inside politely tapped their caps to the shaded windows of the limo.

"We *borrowed* the taxis from their drivers," said Billy the Bean. "No questions asked. Told them to meet us at the plaza and from there to drive to Versailles as fast as they could. Gave each man a week's salary up front and told them whoever made it to the palace first would collect double that."

"Police chasing taxi drivers," said Sid Sawyer. "Now ain't that a pretty race. But what about this fancy rig?"

"Riley swiped it," said Tom Ricks, who had driven the other taxi. "He saw the limo parked at the side of the Louvre and just had to take it for a joyride. Figured it would fool the police. We'll dump it outside of town and pick up some other transportation. Nice, huh?"

"I hate to ask," said Marcus, "but I have to know. Who owns this car?"

"This is Paris, boss," said Billy the Bean. "You can't have the police chasing around crooks in ordinary cars. That would be insulting. The more important the cop, the nicer the car he drives."

"Whose car?" asked Marcus, afraid he already knew the answer.

"The prefect, of course," said Billy the Bean. "Who else could afford a beauty like this but the prefect of the Paris police?"

CHAPTER THREE

The harsh ring of the alarm clock woke Monica Richter promptly at 6:00 A.M. Groggily, she reached over to the nightstand and punched the metal clock to the floor. It continued to ring, a shrill sound loud enough to wake the dead. Groaning, Monica lifted her pillow and threw it on top of the offending noisemaker. Her aim, honed by years of practice, was perfect, but even the goose-down pillow was no match for the alarm bell. It rang and rang like a fire engine until Monica, cranky and wide awake, reached from the bed and pushed the off button. Only then did the noise stop.

Shaking her head in despair, Monica fell back onto the bed and tried to pretend she was still asleep. It did her little good. She knew it was time to get going. Her father, Rudy, who owned the house, had left two hours ago to supervise the early shift at the newspaper. Now it was her time to rise and shine and get working. Ezra Cole was due at seven and she needed to be ready to leave as soon as he arrived. As he had promised weeks before, Ezra was taking her to criminal court today. Several cases he'd been working on were coming up before a judge and he was scheduled to testify. After years of hearing Ezra's stories about corruption in the Paragon City legal system, Monica was going to observe the court in action. If all went well, it was going to be the lead story for next week's edition of the *Paragon City Free Press*. Her father might own and operate the smallest newspaper in the city, but it was also the most honest. When people wanted to read the truth, they read the *Free Press*.

She pulled open the venetian blinds and looked out into the backyard. It was a beautiful summer day. The sky glistened blue, and the morning sun shone brightly. Not a cloud darkened the sky. The rosebush she had nurtured through last winter's snow was in full bloom. A bluebird sang somewhere in the trees. Smiling, she admitted to herself it was too nice a day to be angry.

A quick shower, a few curls to her short dark hair, a cup of coffee and two pieces of wheat bread, toasted, with butter and jelly, and Monica felt almost human. She put on a floral print dress—nothing too fancy, but one that still made it clear she was a very attractive young woman—along with low heels and a dark olive beret. A small black leather purse containing her notebook and a bunch of sharp pencils completed her outfit. She was ready for the day. When Ezra Cole rang the doorbell at seven, a confident Monica was waiting.

"Care for a quick cup of coffee?" she asked the big, bulky man in the policeman's uniform. Ezra was no blood relative, but closer to her than any brother could be. "It's still hot."

Sergeant Ezra Cole looked every inch the law officer.

He stood exactly six feet tall and weighed exactly two hundred pounds, not an ounce of it fat. His wore his hair cut flat, and his shaved jaw was shaped like a box. Gray, grim eyes matched his cold and hard features. His shoulders spanned thirty inches, and his arms ended in wide, strong fingers that seemed to be shaped from granite. Dressed in the blue and gold of his policeman's uniform, he made an imposing rock wall of a man. Ezra looked physically and mentally tough. He represented a rarity among the Paragon City police force—an honest cop.

"Not enough time to sit and chat," he said in a voice much too mellow for a man of his size and occupation. "Judge Harvey runs a tight ship. The old man presides over a hundred cases a week. Today's the day he clears his calendar. It won't be pretty and it won't be by the book, but nobody seems to care. Court starts promptly at eight and will be finished by noon so the judge can get in an afternoon's round of golf. If you want to see Paragon City justice in action, we've got to make tracks."

"I'm ready," said Monica, grabbing her bag and wrapping a scarf around her neck. A minute later, the house was locked and she was seated next to Ezra in his black 1927 Ford. It wasn't anything fancy, but like him, the car was as dependable as the sunrise.

Unlike most Paragon City police officers, Sergeant Ezra Cole lived strictly on his income, with no supplemental payments taken on the side. Doing favors for politicians or looking the other way when bootleggers smuggled their rotgut whiskey into town wasn't Ezra's way. He lived by the book and bent the rules for no one. And yet, strangely enough, it was that straight-and-narrow honesty that had earned him the respect of even the most hardened criminals of Paragon City. There were no frame-ups, no double-crosses, and no stabs in the back from this policeman. Ezra Cole was tough, he was honest, but most of all, he was fair.

"How's your father?" he asked as he steered the Ford through the early morning congestion.

"As well as can be expected," said Monica, "considering that he's sixty years old, his only son is an international soldier of fortune, and his only daughter just took over the crime desk for the one honest paper in town. Rudy didn't want to shift me from society pages to crime, but when Hanratty left for Chicago, Dad needed someone to take over his beat immediately. Besides, with the stock market in ruins, there aren't many social events to cover these days."

"How's his recovery from the stroke?" asked Ezra.

"Good," said Monica. "He can't do much with his right hand. Other than that, he seems to have made a complete recovery. Never ask him about it, Ezra. Rudy gets upset even thinking about slowing down. You know what he's like. He's spent his whole life rushing around. He can't imagine ever taking a break."

"Sure, I'll keep my mouth shut. Though I must admit I'm glad you're helping out more with the paper. Maybe you'll convince him to take a day or two off from time to time."

"I wouldn't count on that," said Monica with a laugh. "He thinks the country is run by an incompetent. He's worried about the economy and the unemployment figures. And then there's the rise of the fascists in Europe. . . ."

"Well, if Rudy wasn't upset about the world's problems, I'd know for sure something's wrong. But, much as I hate to admit it, the situation's not going to improve anytime in the near future—for anyone."

That last comment put a damper on conversation even the bright sunshine couldn't chase away. It wasn't until they were pulling into a parking spot at the Hall of Justice that Monica remembered something else she wanted to mention to Ezra.

"I got a postcard the other day from the French Riviera," she said as they walked from the lot to the court building. "It wasn't signed, but I'm sure it was from Marcus."

"He's still alive, then," said Ezra, his voice suddenly tight. Marcus was a difficult subject for the police officer. A soldier of fortune and notorious outlaw, he represented everything Ezra opposed in Paragon City. Yet, they were still brothers, and blood-ties ran deep. "Did he mention his health?"

"The message was cryptic, as usual. I'm sure he realizes that my overseas mail is screened by the Secret Service," said Monica. "He only scribbled a few lines on the back of the card. Said he was 'feeling ancient, but well' and thinking of you. That's an odd choice of words for him. Do you have any idea what he means?"

" 'Feeling ancient, but well,' " repeated Ezra. "My, oh my. It's been a long time since I heard mention of that place."

"What do you mean?"

"We'll talk," said Ezra. "I promise. When we go out for lunch after court."

The two entered the courtroom and parted, Ezra going to the special section of the chamber reserved for police officers, Monica to the visitors' gallery. Promptly on the dot of eight, the bailiff announced, "All rise. The court of the Honorable Emmanuel Harvey is now in session."

Harvey, a short man dressed in a judge's black robes, entirely bald, with huge baby-blue eyes and thin, bloodless lips, sat down at his podium at the front of the court-room. "Thank you. Please sit down. Be aware that this court serves mainly as a sorting area for lesser crimes so my fellow judges can deliberate on more important cases. I'm going to be quick, so when your case is called, be prepared. You'll find I'm a fair man, but I'm not a patient one. Bailiff, call the first case."

The first case was an odd one. It concerned a fight in a restaurant in one of the city's nicer sections. Two men eating dinner had gotten into an argument that turned from a shouting match into a fistfight involving a half dozen other people. The pair admitted to Judge Harvey that they'd been so drunk at the time they couldn't remember the reason for the fight. The judge fined them each ten dollars and let them go with a reprimand. The restaurant, however, was closed for a week for violating Prohibition, and the judge made it clear that they could only reopen after undergoing rigid inspections by the city. The sentence seemed fair to Monica, but she was caught off guard when she noticed the two fighters grinning and shaking hands after the verdict was announced.

Next was a shooting. The millionaire owner of a meat packing plant, Kurt Farrell, had been cheating on his wife, Joanne, with a chorus girl named Nancy del Rio. Evidently, the affair was known to everyone in the city other than Mrs. Farrell. She only learned of it when she walked into her bedroom at the family mansion and found the two cheaters in a compromising situation. Infuriated, she took the pistol she carried in her purse for protection and shot her spouse twice in the head. Mrs. Farrell was an excellent marksman and Mr. Farrell's life ended immediately. The chorus girl got away and had not been seen since.

The district attorney's office wanted the wife held on murder charges. Mrs. Farrell's lawyer argued that their client had only acted in the same manner as a husband who discovered his wife cheating, and that she was guilty of no crime. Judge Harvey agreed with the lawyer, ruled it a "justifiable homicide," and dropped all charges. Monica never could quite understand the way in which these "crimes of passion" were dismissed so lightly, but at least the judge had treated the wife the same way he would have her husband, had the roles been reversed. By the frown on Ezra's face, she saw that he didn't agree.

The third case was a mugging. One James Rand, a young business executive, had been approached on the street by a much older man, one Nicholas Dwyer, begging for money. Rand had no change and told Dwyer as much. The news evidently enraged the old man and he started beating Rand, breaking his arm, before the police intervened. Rand, his right arm bandaged and in a sling, represented by a well-dressed attorney, made a sympathetic victim. Dwyer, who couldn't afford a lawyer, had already spent several days in jail. Unshaven, dirty, with uncombed gray hair, he looked like a wild man.

"How do you pled, Mr. Dwyer?" asked the judge, staring directly at the prisoner.

"Not guilty, Your Honor," said Dwyer. The words poured out of him in a flood. "I lost my job a month ago and haven't been able to find work since. With a wife and two children to support, I'm desperate. I knew Rand from the office where I used to work. I wasn't begging, only asking him for a loan of a few dollars to help me until I could find a new job."

"And the broken arm?"

"I never touched him," said Dwyer. "He was okay when he called the cop who arrested me."

"Is that policeman here in court today?" asked the judge.

"No, Your Honor," said the bailiff. "He couldn't make it."

The judge nodded and shuffled some pages. "According to his written report, Dwyer assaulted Rand right in front of his eyes. He had to use his nightstick to separate the two."

"Nightstick?" said Dwyer. "No one hit me with a nightstick."

Monica winced. The defendant was clearly out of his league. She'd read some of the arguments made by Progressives to have the city appoint defense counsel for those too poor to pay for their own. Dwyer certainly could have benefited from that help now.

"Your Honor," interrupted Rand's attorney. "The evidence in this case is clear cut. This wretch approached my client, hoping to extort money from him. When Mr. Rand refused, Dwyer savagely attacked him and finally had to be subdued by the police. This is a case of assault and attempted robbery, pure and simple."

"Yes, I'm forced to agree," said Judge Harvey. "Mr. Dwyer, I'm sorry you lost your job, but being unemployed is no excuse for robbery. I'm sending your case to criminal court with a recommendation of a two-year prison sentence and a fine of fifty dollars, plus legal fees, to be paid by you to Mr. Rand."

"But I'm broke," said Dwyer, standing alone. "I don't have the money for the fines."

"You mentioned you had a wife and daughter," said

the judge. "I'm sure they'll be able to raise the money somehow. Next case."

"No!" yelled Dwyer, shaking a fist at the judge. "You can't do this to me. You can't!"

"Add ten dollars more to that fine for contempt of court," said Harvey, betraying not an ounce of emotion. "Guards, remove the prisoner. Bailiff, call the next case."

The fourth case involved drunk driving and Ezra had been the arresting officer. The accused was the mayor's nephew and Monica had a feeling the outcome was not in doubt. Especially when she saw that the young man was represented by Sidney Saunders, one of the partners of Saunders, Saunders, and Lane, the top law firm in Paragon City. The defendant, dressed in a dark suit and tie, seemed bored by the entire proceeding. Every few minutes, he glanced down at his watch and sighed. It was the only sound he made.

"Sergeant, please describe the circumstances of the arrest," said Judge Harvey. "Be brief, please, but specific."

"It was a week ago, on Thursday. I was patrolling the Drive in my squad car when I saw a fancy roadster weaving in and out of traffic. The vehicle's lights weren't on though it was nearly midnight, and it was traveling nearly seventy miles an hour. After flashing my bright lights at the car, I forced it off the road. The driver, Mr. McCarthy, refused to get out of the car, telling me in very colorful language just who he was and how I'd lose my badge for pulling him over. I finally convinced him it would be in his best interest if he exited the car. His breath and clothes reeked of alcohol, Your Honor. When I asked him to walk a straight line, he could not. I also observed several bottles of what appeared to be bootleg gin in the back seat of the defendant's car.

Feeling I had enough evidence to make an arrest, I charged him with drunk driving and a violation of Prohibition."

"Mr. Saunders, does your client deny the charge?"

"Yes, Your Honor. While Sergeant Cole's account, *on the surface*, sounds damning, let's look at the whole story. May I ask the officer a question or two? Off the record, of course."

"I can't see any harm in such actions," said the judge. "Answer Mr. Saunders's questions, Cole."

"You claim that my client was driving drunk, Sergeant. Did you actually see him take a drink?"

"No, sir," said Cole, "but—"

"So you merely assumed he had been drinking," said Saunders, cutting off Ezra. "Were you aware that Mr. McCarthy was taking medication that evening for a bad sinus infection? Medicine that, unfortunately, smells much like alcohol, though it is perfectly safe to use while operating an automobile?"

"Medicine?" replied Cole. "I didn't see any medicine bottle."

"If I may, Judge? Here's a letter from Mr. McCarthy's doctor certifying that he prescribed the medication to his patient that evening. And here's a sworn statement from Miss Rose Gray, who was in the car that night with Mr. McCarthy, testifying that no alcohol was in the car. She says that the bottles observed by Sergeant Cole contained soda pop."

"Hmm," said the judge. "Is this Miss Gray the daughter of Judge Calvin Gray?"

"Yes, Your Honor," said Saunders.

"Sergeant, how do you explain these inconsistencies in your story?"

"Judge, I swear, he was as drunk as a—"

"You can't explain then, Sergeant. Case dismissed. You are free to go Mr. McCarthy, with the city's apology."

Ezra shook his head but said not another word. It was obvious to Monica her stepbrother had been expecting something like this to happen.

"Sit down, Cole," the judge said coldly. "Bailiff, call the next case."

So it went. After an hour, Monica could predict the outcome of the case with near one hundred percent accuracy. The poor never won. They were always fined, found guilty, or sent to a higher court for trial. Those with private lawyers, mostly the rich, were always found innocent. Police testimony, when it contradicted the court's predilections, meant nothing. By the end of the morning, it was clear that in Judge Harvey's court, when money talked, the guilty walked.

True to Ezra's prediction, the judge adjourned court at noon. Monica considered the time she'd spent there a good investment. It was a year's education in graft and corruption condensed into four hours. She realized now why Ezra Cole wanted her to witness a typical day in Paragon City's criminal court. The system was rife with nods and winks and backroom deals. Justice was all but forgotten.

"Well," asked Ezra as they ate BLTs in a diner a block away from the court building, "what did you think of Judge Harvey?"

"Depressingly predictable," said Monica. "What a crook."

"Hold that thought," said Ezra, chuckling. "He's one of the better judges in the system. At least he pays attention to the cases. Some don't bother doing that."

"I thought he made the right decision in the Farrell case," said Monica. "Was I wrong?"

"You need to dig a little deeper," said Ezra. "When a wife finds her husband in bed with another woman, she normally shoots the husband and the girlfriend. Not this time. Miss del Rio escaped unharmed. It seems she took a train to Baltimore right after the shooting and hasn't been seen since. More important, both of Mrs. Farrell's bullets hit her husband right between the eyes, but, despite her attorney's claim, she never took a shooting lesson in her life. And she only bought the gun a day before the shooting."

"So she didn't shoot her husband? She *was* innocent."

"Not exactly," said Ezra. "Kurt Farrell owned the city's biggest meat packing plant. He was also a gambler who never paid his debts on time. Word on the street is one of the city crime lords got tired of waiting for his money. Someone put a hit on Mr. Farrell after making a deal with the wife." He took a sip of his coffee, then continued. "Mrs. Farrell inherits everything. The boss gets his money from her, with interest, and the widow gets revenge upon a cheating husband and gains a nice-sized fortune. Everyone's happy, except the late Mr. Farrell, who should have known better."

"That's outrageous," said Monica. "Why wasn't any of this mentioned in court?"

"All the evidence about the gambling debts and the crime boss was tossed out on a technicality," said Ezra. He finished his sandwich. "Want a piece of pie?"

"Those two men fined for fighting?" asked Monica.

"The owner of the restaurant was getting his bootleg gin from Boston. A local bootlegger decided to teach him a lesson. The two thugs staged the fight so the place would be shut down for a few weeks. If the owner doesn't start buying his booze in the city, it won't be a fistfight next time, but a firebomb."

"How can this happen?" asked Monica as Ezra calmly devoured a piece of cherry pie. What little faith she had in the legal system was gone, destroyed in a few hours.

"Prohibition has a lot to do with it," said Ezra between mouthfuls. "It's a noble experiment, but it's failed miserably. Take something away from people they enjoy and they'll get it back, one way or another. Booze makes small-time hoodlums rich. The more money in crime, the more money spent twisting the law the way the crooks want. Nobody cares, so things only get worse, and worse, and worse. . . ."

"So there's nothing the public can do?" said Monica.

"Repealing Prohibition will be a good first step," said Ezra as he scooped up the last pie crumbs. He pointed his fork at Monica. "The only way to really clean up Paragon City is for the citizens to stand up for their rights. They've got to vote out the crooks, demand the police take action, and fight for what they believe. It won't be easy. Battling evil never is."

"What this city needs is a leader," said Monica. "Someone who's not afraid to stand up for justice." She paused and looked at Ezra.

He shook his head. "Not me. I can't even keep drunks off the road."

Monica sighed in despair. "We need a hero."

"Sure," said Ezra, with a bitter laugh. "But in Paragon City, heroes are in short supply."

CHAPTER FOUR

fter lunch, Ezra drove Monica back to work. "I'm off the rest of the day," he said. "Time for me to pay my respects to Rudy."

"He'll be glad to see you," said Monica. "Rudy doesn't like to admit it, but he misses Stefan and Marcus. You're the only one he has left."

"Hey," said Ezra. "He has you, his annoying but brilliant daughter."

Monica laughed. Ezra had a way of making even the most ordinary statement funny. An even-tempered man with a sense of responsibility a mile wide, he would have made some lucky woman a terrific husband—if he weren't already married to his job. Strange how the Cole brothers had turned out. One inherited all the responsibilities of life and the other none of them. It was a difference nearly as difficult to explain as the chasm between her and her older brother, Stefan.

Ezra found a parking spot a block from the newspaper plant and they walked the rest of the distance. The clear blue sky and the bright sunshine were almost enough to drive the depressing truths about the city's corruption out of Monica's thoughts. Almost. But those dark realities intruded again when she entered the factory and was told by one of the printers that her father was up in his office, meeting with Sammy "the Sledgehammer" Lombardo, one of the city's major crime bosses.

"Good thing I came along," said Ezra, loosening the police special in his holster. "Lombardo's a wild man, capable of doing just about anything if he gets mad. Be careful what you say to him, Monica. You're new to the crime beat. Lombardo's the type who takes any remark he doesn't like as a personal insult."

"Then we'd better get to the office fast," said Monica. "You know Dad. He's not one to mince words."

Rudy's office was located at the far side of the building, a ten-by-ten brick box with two huge windows overlooking the printing presses. Usually, the office blinds were open, letting Rudy watch the newspaper being published while he searched for advertisers by telephone. Printer's ink ran in the old man's blood. Today, the blinds were closed and the voices coming from the office were loud and angry.

"I hope my first scoop as a crime reporter won't be reporting my own shooting," Monica told Ezra. "Here goes." Without knocking, she opened the office door

The situation wasn't as bad as Monica had feared. Her father sat behind his big oak desk, a half-eaten egg salad sandwich on the blotter. His face was beet red, a sure sign he'd been yelling, but his breathing wasn't coming in short, intense gasps through his nose, a tip-off to impending fury.

Standing on the other side of the desk was Sammy Lombardo, known to most people as "the Sledgehammer," possibly the worst-dressed man in Paragon City. Lombardo's nickname came from his notorious habit of personally destroying his rival's whiskey barrels with a sledgehammer, though more than one rake had suggested it was inspired by the shape of Sammy's head.

Standing five feet five inches tall and weighing close to three hundred pounds, Sammy resembled a bull terrier in a pinstriped suit. Tiny ears, a pug nose, and sloped brows over tiny, recessed eyes added to the illusion. An ex-circus strongman, he had made the transition from big top performer to bodyguard to bootlegger in less than ten years. Sammy wasn't known as the smartest mobster in the city, but in some careers, brains weren't as important as brawn.

Standing a few inches back from Sammy, wearing long black overcoats on the warmest day of the year, were Shanks and Grimshaw Fontaine, Sammy's constant companions and personal bodyguards. The Fontaine brothers resembled characters out of a Buster Keaton film. They were big and bulky with bland eyes and a shared expression of absolute ignorance. They actually made Sammy look intelligent.

Monica had evidently walked into the room just as Sammy was about to say something to her father. Slowly, the gangster swiveled his head and looked at her with his tiny eyes. His mouth was still half-open from what he was about to say. "Watcha doin' here?" he managed to spit out in garbled fashion.

"Gentlemen, *mein* daughter, Monica," said Rudy, rising to his feet. His eyes were suddenly twinkling. "She ist the new crime reporter for the *Free Press*. You vill vatch your tongues when speaking around her, understand?"

"A dame covering the mob scene?" said Sammy, his face twisting into an odd shape that Monica guessed was meant to be a grin. "You're kidding, old man, ain't cha?"

"No, Mr. Lombardo," said Monica, "he's not kidding. Women can report something other than society news. We're not all pea-brains like the ladies you associate with. Besides, your criminal activities hurt everyone in this city, men and women alike. I hope to give the crime news a different slant, a woman's perspective."

"Sure," said Sammy, the deep rumble in his barrel chest suggesting some sort of primitive laughter. "Dames reporting crime. Next you'll be saying they should be covering sports, too. Wouldn't that be a laugh, a woman sports reporter?"

"Har, har, har," laughed the Fontaine brothers, taking their cue from Sammy's remarks. Their laughter died as quick as it started. Evidently, Lombardo wasn't paying them enough for more than chuckles.

"Laugh all you want," said Monica. "I'll be the one laughing when they strap you into the electric chair."

"Now dat ain't funny," said Sammy. He pointed a finger the size of a sausage at Monica. "Listen here, girlie, I'll tell you da same thing I was tellin' your dumb old man. You lay off me and my boys. I'm tired of all da stories about bad hootch you've been printing. You keep on with dat, and you'll be—"

Sammy's voice dropped off suddenly as he spotted big Ezra Cole behind Monica. Ezra had been standing silent, waiting for the precise moment to make his presence felt. Not even the Fontaine brothers had noticed his presence, and they were professionals. His appearance—pistol in hand, an angry look on his face—froze Sammy in midthreat.

Caught flat-footed, the Fontaine brothers each reached for the flap of his overcoat. They came to a sudden stop as Ezra's gun hand twitched an inch in their direction. "One wrong move and Sammy's dead, boys. Resisting arrest. And I bet I'd be able to take both of you out before your guns ever cleared their holsters."

"Jeezuz!" snapped Sammy. "I'm paying you goofs to protect me, not get me kilt. Don't do anything stupid."

"Good advice, Sammy," said Ezra, smiling, though the gun in his hand never wavered. "You're not as dumb as you look."

"Watcha doin' here, Cole?" said Sammy. "Why's a cop visiting the offices of da *Free Press*?"

"Oh, didn't you know, Sammy?" said Ezra. "When my mother and father died, their best friend—Rudy here—took me and my brother in, raised us right. Kept us out of the orphanage and all that. He was a father for us." He paused to let the information sink in. "I just thought you'd want to know that if something ever happened to Rudy or Monica, no matter who did it, no matter what the evidence was, I'd hold *you* responsible. And that would be a very bad thing for you and your mob. It would be a disaster for you, in fact. Do you get my drift, Sammy?"

"Yeah, copper, I'm not dumb," said Sammy. "Besides, I don't make war on women. And I especially ain't stupid enough to kill a reporter or a cop. Some people you don't touch. Da bad publicity isn't worth the trouble."

"Then we understand each other," said Ezra.

"Sure, sure," said Sammy. "We understand each other just fine."

The gangster turned to his two shadows. "Come on, boys. I think we made our point. You just remember, Rudy, the next time you write some editorial complaining about the crime in Paragon City, that the garbage always gets picked up on time. There's no union trouble, no labor unrest. This city works like a well-oiled machine. That ain't da case in New York or Chi-town. It takes a little grease to keep the wheels of the city running smooth."

"A little grease?" said Monica. "That's not quite the same phrase most people would use to describe the bootlegging, murder, extortion, loan sharking, gambling, and prostitution that's flooded their neighborhoods. And living with all that is a small price to pay, so long as the garbage is picked up on time every week?"

"Hey," said Sammy, staring at Monica with a new awareness, "you ain't so dumb for a broad. Just remember this—Paragon City ain't ready for reform."

"How poetic," said Monica. She pulled a pad and pencil from her pack. "Do you mind if I write that down? Someday, when you're sentenced to life in prison, I'll quote you. Give you credit in my headline. *Crook who said 'Paragon City ain't ready for reform' sentenced to the Big House.* Catchy, huh?"

"Yeah, sure," said Sammy, grinning. "I like dat."

"Enough small talk," said Ezra, taking a step backward, never lowering his gun for an instant. "I think it's time for Mr. Lombardo and his associates to be leaving."

Ezra watched carefully as the trio of crooks shuffled out the door. Monica noted that the big policeman didn't holster his gun until all three men had exited the building. Ezra wasn't the trusting kind. He took no chances.

"Goot timing," said Rudy, getting up from his desk. He walked around the big piece of furniture and hugged Ezra. The two men, though separated by more than three decades, were nearly the same height and build. Strong and powerful, they both dwarfed Monica, who felt like a child when standing by them.

"Dos bums were getting ready to knock my block off," said Rudy. Though he had lived in America for nearly fifty years, he still spoke with a thick Austrian accent. Monica suspected he could speak perfect English but retained the accent just to trick people into thinking he wasn't too bright. It was a handy way of gaining their confidence. A surprising number of businessmen revealed their secrets when they thought they were talking to an intellectual inferior.

"When you walked in," Rudy noted, "it was a big surprise."

"Well, do me a favor and try to keep criminals like Sammy Lombardo at a distance," said Ezra. "I won't always be around to protect you. Sammy's a cold-blooded killer."

Ezra turned to Monica. "You, young lady, need to carry a gun and know how to use it. Plus, I want you to take lessons in self-defense. A friend of mine, Masahito Mirimoto, teaches a class for rookie cops at Bryerman's Gym. He's an expert in a Japanese fighting technique, *jiu jitsu*, where you use your opponent's weight as a weapon. If you're going to be confronting lugs like that as a reporter, you need to know how to take care of yourself."

That was one of the reasons Monica thought so highly

of Ezra. He didn't tell her to act like a lady. Instead, he was only concerned with her knowing how to defend herself, if the need arose.

"You agree, don't you, Rudy?" said Ezra. "Time for Monica to toughen up?"

"*Ja, ja*, that's right," said Rudy, approving everything with the wave of one big hand. "If she wants to take on crime in this city like a maiden of justice, this is a very good idea."

Monica smiled. Whenever she took some cause to heart, which was actually rather often, her father would refer to her as his brave little "maiden of justice."

"So tell me," Rudy continued, turning to his daughter, "how was the court today?"

"Good," said Monica. She perched herself on the top of Rudy's desk. "Sit down and I'll tell you all about it. I learned more in four hours than I would have reading files for months."

She spent the next half hour recapping the morning's events. Rudy listened carefully but didn't interrupt. Instead, he was mainly interested in what Monica thought about each case. Like Ezra, her father wanted her to look beneath the stories' surface and locate the less obvious truths.

"*Sehr gudt!*" said Rudy when Monica finished. Ezra, who had planted himself in a chair in the corner of the office, also nodded his approval.

"Excellent job, Monica," the big cop added when she was finished. "You evaluated each case fairly and spotted the illegal payoffs and bribes like an old pro."

"Most women have an ear for lies," said Rudy. "They aren't so easily deceived by sweet talk and ridiculous claims. I t'ink you will do a fine job handling the crime news. Each week, in your column, I want you to tell the truth about the law here. The whole truth, not the pack of lies we get fed through the other papers."

Ezra glanced down at his wristwatch. "I'd better get back to the streets. The bookies will be placing bets on which hoodlum shot me if I don't show my face for too long."

The big cop was just reaching for the office door when Monica remembered a promise he'd made earlier in the day. "Wait, you can't leave," she declared. "You were going to tell me about the odd wording of Marcus's letter."

"Sorry," Erza said. "It'll have to be next time. Don't worry, this will wait. The well I think he's referencing has been lost for over three thousand years. Whatever Marcus has planned, I'm sure it can't happen anytime soon."

CHAPTER FIVE

According to Herodotus, the name of the island was Vengeance or, as written in the ancient texts, *Praxidae*. The historian described it as a clump of rock and soil less than a mile square, located north of Crete, south of Melos, and somewhere between the islands of Santorini and Kyhria. Unfortunately, such an island was listed on no modern map, nor could it be found on any of the ancient ones Marcus consulted. Assuming Herodotus had kept to the truth, the island home of the Well of the Furies existed somewhere in the middle of approximately fifteen thousand square miles of water, an area comparable in size to the entire Mojave Desert.

Finding the tiny island required a great deal of patience, and patience wasn't something Marcus could afford. The pain in his chest continued to grow worse. He knew that even if they did locate Praxidae, the chance of finding anything useful being there was incredibly small. He was betting everything he had on a one-in-a-million chance.

With death staring him in the face, he felt that the reward was worth the risk.

Approximately seven months after their robbery of the Herodotus scroll, Marcus Cole and the rest of the Cole gang set sail from Marseilles on a schooner they named the *The Last Chance*, searching for the lost island. Only Marcus and Stefan knew exactly what they hoped to find there, but their comrades were more than willing to sign on for one more mysterious venture. Marcus Cole had never done them wrong and none of them was ready yet to retire from the adventurous life.

On a hot, humid afternoon, on July 1, 1930, after nearly two weeks of sailing back and forth across the Cretan Sea, they found the small isle. "Land ho!" cried Alan Gleason, whose eyes were better than any spyglass. He leaned out from the schooner's crow's nest. "Coming up fast on the starboard bow."

Marcus had spent the night before coughing up blood, and he hobbled from the cabin to the rail a few minutes after all the rest. Stefan cleared a space for him near the bow. "There it is, Marcus," he said, pointing at a gray slab of volcanic rock and stone rising from the sea a thousand yards ahead. There was a touch of astonishment mixed with a pinch of disbelief in his voice. Even Stefan had harbored his doubts about the island's existence. "Just as the old woman described it in her stories. Praxidae, the Isle of Vengeance, the secret location of the Well of the Furies."

Slowly, carefully, Sid Sawyer navigated the schooner around the island. Treacherous shoals made it impossible for the boat to get too close. The island was three hundred feet across at its widest point and stretched for a little less than a half mile in a near-straight line west to east. There was no coast or hint of a beach.

Standing on a solid base of jagged rock and jet-black soil, the island top rose fifty feet up from the sea. The cliffs served as home for hundreds of birds, but there were no other signs of life visible. There was no evidence of a dock or landing. From the sea, the Isle of Vengeance appeared a dismal and unapproachable place.

"I can see why sailors never bothered to land," said Greg Hobart. "Too much trouble for too little reward. With Crete only a few hours away, it was easier for most ships to continue on than to send a landing party to search for a beach. This island wasn't lost as much as ignored."

"All the better for us," said Stefan. "If there's an untouched Greek temple filled with three-thousand-year-old artifacts at the top of those cliffs, we'll all be millionaires. It'll be the greatest archeological find of the twentieth century."

"Well," said Marcus, "let's not start celebrating yet."

He turned to Sid Sawyer. Gone was the pain in his bones, the taste of blood and bile tainting his mouth, the thoughts of death haunting his mind. Finding the lost island had pushed them all away. A warm glow spread from a point on his chest, across his body, energizing him. "The reefs make docking the ship impossible. See if you can find a small break in the cliffs and drop anchor nearby. We'll use one of the lifeboats to ferry the crew and supplies ashore. There's plenty of climbing equipment in the hold."

Using one of the ship's motorized longboats to prowl the shore, Alan Gleason and Billy the Bean discovered a tiny strip of beach on the isle's northernmost tip. It was only twelve feet long and five feet wide, but it was land and it was enough. More interesting was the series of crudely chiseled steps they found carved into the marble-and-rock wall. Though battered by thousands of years of wind and rain, the rock insets were evidence that the island had once been inhabited.

Riley Shaw scrambled to the top of those timeworn steps in less than an hour. With the help of a rope ladder held steady by several tons of marble slab, five more of the gang followed, bringing with them nearly a hundred pounds of supplies and equipment. Marcus insisted that Greg Hobart and Tom Ricks stay on the schooner for the night. He silenced their grumbling only by promising them that tomorrow two others would take their place. Their boat needed to be protected at all costs. One under-sea earthquake could send the ship to the bottom and maroon them on the island for years. Modern-day pirates could do worse. Marcus expected neither to happen, but he felt it was better to be safe than sorry.

They set up a base atop the cliff, not far from where the stone steps ended. The area was blanketed with loose stones and broken shards of ancient pottery. The material scattered around the campground was probably worth thousands on the antique market. Marcus assumed this spot was where the priests who served at the well once lived. Raising tents on three-thousand-year-old ruins gave him the shivers. Memories of his youth flooded his mind. It had taken him most of his life, but he had finally made it to the Well of the Furies. On his chest, he could feel a flicker of warmth against his skin. He was near the end of his quest. Very near.

Splitting up the gang into two teams of three men

each, Marcus and his crew conducted a quick survey of the island. It wasn't a particularly difficult job, considering that the entire strip of land was half a dozen city blocks long. Much of the land was overgrown by tall grass, thick thorn bushes, and slender trees. At the southern end of the island stood the remains of what must have once been a magnificent Greek temple. The forest had grown up thick around it, hiding the few marble columns still upright. Broken white marble paving stones marked the far edges of the building's floor. There was no hint of a roof. Huge clusters of thornbushes, some of them stretching ten feet and higher into the air, covered the temple's courtyard, making easy passage inward impossible.

With darkness falling, Marcus signaled everyone back to camp. Tomorrow, with a full day, they would conduct a proper search, using machetes to cut their way through the undergrowth. Tonight was the prelude of things to come. Tomorrow would be the big day.

Marcus decreed the men use only ship's supplies and not touch either the wild grapes or fresh water on the cliff top. They were ill equipped to deal with any type of poisoning or tropical diseases and he had not come this far to lose someone to such an obvious danger. No one complained. There was something strange about the plateau that gave them all the creeps. None of the crew seemed sure what caused the sense of dread, but they all felt it. Crouched around the fire after a meal of cold rations and bottled water, the usually boisterous Cole gang discussed their concerns in whispers.

"Notice how quiet it is up here?" said Billy the Bean, his eyes as wide as saucers. "The night is dead silent. The land's empty of life. It's unnatural. Ghostly."

"It's strange but not that spooky," said Stefan Richter. He stretched his huge arms over his head, then cracked the knuckles of his immense fingers. "There are no bugs anywhere, at least none we've seen. No animals either, and most of the birds live on the cliffs. From those I spotted climbing up, they weren't the night flyer types. Really, there's nothing around to make noise other than us. We're probably creating more sounds tonight than this plateau's heard in twenty centuries."

"That might well be true," said Alan Gleason, "but my bones say there's something unnatural about these grounds. We may be the first explorers here in years, but the grapevines on the eastern side of the island look like they're planted in straight rows. For wild fruit, they're extremely healthy."

"I noticed that myself," said Marcus. "Very strange."

"Ghosts?" said Billy the Bean.

"I doubt if ghosts would be so neat and clean, Billy," said Marcus. "What self-respecting spook spends time clearing weeds?"

"More than likely," said Stefan, "locals from Crete or the mainland visit the island once or twice a month. Probably for religious purposes. If we search, I'd bet we'd find their old campfires. Remember, this place was once considered sacred ground. Part of their observances might include keeping the island respectable."

"I'm amazed that this island's not inhabited," said Riley Shaw. "The soil seems perfect for growing. Plus, these cliffs provide you with plenty of privacy. Sail an hour and you're in Crete, a bit longer in the other direction, you're in Athens."

"A private island you could rule like a king," said Stefan.

"That sounds almost too good to be true. Master of all you can see and all that. Too bad no one makes that sort of money. Imagine what such an enterprise would cost!"

"Rockefeller could afford it," said Sid Sawyer. "Or Vanderbilt or Morgan."

"I'm not a-caring about the rich," said Alan Gleason. He stared directly at Marcus. "And I'm not worrying if this island's maintained by a bunch of old priests. What I do wants to know, Captain, is what makes the place so important. You've mentioned a certain well more than once. Isn't it time to let the rest of us know why we're here?"

"Fair enough," said Marcus. "I'll talk, as long as all of you promise to remain silent until my story's done. It's pretty incredible and I won't fault anyone for having his doubts. Still, I want to remind you I have complete faith in the tale I'm about to tell."

"Sometimes, my friend," said Stefan, throwing another branch onto the fire, "you talk like a schoolteacher. Tell them the story and try to keep it short."

"The short version it is," said Marcus. Stefan was right. He liked to talk, perhaps a bit too much. Best to keep to the facts.

"You all know me. I'm the son of Tom and Jane Cole, Irish immigrants who came to Paragon City thirty or so years back. My mother died giving me life and my father drowned himself in whiskey. He died a year later, leaving me and my older brother, Ezra, orphans. Lucky for the two of us Stefan's parents, Rudy and Anya, took us in and raised us like their own. Ezra grew up to be an honest cop, and me—well, the results were mixed."

They all laughed at that. Even when keeping it short, Marcus knew how to tell a story.

"Enough about yourself," said Stefan. "Tell them about Mrs. Kallikoros."

"Mrs. Kallikoros," said Marcus, letting the syllables roll off his tongue. "None of us—Ezra included—had much time for formal schooling. My brother took to being a cop, while Stefan and me made our way working on the docks. Mrs. Kallikoros, she ran the bakery near the docks. Little old Greek lady, a widow, she made some wonderful pastries, so damn sticky sweet."

"Get on with it," said Stefan.

"One summer day, a couple of toughs thought to muscle in on her business. Demanded that she pay them protection money or they'd fire her shop. By then I was pretty much running the docks as union steward and I didn't take kindly to thugs threatening anyone in my neighborhood. So Stefan and I hunted down the pair and showed them the error of their ways."

"Fools," said Stefan, smacking one huge fist into the other. "We cleaned their clocks nicely."

"After that, we were Mrs. Kallikoros's favorites," said Marcus. "She was a lonely old woman hungry for company. Many were the nights I spent at her shop. As she prepared the dough for the next morning, she told magical stories about her homeland. Fascinating stuff I never forgot, tales of gods and heroes fighting for glory a thousand years before Christ."

"The Greek myths," said Riley Shaw. "We learned them in primary school—the legends of Zeus and Aphrodite and Perseus and the Trojan War and the River Styx. No big deal."

"To us, they were something special," said Marcus. "We'd never learned that stuff in school, not that we spent much time there. Our education came from the docks. When Mrs. Kallikoros spoke, it was like listening to history. She made those stories come alive."

"Right, right," said Gleason. "When do we hear about the well?"

"The day I enlisted in the army, Mrs. Kallikoros summoned me to her shop. She said she had a gift for me. It was an amulet that had been handed down in her family from generation to generation for hundreds of years. According to her, it protected the wearer from harm. I thought she was a little crazy, but who was I to disappoint an old woman. So I took the amulet and hung it about my neck. I wear it still."

Marcus reached inside his shirt and pulled out a thin silver chain. Looped to the end was a tiny silver face, half the size of a dime. Though the metal appeared worn and old, the eyes of the carving blazed with a piercing gold light.

"Don't stare too long at the rays," warned Marcus. "They're powerful enough to burn a hole in your eye. Mrs. Kallikoros claimed that the gold light is some sort of life energy. It's supposed to keep the wearer healthy."

Billy the Bean shook his head. "Doesn't seem like it did much to protect you against the Boche's gas."

"Depends on the way you look at it," said Marcus. "I got a whiff of mustard gas back in 1918. It's eleven years later. Find me another doughboy who has lasted so long. The charm couldn't protect me from the attack, but it's helped me stay alive while I search for a cure."

"An antidote to mustard gas?" said Sid Sawyer. "You could write your own ticket if you found that."

"That's why we're here," said Stefan. "To locate that cure. To find the source of the gold energy."

"Which is?" asked Alan Gleason, still sounding quite skeptical.

"According to the research I've been doing for the past ten years," said Marcus, "the gods and goddesses of ancient Greece shared only one thing in common—their source of nourishment. They all ate and drank nectar and ambrosia. These magical substances were prepared special for them by three sisters, the women the Greeks called the Furies. The food was made in a secret chamber, known as the Fountain of Zeus, hidden beneath the Well of the Furies. It's that fountain we're looking for."

"Greek gods? Magic food and drink? It all sounds pretty damned outrageous to me," said Gleason.

"There's the amulet," said Stefan. "You can't deny that."

"I figure the eyes are filled with radium dust," said Billy the Bean. "That would make them glow and radiate heat."

"We'll find out for sure tomorrow," said Marcus. "Either we find the origin point of the food of the gods or . . ."

"Or?" prompted Riley after a long and uncomfortable pause.

"I die," said Marcus.

CHAPTER SIX

They rose with the sun, anxious to begin their search for the Well of the Furies, and from there, the Fountain of Zeus. After coffee and hardtack, Sid Sawyer and Billy the Bean went back to the schooner to replace Ricks and Hobart. The two newcomers reported a quiet night on the boat. After bringing the pair up to speed on the hunt, Marcus laid out the day's strategy. They would separate into two groups and, using machetes they had brought from the boat, cut through the undergrowth from the east and the west. When either team came upon something that indicated they were close to the well, they would fire a shot in the air. Then they'd gather in one party to face whatever dangers the ancient temple might hold.

Stefan, accompanied by Ricks and Gleason, attacked the thornbushes from the east, while Marcus, with Hobart and Shaw, approached the ruins from the west. The growth was thick, packed tightly together, and filled with long, painful thorns. Progress was slow, partly because of the wreckage on the ground. The island floor was littered with ancient vases, frescos, tools, and even some weapons, all in beautiful condition. There was no sign that any treasure hunters or archeologists had ever visited the site. It was clean pickings, and none of the men, including Marcus, was entirely able to resist the temptation. They filled their backpacks with thousands of dollars' worth of antiquities. There were enough artifacts on the temple grounds to allow them all to retire in style. Slowly, very slowly, they made their way forward.

As expected, they found the Well of the Furies at the direct center of the ruined temple. Scientifically, it was the location that made the most sense. The word *well* described the pit perfectly, for it was a round hole in the earth approximately ten feet in diameter, framed and walled with white marble tiles. The hole descended into the earth quite a ways.

Stefan bent down and picked up a small piece of marble from the ground. He tossed the stone into the well. It dropped out of sight into the darkness. An instant later, it hit water. "Thirty feet," declared Stefan. "Maybe more."

"It's definitely a well," said Billy the Bean. "Odd though. I smell salt. That's ocean water in the bottom."

"Spread out," commanded Marcus. "Let's not make any hasty decisions. This place sure appears to be the Well of the Furies, but let's be absolutely certain before we invest our time exploring it."

Stefan grimaced, but remained silent. Good old reliable, methodical Marcus Cole. The man who thought of everything, who never let life surprise him. Sometimes Stefan wondered how he had endured Marcus for so many years. Marcus was a smart man, but he was also afraid to take necessary chances. For Stefan, that ability to risk it all was the defining quality of true leadership. Marcus didn't have it, but Stefan did. If he had been running this operation, they'd be at the bottom of the well already, not nosing around the bushes. Sometimes you had to make an instant decision. A man who didn't risked missing the greatest opportunities—and the greatest rewards.

Stefan picked through the ruins like the rest of the gang but his mind was far, far away. As a boy, he had been an avid reader of the weekly illustrated magazine the *Frank Reade Library*. Every issue had told of Frank's exploits with his friends in far-off locations, using the latest advances in science and technology to accomplish some amazing quest. It was those stories and, later, the works of H. G. Wells and Jules Verne that had turned Stefan into an ardent believer in the power of technology. Science, and only science, could save the world from utter and complete chaos.

Stefan's experiences in the Great War and his perception of the political machinations that characterized both the war and its aftermath had convinced him that all the current governments, whether democracies or dictatorships, were corrupt. Big corporations had sold steel to both sides in the conflict, and the great oil fields of the Middle East remained stable, sheltered from the battles raging nearby. Politicians served their own interests, not those of the general population. Deals were made in smoke-filled back rooms, and countries were carved up as war spoils.

Wells's novel, *When the Sleeper Wakes*, had painted a bleak picture of the future. For humanity to survive and grow, a new set of leaders needed to take control. There was a name for such people, men who followed the inflexible laws of science and logic, and rejected the outdated rule of economics and emotion, men who applied the unbending rules of engineering to every aspect of society. They were known as technocrats. Stefan was certain they were the only ones who could set the world right.

Technocracy was an entirely new system of government devised in California in 1920 by engineer and scientist Howard Scott. Stefan had learned about it while in Paris with Marcus. An alternative form of society praised by men as diverse as H. G. Wells and Thorsten Veblen, technocracy was the rage among the Parisian intellectuals and the American conclave on the Continent known as "the Lost Generation." The philosophy had struck Stefan with the impact of a motorcar and he'd never quite recovered.

Technocracy dictated that the government be run on the same principles as a modern engineering firm. Scientific advances would make it possible for people to work less and have more money. Technocracy was a government that didn't believe in artificial boundaries like national borders. It was a system designed to run the entire planet, with the best and the brightest in charge, protecting the masses and keeping them content. In many ways technocracy, with its reliance of a special few to govern the many, resembled another form of government that was just taking hold in Europe during the twenties—fascism. Stefan considered Mussolini a swaggering buffoon, but he admired the secret society that stood behind the dictator and really ruled Italy. According to those who knew, the members of that organization called themselves Arachnos. Someday, Stefan wanted to meet these schemers. Not yet. At least, not until he and Marcus had discovered the secret of the Fountain of Zeus.

"Hey," said Marcus, breaking Stefan's train of thought, "you find anything of interest?"

"No," said Stefan sourly. "Not a thing. Anyone else do any better?"

"Unfortunately not," said Marcus as they walked back to the pit. "I'd be a lot happier if we could confirm that this hole in the ground was the well—and that the Fountain of Zeus is beneath it."

"Maybe we're missing the obvious," said Stefan. "Try holding the amulet over the pit. See what happens."

"Now that makes sense," said Marcus. "Come on."

The results were immediate and dramatic. Amulet held in his right hand, Marcus leaned out over the pool. None of the others made a sound. There was no need. The silver carving glowed like a miniature sun. It burned, but without heat. No one doubted that this was the Well of the Furies. The only question that remained was the location of the Fountain of Zeus.

"It can only be in one place," said Marcus. "We've searched the entire island and there's nothing even remotely resembling a fountain. The ancients must have somehow hidden the fountain beneath the bottom of the well."

"A place where only the gods and goddesses could reach," said Billy the Bean. "Makes sense to me if you believe in the supernatural."

"At the moment I'm not sure what I believe," said Marcus. "Any suggestions on what to do next?"

"We've got plenty of tubing and a good pump back on the schooner," said Stefan. "Let's bring it here and see if we can drain the well."

"I guess so," said Marcus. His complexion was pasty white and his voice cracked in pain. His stamina, though bolstered by the amulet, was fading, leaving him feeling weak. "If that's salt water, though, the well's connected by an underground outlet to the sea."

"Right, I figured that too," said Stefan. "But it never hurts trying."

Two hours and a lot of sore muscles later, their theory was proven correct. The gasoline-powered pump sucked salt water out of the well, but the waterline never budged. As fast as they pulled water out, it filled back up again.

"I gave the hole the once over," said Riley Shaw, who had spent several years studying engineering before volunteering for the army in 1917. "It's a basic ballistic water trap, designed to discourage intruders. More than likely, the water flows through ancient clay pipes buried throughout the island. They feed into the pit at various heights. Three thousand years ago, the well was probably filled to the top. I doubt that anyone at that time could swim to the bottom and make it up to the surface without his lungs exploding. Over the centuries, pipes broke, mechanisms failed, and the water level dropped to where it is today. There's a chance one of us could dive to the bottom, but I'm not certain what he'd find there. There's no practical method to drain the water out of the pit unless we're willing to spend the time searching for each and every hole, plug them up tight, and hope for the best."

"The real problem," said Stefan, "is that we're not attacking the problem head on. We're letting the problem attack us. Playing it cautious cost the Allies a million lives in the war and prolonged the fighting for years. We're following their lead. The only way we're going to discover the Fountain of Zeus is to smash our way to it."

"We've got to be careful," said Marcus. "The ancient

Greeks claimed the Well of the Furies was meant only for the gods. Ordinary mortals weren't welcome to its waters."

"Right," said Stefan. "But that was more than thirty centuries ago. I doubt any booby-traps in the well are still working."

"No wild ide—" began Marcus, who suddenly slouched over onto his knees in the middle of the sentence and collapsed facefirst to the ground. A bubble of blood popped on his lips.

"Like I said, the time for caution is over," declared Stefan. He lifted up Marcus in his arms. His friend's face was white as chalk and his whole body was shaking. "We can't afford to hesitate. We don't have weeks or months to find the fountain. We're down to days, maybe even hours. I'm going to take Marcus back to camp and pump him full of medicine. That should keep him alive. The rest of you try to think of a plan."

Walking slowly, trying not to cause his friend any more trauma than he had suffered already, Stefan carried Marcus back to the tents. The spasms seemed to have passed and Marcus was resting quietly, his eyes closed, half in sleep, half in unconsciousness. Searching through his friend's backpack, Stefan located a half dozen different painkillers. He knew from past experience which ones helped Marcus the most, but he also knew that none of them did a great deal of good. Each attack was worse. Cole had cheated death for over a decade. It looked like his luck was running out.

Lifting Marcus's head, Stefan fed him the pills one after another, each followed by a jolt of water. When they were half finished, his friend opened his eyes slightly and cracked his lips in a wan smile. "So close," Marcus mumbled. "So close and yet not close enough."

"You're not dead yet," said Stefan. For all of his disagreements with Marcus, this man was closer to him than any relative, meant more to him than anyone else in the world. They had fought side by side through dozens of deadly battles, had risked their lives for each other times without number. Stefan had known Marcus all his life. He couldn't imagine a world without him. "You're too tough to die."

"I don't feel so tough right now," said Marcus, his eyes slowly closing. "Do me a favor. Take the amulet from under my shirt and open the clasp. Let its golden light shine on me."

"Keep the faith, partner," said Stefan.

While Marcus believed that the charm given to him by the old bakery lady possessed mystic powers, Stefan had his doubts. He had never disbelieved Mrs. Kollikoros's stories about the Greek gods. He merely attributed their incredible powers to scientific, not supernatural origins. Radioactivity could change men into godlike supermen. That, he felt certain, was the true secret of the amulet—and the Fountain of Zeus, too.

The golden glow relaxed Marcus and within a few minutes, he was sound asleep. Stefan hated leaving his friend all alone at the camp, but there was nothing more he could do. Marcus was as safe here as anywhere else on the island. Better to get back to the rest of the gang and see if they had discovered anything more about the well.

That turned out to be a wise move. When Stefan walked back into the open space around the marble pit, the first person he noticed was Greg Hobart, stripped down to his shorts, a rope around his waist, sucking in deep breaths of air.

"Don't tell me," said Stefan, looking around at the faces of the rest of the Cole gang, "I can guess. Greg's planning to jump into the well and see what he can find."

"Why not?" asked Alan Gleason. "It's a bold attempt, but the right one. I'd have done the same if I were half the swimmer Greg is. You've seen him, Stefan. He's part fish. We figure that the builders wouldn't have constructed this pit without some sort of trick entrance. Sure, they wanted to discourage thieves and such, but making it inaccessible to even themselves don't make much sense. Since there's no entrance on the surface, we be figuring it's beneath the water."

Stefan agreed—not that he had much choice. Greg carried a sawtoothed dagger and wore a pair of rubber goggles with a glass facemask so that he could see through the murk. A recent invention of Guy Gilpatric, an American ex-aviator living in southern France, they were all the rage among divers.

Tying the end of the sixty-foot rope around the pump, they all grabbed hold and began lowering Greg into the well. In less than a minute, he was immersed up to his waist in salt water. It only took him a few seconds to untie himself and dive. They all held their breaths for the next two minutes, until his head once again emerged from the darkness.

"It's cold but I can manage," he called up to them. "The marble walls continue down, and the well is in remarkably good condition. There are plenty of traps hidden in the walls, but fortunately most seem to have been sprung by previous divers. You wouldn't believe the number of skeletons pinned to the stone. Creepy, but it makes things a lot safer for me. If I keep to the center of the pool, I think I can bypass any dangers."

"Spot any underwater pipes we could seal up?" Sid Sawyer yelled down. "Stop the flow of water into the well?"

"Sure, I spotted them," said Greg. "Along with the traps, there's dozens of openings, with bronze bars across them. We'd need to plaster over the entire well to stop the water coming through. I'm going to dive down farther, see what I can discover."

"Be careful," said Sid, but Greg was already underwater.

This time he was gone nearly four minutes and they were all sweating by the time his head once again broke the surface. Hanging on to the rope, Greg spent the next few minutes gulping down deep draws of air. "There's a black marble floor about fifteen feet below the surface," he finally gasped out between breaths. "In the middle of it, there's a trapdoor, also made out of marble, with a heavy metal ring in the center. I tried pulling it open, but no luck. The door's wedged in tight. There's one small crack, with a tiny stream of air bubbles rising from it. So it looks like there's a chamber with air in it beneath the well, just like Marcus guessed. Maybe it's where the fountain is located. If we can get past the water, we're home free. But it's going to take all of us working together to pull that door open."

"You sure it's safe down there?" called Alan Gleason.

"Not a sea monster in sight," yelled Greg. "The bars on the drains keep all but the tiniest fish out of the well.

Traps aren't a problem. Only thing I'm worried about is springing the door open and then not getting it closed quick enough to keep the underground chamber from flooding."

"It won't happen," said Sid. "Air pressure will keep the inner room dry. You'll see. Should be a snap."

A few moments more and Greg was ready once again to submerge. This time, he held the rope with one hand. "I'll tie it around the metal ring and give it a tug. You lugs pull with all your strength. I'll stay underwater and guide the door once it comes free. If I can, I'll climb into the chamber and see if I can find an alternate entrance."

"Stay safe," called Sid Sawyer, still worried, but Greg had vanished once again beneath the water's surface. The four men reached down and lifted the sturdy rope onto a winch raised waist high. In less than a minute, they felt the rope pull beneath their fingers.

"Heave!" cried Stefan, bracing his heels as best he could. "Heave!"

Time froze. The rope tightened as the four comrades pulled with all their strength. The air seemed to crackle with tension as they gave all they could. And, for an instant, a bare instant, the rope moved. Then it jerked back, almost pulling the quartet into the well.

They immediately knew what it meant. The underwater door had shifted upward for a moment, then it had been sucked back down into place. They had failed.

Sid Sawyer was more concerned with Greg Hobart. Lying on his stomach, he inched his body to the well's edge and looked down. "Blood," he declared. "There's blood in the water."

A few seconds later, Greg's body floated to the surface.

There was no question he was dead. There were a dozen wounds in his neck, face, and chest. The stab wounds, like those made by sharp swords, punctured his body, front to back. Greg Hobart had been wrong; not all the traps had been triggered by previous explorers or deactivated by the passage of time. The Well of the Furies had claimed another victim.

CHAPTER SEVEN

Marcus woke to the smell of human blood. It was an odor he'd first encountered in the war, and it was not a smell you ever forgot. He was lying faceup on top of his sleeping bag. He felt like hell. The blood was fresh, only a few hours old. He wasn't sure if was his own. Cautiously, Marcus opened his eyes. He was sprawled in front of his tent, with the rest of his gang crowded around the fire. The sky was dark gray and it looked as if a storm was approaching. Already, thunder crashed and lightning flashed only a few miles away. His men seemed unconcerned about the likelihood of rain. His wits slowly returning, Marcus thought back to the last conversation they'd had, just before he collapsed. Something about using desperate measures. Groaning, he forced himself into a sitting position. There were small flecks of blood on his mouth and nose, but nothing recent. Another near brush with death, he assumed. But he was still alive.

Six men sat around the fire, not seven. He finally

glimpsed a body wrapped and sewn in oilskin. Ready for a burial at sea.

"Who'd we lose?" he croaked.

"Greg," said Alan, handing Marcus a beer. "He went into the pool, found a floor with a trapdoor fifteen feet down. He felt certain there was a room beneath it filled with air. Probably where the fountain lies. It seemed safe enough so we tied a rope to the door to pull it open. A few of the traps in the pool were still active. When we tried the door, we set off a line of spring-driven spears hidden in the walls. Greg died a quick, unexpected death. The best we all can ask for."

Marcus chugged down the beer, and mused on Greg Hobart's demise. Greg had been a good companion for a long time, but Alan was right—a quick death was all any of the gang really expected. "Throw me over an apple, would you," he called to Sid Sawyer after a moment. "I can use a bite to eat."

"You seemed to have made a full recovery," said Stefan. "When I brought you back to camp, I thought I was lying you down for your eternal rest."

"Right," said Marcus. "I was having a nice pleasant talk with the heavenly host when they discovered there was a mistake in St. Peter's journal and I was in the wrong location. By the time they arranged the transportation, my spirit had found my body again and I woke up alive. It's a great trick, but I don't think I'll be able to play it again."

"So, Captain," asked Alan Gleason, handing Marcus a sandwich, "what's the plan?"

Marcus noticed Stefan's frown when Alan asked the question. No surprise, though it was a problem that needed solving. His friend was smart, strong, and ambitious.

He even had a cause he felt was worth fighting for—technocracy. Marcus knew it annoyed Stefan that he led the group—had always led of the group—and as long as he stayed alive, would always be considered the leader by the other members of the gang. Marcus treated Stefan as his strong right hand. But Marcus knew that, sooner or later, being second in command was not going to be enough for his friend. Stefan had never said a word about the matter, but his frowns and sneers made his opinions clear. He hoped the argument wouldn't have to be settled until after they found the Fountain of Zeus.

"Tomorrow morning, we'll take some measurements of the well," said Marcus, answering Gleason's question. "Stefan's right—brute force may be the only method of learning its secrets. But, we have to be smart about how we apply that force." He gestured to the corpse. "Once we have the measurements and the storm blows over, we'll head out to sea and bury Greg. Afterward, we'll stop off at that little fishing village on Kythria. We can buy the supplies we'll need for my plan there—some pieces of sheet metal and a few cuts of wood should do it. Everyone can spend time off ship and talk to the locals. See what they know about this island. If we spend some money in town, they might be a little more willing to chat."

The service at sea the next day was short but meaningful. The men had been together since 1917, and the years had forged strong bonds of friendship between them. A few of the original company had drifted away, but most of them had stuck together. Their experiences together—the hells they'd survived—had made the men closer than even family.

Greg had been a relatively quiet man who enjoyed a

good beer and never stepped away from a fight. He'd been married before the war, but his wife disappeared during his two years of service and he never returned to the States to look for her. He was a man who discovered what it meant to be alive during the great battles of Europe. He enjoyed living on the edge, putting his life in constant danger. There had been no place for him in peacetime America.

Sid, who had known him best of them all, said a few words. Then Riley Shaw played Taps on a harmonica he sometimes fooled with at night. Finally, with the words "Goodbye, Greg. You served your country and your friends with honor" from Marcus, they rolled the tarp-covered body off the schooner into the sea. Greg had made it clear he wanted no religious words at his funeral and they had kept to his wishes. The money he had saved over their years of adventuring he willed to the rest of them, having no desire to cause arguments among relatives he's not seen in years or never met. Greg might have been a quiet man, but he wasn't stupid.

They reached Kythria in the middle of the afternoon. Marcus's plan called for them to split up. Each man had a list of items to buy, everything from food to tools to wood post. Afterward, they were all instructed to spend some money in the local bars and casually inquire about the lost island. None of the gang was trained in spy craft, but nearly fifteen years spent on the run from the law had given them a skill with small talk. They left the schooner at three o'clock and promised to return to the boat by nine that night.

Marcus remained with the ship. He didn't have much energy and the others could buy supplies without him. He definitely didn't have it in him right now to sit at a tavern for hours sipping ouzo with the locals. He had faith in his men, including their ability to stay fairly sober under even the most trying of conditions.

They wandered back in, one by one, around eight-thirty. Riley Shaw staggered up to the ship, looked Marcus in the eyes, said, "See the three sisters," and promptly fell asleep on his feet. Marcus sleepwalked him down to his bunk and returned to the deck just in time to watch Billy the Bean wobble up the gangplank one unsteady footstep after another, his arms spread wide apart to help his balance.

"The three sisters on the hill," said the Bean, his breath unbearable. "They're the ones," he muttered as he folded himself in half, his back to the cabin deck, eyes wide open but seeing nothing. "Take my word for it."

Sid Sawyer was next. He seemed fine until he came across Billy the Bean lying on the deck. "Obviously, the Bean overestimated his capacity for liquor," stated Sid in his usual solemn tone. Without another word, he sat down next to the unconscious man, put his head on his shoulder, and fell asleep.

Tom Ricks and Alan Gleason danced a path along the pier, performing an Irish jig while singing "Auld Lang Syne" in perfect harmony. Ricks only sang when he was drunk, which was a shame, as he had a beautiful voice. Watching the two try to dance their way up the gangplank was amusing, but Marcus was growing impatient by the time they finally made it on board. "It's definitely the three sisters you need to see, Marcus," proclaimed Gleason, with a wink and a nod, then joined Ricks on the bow of the boat to continue singing traditional Irish drinking tunes.

Stefan arrived at the boat promptly at nine. Looking at the rest of the crew, he shook his head and laughed. "They forgot how powerful ouzo is. Stuff has the kick of a mule. It's more than forty percent alcohol. Got to sip it, and eat plenty of *mezedes* while you're drinking."

"You okay?" asked Marcus.

"Comparatively sober," said Stefan, "though I could probably light a cigar with my breath. Any of them mention the three sisters?"

"Just about all of them," said Marcus. "At least the ones who could still talk."

"Well, everyone agrees that they're the ones to talk to about the island," said Stefan. "Sounds like we're not the only ones who've found it and talked to them. There have been others. Some Italians came asking about it about twenty years ago. Another old-timer remembered a crew of Spaniards maybe ten years earlier than them. Same story—asked some questions in town, then went to see the sisters."

"Maybe sailors from one of those expeditions planted those grape fields," said Marcus.

"Maybe," said Stefan. "Though I doubt it."

"These three sisters must be rather old ladies by now."

"I commented in that, too. That's when everyone I was drinking with suddenly found something else to do. End of conversation, period, poof, no more. There's something *really* strange about them, Marcus. More than isolated fishing village strange."

"I think we need to visit these mystery women. First thing tomorrow morning."

"They're waiting for us now," said Stefan.

"What?" Marcus, who disliked being surprised, was surprised. "Why are they waiting for us?"

"One of the sisters came down from their villa this morning to buy bread and cheese," said Stefan. "She told the baker to pass along a message that we should come to see them tonight. No matter what the hour."

"We didn't decide to come to this island until last night," said Marcus.

"Right," said Stefan. "I know. I told you—*strange.*"

"Weird," said Marcus. He waved a hand at the rest of the crew, most of them asleep. "Safe to leave them here in this condition?"

"Do we have a choice?" replied Stefan. "Ricks and Gleason are awake, even if they're singing. They'll keep an eye out for thieves. Besides, we've done it before."

"Right. You know the way?"

"Follow me," said Stefan, and off they went.

Thirty minutes later, they were a mile inland and a half mile up from where the boat rested in the harbor. A huge old villa, more of a fortress than a home, stood perched on a solid rock foundation. A six-foot-tall wrought-iron fence enclosed the entire grounds. The lights in all the buildings were off, and the villa looked deserted. There was nothing to do but search for the gate.

Three women, each only a few inches shorter than Marcus's six feet, dressed in identical black gowns that perfectly matched their long, curly black hair and deep black eyes, waited for the two of them at the gate. Their faces were the white of fine marble, and they had thin black eyebrows, ruby-red lips, and well-defined, almost needle-thin features. They appeared perfectly proportioned beneath their silk gowns. None of them wore any jewelry, and they needed none. Though their features shared many similarities, there were minor differences that marked them as sisters but not identical siblings.

"Welcome, strangers," said the first woman, slightly taller than the other two. "My name is Megan. We have been expecting you." She turned and disappeared into the darkness enshrouding the house.

"Welcome twice, Mr. Cole and Mr. Richter," said the second woman, her voice a shade deeper, making her sound slightly older than the first. "Your fame precedes your visit. I am called Alexis." She beckoned them follow.

They climbed a steep path that brought them to a ledge looking out on the sea.

"Welcome a last time," said the third sister. There was something about the way she arched her eyebrows as she spoke, as if she found everything in the world amusing. "My name is Phoebe. You've had a long walk from the dock. Would you care for some wine? We make it ourselves, using some very special grapes."

She gestured with one hand, the wind blew, some leaves shifted, and a large wood table with five heavy wood chairs appeared out of the shadows of a nearby tree. Marcus smiled at the theatricality of it all, though he also recognized how much more was at work here than simple stagecraft.

"Please, sit," said Alexis. "Our wine is famous throughout the world. Kings and dictators and presidents fight for the honor of owning a bottle, but we are very careful to whom we give a drink. Very careful."

Megan returned, carrying five chilled glasses, a bottle of wine, and a bottle opener. She uncorked the bottle and poured them each a half glass. Marcus wasn't surprised to see that the liquid glowed golden in the starlight. These women were no ordinary winemakers.

"You carry something that was once ours, child," said Phoebe. She looked years younger than Marcus, but he wasn't going to correct her. "May we see it?"

Reaching beneath his shirt, Marcus pulled out the amulet presented to him by Mrs. Kallikoros. Its glow matched the golden light from the wine.

"So it returns," said Megan. "Full circle."

"The woman who gave it to me said this charm had been in her family for hundreds of years."

"So it has," said Alexis. "A young girl showed us a path through the mountains."

"We were being pursued," said Megan.

"By priests who wanted to do us ill," said Phoebe.

"It was a small reward for saving our lives," said Alexis. "We are glad to see it served her well."

"One drop," said Phoebe. "That is all that remains pure."

"Remember those words," said Alexis, looking first at Marcus, then at Stefan. "Keep the token. When you no longer need it, pass it on to another who does."

"Enough of the past," said Megan, raising her glass. "Let us drink to the present. And to the future, whatever it made hold."

"This wine is made from the grapes grown on the slopes of Praxidae," noted Marcus, swirling the liquid in the goblet. He had never smelled wine with such a delightful aroma. "Can it be nectar, the drink of the gods?"

All three women laughed, tinkling soft sounds filled with humor. "A poor imitation of nectar, I'm afraid," said

Megan. "Think of it as a distant cousin to the fruit of the gods. Drink, Marcus Cole. You will be better for it."

Marcus raised the glass to his lips and drank. The wine rolled over his tongue, into his throat with a light, smooth touch. It was enchanting, bewitching, erotic, and incredibly sweet. It was the most amazing wine he had ever tasted. The pain in his chest lessened to a dull ache and new strength surged through his arms and his legs. It felt as if a giant weight had been lifted off his shoulders. Most of all, he felt content.

"That was just your first taste," said Alexis, smiling. "Finish the glass and you'll understand why kings would give up their countries for a bottle of this wine."

"Who are you?" asked Stefan. The glass in his hand was empty, but the expression on his face was one of curiosity, not contentment. Obviously, the wine didn't have the same effect on him as it had on Marcus. "We're looking for information about Praxidae. Do you own the island? Or, perhaps, you're the owners' agents. . . ."

"No one owns Praxidae," said Phoebe. "It belongs to the earth. From time to time we travel there to tend the grapes and trim the trees and clear the debris. We do nothing more and nothing less. We work for no one but ourselves."

"We are merely three sisters who went on a search," said Megan. "And found a dream."

"We search still," said Alexis. "But now we look for answers."

"We're searching also," said Marcus, taking another drink. "We're looking for the Fountain of Zeus."

"A legend," said Alexis. She smiled, sipped the wine from her glass. "A myth."

"A tale from ancient times," said Phoebe. "A child's fable."

"Fantasy," said Megan. "Pure fantasy."

"We believe it exists somewhere beneath the Well of the Furies," replied Marcus. "We were hoping you could tell us an easier way of getting to the fountain than down through the well. We've lost one man already and don't want to lose any others."

"Not all questions have answers," said Alexis.

"The obvious answer is not always the right one," said Megan.

"The right answer is sometime obvious," said Phoebe.

"Riddles," Stefan spat. "I hate riddles. Can't you just tell us how to find the Fountain of Zeus?"

"We've seen many things," said Alexis.

"We're older than we look," continued Megan.

"We know many secrets," Phoebe noted. "But we answer all those who seek answers with the same words. That is our way."

"So you won't tell us anything?" said Marcus.

"We cannot," said Megan. "You are not the first."

"We dare not," said Alexis. "Most likely, you will not be the last."

"We are bound not to speak," said Phoebe. "But there is a warning—"

"We heard it from another—" continued Alexis.

"So we can pass it along to you—" said Megan.

"There is a price for the pain," they intoned. The three sisters dressed all in black rose to their feet. "For each one who enters, another must be slain."

CHAPTER EIGHT

The brightly tiled floor of the bank trembled beneath Monica's feet. The vibrations made no sound but sent a flurry of dust from the crossbeams into the lobby. Flustered, Monica dropped her pen to the floor, while her checks and deposit slip flitted across the glass counter. Hurriedly she gathered her material together, then glanced to the right and left. No one else seemed to have noticed. The quake had been so sharp and so sudden that, like most city dwellers, the people in the bank appeared willing to ignore it. Anything that would take time away from their busy schedule they preferred to pretend never happened.

Thwump. This time the bank floor shook more noticeably, and a few tiles popped loose on the floor. An alarm sounded in the rear of the bank, and one of the glass deposit counters cracked and then shattered into jagged pieces. The cracking glass sounded like gunfire. "Earthquake," someone yelled. "Earthquake!"

Monica had experienced an earthquake on her visit to

California last summer, and this wasn't one of those gut-wrenching shifts in the earth's surface that left you feeling like you were in two places at once. These shock waves moved up and down, not side to side. Something heavy was pounding the street outside the bank, sending tremors through the building's foundation. It wasn't the earth moving, but the ground shaking.

The floor and walls of the First National Bank shuddered a third time as whatever approached drew closer. The huge glass windowpane facing the street shivered in its frame. A web of fine cracks radiated outward from the window's center. In seconds, the entire pane was frosted white.

"Get down!" screamed Monica, dropping to the floor. Most of the people around her seemed unaware of their danger. "Down! Now!"

Then the gigantic window exploded inward, sending pieces of glass hurtling like missiles at the people in the lobby. Dozens of customers shrieked in agony, and their blood spattered the floor. Only Monica and a few others wise enough to realize what was going to happen were unharmed.

"Fast thinking," yelled Joe Grisham, the staff photographer who accompanied Monica to the bank every Thursday to deposit the week's checks into the newspaper's account. No crook had ever threatened Monica during the six-block trip from her office to the bank, but Rudy was always cautious. His paper ran on a shoestring budget, and every payment he made kept the wolf away from the door a day more.

Grabbing Monica by one arm, Joe dragged her behind a heavy table. People were screaming now and rushing madly from the bank's lobby in a wild charge for the street. Moving in a panic that could only get worse. "We've got to stop them, Joe," said Monica, trying to stand up. "These people need our help."

"Make a move and you'll be trampled," said Joe, not letting go of Monica's coat. "I feel sorry for them, too, but there's no reasoning with a mob. We stay here until things calm down."

The pistonlike thumping grew louder. The shattered glass on the floor jumped into the air with each thud. Above the noise, Monica could hear the sounds of horns honking, of metal crashing into metal. Something was happening outside. Cars were smashing into cars. There was panic in the streets, as well as inside the bank. She muttered a very unladylike curse. A big story was occurring not fifty feet away, and she couldn't see a thing.

Someone screamed, and the crowd surging just beyond Monica and Joe suddenly froze in place. All heads turned to where the glass window had been and a collective moan of fear rose inside the building. Seizing the opportunity, Monica, with Joe at her side, stood up. Her eyes grew wide with shock and disbelief when she caught a glimpse of the metal thing framed by the broken window.

She glanced at Joe and found him frozen with fear. "Take a picture," she whispered, elbowing him in the ribs. "Take a damned picture!"

The machine stood nine feet tall and was shaped like a man, with two legs, two arms, and a head. It looked as if it had been constructed out of battleship steel, and its chest was a huge cylinder, perhaps four feet in diameter. Its arms, which stretched almost to the ground, were equally gigantic cylinders, a foot in diameter, each ending in a massive pincher ten inches long. The automaton had short, stubby legs and wide boxlike feet that appeared to be made of solid steel. Monica guessed the heavy shoes helped the machine keep its balance.

Its head was a foot high and a foot thick, and was perched at the center of its cylindrical body. Two small yellow searchlights served as its eyes. A grotesque parody of a human being, it dripped red blood. Not its own blood, but that of others. Beyond the monster, in the street, Monica could see a line of crushed and smashed cars stretching halfway down the block. In the distance, she could hear the whine of police and fire sirens.

With a whirring, clunking sound, the robot monster stepped forward, its huge foot coming down hard on the bank floor. Floor tiles crunched, ground into dust. The machine was so heavy that it sank inches into the ground with each step. Moving slowly, deliberately, the robot took another step forward, heading toward the trapped customers.

"Keep calm!" Monica called. "Don't panic!"

"It's after us!" screamed a woman in the crowd. She drowned Monica's more reasoned plea, and, in an instant, dozens of others had taken up her cry. With shrieks of panic, the horrified bank patrons scattered in all directions like a flock of sparrows being chased by a hawk.

Monica turned to Joe. "Did you get those photos?"

"Sure," said Joe. "Question is, will we get out of here alive so I can develop them?"

"We're not leaving yet," said Monica. "That machine's not interested in us. It wants the cash in the clerk's drawers. See."

Monica was right. The automaton had stopped at the tellers' cages and was using its claw hands to dump drawer after drawer filled with cash into a sliding compartment that had emerged from its chest. It totally ignored the people running by. The machine was merely a bank robber made of metal.

"Keep taking pictures," said Monica. "We'll run it on the front page of tomorrow's edition. Quick, before the thing decides to leave."

Joe was no fool. He knew a picture of the steel behemoth robbing a bank would make the front pages of newspapers all over the country. Not only would it boost the *Free Press*'s sales, but the photo would sell for lots to the wire services. It might even win a Pulitzer.

"Uh-oh," said Monica. "I think the thing hears the police sirens. It's getting ready to leave."

Joe was busy snapping his pictures. As if suddenly sensing the camera's flash, the robot took a half step toward Monica and the photographer. Before she had time to panic, it stopped, raised its two immense arms over its head, and spoke.

"I . . . am . . . Nemesis," the robot declared in a mechanical voice crackling from a loudspeaker somewhere on its metal frame. "Fear . . . me."

Monica's jaw dropped in astonishment. She had thought for a moment the machine was going to smash the camera, or them, but it had announced its name. The thing—or whoever was controlling it—wanted publicity!

Then the massive steel construct marched out of the bank. A heavyset police officer, one of the two normally stationed in the bank, raced from behind one of the tellers' counters, a pistol clutched in both hands. He closed to within a few feet of the giant machine. Taking aim at the back of the metal monster's head, he squeezed the gun's trigger. Three times he fired. The bullets sped quick and true and slammed into the automaton's skull—then bounced off. The gunship steel wasn't even scratched.

The machine kept walking. "Come back here, you thieving monster!" the cop shouted.

Without warning, one of the automaton's arms swung backward, moving like the clapper of a gigantic bell. Metal claws extended full length, the immense arm couldn't miss. The monster's hand slapped the cop right in the chest. A blow with the power of a dozen sledgehammers lifted him high into the air and knocked him across the room. His lifeless body left a bloodred blot on the far wall, then he crashed to the floor, every bone in his chest crushed.

"I . . . am . . . Nemesis," intoned the automaton again. "Fear . . . me."

Monica spotted three police cars pulling up outside to form a barricade. Twenty cops armed with Thompson submachine guns waited, while a senior officer handled a bullhorn. "Surrender, now," he commanded. "We have the bank surrounded. You can't escape."

"Be careful," Joe snarled as he tried to yank Monica down to the floor besides him. Most of the other customers had escaped the bank or fled to the safety of the basement with the employees. Those few that remained were flat on the floor like Joe, cowering from fear or cringing in pain. Monica didn't budge. This was the biggest story of her life. She wasn't going to miss a second of it, even if it meant standing in the midst of a gun battle.

"If the cops start firing," said Joe, "drop to the floor. Nobody shooting a Tommy gun aims that well."

"I can take care of myself," said Monica. "You just keep that camera busy."

"Surrender, or we'll shoot," said the officer, whose

voice seemed to waver only slightly when he discovered he was not facing a gang of bank robbers but a solitary thing of metal some nine feet tall.

"Put your hands over your head and step away from the building," the policeman commanded. "Now."

Unfortunately, the automaton did exactly that. It hoisted its huge arms high over its head, the massive claws on its hands wide open. The bank's ceiling was fourteen feet off the ground and the metal pincers grabbed hold of the wood crossbeams. Mortar and wood cracked and tore as the robot dragged its arms straight ahead, and sent a hail of debris hurtling onto the street. Machine guns blazed but they were useless against the falling wood, brick, and mortarboard. The debris crashed onto the police cars and the men standing around them with horrific impact. None of the officers had a chance to move, not one had a chance to flee. Twenty lives were wiped out in an instant. Blood ran in the street. Clouds of dust filled the air. Horns blared and onlookers screamed in terror as the automaton marched forward, disappearing into the dense haze.

Monica clenched her teeth. She wanted to scream, wanted to run shouting from the bank, but now was not the time to lose control. "Where's it going?" she called to Joe, who had raced to the twisted window frame. A cloud of dust hung over the street, cutting visibility to near nothing. The thunder of the robot's footsteps grew softer as it marched away from the bank.

"I can't see too well," said Joe, peering into the haze. "But I think it's climbing down the stairs leading to the subway."

"Well," said Monica, "what are we waiting for?"

Following the killer robot proved simple enough. A

trail of dead bodies marked its passage down the subway steps and past the ticket office. Three demolished turnstiles indicated which tunnel it had chosen for its destination. A solitary commuter—a man in his sixties, with gray hair and startled blue eyes—was the only figure on the northbound platform. He appeared unharmed, just frightened beyond belief.

"Did a mechanical man come through here?" Monica asked. "Just a few minutes ago?"

"Yes," the man replied, his voice trembling just a little. "There were only a few other people here. They all ran up the other stairway. I tripped and fell. The thing ignored me."

"Where did it go?"

The man pointed into the northbound tunnel. "That way. It jumped onto the tracks and walked off into the darkness."

"I'm not following no damned mechanical *thing* into a subway tunnel," declared Joe. "Newspaper doesn't pay me that well."

Monica was tempted to go on alone, but she decided against it. Best to wait for the police and see what they could find.

The riot squad arrived five minutes later. Though they stopped the trains and searched the tunnels for hours, they found no sign of the mechanical monster. Somehow, it had vanished without a trace.

CHAPTER NINE

"We've got the biggest story in Paragon City history," said Monica to her father, late that afternoon, "with photos to match. But that's not good enough for our readers?"

"It's not enuff," said Rudy, waving his blue pencil in the air. "It's very nice, but we must give the people of this city all the news, not part of the news. You know that. I know that. They know that. So, stop arguing with me. You're wasting valuable time. Go find me the rest of this story, Monica. You haff a few hours before we go to press."

Monica had been raised right, so she didn't curse her obstinate father. Besides, she knew in her heart that he was right and she was wrong. It wasn't enough that she had delivered a major scoop only a few hours before. Even the photos, good as they were, were not enough. For the story to resonate with the readership, it needed to be grounded in facts. Otherwise, it was just a headline with some nice pictures. The news was more than just a few lines of type stating the obvious. A good newspaper writer took those headlines and wove them into a piece that you couldn't forget. That's what her father wanted, and that's what she was going to deliver. Assuming she could find out something about this Nemesis.

Determined to get the story right, Monica marched up the concrete steps leading into the main library. Head down, staring at the floor, she made eye contact with no one. The set of her shoulders and the determined thrust of her hat made it clear she didn't wished to be disturbed. Step after step, aisle after aisle, she marched through the library like Wyatt Earp heading for the OK Corral. As she passed each section, the librarian in charge of the area breathed a sigh of relief. They had all dealt with Monica when she was in one of these moods. They had no desire, no desire at all, to deal with her when she was in such a mood again.

An audible sigh drifted through the library when Monica disappeared into the basement, where stacks of newspapers from the past century were kept in watertight binders. Jasper Johnston ran the newspaper morgue and anyone who wanted to sift through the bound newspapers did it with his permission. An old man, nearly a hundred, with skin as yellowed and crinkled as any of the newsprint he handled, Johnston was a crime news junky. If you were interested in some obscure murder from the nineteenth century and it had been reported in any of the major newspapers published in the U.S.A., Jasper Johnston knew all about it. He knew the criminals, the victims, the cause of death, and the motives. Historians from all over the country came to learn about crime history from him.

The *New York Times* had dubbed him "Crime History's Homer," a title he told everyone he met. Having visited the basement numerous times with her father, Monica knew Jasper better than most. They got along reasonably well, meaning they talked when Jasper felt like talking. Still, Jasper was old-fashioned enough that he wasn't all that comfortable with a woman covering crime.

"It's a big story," said Monica, sitting on the small chair that served as the only guest seat in Jasper's office. "Twenty policemen killed, and no solid leads on the real murderer. But I bet you have information that will bust the case wide open."

"Me?" said Jasper in a wheezing voice, pointing a long gnarled finger at his chest. He smiled, exposing a mouthful of yellow teeth. With his pure white hair, wrinkled skin, and light gray eyes, he looked like a mummy. "You think I have information that can help break this case?"

"Most likely solve the case and point the finger at the man behind the murders," said Monica. She knew that Jasper liked to feel he made a difference. He considered getting his name published in a newspaper a high honor. "The thing that tore apart the First National Bank today was a metal man, an automaton, possessing the strength of ten. It bragged its name was Nemesis right before it disappeared."

"Nemesis. . . ." said Jasper, his face crinkled in deep thought. "I remember that name, but he's no run-of-the-mill thug. No, this crook's a special one. I'm thinking I first heard about Nemesis fighting for the South during the Civil War."

Despite her inner vow to be ready for anything, for any

revelation or surprise, Monica drew in a slow, deep breath. "Nemesis fought in the Civil War, over sixty years ago? That would make him at least eighty years old today."

"Possibly older," said Jasper Johnston, chuckling. "I doubt that he started constructing these automatons when he was just a teenager. He needed years and years of practice to make them work efficiently. Let's wander through the newspaper files and see what turns up."

It took very little time for them to locate an old reference to the criminal mastermind. And from there, with Jasper's expertise, the investigation proved even easier. They broke the job into two parts. Jasper located references in the huge bound volumes of old newspapers, skimmed the articles and stories, and then dictated the important information about Nemesis to Monica, who transcribed it in her notebooks. Fortunately, many of the stories covered his history in depth, providing them invaluable cross-references about his early life. Slowly but surely, they constructed a detailed portrait of the genius known as the Prince of Automatons.

Like many of the criminal masterminds in history, the man who called himself Nemesis began life as a toy maker. His real name was Gerhardt Eisenstadt and he was born in 1804, the youngest son of the Prussian house of Eisenstadt. For centuries, his noble ancestors had supplied swords and armor for the kings and nobles of all the major kingdoms of Europe. The nineteenth century was a period of unprecedented growth for the company. They expanded their inventory to include guns, rifles, and other modern battlefield weaponry. Their fortune was estimated to be one of the largest in Europe.

Gerhardt grew up during the Napoleonic Wars, a

period when his family progressed from very rich to un-believably rich, as they supplied arms to the Prussian, Austrian, and Russian armies. Gerhardt was raised as a spoiled, pampered child. As best Monica could tell, from consulting detailed newspaper accounts of the time, Gerhardt was not noted as being particularly intelligent or ambitious. That changed when he was twelve.

All accounts of Gerhardt Eisenstadt's career in crime described his twelfth birthday party as the turning point in his life. It was at this family celebration that his parents gave him a life-sized clockwork horse. The machine, designed by a team of Swiss clockmakers, could walk, run, even jump. It was perhaps the most sophisticated piece of machinery produced in nineteenth-century Europe. The toy, if such a marvelous invention could be so catego-rized, fascinated Gerhardt. For weeks, then months, he did nothing other than play with his fabulous gift.

Even the greatest inventions last only so long under constant use. So it was with Gerhardt's mechanical horse. One day, the machine ceased to move and no amount of winding, pounding, or tearful entreaties could make it run again. Gerhardt's parents assumed the boy's atten-tion would, as usual, shift to the new playthings they bought for him. To their surprise, that wasn't the case. In-stead, Gerhardt told his father he wanted to learn how to build clockwork devices. He wanted to create mechanical beings just like his horse. And build them so they lasted forever.

Delighted with their son's interest in science, the Eisenstadts hired the clockmakers who had constructed the mechanical horse to come to their estate and tutor Gerhardt. The boy's intelligence surprised everyone, as did his drive, and within a year, he had learned everything the clockmakers could teach him, and more. Following as rigid a schedule as any college student, the teenager investigated clocks, gears, mechanics, and metallurgy. By the time he was twenty, Gerhardt was producing incredible mechanical devices that mimicked the actions of every animal he had ever seen. However, not everyone in his family was impressed by his newfound engineering skills.

Jealous of the attention Gerhardt was receiving from their parents, his elder brother, Tobias, challenged the young genius to invent something practical, some weapon of war that would earn the family money. Gerhardt refused. He had no interest in the mundane concerns of business. He invented for the sheer joy of inventing. Still, Tobias continued to taunt Gerhardt. For five years, the feud continued. Then, finally tiring of his brother's ceaseless criticism, Gerhardt built his first automaton—a human-shaped robot—which promptly killed Tobias. From that point on, Gerhardt refused to acknowledge any laws but his own. Willingly, he abandoned human society and took to a life of crime.

During the next ten years, Gerhardt's infamy grew. Though forgotten in modern times, he had once been feared throughout Europe. From 1825 through 1837, he conducted a one-man crime wave that killed nearly a thousand people, including hundreds of nobles. He took to calling himself "the Prussian Prince of Automatons." The rich hated him while the poor loved him, because Gerhardt only seemed to target the wealthiest for his victims. It was during this same period that a newspaper in England started calling him "the Nemesis of the Nobility." Of course, Gerhardt didn't show mercy to anyone who got in his way, and it soon became clear that his reputation for sparing the poor was inspired more from his contempt for them than any sort of social conscience. Before long, he was known simply as "Nemesis."

According to the European newspapers, Nemesis was surrounded and killed in 1837, when three British warships trapped him on the island of Malta and bombarded his fortress for an entire day. The Prince of Automatons perished when he was hit by cannon fire during an assault on the base by squadrons of Royal Marines. His body, however, was never recovered.

Monica stopped writing for a moment, and Jasper, seeing her caught up in thought, paused in his reading. She'd realized something. Despite the Prussian's long list of terrible crimes, he was totally forgotten today. Remembered only in these musty old newspapers. A century of death and destruction leading up to the most violent conflict of all time, the Great War, had relegated him to this obscurity. Perhaps Gerhardt—if he was somehow still alive—or whoever had taken on the name Nemesis was hoping to change that; certainly he was not shy about publicity, as she'd seen at the bank. She signaled to Jasper to continue, and he did so eagerly. Nemesis's story, it seemed, was far from over.

In late 1863, reports started to filter into Union headquarters from the mountains of North Carolina about a group of rebel raiders—"armored men, riding steel horses"—who were wrecking havoc upon army patrols. These stories continued over the next year, and included metal men on mechanical horses fast enough to outrun a locomotive and rifles capable of firing cannonballs. It was a British paper that first raised the possibility the inventions might be the work of some former assistant to Nemesis who had made his way to America. Never one to retreat on the field or off, General Grant offered a $10,000 reward for the capture of the mastermind behind the mechanical marvels.

No one claimed the bounty, but the South, even with the help of the strange inventions, wasn't capable of winning the war. Once the treaty was signed at Appomattox, Grant immediately sent General Sherman and his army to hunt down and destroy the metal brigade.

Meanwhile, British and French intelligence had concluded that the person behind the inventions was none other than Nemesis, who had somehow escaped from Malta. Several retired military men who had battled the Prince of Automatons were sent to advise Sherman on his march to North Carolina. Relying on their judgment, Sherman cancelled plans for an all-out ground assault on the rebel base and, instead, commenced shelling the mountaintop. Caught totally by surprise, the metal army was chopped to pieces by artillery. Afterward, a thorough search was conducted of the enemy headquarters. Investigators discovered recent letters written by Gerhardt, proving he had been the mastermind guiding the robots, but once again his body was never found. It was optimistically assumed he died during the shelling.

"Perhaps not," declared Monica, closing her notebook. She had pages upon pages of notes on Nemesis, and she doubted she could fit all the material into one background article. But, she'd try.

"He sounds like a pretty dangerous fellow," drawled Jasper Johnston as Monica made ready to depart. "Hard to kill."

"Maybe," said Monica. "If Gerhardt was born in 1805, that would make him over one hundred and twenty-five years old today, assuming he'd survived both bombardments. It's more likely that several men have been using the name, and the plans for the mechanical marvels. Still, after seeing that thing at the bank, I wouldn't rule out something more fantastic. Maybe Gerhardt's discovered the secret of eternal life."

"Damned if I didn't think of that," said Jasper with a wheezing laugh. "I wonder if the old coot would tell me his secret."

"If I interview him, I'll ask," said Monica as she grabbed her purse and started walking up to the first floor.

"Ask who?" came a voice from the top of the stairs.

Inwardly, Monica groaned. It was Jennifer Nayland, girl reporter and general busybody for the *Paragon City Times*, the city's biggest daily paper. Jennifer was a few years older than Monica, blond as Jean Harlow, with blue eyes and a baby-doll complexion. She was also a damned good reporter. She could spot a major news story a mile away and she wrote in an easy, chatty prose that Monica only wished she could duplicate. Worst of all, despite all of the sharp tactics she used to get a scoop, Jennifer was actually a pretty nice person. She and Monica were friends and sometimes sparring partners at the gym Ezra Cole had recommended.

"Monica," said Jennifer with a sly grin as she bounced down the stairs. Wearing a long black skirt, slit down the side, a white blouse, and a checkered vest and matching cap, Jennifer was the soul of good taste and high fashion. "What a surprise running into you here. Were you talking

to my good friend Jasper? I bet I can guess about what—
or, should I say, who?"

"You're too late, Jenny," said Monica, trying not to
sound petty. "You'll never catch up in the research and
make the morning edition in time. This is my scoop."

"Is it?" said Jennifer. "Maybe. I did mention something at the city desk about having a late story. I think
they might hold the presses for news about Paragon's
newest crime lord."

"Nemesis is my story," said Monica, a sinking feeling
growing in her stomach.

"Only if you get it into print first," said Jennifer. "Our
paper comes out an hour before yours. See you later,
kiddo. I've got to do some research."

Monica hurried up the steps to the main floor. For an
instant, she considered locking the door to the basement,
trapping Jennifer and Jasper downstairs for a few hours.
But that wouldn't be ethical, and Monica prided herself
on her ethics. Besides, the basement had three exits and
locking them all would take too much time. Sighing,
she left the building. Rudy was waiting for her story. She
didn't want to let him down, even if the same story would
appear in the *Times* under Jennifer's byline.

Yet, to Monica's great surprise, when she picked up
her copy of the *Times* the next morning, there wasn't a
word about Nemesis. It was her story, in the *Free Press*,
with the scoop. Jennifer's column covered fall fashions.

"What happened?" Monica asked Jennifer as the two
of them ate lunch at a local reporters' hangout. "Where's
the story?"

"In the trash," said Jennifer with a mournful look.

"Too bad, as I gave it a swell write-up. My editor read one paragraph and canned it."

Jennifer's voice sank to a whisper. "The city editor was told to downplay the story. Makes no sense since crime sells papers. Pressure like that only comes from the top. I think a certain big-shot politician didn't want a massacre leading the front page on the same day he announced that he was running for another term. Stuff like that might jeopardize his chance of getting reelected. . . ."

Monica's eyes widened, but just a little bit. Jennifer had more than once complained about her work being censored by the city desk manager, as part of some vague political agenda. But this was the first time she had come right out and stated that crooked politicians controlled the paper.

"Besides, Mon," said Jennifer, her voice slightly louder but equally concerned. "This Nemesis guy sounds like trouble."

"Actually," Monica said. "I got a note from him this morning. I guess he reads the *Free Press*."

She drew a small piece of paper from her purse. In a neat, cramped hand was written: *Do not mistake me as a pretender to the title Prince of Automatons. There is only one Nemesis, one genius worthy of that name. I have conquered time just as completely as I will conquer this city.*

Jennifer handed the paper back to Monica. "He wants publicity, sure, and maybe he really is the same old geezer who fought in the Civil War. But can't you see the threat implied here? If he doesn't like what you write next time, he could turn on you. Creeps like him get mad real easy, Mon. Mad enough to kill."

CHAPTER TEN

The boat trip back to the Isle of Vengeance was notable for its absolute silence. Most of the crew were battling hangovers that could be conquered only by a total lack of noise and the absence of food or drink. Stefan, who felt better than most, sat in the rear of the schooner's cabin, mulling over the words spoken by the three strange sisters.

He still wasn't completely sure if he believed what he had been told last night. All his life, he had accepted science as the basis for all truth. He had dismissed superstition and religion as foolish, something based on dreams and illusion, not on facts and figures. Now, for the first time, he was confronted by beings who seemed to make mockery of all that he believed. Could humans actually predict the future? Were ancient curses really true?

Nonsense, Stefan decided. He felt certain that, given enough time, he would find logical explanations for everything he and Marcus had seen and heard.

They reached the island late that night and ate a leisurely dinner. No reason to start carrying the supplies from the ship to the cliffs just yet. There would be plenty of work for them all tomorrow. Instead, Marcus gathered everyone around the fire for a short meeting.

"Stefan and I talked to three very unusual women last night on Kythria, and while we can't verify what they said was true, the peasants on the island seemed to think these women possess supernatural powers. They definitely acted strange enough. Unfortunately, they didn't tell us any of the secrets of the Well of the Furies. They did, however, reveal an ancient curse that affects those who try to take the treasure. According to them, for each man who finds the fountain, another man must die."

"You think they might be wrong, Captain?" asked Alan Gleason.

"It's all nonsense," said Stefan with more certainty than he felt. "Meaningless gibberish. The women were frauds. The wine was drugged. They treated us like fools."

"Hobart's dead," said Marcus Cole.

"No one's seen the fountain," said Sid Sawyer.

"Not yet," said Marcus.

"We never let a curse scare us off any job before," said Sid Sawyer. "You've stood by us over the years, Captain. Put your life on the line for us more than once. Seems the least we can do is pay you back in kind. If this is going to be our last mission, it's a poor time to start running scared."

"If we continue, it could mean another member of the gang will die," said Marcus. "Or more."

"If we stop, then you die for certain," said Gleason.

"Would you do any less for us if it was our lives on the line? Besides, I'm willing to tempt fate once or twice more. What would life be without taking a few chances?"

"Right," said Sid. "I'd rather gamble on a chance at eternal life than just pack it up and go home. I say we keep on working. Anyone think otherwise?"

No one objected. Stefan wasn't surprised.

"It's your decision," said Marcus. "But I think you're all crazy."

"Yeah, yeah, save it," said Billy the Bean. "You want to explain how we're going to get beyond this water trap?"

"Stefan had it right," said Marcus. "Trying to avoid or disarm the traps in the well is a waste of time. Assuming that it could ever be done. Someone once told me about a water trap on Oak Island, where Captain Kidd supposedly buried his loot. Treasure hunters have been trying to solve the mystery of that pit for a hundred years without success. We've got to throw out the book and start playing the game by our own rules."

"About time," said Stefan, trying not to sound too smug.

"You were right and I was wrong," said Marcus. "I admit it. Sometimes brute force is the only answer."

"So, what are we going to do," asked Alan Gleason, "blow up the well?"

"Not blow it up. Plug it up," said Marcus. "Plug it up tight."

Which was exactly what they proceed to do the next morning.

The well was ten feet in diameter and circular in shape, so it had a circumference of just under thirty-two feet.

Marcus, wanting a good amount of overlap, had purchased eleven sheets of steel four feet wide by twenty feet long. One by one, the gang hauled the sheets from the schooner up to the well and dropped them in, standing up lengthwise. Since the pool was fifteen feet deep, five feet of metal remained exposed. Working on a makeshift scaffold, Stefan and Alan Gleason attached the exposed section of the steel sheets to the marble walls using dozens of jagged spikes. Slowly but surely, they created a metal cylinder pressing firmly against the inside of the well.

Next came the wood beams. Marcus had ordered them cut so that they fit perfectly in the well, stretching from one side to the other. Wanting to insure that the metal plates couldn't be dislodged, Marcus had bought the most porous wood he could find. After a day in the well, they would be wedged in so tightly between the metal sheets that nothing less than an earthquake could shake them loose.

At sunset, their work done, Marcus lowered a hose into the well water and turned the pump on high. With a chugging sound, the machine began sucking seawater from the pit.

Twelve hours later, the well was relatively dry. The steel walls bulged where water was pressing against the panels from the inlet pipes, trying to break through. There were small leaks everywhere, since the cylinder wasn't sealed tight. But the metal held.

The bottom of the pit was a floor made of copper and marble. Once there had been pictures on it, but three thousand years of exposure to seawater had wiped away the designs. All that was visible was a large trapdoor, made from bronze, with a large metal handle.

"So much for the curse," said Stefan. "I told you those sisters were frauds."

"Don't tempt fate," said Marcus, smiling. "At least, not yet. Are you ready?"

"Ready as I'll ever be."

The two of them stood in semidarkness on the pit floor. They were dressed in khaki. Two flashlights hung from their belts. Each of them carried a knapsack filled with canteens and glass test tubes on their back. With luck, those containers would be filled when they returned to the surface.

The rest of the gang were bunched together on the edge of the pit. The boat was unguarded; no one was willing to stay on board when the secret of the well was so close to being revealed. All five of them grasped a rope set on a winch and tied to the trapdoor's metal ring. On Stefan's signal, they were all going to pull. The hope was that they'd get the door to open long enough for Stefan and Marcus to enter. If, by chance, the door remained open, all the better. But none of them expected such luck.

"Stand back," warned Stefan as he raised one arm. He stepped away from the door. Marcus took a position to his right.

"Ready above?" Marcus called.

"Ready," replied Alan Gleason.

"This one's for you, Mrs. Kallikoros," murmured Marcus.

"All right, heave!" cried Stefan and brought down his hand in a chopping gesture. High above, all five men strained, pulling the rope with all their strength. The winch groaned but held. The trapdoor started to move.

Down in the well, something shook the steel plate, causing it to shift an inch and sending a spray of seawater across the bottom of the pit. No doubt it was another one of the many spears hidden in the pit's wall. An instant later, another of the steel plates jumped. Then another, then another. Still, the heavy-duty steel held, though a half dozen new leaks spilled seawater onto the floor of the well. Sooner or later, Stefan realized, the water pressure was going to rip the steel panels free. They were only going to have a little to explore the chamber beneath the well.

"Door's almost open," said Stefan, watching the slab of carved marble nearly a foot thick rise from the floor. "Be prepared to move."

"Watch out for another trap once it's open," said Marcus.

"Right," said Stefan. If the Greeks had booby-trapped the walls, it was equally possible they'd planted a similar device in the opening.

With a screech of marble on marble, the heavy door swung free. Five short bronze spears, points shaved to needle tips, flew out of from the pit, missing Stefan's toes by inches.

Marcus switched on his flashlight and peered into the opening. "It's a cave. There's a drop of twelve, maybe fifteen feet to the floor. I'm going in."

With a wave to those up above, Marcus gripped the edge of the hole with both hands and disappeared into the darkness. A moment later, he called up to Stefan. "Come on down. Be careful, though. There are rocks under the sand on the floor."

Stefan edged himself into the hole, feet first. Hanging on to the marble rim, he lowered his body into the cave. "Watch out below," he called and let go.

He dropped. Marcus hadn't exaggerated. The sand was soft but there were sharp stones beneath the surface. Still, Stefan was up on his feet quickly. The chamber was totally black. Pulling his flashlight from his belt, Stefan switched it on. He was in the middle of a small cavern, approximately the same dimensions as the well, but with rough stone walls and a sand floor. The cave appeared to be completely natural, not marked in any way by man's presence. There was no sign of any fountain, but a narrow pathway led south from the chamber. As Stefan watched, Marcus disappeared into the tunnel.

"Come on," Marcus called a moment later, an odd sound in his voice. "Quick."

Stefan squeezed into the tunnel. It ran straight for about fifteen feet, then turned to the left. It seemed to be growing brighter ahead, and Stefan recognized a sharp smell. Salt. Another water trap, or the sea itself? He rounded the bend and that's where he found Marcus, standing at the edge of a much larger cavern. The cavern was huge, approximately forty feet by sixty feet, with a roof twenty feet high. A single structure filled most of the space—a small, open temple built completely out of marble.

At the temple's heart stood a statue, again, hewn from the purest white marble. The statue depicted a divinely proportioned man, his right hand grasping three thunderbolts, his left empty and pointing down. At his feet lay a small, gurgling pool with water that glowed golden.

They had found the Fountain of Zeus.

CHAPTER ELEVEN

"**A**mazing," said Stefan, clicking off his flashlight. Light suffused the massive chamber, not just from the glowing water of the fountain, but from another tunnel that led from the cavern. Though they could not see where the tunnel led, the not-too-distant drum of the surf suggested they were close to the surface.

Marcus grinned. "That's the real pathway to this temple. Remember what the three sisters said the other night, how the right answer is sometimes obvious? Can you imagine the temple priests navigating their way through the water trap each time they were supposed to conduct a ceremony here? Not likely."

"Yeah, I get it," said Stefan.

"The real entrance must be disguised or maybe it just blends in right against the cliffs. The stories about the well would have kept treasure hunters from looking for it. So long as it's nowhere near a beach, sailors wouldn't have stumbled over it, either."

"So the secret of the Well of the Furies—" began Stefan.

"Is that it's nothing more than a diversion," finished Marcus.

"Well, we'd better get a move on," said Stefan. "Only so much time we can stay down here before the rest of the gang starts worrying."

"Right," said Marcus. "Plus, we left the trapdoor open and those metal sheets aren't going to stay in place forever. If they buckle under the pressure, the seawater will flood this place."

"Then it's time to take a drink and see if we've wasted half our lives on a wild goose chase. . . ." He started toward the statue.

Marcus nodded, suddenly unable to speak. Stefan's words put everything in stark perspective. He'd been searching for this location since the end of the Great War. Over the past few years, as his health deteriorated, all his waking hours had been devoted to finding this spot. Now, he was here, and the moment of truth was at hand.

Neither of them bothered using a cup. A slender stream of gold water emerged from a break in the rock floor supporting the statue of Zeus. The liquid flowed through a narrow channel into a small marble pool, only a few inches deep and two feet in circumference. The overflow for the stream never ceased running and drained over a small stone barrier straight into the sea.

"Radioactive water, I bet," said Stefan Richter. "As I predicted long ago, my friend, it's science not magic."

"Perhaps," said Marcus. "Though I'd like to find the origin point of this stream. Later."

Kneeling down, Marcus and Stefan each scooped up a handful of the water and drank. The fluid sparkled like fine gold though it had the feel and consistency of pure spring water. It went down smooth with a taste like honey. But lighter and less cloying and, as Homer had claimed of nectar, nine times sweeter. From the first taste, from the first touch of the liquid on his tongue, Marcus knew that his quest had been fulfilled. Not all questions had answers, the three sisters had said. But this one did.

Four handfuls Marcus drank and then he knew he'd swallowed enough. His body felt as if it were on fire. He could sense changes taking place within him, profound changes that were reshaping every cell of his being, molecule by molecule, in a manner far beyond the understanding of the world's greatest scientists. No words could describe what was happening to him and thus he stopped trying. The transformation took an infinite amount of time—an age, an epoch, a century, a week, a day, an hour, a minute, yet it began and ended in the same second. It was science that transcended space. It was magic that eliminated time. Most of all it was a mystery.

He blinked, opening and closing his eyes in astonishment. Nothing around him had changed and yet everything looked different. His vision was sharper, clearer than ever before. He could see grains of sand in the rock, flaws in the marble, motes of dust in the air.

Somewhat shakily, he rose to his feet. A million cells sang with renewed life and energy. His body felt like it had been brushed by a star. The three sisters had been right. While their wine had been magnificent, its taste was a shallow hint at the magnificence of the fountain's elixir. This was truly the drink of the gods. Nothing in the world compared with true nectar.

Stefan was still on his knees, staring at the sparkling

liquid cupped in his hands, as if trying to read his future in the golden glow. "You okay?" asked Marcus.

"Never felt better," replied Stefan. "Never, *ever* felt better. What about you? How do you feel?"

"Never better."

He pressed a hand to his chest, closed his eyes, and listened. Listened with senses a hundred times clearer than any doctor's tool. "The poison is gone from my lungs. I can breathe without pain. The toxins in my blood have disappeared, been destroyed. The legends didn't lie. I'm cured."

"I figured as much," said Stefan.

"I'm going to look around a bit," said Marcus. "You going to stay here?"

"Sure," said Stefan. "There's work to be done."

He sounded like he was in a daze. Marcus understood. How could anyone fully comprehend the transformation that had just taken place? He surely could not. Before the drink he had been human. Now, he was something else. He wasn't sure exactly what.

"I need to fill up some bottles and test tubes with this stuff," said Stefan. "Take it back to America to be analyzed. It'll be nice to have the rulers of the world begging at my feet for a taste of immortality. See what else you can find. I'm in no rush."

They had been in a hurry but Marcus was so filled with new sensations that he couldn't remember exactly why. At the moment, he was having enough trouble adjusting to his new, improved senses to worry about anything else. It was a wall of sound, sight, and feeling that threatened to overwhelm his mind and short-circuit his emotions.

He could see tiny cracks in the temple's white marble columns and follow the oxygen bubbles rising to the surface from the water. He could hear the beating of his heart, the compression of his lungs, the squeaking of his skin as one finger rubbed against another. The smell of the sea broke down into a hundred different odors, most of which he could not recognize but knew he would never ever forget.

Concentrating, Marcus could hear Stefan's breathing and the sound of the ocean waves pounding against the island's rocky perimeter. The sound of tiny shells cracking beneath his feet echoed like thunder. Each breath of air filled his lungs with a dozen new sensations that his mind scrambled to categorize and identify. Every glance he took revealed new marvels. It was too much information for any man to handle, and he knew if he could not adjust he would go insane.

Enough, he thought, focusing his will. *Enough*.

And, it was.

Marcus drew in a deep breath, then another. Heightened senses meant heightened control. It would take time to learn how to use his senses properly, wisely, but he knew he could do it. Some miracles required patience. For the first time in more than ten years, he didn't taste blood in his mouth. The pain in his chest was gone. The golden elixir had healed him and made him strong. He wasn't sure exactly how strong, but he meant to find out. But patiently, not in a wild rush.

Marcus walked around the temple to a smaller building at its rear, a sanctuary for the priests. Here he found the final resting place for those who had served the gods. The graves were aligned in perfect rows. Atop each rested a small altar piled high with four-thousand-year-old carvings and jewelry. The light streaming in from the tunnel leading to the surface was strongest here. It glinted off the gems, creating sparkling prisms that danced across the artwork covering the cavern wall. Marcus's gaze focused on one of the frescos, the figures at its center, and a smile slowly spread across his lips.

"Stefan," he called. "Come in here. Right now. There's something you've got to see."

"Can't it wait?" came the reply. Stefan no longer sounded so cheerful. There was an edge to his voice that hadn't been there a few minutes ago. "I'm having a problem or two with this water."

"You'll want to see this," said Marcus. "I guarantee you won't be sorry."

Stefan, face red with suppressed fury, his eyes narrowed in anger, stomped over to the sanctuary and the graves. "Okay," he growled, "surprise me."

"Look at the far wall," said Marcus.

Stefan's eyes widened in surprise. He took a step closer, then another. Reaching out, he touched the marble fresco. Though it had to be well over three thousand years old, it had lost none of its luster. "Impossible," he said, after a moment of deep thought. "It can't be."

"But it is," said Marcus.

The picture on the wall showed three goddesses. Except for their hair, which was rendered as masses of small, deadly snakes, they appeared almost human. They were young, and they resembled each other enough to confirm they were sisters but not identical siblings. There was absolutely no doubt that the portraits depicted the three sisters they had spoken to the other night in Kythria.

Beneath the picture was inscribed a word in ancient Greek, a language Marcus could read. " 'The Kindly Ones,' " he said. "Or as they are known in modern times, 'The Furies.' "

Stefan shook his head. "It's a coincidence. Or maybe a trick. Simple as that. Put here last week, maybe. It's a hoax, Marcus, a gigantic hoax."

"A hoax?" repeated Marcus. "You're kidding, right? After what happened when we drank the water, you're still—"

"I still say the water can be explained away by science," Stefan snapped. "And I can prove that, if you'd let me get back to work. In fact, I could use your help. . . ."

Realizing there was little use arguing, Marcus accompanied Stefan back to the fountain. Six test tubes and four canteens were lined up in a circle at the edge of the golden pool.

"I want to take a sample so I can analyze it," said Stefan. "If we can break it down, maybe we could mass produce it. Bring health and happiness to everyone in the world—for a reasonable price, of course."

"I'm not concerned about the money," said Marcus. "Not after regaining my health. But I'm willing to help. What's the problem?"

"I dip the test tube in the water, holding it by a pair of metal tongs. I should be drawing a perfect sample, clear and golden. But, when I remove the tube from the stream and cap it, there's always a tiny black spot, some little impurity. Try as I might, I can't get it out. And, no matter how many times I try, even corking the tube in the stream itself, that damned impurity always appears."

"Let me try," said Marcus. Bottle after bottle, tube

after tube, he immersed in the water. Each time he did, the liquid he captured appeared perfectly pure. Yet, within a minute, a black blotch had somehow appeared in the sample.

" 'One drop remains pure,' " said Marcus. "That what the three sisters said. I suspect that's what we're witnessing here, Stefan. Remove more than a drop from the fountain and the water begins to decay."

"That's insane," said Stefan, his face flushing crimson. "A drop? How can you measure a single drop? Scientifically, that makes no sense. Water isn't sentient. It's not alive. How can a stream know if I take a drop or a spoonful or a gallon?"

"Perhaps," said Marcus, "science doesn't have all the answers."

"Science always has the answers," said Stefan. As quickly as it had risen, his temper disappeared. "And you'd better hope that the water retains its power after being removed from the stream. The elixir cured the poison in your lungs. Plus, it heightened my awareness and strengthened my mind."

"What do you mean?" asked Marcus.

"The water, it cleared my mind," said Stefan. "The liquid boosted my intelligence, broke down the artificial barriers of morality that clouded my thinking. Didn't it do the same for you?"

"Not exactly," said Marcus. "What do you mean, 'artificial barriers'?"

"It doesn't matter," said Stefan. His eyes widened as if astonished, and he smiled. "You mentioned decay. That makes sense. Quite a lot of sense, actually. Help me fill up these canteens and test tubes. If this water is highly radioactive, it will appear to decay faster when it's removed from the source of radiation."

"What about the water we drank?" asked Marcus.

"It's been absorbed into our systems," said Stefan. "Our cell structure has been altered—irrevocably, I would think. We're in no danger of reverting to our ordinary selves."

"We'd better head back to the well," said Marcus as they finished filling the last of the canteens. "We can send down the rest of the gang two at a time to drink from the stream. Make sure they experience the full effect of the elixir."

"Not yet," said Stefan. He looked around the cavern, as if seeing it for the first time. "We're not finished here, Marcus. We need to find the elixir's source. That's the real secret of the Well of the Furies, and the Fountain of Zeus. It's nearby, it must be. I can sense it. Can't you?"

Stefan inhaled deeply, as if he could smell the elixir's source in the air—and perhaps, with his heightened senses, he could.

"This substance is like nothing on earth," he murmured. "If drinking this water changed us, imagine what power we could gain from its source. We're not talking about healing old wounds now, Marcus. We're talking about the secret of eternal life!"

CHAPTER TWELVE

"**H**ere it is," said Marcus. He stepped back from the section of cavern wall he'd been examining and pointed to a spot about five feet off the ground. "These rocks don't belong here. There's a hollow space behind the stones. I can feel the air flowing through the cracks."

"Stand back then," said Stefan. He wore his backpack on his shoulders and in his arms he carried a slab of marble six inches wide by two feet long. Most likely it had once served as the leg for a small table. Today, it took the place of a sledgehammer.

Stefan drove the chunk of marble into the rock wall. Chunks of stone dropped to the cave floor and a cloud of dust rose. "Looks promising," he declared and swung the makeshift battering ram into the wall a second time. Then a third. Once more, and the entire section of the wall collapsed into fragments.

"Another tunnel," said Marcus, holding his flashlight over his head and peering through the dust and debris.

"Narrow and not very high. We'll have to duck to get through."

"I'll manage," said Stefan. He dropped the slab of marble to the floor. "You lead, I'll follow."

"Odd," said Marcus, as he entered the cramped walkway. "This path leads away from the sea, but there's a glow up ahead. Not sunlight, but it can't be artificial. Nothing stays lit for more than three thousand years."

"You just drank a potion that cured lung disease," said Stefan from a few steps back. "Don't tell me what's possible or impossible."

"Point taken," said Marcus.

Carefully he inched his way forward into the cavern until he found himself out of the tunnel and in a small room, perhaps seven feet long and five feet wide. The roof rose forty feet into the darkness of one of the island's few peaks. There was only one object in the room, and it was not something Marcus was expecting.

"Marcus, is something wrong?" asked Stefan. Then, he squeezed into the same cave with his friend and understood the silence.

It was a box, jet black in color and made out of a substance that resembled no rock, no metal, absolutely nothing known on earth. It seemed to pulse with inner power. The box was four feet wide by six feet long by four feet high. There was a lid of the same strange material resting on its top. The lid was approximately an inch thick and was slightly askew, leaving a small sliver of the inside of the box uncovered.

A brilliant golden light flowed upward from that uncovered sliver, illuminating the entire cave. Strange objects, ghostly beings seemed to move in the radiance, hurtling up, splashing into the cave's roof, then vanishing. Tentatively, Marcus reached out and touched the box on one side. It was cool and smooth to the touch. It was definitely artificial, but for something crafted four thousand years ago, it was remarkably free from even the slightest scratch. Marcus stared at the object using all the new-found powers of his extraordinary eyes. Strong as they were, he could not see any cuts or marks on the outside of the box. The golden glow escaping from inside was so bright, so powerful, that Marcus's eyes burned merely from staring at the glimmer for an instant. There was no way he could see inside the box.

Stefan pulled out his knife. "Let's see how tough this stuff really is," he said, and before Marcus could stop him, slashed at the black box with all his strength. The knife was made from the finest carbide steel and Stefan kept it razor sharp. It made no mark on the black substance. Marcus knew it wouldn't. Stefan only grunted.

"The Greeks didn't construct this," said Stefan, sheathing his knife.

"I think we both agree on that," said Marcus.

"And whatever this is, this is the source of the fountain's power," said Stefan. He gestured at the rear wall. A slow but steady stream of water flowed down the stone. "See. Water seeps into this cavern." He gestured again to the cave floor, to a small sinkhole. After running under the box, the water disappeared into the hole. "I'm betting the water reemerges in the Fountain of Zeus. It's the radioactivity in the box that transforms it into elixir."

Marcus nodded. His friend might not be subtle or poetic, but he was no fool. He was the one who had guessed the existence of the box and its true power. Stefan was right. The content of the box was everything.

On the wall where the water descended, about six feet off the floor, were engraved three words in ancient Greek. Crudely etched into the rock, bracketing the words, were pictures of two faces. One was a woman's face, ageless, eternal, serene. The other a man's face, dark and sinister, his teeth bared in anger and hatred.

" 'Here lies power,' " translated Marcus. Were the faces merely symbols, he wondered, or did they mean something more?

"Power to rule the world," said Stefan. "Power to do anything."

"Power to be a god," replied Marcus. "Or power to be a devil."

"I don't believe in either. Humanity needs to throw off the shackles of the past and accept the promise of the future. In a world ruled by science, not emotion."

"And if you're wrong?"

"But, I'm not wrong," said Stefan, smiling. Then, before Marcus realized what his friend intended, the big man stepped up to the box, grabbed hold of the lid, and, with a jerk of his arms, threw it off.

Light brighter than a thousand suns poured out of the box. A fire that burned but did not consume engulfed Marcus and Stefan, whispering to them in a voice that spoke no language and yet spoke all languages at once. Einstein claimed that matter and energy were one and the same. Here was strong evidence that energy, thought, and life were identical.

Contained within the box was a spark of divinity that set man apart from animals.

Here, too, resided the spirit of creativity responsible for unleashing the innermost powers of the human mind.

From this light had emerged many of the ancient beings of legend, the gods and demons, the heroes and villains of a thousand cultures, a hundred lands. Here was their beginning, and here, too, was their end.

In the light's center spoke the voice of the storm and the screams of chaos.

Here swirled the energy of love and honor and duty and responsibility. And here, too, raged deceit and treachery and hatred and despair.

Here, as the words etched in stone proclaimed, was *power*.

Within the firestorm, in the heart of the burning, lurked the bizarre entity Marcus and Stefan recognized as the box. Sentience was a child of electricity, and electricity formed electrons and neutrons, which built atoms, and atoms served as the blocks that constructed the universe. So even the most inanimate of things contained a spark of electricity and, thus, life. Given the power the box contained, it was little surprise that it was more aware of itself and its destiny than other, more mundane objects.

The box, which was alive but not sentient in the way humans understood, spoke, and Marcus and Stefan listened. It described its voyage to this spot from somewhere else. It had come from somewhere different, where thoughts and feelings were alive and had shape and form. Another world, another planet, a parallel universe, a land of magic— it could not remember. The box spoke of its mission. It had been sent to capture the essence of creativity, of ambition, of greatness, from the minds of men and women. The box was designed to trap as much of that power inside its walls as possible, keeping it stored in active form until it received further orders. Those orders had never come. Yet, it had remained true to its mission for the past ten thousand years.

Twice before, the box had been opened and much of the captured energy had escaped. The world, of which the box was only vaguely aware, had gone through many changes in the years that followed its opening. Men and women gained powers, fought wars, raised great empires, and then destroyed them. In the end, always, someone had returned and closed the box and the process had begun again. It assumed the same thing would occur this time.

Slowly, very slowly, the golden waves of energy flattened into straight lines, lost their power, and disappeared. The room was dark, except for the thin white glow of Marcus's flashlight.

"Shine it inside the box," said Stefan. "Remember the story of Pandora and the box? We need to check to see if anything remains."

There was nothing. The box was completely empty. Not even hope remained.

Dazed and confused, the two men slid through the narrow tunnel leading back to the larger cavern in which they had found the Fountain of Zeus. The magic, the science, the motivating force—whatever it was—had left this place, had fled the Isle of Vengeance. Already the golden water had changed to a bland yellow tainted with streaks of black. In the distance, the earth rumbled and shook. Marcus wondered what might be the cause.

Stefan knew. His face turned white with fear.

"The door in the water pit," Stefan declared. "We were so focused on the fountain and the box that we forgot about it. The steel plates must be buckling under the water pressure. We have to get out of here or we'll be swept away by the flood!"

The entire cavern shook. "It's more than that," yelled Marcus, letting his senses expand through the cavern. "The island's being battered by a storm. The rain's falling in buckets, filling up the well. Grab hold of something sturdy. Right now!"

There was no chance to act. Like a speeding locomotive, a wall of water swept into the cavern and smashed into the two of them. Marcus didn't even have time to blink. The wave picked him up and slammed him into the temple's pillars, then heaved him up to the ceiling. He struggled to keep his head above water, tried to grab something to anchor himself in the flood's fury. He fought to remain conscious, but it was a battle he could not win. His head slammed against something hard, and he sank down into darkness.

CHAPTER THIRTEEN

There had been fireworks all evening in Paragon City, celebrating the Fourth of July, so no one complained when, at 2:00 A.M., a flurry of gold lights suddenly lit up the summer sky. The few people still awake assumed it was some prankster lighting his last Roman candle before calling it a night. No one noticed that there was no accompanying gunpowder explosion. Nor that the lights seemed to drift down through the city to specific homes, as if they had been drawn to those locations. The great events in world history don't always take place during the daytime and aren't always announced with trumpet fanfares. Sometimes, important events happen at night, in silence. Often, they occur in solitude.

Devon Wilcox couldn't sleep. That was nothing new. He rarely slept well anymore. His nights were troubled with terrible dreams, nightmares where he roamed the city as an invisible demon, witnessing crime after crime, helpless to prevent them. Terrible, horrible dreams, made infinitely worse because they seemed so real.

Sitting alone in his room, his legs crossed on his bed, Devon wondered for the thousandth time why this was happening to him. He only wanted to be ordinary, a normal teenager, not some freak who could shift locations as easily as most people could walk. Devon didn't want the powers he possessed and hated what they did to him. He only wanted to fit in, be like everyone else. He didn't want to be different.

But he was different. So different that his parents wanted to send him to Tibet to study with some oddball monks they had read about in the newspaper months before. The monks of the Order of the Four Winds were supposedly experts on unusual powers, teachers of specially gifted children who they claimed had been touched by the divine. Devon didn't care what the monks believed or what they taught or what they claimed they could do. He just wanted to be left alone.

For two years now he had been trying to pretend his powers didn't exist. Two years of struggling and hoping and praying they would go away. But he couldn't deny that he had the ability to transport himself from place to place by thought alone, or that he could form a shield around his body and even make himself invisible. Maybe they were powers other people wanted, wanted desperately, but all Devon wanted was to be like everyone else. It didn't seem too much to ask

Angry at the world, he stared out his window at the clear skies. Though it was just past two in the morning, the city looked brighter than normal. Some sort of golden haze hung in the air. It was as if thousands and thousands of bright golden lanterns had suddenly descended onto the skyscrapers of Paragon City, turning the metropolis into some gigantic carnival. He could almost hear the music.

A soft undercurrent of sound seemed to fill the night. Devon listened closer. That was strange. He could swear he heard voices chanting. Voices that rose from the night itself, from the darkness. *Devon Wilcox*, cried the wind, *Om Mani Padme Hung.* Above it all, one man's voice was clear. *Reveal your powers*, it said. *Demonstrate what you can do, child.*

Child? Devon grimaced. He hated being called a child. No child could deal with what he'd been experiencing for the past two years, much less most adults. He was anything but a child.

Not exactly sure what he was doing, or why, Devon slid off his bed and stood up. Quickly he pulled on a pair of slacks and a shirt. Shoes and socks for his feet. For his head, one of his father's old hats, pulled on tight, covering much of his face, so he wouldn't be recognized. Fully dressed, he stared out the window, letting his subconscious mind take over. The only thing required was a little mental push. Devon pushed, and he was gone.

He reappeared on the street in front of Independence Plaza an instant later. It was the middle of the night, but the lights were still on at City Hall. No doubt the mayor was having a big Fourth of July celebration. Though he complained constantly that the city didn't have enough money to help the poor, the mayor and his cronies never seemed to suffer any want themselves.

Two police officers walked by, patrolling the plaza. They didn't notice Devon. No one noticed him unless he wanted. Devon watched but could not himself be watched.

When he used his power of teleportation, he was invisible to the human eye.

Show me, the voice whispered, and the chant echoed, *Om Mani Padme Hung*.

Devon disappeared again. This time, he materialized a few feet away from the entrance to the Jack Johnson Bar and Grille, one of Paragon City's finest restaurants. When he felt particularly down, Devon liked to hang out in front of the grill and watch the city's celebrities arrive and depart. The restaurant was open until 4:00 A.M. and it was always busy. This was the second of the half-dozen stops he made on nights when the urge to use his powers grew too strong, observing people, but never revealing himself. He didn't think it was his job to interfere, merely to observe. He was a watcher in the dark.

A glitzy couple walked out the main entrance shortly after Devon appeared. He recognized them from a photo that had appeared yesterday in the *Paragon Times*. Doctor James Nelson, the famous brain surgeon, newly appointed head of the neural unit at the Paragon City Hospital, and his wife, Vivian. Nelson was one of the finest surgeons in the United States, and the hospital had been trying to lure him to their staff for years. His wife was famous for her charity work in poor neighborhoods. The Nelsons were the type of people who used their money to benefit all.

"Cab, Doctor Nelson?" asked the doorman.

"No, thank you, son," replied the doctor, handing the young man a five-dollar bill anyway. "Such a beautiful night, the Fourth of July, a new city, I think my wife and I would prefer to walk to the hotel. It's only two blocks from here."

"Uh, sure, Doctor Nelson," said the doorman, "but you folks are dressed mighty nice. Not a lot of police on the street this time of night, if you catch my drift. Might not be the safest choice."

"Nonsense," said the doctor, chuckling. "We need the exercise, don't we?"

"Whatever you wish, dear," said Vivian Nelson. She pulled a thin pair of leather moccasins out of her purse. Then she reached down and removed her high heels. Slipping on her moccasins, she squeezed the heels into her bag. Evidently, Mrs. Nelson knew her husband's preference for walking. "As you say, it is a nice night."

"There you go," said Nelson. "It's only a couple of blocks. I'm sure we'll be safe."

"You're the boss, Doc," said the doorman. Another couple was exiting the club and he had to hustle over to open the door. "Have a good night."

Off went the Nelsons, walking down the street at a good pace. Devon watched them depart with mixed emotions. They were adults and he was just a teenager. It was none of his business if they wanted to act foolishly. Still, they seemed like a nice couple and earlier in the day his dad had commented on how good it was that a talented man like Doctor Nelson had come to City Hospital. Besides, the voice he was searching for was silent. Keeping an eye on the Nelsons would only take a few minutes. Then he could continue his travels.

Devon hurried along the street to catch up with them. He'd never noticed before but when he was invisible, his footfalls made no noise. He was more than merely invisible—he was undetectable. Something to ponder, when he had some free time.

Everything seemed fine with the Nelsons when he caught up with them. Doctor Nelson was telling his wife how he'd like to create a children's ward in the hospital, so that young patients could be treated separately from adults. His wife agreed that it was a magnificent idea, and that it would serve as a good theme for her next fund-raising banquet. These were good people, Devon decided. Very good people.

Not like the man who suddenly stepped out from an alley five feet ahead. Dressed in black, wearing a mask over his nose and mouth, he held an automatic in one hand, a worn cloth bag in the other. He waved the pistol at the Nelsons and held out the sack.

"All your money," the man said. "And her jewelry. Quick. Try anything funny and I'll shoot."

"No reason to do that," said Doctor Nelson, reaching slowly, carefully, into his suit pocket. "We're not fools. We won't cause any trouble for you."

Devon looked around for the police. The city streets were deserted. There wasn't a patrolman in sight, and police cars were rare this late.

Doctor Nelson tossed his wallet to the crook. Holding it in his left hand, the gunman riffled through the contents with one finger. "Nice," said the man, "lots of cash. Hurry up with that necklace, babe. I ain't got all night."

"The catch—it's stuck," said Mrs. Nelson, her features frozen in fear. "Please, give me a moment. I'll get it undone."

"Break the catch," said the crook, waving his gun in the air. "You've got three seconds. Three—two—"

Devon could no longer just watch. These were good

people and the city needed them. The world needed them. Tonight, he had to act. So Devon did the only thing he could. He let himself become visible. "Put down your gun," he commanded.

The crook appeared stunned for an instant, then, instead of dropping his weapon, he leveled it at Devon and fired three times.

Three bullets dropped harmlessly to the pavement. Though he was no longer invisible, Devon was still untouchable. "Your weapon cannot hurt me," said Devon, trying to sound confident. "I warn you. Put down your gun."

Devon stretched out his right hand, fingers open, like a magician casting a spell. He waved his hand at the crook, repeating the words of the chant he had heard. "Om Mani Padme Hung." He wasn't sure why he did it, but some phrases sounded right no matter what the situation.

The mask slid off the robber's contorted features. His eyes bulged like they were about to explode. The gun dropped from his fingers as he flailed at the empty air in front of his face. "Take them away," he shrieked. "Take them away."

Stinging, flying insects. The crook feared them, had a mania about them. Without knowing how he did it, Devon had reached into the man's subconscious mind, pulled out that fear, and projected it before his eyes.

Hurriedly, Doctor Nelson picked up the crook's gun. In the distance, a siren howled. The shots had drawn the attention of the police. In the meantime, the crook, down on his knees, babbled frantically about gigantic bees buzzing around his head.

"You saved our lives," the doctor said to Devon. "Thank you. Thank you a hundred times."

"Who are you?" asked Mrs. Nelson. "What's your name?"

Giving them his name, Devon realized, would raise a fistful of questions he wasn't ready to answer. "Call me the Dark Watcher," he said, and then, as the police car pulled up to the curb, teleported away.

He materialized at the pond in Gemini Park, another one of his favorite locations in the city. It was peaceful here, serene. The voices were here, too. *Om Mani Padme Hung.* They, too, sounded peaceful, serene.

From out of the mist wafting around the pond's edges walked a little old man, a shade over five feet tall, dressed in a white wool robe that was tied together by a black sash. Entirely bald, the man had skin the color of burnished bronze. For all of his immense age, his face was free of wrinkles. Blue eyes, bright as the sky, stared at Devon, and the old man smiled.

What a great pleasure, he began, though his lips did not move. *We have been trying to contact you telepathically for months, Devon. We have managed to exert some influence over your parents, to plant suggestions in their thoughts about the best path for your education, but your mind has been shielded against us. Tonight, for some reason we don't quite understand, we were finally able to touch your mind, even send this image to speak with you.*

"An image," said Devon. "You're not real. . . ."

You are seeing an astral projection. My physical body resides, at the moment, in Tibet, said the old man. *My name is Pa Soong, leader of the Order of the Four Winds. For two years, we have sensed your struggles, your un-*

happiness with your powers, your fight to remain sane. Tonight, the link between our minds and yours was made complete. You possess great and wonderful powers. These powers can help all mankind. Come to us in Tibet and we will teach you how to control your talent, discover how to be a man of great destiny.

"Last night, I would have refused," said Devon. "Last night, I wasn't ready. Tonight, I realized for the first time that I shouldn't be afraid of my powers, but proud of them." Devon raised his eyes to the stars. "It was the golden glow in the sky that that cleared my thoughts, made me aware of my destiny."

Then you will come to study with us in Tibet? asked Pa Soong.

Devon nodded solemnly. "I'll be on my way in the morning."

CHAPTER FOURTEEN

Getting a cab at 3:00 A.M. in Paragon City was difficult enough. Finding one unoccupied at 3:00 A.M. after a wild Fourth of July was impossible.

Resigned to the fact that they were stuck getting back to their campus apartment on their own, Brandon Warfield and James St. John-Smythe made the best of it, humming the Paragon City University fight song as they progressed along the street. The two young men, both twenty-one, had been at an off-campus celebration that had lasted longer than expected. Fortunately, tomorrow was Saturday and they had no demanding responsibilities. Brandon was helping Coach Reardon run the university's summer football league for kids from some of Paragon's rougher neighborhoods, while Jimmy was tutoring classes for disadvantaged children in the science lab. Though they looked very different, the duo thought very much alike. They cared about people and wanted to help those less fortunate than themselves.

Brandon had come to Paragon on a full athletic scholarship. A star high school football player from the Midwest, he had been one of the most sought-after young linebackers in the country. He had chosen Paragon not only because of their generous scholarship offer, but because, coming from the Chicago area, he liked life in the big city.

James, who was half the size and weight of Brandon, had also received a full scholarship to Paragon. His specialty was science and he, too, had been offered scholarships from great universities throughout the world. Why he had selected Paragon was a carefully guarded secret between him and his father.

James came from London, England, but his father, John, a well-known investment banker, had made his fortune in Texas oil. According to John, he wanted his son to receive an American college education so he could manage the family oil business. At least that was the explanation he'd given his wife and all their relatives in England. No mention was made of the deal between father and son to free James from his mother's overprotective attention. The younger St. John-Smythe had suffered from polio as a child, and his bent and twisted body was bound to a wheelchair. Julia had smothered her stricken child with love and affection, and while he appreciated her attention, James wanted to lead his own life.

In one of those odd coincidences that only happen in real life, Brandon and James were booked together as roommates their freshman year. The football player had never met anyone like the young scientist, and vice versa. The two men had bonded and become closest of friends.

"Great party, huh, Jimmy," said Brandon, his voice echoing eerily down the empty streets. "Super fireworks, too."

"You Americans love your sparklers," said James, nicknamed "Jimmy the Smith" by his friend. "An amazing display for sure. I'd swear there are still some up in the atmosphere. Notice the golden glow in the sky?"

"Yeah," said Brandon. "Weird, how long it's—"

A woman's scream cut off Brandon's reply. A teenage girl, no more than fifteen, struggled with three hoodlums in the shadow of an old warehouse. "Help! Please!" the girl shouted, as the trio pummeled her with their fists.

"No cops, as per usual," said Brandon, and without hesitation, plunged down the alleyway, leaving Jimmy in his wheelchair far behind.

"Let her go!" Brandon roared, and in his best football form, tackled two of the three thugs. The men crashed to the pavement in a heap, with Brandon on top. Huge fists flailing, he fought like a human tornado, battering his two opponents. Stunned by the sudden, intense attack, the pair scrambled from him and dashed down the alley, never once aware they had been routed by just one man.

"Wise guy," said the third thug, who had sidestepped Brandon's initial attack. Pushing the girl aside, the hoodlum pulled a snub-nosed automatic from his pant's pocket. He pointed the gun at Brandon's chest. "Let's see how smart you really are!"

A police siren howled less than a hundred feet away. Bright lights caught the crook dead on, the beams hitting him in the eyes. "Drop that gun," a voice snarled in the night, "or you're a dead man."

"I'm dropping, I'm dropping," yelled the terrified crook. The gun fell to the ground. The next instant, a massive hand clamped down on his shoulder and a ham-sized fist sent him into dreamland.

"You can shut the lights and siren," Brandon shouted to Jimmy the Smith. "Great job, as always. Almost convinced me the cops had arrived."

"Wh-where are the police?" asked the teenage girl, trying to straighten her torn clothing.

"At the local donut shop, I suspect," said Jimmy, rolling up to the young woman in his wheelchair. "The lights and siren are a little trick I rigged up in case someone decided to take advantage of my condition. The voice of doom was my own."

"It helps when dealing with trash like the hoodlums who attacked you," said Brandon. He lifted the still-unconscious gunman, sans revolver, and tossed him head-first into a garbage drum.

"What, if I may ask, were you doing out at this time of night, young lady?" said Jimmy.

"My—my cat," said the girl. "The fireworks scared him and he ran out of our apartment. I've been searching for him for hours. Those three men, they laughed at me. Said I was crazy. Started hitting me. I don't know what they would have done if you hadn't come along."

"Best if you head home," said Brandon. "Cats have a habit of turning up the next morning. I know—my sister's ran away lots of times but always showed up in the morning when it got hungry."

Ten minutes later, after escorting the teenager back to two very worried and thankful parents, Brandon and

James finally made it to their campus apartment. Before entering the building, Jimmy looked his friend directly in the eyes.

"That was wrong tonight, my friend," he said. "Very wrong. Things like that should never happen in a civilized society."

"Tell me about it," said Brandon. "Looking at that girl, I couldn't help but think—what if she had been my sister? Would someone have been around to save her?"

"Not the police, obviously," said Jimmy.

"That's the truth," said Brandon. "This city's corrupt through and through. From the mayor and chief of police down to the cops on the beat, there's hardly an honest man among them. Everyone's been telling me that since I got here, but tonight I've finally seen the light. If no one else is willing to make a difference, it's time for us to act."

"Us?" scoffed Jimmy. "I'm hardly the one to fight criminals."

"Maybe not with your fists, but with your mind," said Brandon. "Working together, the two of us can make things better around here. I know we can."

"Well, my father told me I needed to think like an American," said Jimmy. "I've always wanted to be the cowboy on the white horse. Count me in, partner."

CHAPTER FIFTEEN

He awoke in darkness. At first, he could not see, and for a second, he worried he might be blind. Then, slowly, his eyes adjusted to the night sky, and he saw stars, thousands and thousands of stars. And he saw a golden mist. He recognized the color immediately. It was the same brilliant gold that had filled the strange black box he had opened. Tonight was the first night of a new age, and he was the one responsible for it happening. Would his name someday be worshipped in the temples and churches of the future? He doubted it. If anything, he'd be cursed. Which suited Stefan just fine. What he had done wasn't for those fools who believed in the old morality. What he had done was for the future, for a new order in the world.

He was floating on his back in the Cretan Sea. His last memories were of being swept out of the cavern and over the shattered cliff wall leading to the sea. Falling debris knocked him unconscious but his body had never sunk. He was stronger than he had been before. His mind, working on the subconscious level, had refused to let him be pulled under. What would have killed any ordinary man had barely bruised him. Even his pack, still on his back and loaded with bottles, had not pulled him down. He had been drifting in the current for a long time. How long didn't matter. All that really mattered to him now was that he was still alive.

He wondered for an instant if Marcus had survived. He suspected so. The fountain's water had transformed them into something barely human. Exposure to the escaping energies of the black box had heightened the effect. They were no longer ordinary men. His mind, a hundred times more powerful than before, told him so. They might not be gods, but they were awfully close. At the least, they were super humans, men with powers unlike anything seen on the earth in more than three thousand years.

Science, not sorcery, had transformed him. Stefan sighed with relief. The three sisters might be immortal but he felt certain they were not supernatural. No doubt they had also been changed by the black box, thousands of years ago, but the box had not bestowed on them any magical powers. They had claimed two would die if two entered the secret chamber, and that hadn't happened. Some inner sense told him that the rest of the gang, including Marcus, was still alive.

Feeling very pleased with himself, Stefan turned onto his stomach and began to swim for the island. He knew without thinking which direction to go. Another small benefit of his transformation, he realized. He suspected he possessed numerous powers unimagined by normal men. And he would have centuries in which to discover the scope of those powers.

It took a little more than an hour of strong swimming to return to the island. Miles and miles of water he covered, the backpack hardly noticed, and never once did he feel tired or winded. At first, hundreds of yards from shore, he wasn't even sure that he had found the right place. The Isle of Vengeance looked different from what he remembered.

Half the plateau was gone, collapsed in on itself from the devastating impact of the subterranean flood. The entire temple grounds on the top section of the isle had dropped fifty feet. What had been a seemingly solid cliff was now a patchwork of rocks and ruins, smashed marble columns, mounds of dirt, and small patches of greenery. The Fountain of Zeus, and more important, the box that had created it, were buried beneath tons of earth and stone.

A huge bonfire burned on the section of the island where they had made their camp and, even from this distance, Stefan could see several members of their gang searching the ruins for something. Remains of the lost temple, he assumed, though as he swam closer, he could hear their shouts and realized his mistake.

"Find any trace of him?"

"No luck. Maybe he was swept out to sea."

"Keep searching. He has to be somewhere in the ruins."

The last voice he recognized as belonging to Marcus. That's when he understood: They were hunting for him. Marcus hadn't been swept out to sea and had somehow survived the ensuing rockslide. He evidently thought Stefan had survived, as well.

Stefan started to raise an arm out of the water, began to call attention to himself, then thought better of it. He lowered his hand and stopped swimming. Floating in the water, he considered if he wanted to be rescued.

He was different—smarter, more powerful, more sure of himself than he had ever been before. His body burned with energy. The nectar and ambrosia, combined with the golden light from the black box, had transformed him into a super human. Tonight, he and Marcus had changed the course of history. Because of them, a new age was beginning. The question was, whose vision of the future would shape that new age?

Stefan swam for shore, keeping out of sight of the gang. He and Marcus had been friends for most of their lives. They made a great team, but Stefan was tired of being the one who did most of the work and got none of the credit. It was time for him to strike out on his own. Time for him to prove he was capable of anything, without the help of a partner. Marcus thought technocracy— that Stefan himself—was some sort of joke. Stefan was determined to show him just how wrong he was.

The relics in his backpack would make him rich. Very rich. Plus, the water samples he'd taken from the fountain, slightly tainted as they might be, were still worth more than any other drink on earth. There were those who would give anything for a sip of that liquid. Perhaps, such people weren't among the most ethical in the world, but Stefan didn't care. They were among the most important. Thinking about the golden elixir made him realize that he had been stifling his own ambitions for far too long. He'd been so determined to help Marcus that he'd never given his own needs proper consideration.

Now was the time to change all that.

The approach of one of the schooner's two motorboats

caught him by surprise. It chugged closer, on low power. Only one man was aboard.

"Stefan?" called out Billy the Bean. The ex-ambulance driver was in the front of the boat, leaning over, peering into the dark sea. "Stefan? Is that you?"

A dozen emotions flickered through Stefan's brain. He had known Billy the Bean for nearly fifteen years, and they had escaped many a tight situation together. A good man to back you up, the Bean had a way of making you laugh at your mistakes without being insulting. There was no question, he was one of the finest men Stefan had ever met. But, at this instant, he was primarily a man blocking the fulfillment of Stefan's dreams. That could not be tolerated.

"Hey," said Billy, searching the water with a flashlight, "are you—?"

Stefan erupted from the water, grabbed the Bean's head with both hands, and pulled him facefirst into the sea. Billy struggled for an instant, but only an instant. Stefan twisted his wrists and, without effort, broke the other man's neck. The Bean was dead before the ripples caused by his plunge into the sea had spread more than a few yards.

Hauling himself into the boat, Stefan turned up the motor a notch. With a little luck, he'd be in Athens before morning. Let Marcus continue to wonder what had happened to him. Let him wonder what happened to the lifeboat and Billy the Bean, as well. Curiosity was good for the soul.

Stefan looked down at his hands. Killing the Bean had been unfortunate but necessary. He felt no regrets. If anything, the murder had made him stronger. It proved that he would sacrifice anything, including friendship, for his goal.

"Here lies power," he stated softly, remembering the words carved in the chamber of the black box. His massive hands curled into fists. "*Here lies power.*"

It wasn't until Stefan was two hours away from the Isle of Vengeance that he realized killing Billy the Bean had fulfilled the strange sisters' prophecy. By then, he no longer cared. It didn't matter. Nothing mattered other than power.

CHAPTER SIXTEEN

The phone rang a little after one in the morning. Monica's bedroom was situated a floor above the living room where the house phone was located, so its ringing woke her first. Still, her father slept with one eye and one ear open, and a second after the ringing started, she could hear his feet pounding down the stairs. It always took Monica a few seconds to throw on a robe and rub the sleep from her eyes. Only on a rare occasion did she ever get to the phone before Rudy. Tonight wasn't one of those occasions.

Standing on the landing leading down to the first floor, she listened to her father talk to whoever was on the other end of the line. Rudy's answers were slow, mechanical. He didn't say much, just answered a few questions, shook his head in bewilderment once, and then, when he placed the receiver back on the hook, sighed deeply.

"Monica," he said, his features grim, tears forming in his eyes, "you better get dressed. We haff a ride to take downtown. There's been a shooting. A bad shooting. They want us to come to come identify the body at the morgue."

"A shooting?" repeated Monica, her face going blank. "Identify the body? But we don't know anyone who might get—" And suddenly she knew exactly whom her father was talking about and she stopped talking. Instead, her eyes burst into a storm cloud of tears. The drops ran down her cheeks, across her neck, onto her thin silk nightgown. She paid them no attention. "It can't be," she said. "It can't be."

"But it iss," said Rudy, trying to keep a strict control on his emotions. In all his years raising Monica, he had never cried, though he had faced some terrible news in his day. "Der crooks, dey finally got Ezra trapped in a warehouse without any backup. He was kilt a few hours ago. Shot in the back."

"Do they have any suspects?" called out Monica from her bedroom, where she was changing into a skirt and blouse and light jacket. It was late August, and the summer was slowly turning into fall. Last thing she did was check to make sure her automatic, fully loaded, was in her purse. Having worked more than a year now as a crime reporter, Monica knew that a girl's best friend was her gun.

"I don't know," said Rudy, pulling on his worn overcoat. "Ezra was just about the only clean cop on the force. He didn't haff a lot of friends. And der were a lot of gangsters who would have been happy to see him gone."

Rudy drove an old Packard, and while it wasn't very fast, it was dependable.

"Most gangsters know better than to kill a cop," said

Monica. "That's one of the unwritten laws around here. Kill a cop or a reporter and your life is worthless. Those murders get too much press, put too much heat on the crime lords. Lots of times they'll give up the killer just to save themselves from further investigations."

"I know, I know," said Rudy. "And Ezra knew it, too. Tonight, he must haff run into someone who didn't know the rules."

"Or didn't care about them," said Monica. She sniffled, repressing another bout of tears.

"Maybe it was that big lug, Sammy Lombardo. He had it in for Ezra after ever since that time in *mein* office."

"Sammy's tough and crude," said Monica. "But he's not as stupid as he acts. He would never have shot Ezra. Especially in the back. Even the most corrupt cop in the city is going to break heads to find out who committed this murder. It's hard to believe any crime boss would have been this dumb."

"Den maybe there was another reason for killing Ezra," said Rudy. "Maybe he found out something tonight that made him too dangerous to leave alive. Or maybe there's some reason we don't even know."

"I'm not sure, Dad," said Monica, brushing away tears. "I'm just not thinking straight. Ezra's dead. It's hard to realize that I'll never talk to him again, never see him again. It's not fair."

"Life ist not fair," said Rudy. "Monica, you must write to Marcus. And to your brother, as well. Maybe now they will finally come home."

"I haven't heard from either Marcus or Stefan in more than a year, even though I've written them once a month without fail. The post office drop box they used in Paris is still open and the mail's never been returned, but they never answer. Even when I told them how badly the newspaper's been doing due to the bank closing. I hoped they would send some money, or at least write back, but nothing. It's as if they've vanished from the face of the planet."

"I can't believe that Marcus would not want to find his brother's killer," said Rudy. "The same with Stefan."

"Okay, I'll write. But don't get your hopes up."

All talk came to an end as Rudy pulled into the city morgue parking lot. Ezra, in death, looked cold and forbidding, all of the warmth and personality fled from his body. He had been shot six times, with at least four of the bullets fired into his body when he lay dying on the floor. It had been a particularly brutal murder.

Monica, who had seen her fair share of dead bodies after a year as a crime reporter, could only look at Ezra's corpse for an instant. She didn't want to remember him as a lifeless body but as the upbeat, funny, and, most of all, heroic figure she had known all of her life. Ezra Cole had become a cop because he wanted to bring justice to the world. He deserved a better end.

Rudy stood looking at the body for several long minutes. He didn't move, didn't say a word. He just stared, as if memorizing every inch of Ezra's face. He only turned away and rejoined Monica when the coroner covered the body.

"He was a fine man," said Rudy softly. "He was a very fine man."

Waiting for them in the front office of the morgue was the Paragon City police chief, Andrew Mooney. A heavyset man with beet-red cheeks, tiny pig eyes, and shocking white hair and eyebrows, he looked like a typical dime novel flatfoot. But Mooney was a career cop who had made it to the top of the force by knowing when to look the other way and when to act against small-time hoods and grifters. "A terrible crime," he said to Rudy. The flesh sagged on his massive cheeks, and his voice trembled when he spoke. The chief seemed genuinely shocked by Ezra's murder. "A terrible, vile crime. It was a routine assignment—destroy some illegal hooch in an East Side warehouse. Ezra went in first to scout around. The killer must have been waiting for him. He never had a chance. By the time the rest of the squad rushed in, the murderer was gone."

"Dere were no clues?" asked Rudy.

"Nothing other than some sort of oil on the floor where we think the assassin was waiting. I have our chemist analyzing the stuff now. It's nothing definite, but makes me wonder if Nemesis isn't involved somehow."

"Nemesis?" said Monica. "Why would he want Ezra dead?"

"Good question, young lady," said the chief. "Find a motive and you've got your killer. That's what I always say—find the motive."

"You will let me know those test results, Chief?" said Rudy.

"Immediately." The chief brushed a trickle of sweat from his forehead. "Now, you go home and take it easy. I know how much Ezra meant to you. He was a good man, a very good man. He was the heart of the Paragon City police force. He'll be missed."

"Thank you, Chief. Good night."

Leaving the morgue, Rudy handed Monica the car

keys. "Please drive, Monica. You can drop me off at the newspaper. I want to change the main page for tomorrow's edition. We will lead with Ezra's murder. I want to write that piece myself. It will take me hours to get the page torn up and reset. You go home and get some sleep. I will see you in the morning."

"Are you sure, Dad? You need rest, too. This has been a big shock to both of us. We can always run Ezra's death as the lead story next week."

"No. The article will run tomorrow. There will be no sleep for me until I get it done. Please do as I say."

"Yes, sir," answer Monica. When Rudy said no in such a manner, Monica knew there was no use in arguing.

It was nearly four in the morning when she finally pulled the Packard into the driveway. She didn't think she'd be able to sleep, but she was totally exhausted and collapsed on her bed fully dressed.

Two hours later, Monica awoke in a sudden panic. She had the feeling that something terrible had happened. Instantly, she remembered Ezra's murder. But that wasn't what had woken her. The fear she felt was immediate, real, and urgent. Anxiously she rushed to the telephone, dialed the newspaper office. The regular morning crew didn't start work until seven, so Rudy should answer. The phone rang and rang but no one picked up. Monica's concern inched up another level. What was going on?

Still, it was possible that Rudy had been more tired than he had let on. Maybe he'd just curled up on the cot by the printing presses for a short nap. He'd done that more than once over the years. Or maybe he'd gone out for an early cup of coffee and a donut. Anything was possible. It didn't have to be the worst.

Still, all the reasoning in the world couldn't stop her heart racing at twice its normal rate. And the same fear that motivated her allowed her to stay clear of the traffic squad as she sped to the newspaper office at seventy miles an hour on the deserted city streets. The door to the building was open, a bad sign. When he worked alone, Rudy Richter always kept the door locked.

"Dad," she called as she entered the dark building. Reaching over to the control panel, she switched on the plant lights. "Dad, are you okay?"

No answer. The printing plant was silent. Other than the overheads, the only lights visible in the building were in the office upstairs. Rudy's office.

"Dad?" she called again and again as she walked through the plant and up the stairs to the office. The door to the room was half open. But the room was silent. There was no sound of typing, nor any other hint of life. Slowly, Monica pushed the door wide open and looked inside.

She screamed, but only once. In her heart, in her soul, she had somehow already known that her father was dead. He lay sprawled out across his desk, a bullet hole in his head and a revolver clutched in one hand. It looked like suicide, but Monica knew her father too well. Ezra's death had angered, not depressed him. Suicide was the easy way out and Rudy Richter never did things the easy way.

More damning was the fact that the gun was clenched in Rudy's right hand. It wasn't common knowledge, but the old man had suffered a mild stroke earlier that year. Rudy had recovered, but he'd lost some of the feeling in his right side. Ezra, Monica, and the doctor knew about his weakness. So did the foreman and a few top officials at the plant. That was it. Obviously, the person intent on framing Rudy hadn't known that it would have been impossible for him to squeeze the gun's trigger with the fingers of his right hand. This wasn't a self-inflicted wound, but murder.

Holding back the tears, Monica dialed the police. The officer on duty recognized her voice and offered sympathies for Ezra's death. The cop wasn't prepared for Monica reporting a second death. He promised immediate action. He was true to his word; in less than ten minutes, three police cars filled with men pulled up to the newspaper building. Even Monica was taken by surprise when Police Chief Mooney came up the stairs, leading a crew of experts.

"I know it looks like suicide, Chief—" Monica began, but Mooney stopped her in midsentence."

"Suicide? Rudy Richter?" said Mooney, his face twice as red as normal. "Monica, your father and I had our differences over the years on how the police department should be run, but that was strictly business. I knew your dad for a long, long time, and he's the last man in the world who would ever commit suicide. You know it, and I know it. Rudy was a fighter. He never gave up. You could show me a five-page handwritten suicide note signed by your father and I wouldn't believe it. This was murder."

Monica nodded, caught by surprise. Mooney was not someone known for his great admiration of her father or the *Free Press*.

"Chief, look at this," said one of the detectives. "Here, on the floor, a foot or so behind the body."

The officer pointed to a small pool of liquid. Kneeling down, Mooney touched the edge of the puddle with his first finger. "Just as I thought," he said, a note of satisfaction in his voice. "Machine oil. I'll bet my last nickel it's the same stuff we found by Eza's body tonight—and that Nemesis is behind this. Probably has a grudge against your family for that story the paper ran about him. You should give some thought to leaving town, little lady. If I'm right, you're in danger, too."

"I appreciate your concern, Chief," said Monica. "But my dad raised me to run a newspaper. I'm not leaving, and the *Free Press* will keep on publishing. That's final."

"You're a brave young woman," said Chief Mooney. "Braver than most of my force, I'll tell you. I only hope you're not making a big mistake."

A few hours later, after the crime photographer and the medical unit had left the building, Monica pondered the same thought over and over. The Depression, now pounding at banks and businesses with the full force of a Florida hurricane, had hit the *Free Press* hard. Advertisers mostly stuck with the *Paragon City Times*, and gave up on the once-weekly *Free Press*. The only thing that had kept Rudy's newspaper alive was his no-holds-barred journalism and unflinching commitment to the truth, no matter what politicians it hurt. Still, the paper was barely paying its bills. With Rudy's death, it could easily go under. Moreover, while she wasn't as convinced as Chief Mooney that Nemesis had orchestrated the two murders, Monica had no doubt that her own life was in danger. The situation looked grim.

She planned to stick out the troubles as long as possible. But that didn't mean she couldn't ask one last time for help.

Sitting at her typewriter, she hammered a short letter

to the mailbox drop in Paris used by Marcus and Stefan. They were her only hope. Perhaps her only chance.

In short, clipped paragraphs she described the murders of Ezra and Rudy, and detailed Chief Mooney's suspicions. She also mentioned the newspaper's precarious financial position. A half-page typed letter, it told the whole story. At the bottom of the page, in dark, bold strokes, she closed with two handwritten lines:

Please come home. I need you.
Paragon City needs you.

CHAPTER SEVENTEEN

The French had a phrase for it: *la bonne vie*. To the Spanish, it was *la vida buena*. The Italians called it *la vita buona*. All translated the same: *the good life*. Which was what Marcus Cole was living in Paris, the City of Lights, in late August 1931.

The past year had flown by amazingly fast. Marcus's discovery of the black box had changed his life, completely and utterly reshaped him. The Marcus Cole of August 1931 was an entirely different man from the Marcus Cole of June 1930. One had been a daredevil adventurer, on the run from the law and on the run from ever-approaching death. The new Marcus was a man-about-town, a millionaire on good terms with the law enforcement agencies of Europe, as well as a patron of the arts and letters. Most of all, he was a handsome, healthy young bachelor possessing rugged good looks and a subdued but nearly overwhelming force of personality. When he wanted, Marcus dominated conversations with just a word, a casual nod, a smile. When he walked into a room, all conversation stopped for an instant. There was an aura of intense energy about Marcus Cole, a vitality beyond that of normal men. There was something special about him, but no one could say exactly what.

Tonight, he was returning from a day spent touring the magnificent Colonial Exposition located in the Vincennes Park area. One of the largest expos ever to be held in Paris, the fair contained over twelve thousand exhibits spread out over five hundred acres. Dozens of European nations, as well as the United States, had set up major exhibits alongside more minor ones from all of their colonies. It was a fascinating tour through much of the world. Privately, Marcus thought celebrating colonialism was like celebrating slavery. He also found it amusing that the most popular area of the United States display was a reproduction of General Lafayette's quarters at Mount Vernon during the Revolutionary War. No one commented on the ironic fact that the war had been waged by a colony fighting for independence from a European power.

No matter. Marcus wasn't interested in making trouble for the French. He had recently been granted a full pardon from the government for his shadier activities in years gone by, wiping his slate absolutely clean throughout Europe and England. It had taken huge monetary donations to the right people and proper institutions, but as of a few months ago, he and all of the surviving members of the Cole gang were once again considered honest citizens of the world. England, of course, had posed the most trouble, but returning the Herodotus scroll, along with his notes and a detailed translation of the work had gone a long way toward repairing his relations with Colonel Turnbull. A secret expedition to the Isle of Vengeance with a British archeological crew had sealed the bargain. Marcus hadn't been surprised to discover that no trace of the Fountain of Zeus or the black box could be found. Not that he had informed the researchers of their powers.

Still, the expedition had been labeled a huge success due to the discovery of hundreds of stunning Greek artifacts from the first age of heroes. All was forgiven, and Marcus had even been invited to lecture someday at the British Museum about his days as an archeological outlaw. Someday, but not right away. He had plenty of time, lots and lots of time.

The first thing he had done upon returning to Paris after his adventures on the island was to visit a series of leading specialists in lung ailments. One and all agreed that not only was his cancer cured, but several expressed doubts that he had ever been stricken. In every case, Marcus left the doctors with the impression he was a crazed American hypochondriac with an excess of money. He made no mention of his previous visits to other lesser-known doctors over the past decade and a half, nor did he ever once speak of his service in the Great War. Some remarks were best left unstated.

The quiet black market sale of Grecian antiquities to private collectors in Europe, Asia, and the United States had made the members of the Cole gang incredibly rich. The money had been split equally among the survivors, Marcus insisting that each man take a full share of the booty. Despite the money, he hadn't been able to deliver them perfect health and, while the others expressed extreme doubts abut the reality of that gift, none of them could argue that the nectar and ambrosia had cured Marcus's ailments.

None of their money had been able to solve the mysterious disappearance of Stefan Richter or Billy the Bean. Marcus had hired some of the finest detectives in Europe to search hospitals, mental institutions, and even Greek fishing villages in the hope that either one or both of the men had turned up, amnesiacs, in those locations. Not a trace of either had been found. Alan Gleason, who'd never had much to do with Stefan, had once or twice raised suspicions about the big man, but he had no proof and Marcus was loathe to believe anything bad about his closest acquaintance. Stefan's powers should have matched his own, but perhaps even they had not been enough to save him from the cavern's collapse. It was just hard for Marcus to believe that he had escaped, where the ever-resourceful Stefan had not.

Banishing such dark thoughts from his mind, Marcus nodded to the doorman who pulled open the entrance of the sumptuous hotel were he was living. The place was located a half block from the Champs-Élysées. Marcus didn't recognize the night clerk, which was no great surprise. Marcus spent as little time in the hotel as possible. He was out most days and many evenings, living life to the fullest, meeting the rich and famous during the day, and attending the opera, the ballet, and theatre at night with one or more of his many female friends. Fabulously rich and quite handsome in a dark and dashing way, Marcus was already considered one of the most eligible bachelors in Paris.

Despite the attentions of dozens of beautiful and sophisticated young women, Marcus still wondered what had happened to his lifelong correspondent and friend, Monica Richter. He had continued to write to her month after month, but Monica had stopped answering his letters more than a year ago. The last time he had heard from her was shortly after his exploits in Greece. He had written and written, but his letters had all gone unanswered, as had his queries to Rudy Richter. It was Sid Sawyer who suggested a depressingly logical answer. Most likely, Monica had met a nice young gentleman in Paragon City and gotten married. As a new wife, she probably considered correspondence with a known adventurer and unmarried man less than proper. That Rudy Richter felt uncomfortable explaining the situation to his adopted son made sense, too. That was all there was to it. Marcus had his doubts, but the explanation calmed his worries. Someday, he would return to Paragon City, find Monica, and explain to her how much her letters had meant to him, especially in those grim years after the war when they had been like an anchor to a man drifting away from life toward death.

Marcus turned the ornate key in his door, pushed it open, and stepped into his apartment. And his life changed forever.

They moved in silence, rags tied on their shoes to muffle the sounds made of their footsteps. Six of them, armed with pipes and chains, and not hesitant to use them. Six, big, powerful men who attacked with an overwhelming fury and a precision that marked them as professional killers. Six men against one. It could have been sixty or six hundred. Against Marcus Cole, such odds meant nothing.

He moved with lightning speed, catching two iron bars as they descended, ripping them out of the hands of the wielders and swinging them down to block the thrusts of two others aimed at his stomach. Continuing the same motion, he thrust out with both elbows, catching the last two men in their heads as they bent down trying to slam the pipes into his feet. Moving with the grace of a ballet dancer, he spun forward, battering the three men on each side of him with blows powerful enough to send them flying across the room. In the blink of an eye, he was master of the situation. Until a man spoke, slowly and deliberately, from across the room. The familiar voice caused Marcus to freeze in place.

"I expected as much, but I had to know for sure. Amazing, watching you move, Marcus. A little faster than me, but not as powerful. Still, quite impressive. Time to stop fighting and surrender. Otherwise, I'll blow the whistle around my neck. That noise will signal the twenty agents I've stationed throughout this hotel to kill an innocent bystander. If you resist in any manner, those people will perish and their deaths will be on your head."

With any other man, Marcus might have gambled. With his superhuman speed and strength, he should have been able to overpower his enemy before he could use the whistle. But, there was no gambling with a man whose powers presumably matched his own. "Stefan," he said. "Somehow I knew you'd survived. What's this all about? Is this some kind of joke?"

"No joke, I assure you."

Stefan switched on the table lamp that rested on Marcus's desk, located a few feet in front of the double glass doors leading to the apartment's balcony. The desk light cast an eerie glow on the big man's face. "First we make certain you're not going anywhere," he said, folding fingers in front of his face, as if in prayer. "Then we talk."

Stefan's features had coarsened, and his expression was cruel, without humor. He was dressed in a heavy black sweatshirt despite the warmth of the evening. A black cloak was wrapped around him like some gigantic web. Hunched forward, huge arms resting on the desk, massive shoulders bunched up around his neck, he reminded Marcus of Lon Chaney in *The Hunchback of Notre Dame*. Always a big man, Stefan looked bigger—much bigger. And much more menacing.

Groaning and cursing, the six killers Marcus had scattered through the apartment staggered back to the door. Out of a huge painter's box, they pulled a tightly woven fisherman's net and tossed it over Marcus's body. Hundreds of tiny but incredibly sharp hooks barbed the net and a several dozen steel balls weighted it to the floor. "That should hold him," said one of the assassins. "This stuff is nearly indestructible."

"I've tested it myself," said Stefan, nodding. "It should serve. But keep your guns aimed at him. Just for insurance."

"I'm still waiting for an explanation for this attack, old chum," said Marcus. He was anxious to get Stefan talking. "Is this about that bar tab I stuck you with in Monaco?"

"Same old Marcus," said Stefan. "Never at a loss for words. Always ready with a joke, no matter how dangerous the situation. I always found that pretty tiresome, but it amused the others. I hope you retain that same sense of humor when I start torturing you. Poor Tom Ricks, he never laughed once. He died screaming."

Marcus struggled to comprehend what Stefan was saying. "Tom Ricks was one of the finest, bravest, most loyal friends a man could have," he said through gritted teeth.

"He saved your life at least twice. Once in Venice, once in Bavaria. Why would you ever—"

"Torture him? For information. I thought Ricks would betray you," said Stefan. His leer revealed his total lack of remorse. "I knew you lived in Paris, but there were some other things I wanted to know about your situation—whether you had hired bodyguards, that sort of thing. By the time I was convinced Ricks didn't know anything my agents hadn't already discovered on their own, he was past help. Killing him was a favor for his past good deeds."

"I wasn't trying to hide from anyone," Marcus said. "I moved frequently because I liked staying in fancy new places. That's the only reason. I would have been glad to see you."

"Glad to see me?" Stefan scoffed. "Glad to take advantage of me again, you mean. I finally came to my senses when we were on the Isle of Vengeance. That's when I realized how you had cheated me for years, shared my rewards with the others, held me back so you always got the best. Nothing changed with me. I'm the same man I was, only better. Much better. And now, much more appreciated."

"Stefan, you're talking—"

"I'm talking truth, Marcus, and you know it. The elixir helped me recognize the lies you used against me. Afterward, the radium rays—the golden light—showed me the right path, the only path to my true destiny. I've been pursuing that path ever since. Right up to tonight, when I intend to even the score between us."

"Your true destiny?" said Marcus. The longer he kept Stefan talking the better. The six killers were standing at attention, their pistols raised and aimed at his head.

Sooner or later, they'd drop their guard. That's when he'd move. Stefan might think this net could hold him but Marcus felt otherwise. The trick was to get out of its tangles before the gunmen could react.

"I've become an important member of a very important society, one with great plans for mankind's future," said Stefan. "A vast organization that understands humanity needs proper . . . *supervision* if it is ever to reach its full potential."

"There's a secret order of technologists?" said Marcus said with a bitter chuckle. He knew his friend's weaknesses, his soft spots. After fifteen years of adventuring, he knew Stefan Richter better than anyone else in the world. "Do they speak Esperanto?"

For an instant, Marcus thought he had gone too far, had angered Stefan so intensely that he was going to order his underlings to fire. His friend's face twisted with raw, unadulterated hate and his eyes seemed to flare brilliant crimson. Stefan drew in one deep breath, then another, hunching his shoulders forward like a wild beast about to spring. Even his own men took a step back. Time seemed to stop, paralyzed by the fear in the room.

"Ricks took five hours to die," said Stefan, his voice emotionless. "Five very painful hours. Wait till you discover what I have planned for you, Marcus."

Not tonight, I won't, thought Marcus. He said nothing in reply but his mind was spinning. If Stefan really intended to kill him, he would have done so already. There was no reason to supply all this information to a man you were abut to murder. Stefan was no fool. He was staging this show for a reason. Something more than merely telling Marcus that Tom Ricks was dead. Sooner or later, the big man would reveal his true intentions. All Marcus had to do was play along, and convince Stefan that he had no idea what was really happening.

"I joined Arachnos, a secret society based in Italy," continued Stefan. "Our gang avoided working for them because of your baseless fears of fascism. I always considered that one of your many blind spots. I was right. Under the guidance of Arachnos, Mussolini has gained incredible power in Italy. And their plans stretch far, far beyond anything imagined by the powers in Europe and America. Working with them, my dreams of a better future for mankind will come true."

"Your dreams?" said Marcus. "Not theirs?"

"My dreams will become their dreams," said Stefan. "Already, I've risen to one of the organization's top leadership posts. Don't forget those samples I took from the Fountain of Zeus, my old comrade. Those vials are worth more than their weight in gold, a hundred thousand times more than their weight. I labor with all my strength for Arachnos because I know for certain, one day, when the time is right, I will be Arachnos."

"Your dream sounds like a nightmare," said Marcus. "But it'll never happen. Not as long as there's an America to stop madmen like you."

"America, sweet land of liberty," snarled Stefan. "Land of the pilgrim's pride, and so on and so on. Italy is merely the beginning, Marcus. Arachnos has turned its eye on our homeland. With the United States deep in this Depression, there's a hunger for new leadership, for change. Exactly what Arachnos can offer, to those willing to swear loyalty to us. I've been selected to supervise the first wave of our American operation. Can you guess where I'm planning to begin?"

"Paragon City," said Marcus. Now, he suspected, he would learn the true motive for this attack. "Won't your father be proud, you traitor?"

"Ah, my father," said Stefan. "I think he would have understood. At least, I like to think so."

" 'Would'?"

"Oh, that's right," said Stefan. His face glowed with ghoulish delight. "You don't know. You haven't heard anything from my dear sister in, let's see, a year or more. She stopped writing, stopped answering your letters. How disappointed your letters sounded. They were so sad."

"You stole my letters," said Marcus. A feeling of absolute stupidity swept over him. "You stole her letters to me."

Stefan laughed and laughed. "Not me personally, of course, but Arachnos has agents throughout Europe. They're very reliable. My men even intercepted the two telegrams you sent to her. You absolute, arrogant fool."

Stefan held out one hand, waved at one of his assassins. "Rocco, did I ever mention to you that Marcus had an older brother in America? A policeman named Ezra."

"Yes, leader," said the man. He was two inches taller than Marcus and twice his weight. He had a voice that sounded like gravel rattling in a coffin. "You told me he was killed by Nemesis. The same criminal genius who murdered your father."

"Exactly right," said Stefan. "Nemesis, the leader of Paragon City's criminal gangs, and the man who I will personally execute once I've returned to the city of my birth. Marcus really should have been the one to do that, months ago, but then again, he never even answered any of Monica's letters. How terrible of him, disappointing my sister, the young woman who thought of him as some sort of noble hero. How truly heartbreaking."

Marcus prided himself on his self-control. All of his life, from his years on the docks of Paragon City, to the bloody trenches of France, to his long years battling the aftereffects of the poison gas he'd inhaled, he had managed to keep his emotions in check. He had fought and even killed, but never out of rage. Marcus believed that losing control was the first step in losing your life.

Stefan, Marcus knew, didn't share this philosophy. His one-time friend had always thought Marcus's self-restraint, his reluctance to kill, was based on weakness not strength. The big man never could grasp the concept that the only way to truly master your emotions was not to yield to them. No doubt Stefan felt certain now that Marcus would maintain his control, would never give him the satisfaction of rising to his bait. But Marcus knew, too, that surprise was the great equalizer in grim situations like this.

"You bastard!" Marcus suddenly bellowed at the top of his lungs. He grabbed the steel net with both hands and ripped it to confetti. Two swings of his arms smashed the gunmen surrounding him to the floor. Bullets roared but none of them came close to hitting him. Marcus smiled inwardly; this proved Stefan didn't want him dead. His former friend wasn't fool enough to bring any but his best marksmen on an assignment like this. Marcus knew, too, that it was to his advantage to play along, to conceal his understanding of the game Stefan was playing here.

With a theatrical roar of outrage, Marcus leapt the dozen feet across the room separating him from Stefan and seized his closest friend, now his worst enemy, by the throat and squeezed. Squeezed with the power to bend steel, to twist muscle and bone like putty beneath his fingers. Only to have Stefan's massive arms smash into his wrists and break the hold. Marcus knew he was stronger than most men alive. So was Stefan Richter.

"No more talk," said Stefan, rising to his feet. He was immense, a giant of a man who towered over Marcus by a head, with shoulders wider than a doorway and muscles like bands of steel. "Only death remains for you."

Behind them, the door of the apartment slammed open. "Leader!" cried a voice. "We heard shots!"

For a second, Stefan's eyes shifted from Marcus to the men pouring into the apartment. It was an instant that Marcus used to his full advantage. A dodge to the right, a step forward and, like a human missile, he hurtled the remaining few feet straight into the window leading to the balcony. Haloed by shattered glass, he dropped to the street. He hit the pavement running. The streets of Paris were packed with the late-night theater crowd. Having spent months wandering through the city, Marcus knew many of its alleys and shortcuts. There was no way that Stefan and his men would find him.

Then again, Marcus understood that finding him was probably the last thing Stefan intended to do. The trap had been baited and set; that's what the drama this evening had been all about. Now, it was for Marcus to decide what to do about it.

CHAPTER EIGHTEEN

Five hours had passed since Marcus's escape from Stefan. He sat in the parlor of the small house that Alan Gleason and Sid Sawyer shared near the Seine. Marcus had spent an hour carefully checking the area for suspicious characters before making contact. As best as he could tell, the agents of Arachnos knew nothing about this location.

"So, you've heard the whole story," said Marcus. "How much of it is true and how much is lies?"

"It's a grand mix," said Sid. The quiet one, the calm one, the devious one of their group, he possessed a keen eye for separating the truth from fiction. "The way I see it, everything devolves from the end of the action to the front. Stefan's no fool. As you surmised, the entire scene was carefully planned and well executed. He did a good job of it and if we weren't experts in the same line of work, we might have fallen for the bait totally aware of the hook."

"As usual, I'll follow Sid's lead," said Alan Gleason. The Irishman stood at the opposite end of the living room.

"This drama was never planned as a murder, Marcus. Stefan knows the rules of combat. You want a man dead, you take care of it immediately. That you escaped was no accident. He wanted you free and gone. Not for any love left between the two of you. The man has turned into a killer. Reports I received earlier in the day from Tom's dad indicated that Stefan hadn't lied about the torture. He needs to be stopped. And I suspect you're the only one he'll ever let close enough to him to perform that act."

"I'm fairly certain I can follow Stefan's thinking," said Sid. "The only question, really, is whether he's underestimated Marcus's powers. There's really only one way to discover that." Without another word, Sid fired three shots from the revolver he had slipped into one hand.

Fast as Sid was, Marcus moved even faster. Like a man swatting flies, he waved his right hand through the air, though that hand moved in a blur no eye could follow. "That trick won't work," he said, opening his fist and letting the three bullets fall to the carpet. "My reflexes are too good. They only caught me in that net in the apartment because I let them."

"You've been shot at before tonight?" asked Sid.

"One or two minor disagreements with gentlemen over ladies in the past year," said Marcus. "I have been trying to live a fuller life."

"What about a knife?" asked Alan Gleason, then tossed a gleaming silver missile. A six-inch stiletto quivered in the back of the wood chair in which Marcus was sitting. An abrupt shift of his shoulder as the blade flew through the air had allowed him to evade the blow.

"I'm hard to hit," said Marcus. Casually, he yanked the knife out of the chair, flipped it up in the air, grabbed it with the same hand, and plunged it with all of his strength straight down into one thigh. The blade snapped with a loud crack. "I'm also hard to hurt. I hope this wasn't your only one, Alan."

"A Gleason without a knife," said Alan, another blade slipping into his left hand then disappearing equally as smoothly. "I doubt that. So, you've got skin like steel?"

"I'm invulnerable to a gunshot or knife blade," said Marcus. "That much I've discovered. Indestructible is another matter. I'm not planning to juggle sticks of dynamite in the near future. Better safe than sorry."

"Still, assuming Stefan's abilities are anything like yours, I think his scheme is clear," said Sid Sawyer. "He wants you to follow him to Paragon City and put this Nemesis character out of action. In effect, do the heavy lifting for him. Meanwhile, he'll concentrate on corrupting the city officials and taking over the city government. Once that's done, he'll finish the job by eliminating you."

"Nice, neat, and tidy," said Alan Gleason. "You'll go, of course?"

"Of course," said Marcus. "Monica's in danger and Stefan needs to be stopped. Would you have me do otherwise?"

"Not if you're Marcus Cole," said Sid. "What do you want us to do?"

"I think some research is in order," said Marcus. "And I'll need some help quietly closing out a few bank accounts. For one night, the Cole gang rides again."

The next morning, Marcus, dressed in a street peddler's clothes, selling roses to departing tourists, watched as Stefan Richter, wearing a heavy black cloak, slouch hat, and dark leather boots, boarded the ocean liner *Grand Royal*.

Neither Stefan nor the lackeys surrounding him gave any indication they knew they were being watched, yet Marcus felt sure his old friend knew he was on the docks. There was a bond between them built over a lifetime, an almost supernatural link that only death could shatter. Marcus understood that he was perhaps the only man alive who could stop Stefan's plan for Paragon City. But it wouldn't be easy.

A day later, under an assumed name, Marcus set sail on a liner, the *Queen Vic*, bound for Havana, Cuba. A quick check by Sid Sawyer had established that Arachnos agents were watching every voyage departing for America. Marcus preferred to keep his movements secret for as long as possible. A detour to Cuba, a smuggler's ship to Miami, and then a train trip up the East Coast to Paragon City should allow him to evade any of Stefan's agents. The time spent on the train would also provide Marcus the opportunity to set into motion certain necessary plans. Or so he hoped.

Saying goodbye to Sid Sawyer and Alan Gleason was difficult. These men were his family, would always be his family.

"I finally was able to contact Riley in Denmark, Captain," said Gleason, as the three of them stood on the ship deck, waiting for the last call ashore. "He's fine, living in a chateau in the North Country. He'll keep his eyes peeled for unwanted visitors. He asked me to pass on a message— if you need his help, don't hesitate to let him know. He's building some sort of new automobile. Claims it will revolutionize travel. Knowing our Mr. Shaw, it might do just that."

"I'm glad to hear he's okay," said Marcus. "I worry that Stefan's agents have our entire crew on their execution list."

"Maybe they do, sir," said Sid Sawyer, with the briefest of smiles gracing his face. Then his features returned to unreadable stone. "Gleason and I plan to do some hunting this fall. We heard the shooting in Italy's excellent."

Marcus laughed. "And to think, Turnbull once said we hunted only for booty, never for revenge."

"Life changes," said Alan Gleason. "So do we. But some things remain the same. If you require aid, Captain, you know I'll be there."

"And me," said Sid Sawyer.

"I know," said Marcus as he shook hands with each man. "I know."

An hour later, he was Cuba bound.

He spent the rest of the day in his first-class cabin reading a book of short stories by Ernest Hemingway, an American author and friend of Riley Shaw who had met him in Paris some years before. The writing was crisp, clean, and dynamic and made Marcus wonder if Hemingway had tried his hand yet at novels. He'd have to look up his work in the Paragon City Public Library when he arrived home.

After a fine dinner at a table filled with Cuban businessmen and their wives returning from a dream vacation to Paris, Marcus decided that a stroll on the deck would serve him well before he retreated to his room for the night. A mellow dance band played on the promenade deck as he walked casually along the railing. He'd done more than his fair share of sailing in life, but he'd never gotten bored with the majesty of the sea.

As he neared his cabin, Marcus spotted four men clustered at the rail, pointing to something off the ship's stern. The electric light over them was out and the quartet moved in near darkness. They seemed excited and he couldn't help but wonder why the commotion. Sensing nothing amiss, he walked closer.

"I think she's sinking," said one man.

"Maybe we should call the captain," suggested another.

"I'm not sure if that would be right," said the third.

"Gentlemen, what's happening?" asked Marcus, trying to follow their gestures. In the distance, he could see what appeared to be a flare glowing on the water.

"A small boat capsized," replied the first.

"Take a look," said the second.

Marcus leaned farther over the rail, hoping to make out details. "Best to inform the—"

"No need," said the fourth man, the biggest of the group, as he swung a slip-knotted noose around Marcus's neck. "Nemesis sends his regards."

The other three immediately pushed the iron anvil at their feet over the rail. It dropped like the proverbial stone, more than enough weight to snap any man's neck and drag him overboard to a watery grave before anyone would notice the splash.

Marcus Cole was no longer any man. He was a man of superhuman strength, speed, and agility. More than that, he was a man who had learned to think on the field of battle, make a split-second decision, and implement that decision without the least hesitation or doubt.

Instead of grabbing the railing, an instinctive action that would have done more harm than good, he whipped both hands to his neck and the noose around it. At the same time, he smashed one foot as hard as he could into the deck, splintering a wide circle of wood to kindling. Through this hole he half dropped, half collapsed to the lower floor. In the instant before the rope was pulled tight, he ripped the noose from around his neck and let it go. The rope hissed up through the hole and followed the anvil into the ocean.

Screaming curses, the four attackers swarmed down the ladder to the lower deck. Marcus might have been able to escape if he immediately turned and ran. But Marcus had no plans to retreat. He'd escaped injury so far, save to his pride. He was annoyed with himself for being so easily fooled and was not in a forgiving mood.

The first man, the big one who had handled the noose, jabbed at Marcus with a boat hook, holding it with both hands like a pike. At the same time, two men armed with machetes leapt forward, swinging their blades—not at Marcus, but at the place they thought he'd retreat to in order to avoid the hook's thrust. The fourth man, armed with the second hook, stood well to the rear. Strong in the wrist, he held the boat hook raised to shoulder height like a harpoon, ready to toss it at the right moment.

The plan didn't work because Marcus didn't react the way the assassins expected. A quick turn of his body allowed him to avoid the first boat hook altogether. Grabbing the pole with both hands as it passed, Marcus twisted the wood to the left with a snap of his wrists. The beam cracked under the strain, but not before the angular momentum imparted to the wood sent the largest of the would-be killers flying out over the railing.

The machete men, slow in reacting to the loss of their leader, proved no more of a challenge. They ran at Marcus, swords raised high. He ducked their charge and used his hands on their backs, and their own momentum, to continue their journey over the railing and into the sea. The fourth man, the one primed to use the boat hook as a spear, swung his head about and checked to make sure none of his companions had somehow regained the ship. Realizing he was alone, he quietly laid the boat hook down on the deck and jumped overboard before Marcus could lay a hand on him.

Standing at the rail, Marcus could see the four men treading water. Not far away came the muffled clank of a boat bell—prearranged transportation for the assassins. Marcus could imagine the panic the would-be killers felt, anticipating the reception they'd receive after failing their mission. But they hadn't failed, not in the way they envisioned, anyway. Nemesis had no reason to know who he was, let alone reason enough to want him dead. Not yet, anyway. No, this was Stefan's work, and the assassins' real purpose, whether they knew it or not, was to provide one more reason to set Marcus against the mysterious crime lord Stefan wanted out of the way.

A flicker of motion, a hint of black lace, and, as if from nowhere, three young women appeared on the walkway. They were dressed in ultra-fashionable cocktail dresses, high-heeled shoes, and long silk shawls. Their voices, whispering softly behind Chinese-style fans that were much the rage on the Continent, sounded very familiar. Equally familiar was the look of their thick black hair, artfully woven into long braids decorated with fine gems.

As the trio reached Marcus, one of them peered over her shoulder and smiled. "Mr. Cole, what a pleasant surprise," said the young woman who had called herself Alexis. "Perhaps not exactly a surprise, but pleasant nonetheless. Would you care to join us for a drink of wine? I think we have much to discuss."

"Ladies," said Marcus, straightening out his badly mangled suit and tie as best could be expected. "I'd be honored."

CHAPTER NINETEEN

Entering the women's quarters, one of two suites on the ship reserved for royalty, Marcus came to the immediate realization that the three sisters were not afraid to reveal the substantial wealth at their command. His spacious cabin was a closet compared to their accommodations. As befitting royal quarters, the suite was comprised of a large sitting room; three separate bedrooms, each with its own bath; and a small, but well-appointed kitchen

"Tonight, I think, would be a good night for the red," said Phoebe to her sisters as Marcus settled down in one of four luxurious chairs arranged in a circle around an elegant coffee table in the parlor's center. On it rested an exquisite china bowl filled with the reddest apples Marcus had ever seen. As did four coasters for glasses and a grouping of white silk napkins. Evidently, he had been expected.

"Do try an apple, Mr. Cole," said Megan, seating herself in the chair across from him. "They grow on a tree on our patio. Whenever we travel, we like to bring some along—a taste of home so to speak."

"Will I turn into a pig if I eat one?" asked Marcus with a smile.

"A pig?" Megan frowned. "No, no. Forget those old stories about Circe. She did turn Odysseus's men into swine, but that was because they behaved so badly at her farm. Besides, that was thousands of years ago. My sisters and I never resorted to such foolish tricks. And we certainly mean you no harm."

"No harm at all," said Phoebe, returning to the table bearing a bottle of red wine. Behind her came Alexis with a tray of grapes and cut cheese. "We would like it if you thought of us as your friends."

"When we spoke the other night, you talked in riddles," said Marcus.

"The other night you had not tasted nectar and ambrosia and had not bathed in the golden light of Creation," said Phoebe. "Those secrets must be discovered on your own, without any help. So it was for us and so it is for those we follow."

"We keep to ourselves," said Alexis. "We've seen how envy and desire turn the noblest men mad. So, when we discuss our gifts and our history, we only converse with other immortals. I can assure you that, over the centuries, the number of true eternals has been very, very few."

Marcus slowly lowered the wineglass to the table. "Are you saying that by drinking the water from the fountain, I've become an immortal?"

"Immortality lasts a long, long time," said Phoebe.

"Immortality does not mean invulnerability," said Megan.

"Some people find immortality boring," said Alexis.

"How about a straight answer?" said Marcus.

"A drink of the golden water and exposure to the open box confers long life," said Alexis. "Perhaps not eternal life, according to the literal definition of the phrase, but something close enough to merit the name. There are beings that have walked this world for eighty centuries—eight thousand years—though they are usually quite reluctant about sharing their true ages, even with us."

"Then, is it true?" asked Marcus, "Are you the Furies of Greek myth?"

"We have used many names," said Phoebe as she poured Marcus a glass of wine. He could not resist taking a taste. It was even finer than the bottle they had shared at the villa, a lifetime before. "We've been given so many titles. Some names were less complimentary than others. Listen and we will tell you our history."

Marcus felt as if he were living in a dream. Any moment he expected to wake up and find himself in prison or in a hospital for the criminally insane. This entire episode had such a feeling of unreality, he wished there was some way he could prove to himself that it was not some vivid delusion. In the end, though, it was a matter of faith.

"Pay attention and you will know the truth," said Megan.

"We were born in the great city-state of Mycenae nearly four thousand years ago," began Alexis. "Near identical triplets, we were considered chosen of the gods by the city's rulers and raised as vestal virgins in the Temple of Gaia, earth goddess. Our lives would have been short and uneventful were it not for a disagreement over a grape

orchard between our father, one of the city's most promi-
nent citizens, and the king. Father owned it and the king
wanted it. Our father was a stubborn man who considered the law greater than any man. The king considered
himself above the law, so he seized the orchard and had
father killed. We fled for our lives."

"In those times, women were considered their hus-
bands' property and we three became outlaws," said
Megan, taking up the story. "We roamed the land, looking for those who would champion our claim against the
king, but found no one. The law was the law, but the king
was the king and his power was great. Or so it was until
the goddess Gaia herself visited our camp one night."

"She came in silence," said Phoebe, "and surrounded
by wild animals."

"She glowed with golden light," said Megan.

"She cast no shadow, even in the brightest moonlight,"
said Alexis.

" 'If you merely seek vengeance,' she told us," said
Phoebe, " 'find the Fountain of the Titans. If you want
justice, open the black box.' "

"She disappeared as suddenly and as silently as she
had arrived," said Megan. "But she left us with a quest
that we pursued for the next decade."

"The search finally ended at a cave on a nameless island,
where a trickle of golden water emptied from the base of
a statue of Cronos, the first god, to the sea," said Alexis.

"There was no temple around the statue then," said
Phoebe. "No guardians. It was a lost spot, an unknown
place. We were the first to step on the sand floor of that
cave in thousands of years. The black box was there also,
in the second cave, its lid opened the slightest amount."

"On the wall behind the box?" asked Marcus, not wanting to interrupt, but the question had to be asked.

"Carved in the rock were the faces of a man and a woman. The woman was Gaia, as we had seen her. Between the two faces, the same words: *Here lies power.*"

"We drank," said Megan.

"We opened the black box," said Alexis.

"We transformed," said Phoebe. "We became . . . *more.*"

"Combined, the water and the light gave us powers that rivaled those of the Titans," said Megan. "We became immortal, nearly invulnerable, and possessed of the power to sense the good and evil in all those we met. We were also gifted with the ability to kill with the single touch those who deserved to die."

"We returned to Mycenae," said Phoebe, "no longer fugitives, but judges. The king remained the king, but now, the state was ruled by the law. We became guardians of the state, protectors of hearth and home. Those who thought to break the law, offend the state, we punished."

"Our original names were soon forgotten," said Alexis. "We became known as Erinyes, the Angry Ones. My sisters they called Megaera, the jealous one, and Tisiphone, the blood avenger."

"And you?" asked Marcus.

"Because of my determined ways," said Alexis, with a savage grin, "they named me Alecto, the unceasing pursuer."

"The force we released from the black box, the energy it had somehow been collecting for thousands of years, affected people throughout the world. Men and women were transformed into gods, goddesses, and strange half-human things. Not all of the beings of legend were creations of that mysterious light, for many other powerful forces were working in those times. Still, only we three knew the power behind the changes, knew the secret of the Fountain of Cronos."

"Hundreds of years passed and most forgot that the gods had once been humans. Memories grew dim and legends arose to explain the gods' origins. Over time, the powers granted by the golden light slipped away from some of the lesser gods and they began to vanish. They turned to dust, the result of living long beyond their time. With the passing of each god and hero, the golden energy returned to the black box."

"Then all of my struggles were for nothing?" asked Marcus. "A few years of greatness and then a handful of dust?"

"We do not know," said Alexis. "If that is the fate awaiting you, you cannot escape it. But not all the beings changed by the box's power have lost their might. We remain unchanged."

"And because we have outlived so many of the others, we have taken upon ourselves the task of protecting the island and the secrets it holds," said Megan. "We commanded laborers to clear out the ancient cavern. To protect the box and the spring, we built a new temple, with a statue to Zeus replacing that of Cronos, then built a trap to frighten off the unwary or kill those who refused to be warned."

"Did you ever learn who or what put the black box in the cave, and what purpose it serves?" asked Marcus.

"Gaia whispered to me in a dream that she and her brother, Tartarus, found the box four thousand years before us," said Phoebe, "with the same words written on the wall. They etched their faces on the stone. So the box dates back more than eight thousand years. As best we can tell, it collects creativity and genius, along with ambition, drive, and intensity from the vast ocean of humanity. In some unknown manner, it transfers huge jolts of power to those throughout the world best suited to use those gifts. Whether it works by magic or advanced technology, we don't know. The only thing we know about its origin is that we don't know anything."

"But all those years, after the power of Greece waned and the Roman Empire grew strong—what happened to you?" asked Marcus. "What did you do?"

"We waited." said Alexis.

"And waited," added Phoebe.

"And waited more," concluded Megan.

"Why?" asked Marcus. "Waited for what? For whom?"

"Surely you've guessed, Mr. Cole," said Megan. "We waited for you and Mr. Richter to appear and open the box and start the cycle once more."

"Planning to deal out some more justice?" asked Marcus.

"No," said Phoebe, her expression serious. "We swear we will not interfere in your plans, your wars, your lives. We only want to observe. Watching how you act will help us judge how we acted thousands of years ago."

"It has been a question that has haunted us for forty centuries," said Alexis. "No history book has an answer, for they treat us as legends, not reality. Only by observing your activities, studying your decisions, will we be able to tell if we acted like gods—or foolish children."

"One thing I don't understand," said Marcus when the

women finally finished speaking. "Both Stefan and I drank the water and were bathed in the light from the box. Why aren't any of you following him?"

"*His* kind we've seen before," said Megan, with a very modern, quite dismissive flip of the wrist. "The greedy ones, the ambitious ones, the ones who dream of unchecked power. We know them all too well. In our time, we watched them regress into brutal, merciless creatures, devoid of all humanity. Sooner or later, their lusts betray them and turn them into beasts. That sort of man never changes."

"You, on the other hand," said Alexis, raising the long-stemmed wineglass to her lips and taking a drink of the rose wine. "A wise, introspective man like you should make for much more interesting observation."

CHAPTER TWENTY

rachnos's headquarters in Paragon City was located in an old tenement building, built during the 1900s and abandoned some twenty years later. Stefan's advance team had been able to buy the place for a pittance. They had been working on it for weeks, shuttling in construction crews from out of town to make major improvements on the building interior while leaving the exterior unchanged. By the time Stefan arrived from France, the tenement had been transformed into an armed fortress with an up-to-date communications center, all hidden within a facade of crumbling brick, rotting wood, and old concrete. With a half dozen entrances on the street, and another five doorways hidden beneath street level, it was the perfect hideaway.

Stefan controlled the organization from a well-lit, comfortable office in the basement. Hanging from the walls of the office were huge street maps of Paragon City, with large sections outlined in red ink. Each area had a name like Founders Falls or Kings Row, the designation given to that part of the metropolis by the people that lived there. Paragon City, like Chicago, was a city of neighborhoods, a network of zones. The secret to controlling the megalopolis was in those zones.

"The city's strength is greater than the sum of its individual parts," Stefan said to his right-hand man—the heavyset, bearded assassin known as Rocco Tutoro. "Paragon is governed much like medieval England or France. The mayor is the titular head of the city, similar to the kings who ruled those countries. The true power, however, rests with the gangs and the politicians who direct the neighborhoods. They're the ones who make certain the police patrol the streets, the garbage gets picked up on time, and the gangs keep their predations to acceptable levels. They're the noblemen of Paragon, and the police and firemen their soldiers."

"So, we need to replace the independent aldermen with men loyal to Arachnos," said Rocco in his gravelly voice. "As for the gangs, we either put them on the payroll or put them in the graveyard."

"Exactly correct," said Stefan, with an expression that slightly resembled a smile. "We need to weave a web across the city, a web of treachery and deceit. A web of bribery and payoffs, backed by threats and scandal and mistrust. I like to think of it as the Web of Arachnos, with me as the spider pulling the strings."

"It is an ambitious, brilliant plan," said Rocco. "It cannot fail."

"You know the right things to say, Rocco. That's a rare talent. Don't ever make the mistake of thinking I believe your flattery. I trust no one, no matter how loyal they appear to be—to me or to Arachnos."

Rocco nodded. "I serve Arachnos. I serve you. But I serve myself first."

"A wise philosophy. Make sure you don't forget my eyes are upon you, or that I have a long reach."

"I know my place."

"Good," said Stefan. "Tomorrow, I'll have my first meeting with our sector agents. Tonight we are free from responsibilities. Get one of the cars. There's a party I want to attend. A very special party."

Rocco rose to his feet. "I'll be at exit three in five minutes."

"No delays," said Stefan. "You know how I hate to be late."

Rocco pulled the white touring car up to the designated door in four minutes. As Rocco maneuvered through the city traffic, Stefan huddled alone in the auto's backseat. He made a frightening, imposing figure—six and a half feet tall, weighing near three hundred pounds, dressed entirely in black, with a huge dark cape that wrapped completely around his shoulders and torso, and black slouch hat that almost hid his face. Only his eyes were visible. They burned like charcoal, dark with hints of crimson flame.

The neighborhood was called Kings Row, their destination a warehouse on a lonely and deserted street near the garment district. The building's parking lot was packed with expensive limousines and touring cars. Three young toughs, armed with pistols and machine guns, kept watch.

"You here for the party?" one asked, flashing a light in Rocco's face. He held the Thompson diagonally across his chest.

"No, I just like driving around the city looking for new

places to park," said Rocco. His gun, a long-barreled automatic, rested on the sill of the car window. It was aimed directly at the man's chest. "By the time you got that Thompson in play, I'd have put five bullets in your gut."

"Sure," said the man with the flashlight. "But my buddies would have turned your car into Swiss cheese. So we'd be all even." The mobster flashed a grin, revealing a gold tooth in the center of his mouth. "Fifty bucks, tough guy. In this neighborhood, parking's cheap at that price."

Rocco handed the crook a hundred-dollar bill. "Keep the change."

"Thanks. You know where the party is. The password's 'big shot.' Stay away from the bathtub gin. It's rotgut."

"Thanks for the tip," said Rocco. He opened the car's back door for Stefan. At the same time, he slipped the man with the gold tooth a business card. "You get tired of parking cars for a living, give me a call."

"Yeah," said the crook, dipping his head a fraction of an inch. "I just might do that."

Stefan, a huge shadow in the moonlight, raised a hand and they were off. Despite his tremendous size, Stefan moved quickly and his second-in-command had to trot to keep pace.

"Big shot" got them inside the door and into another world. The deserted warehouse was a front for a hot bootleg club. The room was complete with dancing girls on a raised stage, a huge buffet table loaded with everything from shrimp to caviar to sautéed frog's legs, an immense bar with three bartenders serving what they called "the best bourbon in the city," and a swing band. A thick, grayish-green cloud of cigar smoke hung over a crowd that numbered nearly three hundred.

About two-thirds of the attendees were women. Not one weighed over a hundred twenty pounds and none of them looked anywhere near thirty. They wore diamonds, emeralds, and fine pearls. Most likely, none of the gems had been acquired by legitimate means and none of them were insured. Other than by bullets.

Stefan found a table to the back of the room where he could sit and watch the rest of the crowd without them watching him. He wasn't paranoid, merely prudent. There was enough firepower in this one room to overthrow a South American government. The men carrying the guns— seventy or eighty mobsters in all—had probably killed enough people to fill a small town. Stefan knew from tests he had conducted that he couldn't be harmed by a knife or bullet. Still, he wasn't confident enough about his invulnerability to risk being shot several dozen times in the head.

Stefan stationed Rocco a few steps behind him, a good location from which he could keep any uninvited guests from getting too close to the table. If someone could get past Rocco, he was dangerous and Stefan would react accordingly. So far, though, he hadn't encountered anyone Rocco couldn't handle. He doubted he would anytime soon. Of all the men working for him, Stefan considered Rocco by far the most ambitious. Which was another reason he kept the big man close.

"What do you think of the celebration, Rocco?" asked Stefan.

"I'm not easily impressed," said the assassin. "Who's paying for this blowout? And why?"

"In a sense, we are. As to the reason, I believe that will be announced in a moment. Listen, watch, learn."

The band ceased its wailing and the chorus girls

stopped dancing. A small, mousy man with thick blond hair and baby-blue eyes stood on the nightclub stage holding a microphone. "Friends, friends," he shouted into the microphone, the sound blaring through the room, "can I have your attention?"

The crowd paid him no mind. If anything, with the band quiet, the volume of talk in the room rose to new heights. Showgirls laughed shrilly at bad jokes told by gangsters, while crooks blustered and bragged about their latest crimes. The little man on stage shook his head in frustration. Reaching into his suit pocket, he pulled out a .45 automatic. He aimed the gun straight up at the ceiling and squeezed the trigger three times. By the third shot, the crowd was silent.

"Next time," he said, waving his automatic in the direction of the crowd, "I'll aim a little lower."

"Get on with it," shouted a hoodlum more drunk than the rest. "Or shut your face."

The small man swung his gun around, aimed it at the heckler, then reconsidered. "Why waste a bullet? Folks, without further delay, let me present to you the man throwing this swell party—your friend and mine, boss of the Kings Row mob himself, Sammy Lombardo."

From the rear of the room came Sammy the Sledgehammer, dressed in a tuxedo, flanked on each side by one of the Fontaine brothers, who were wearing their everpresent black trench coats. The diminutive, pug-nosed gangster walked to the center of the stage and raised his arms over his head, fingers clenched together in a gesture of triumph. Though Sammy looked like a penguin in need of a shave, no one laughed. Not with the Fontaine brothers hefting Tommy guns in their arms.

"Hiya, folks," said Sammy, a huge grin stretching from ear to ear. "Glad you could make it to my big surprise party."

"Happy birthday, Sammy!" cried one of the chorus girls. Several other girls and gangsters took up the cheer. "Happy birthday!"

"Nah, shut up," said Sammy, losing his smile. "It ain't my birthday. That's not the surprise. I threw dis party tonight for another reason. Things are changing in Paragon City and I'm changing with dem. That's what the surprise is about. So keep your traps closed and listen carefully."

Lombardo reached up and yanked off his black tie. "First, I gotta get comfortable."

"Keep your eyes open," whispered Stefan to Rocco. "I'm expecting visitors."

"You knows me," said Sammy, looking out at the crowd, nodding at faces he recognized. "I've been involved in da rackets for fifteen years, with never a conviction. That's 'cause I'm smart, smarter than most of you bums. I got buddies in high places and I keep one step ahead of the law. Fifteen years, and not one night in jail. That takes brains.

"Now, for the last couple years, the big guy in town's been Nemesis. Even our former mayor was on his payroll—until His Honor got shot dead and Gryme was elected to take his place. We've all dealt with Nemesis, paid our protection, kept out of his way. Not that we had much choice. You crossed him and you were dead."

"Tell us somethin' we don't know," shouted Luke Molineri, a gang leader from the west side of town. "Nemesis is poison."

"I'm tired of dealing with poison," replied Sammy.

"There's a brand new mob in town—the Web—and they're moving quick, taking charge of territories nice and smooth, without any violence. These guys are paying off the right people, buying the smart politicians. They're tough, but they're also smart. They got it figured out that there's nothing wrong with a steel fist, but it should be wearing silk gloves."

Sammy paused and let the murmuring in the room subside. "Which gets us to the reason for this little get-together. I'm celebrating because I wised up and changed sides. I did some negotiating with this Web. I liked what they had to say. Enough so that I'm shifting my mob over to them. If the rest of you are as smart as you like to think, you'll do the same."

"I think not," came a mechanical voice from the rear of the building.

Stefan shivered. Though he had read about automatons for years and years in science fiction magazines, he'd never imagined what they would sound like in real life. The noise made by metal parts grinding on other metal parts was not pleasant. There was no soul, no humanity in that voice. It was the cold, relentless sound of a machine. Something that had never been alive was speaking.

From out of the back room of the warehouse walked an automaton, seven feet tall, with cable-like arms ending in huge pinchers. The wood covering the cement floor cracked like old paper beneath its weight. A single red eye swiveled back and forth in its head, like a searchlight. The thing had no mouth, only a voice box that resonated with mechanical speech.

No one in the audience moved. Sammy appeared

shocked, caught totally off guard. The Fontaine brothers raised their Thompsons, but didn't shoot.

"Fire your weapons and be destroyed," declared the mechanical man. It pushed crooks and showgirls out of its path. Each step brought it closer to the stage.

"Shoot it, you idiots!" screamed Sammy. He slapped Grimshaw Fontaine across the back. "You think it's gonna let the three of us walk away?"

Grimshaw squeezed the trigger. The Tommy gun bellowed like an enraged lion, spewing bullets at the metal monster—only to have the slugs bounce harmlessly off the automaton's armor and tear into the crowd. Men and women dropped to the floor, dead before they hit the ground. Death by ricochet!

Shanks Grimshaw fired at the automaton's head. The Tommy gun had been designed for laying down intense fire over a wide area, not accuracy, and only two slugs came close to hitting the robot's eye. The rest of the bullets flew into the crowd, killing another half dozen.

Outlaw guns roared in return, and the two Grimshaw brothers danced a horrible dance of death as they were pounded by bullets from the weapons of a dozen different criminals.

Sammy Lombardo wasn't as lucky. The automaton grabbed the gangster by one shoulder and lifted him ten feet off the floor. "No!" screamed Sammy, his face white as a sheet. "Don't do dis!"

The automaton reached up with its other arm and opened its huge pincher. With a fearsome snap it cut through the flesh, muscle, and bone of Sammy's right foot. Four more cuts and the automaton dropped the torso of Sammy Lombardo to the warehouse floor.

"This is the fate of those who try to stand against Nemesis," said the automaton.

The bloodstained crowd stood perfectly still. Frozen with fear, they dared not move. The automaton's red eye glared down at them.

"Remember this," said the machine. "Nemesis does not believe in mercy."

With those words, the automaton marched out of the club, leaving smashed doors in its wake. Once the machine was gone, the crowd scattered. Stefan swung around on his chair and stared at Rocco. The killer's features were gray and drawn, but in each hand he held a gun. He was ready to die fighting, if he must.

"So much for the celebration," said Stefan. He smiled. "That was nicely done. But, we can do better."

Slowly Rocco holstered his guns. "Permission to speak, leader."

Stefan nodded, the sly smile still on his face.

"Lombardo switched sides and Nemesis killed him. Why should the others trust the Web to protect them if they join us?"

"We will make Nemesis pay for this, of course. Kill ten of his underlings for each man killed here tonight. Nemesis rules by fear, and we will show Paragon City that they have more to fear from us. But there's more to it, something I understand that Nemesis does not."

Stefan's smile widened to a monstrous grin. "According to Machiavelli, fear is stronger than love. Yet there is a force even mightier than fear—one that will deliver to us control of the city. *Greed.*"

CHAPTER TWENTY-ONE

Monica Richter stood five feet six and weighed a hundred and three pounds fully dressed. She had long legs, a narrow waist, and a shapely bust, giving her a figure that attracted admiring looks from most of the men she met. One smart-aleck crime reporter had gone so far as to say Monica reminded him of the well-known cartoon character Betty Boop, but in living color. Monica took the remark as a compliment, but she refused to date the reporter. She wanted to be known for her brains, not her good looks.

Joe Sherman, nicknamed "the Mangler," stood six feet five and weighed three hundred pounds. He had no visible waist and his chest was shaped like a barrel. The only cartoon character Joe even vaguely resembled was Pegleg Pete, the villain of a series of musical short subjects starring a talking mouse named Mickey. Sherman had the grace and style of a steamroller.

"Your money or your life, babe," growled the big

man, as he closed a massive arm around Monica's neck. "And be quick about it!"

"You brute!" said Monica. The purse she was carrying dropped to the floor as both of her hands flashed up and grabbed Sherman by the wrist and elbow. A quick tug by her fingers, a slight twist of her hips, and her assailant went flying over her head, crashing onto the conveniently located gym mat. Despite the padding, Sherman groaned in real pain. Monica had retained her grip on his wrist, and with a quick step-over shift, had his hand bent in a reverse armlock submission hold. The slightest turn of her fingers would snap Sherman's wrist like a piece of dried wood.

"I surrender," gasped the big man, wiggling his fingers. "I give up."

"A nice throw, Miss Monica," said Masahito Mirimoto, the resident *jiu jitsu* master of Bryerman's Gym. "Executed with style and grace. You have a natural gift for the martial arts. At times, I swear that your body glows as you fight."

"Thank you, Mirimoto-san," said Monica, with a short bow. "Whatever skill I've developed is merely a reflection of that of my instructor."

The small but compact Japanese gentleman bowed his head in return. "I do my best. Unfortunately, some clay cannot be so easily molded. Your dear friend Jennifer, for example, exhibits little talent for the gentle art."

"Jennifer's not the type to defend herself," said Monica, smiling and waving to her friend and fellow reporter on the other side of the gym. "She's looking for a handsome young prince to keep her safe."

"Yeah," said Joe Sherman, gingerly rising off the practice mat. "Nobody with any sense would jump that dame anyway. She'd talk you to death." Sherman prodded his chest and arms in a half dozen spots, wincing whenever he found a sore spot. "Boss, I'm a mass of bruises. Time for me to hit the showers."

"Go," said Mirimoto. "Thank you for your assistance, Joe."

"Yeah, no problem," said the big man. " 'Night, Miss Monica. Boss is right about that glow. When you get like that, I know I'm toast."

"Goodnight, Joe," said Monica. "And thanks for the compliment."

She'd been training for almost a year now at Bryerman's Gym, working out twice a week without fail with Masahito Mirimoto. At first, the *jiu jitsu* instructor had been hesitant about teaching women, since Jennifer had declared that if Monica trained with him, she wanted to, as well. But Ezra Cole had somehow convinced the instructor and Monica had developed into one of his prize pupils. If anything, her success with unarmed combat had helped land Mirimoto many other students anxious to learn the art of self-defense.

Mirimoto had learned his art from Mitsuyo Maeda, the first Kodokan judo instructor ever to practice in the United States. Maeda had come to the States only to demonstrate *jiu jitsu*, but there was little interest in seeing martial arts demonstrations, just fights. So the teacher had become the warrior. Maeda participated in over two thousand freestyle fighting matches. He never lost one. Though not as skillful or as deadly as his master, Mirimoto was an exceptional teacher, and he was passing on all of Maeda's special techniques and fighting skills to Monica. At twenty-three years old, she was probably the most dangerous woman hand-to-hand fighter in America.

A quick shower and she and Jennifer were out for their usual cup of coffee flavored with the latest news of the city's rich and powerful. Occasionally Jennifer got stuck covering high society for the *Times* these days, while Monica, though she was acting as editor for the *Free Press*, still handled the crime scene whenever possible. Taken together, their bylines recorded the city's scandals.

"Anything new on the Lombardo massacre?" asked Monica as she bit into a cheese Danish. "We're devoting the front page to the killings. I'm writing an editorial asking the governor to send in the National Guard to deal with Nemesis."

"Nice touch, Mon," said Jennifer. Her sin of choice was apple pie with a scoop of vanilla ice cream. Jennifer considered herself a patriot and nothing was more American than a slice of apple pie. "Won't do any good—other than sell papers, though. The governor won't send in troops unless the mayor requests help. You know the chance of that happening is zero. Gryme would have to admit publicly that the city's crime problem is out of control. With an election next year, that would be bad politics. And if there's one thing Gryme knows, it's politics."

"But twenty-two people were killed," said Monica.

"To you and me, they were twenty-two people. To Mr. and Mrs. John Q. Public, they were twenty-two crooks and their molls who got caught in a gangland shootout. Face it, Mon. Ordinary citizens don't care what happens to criminals. Out of sight, out of mind. That's why they keep electing guys like Rabinowitz and Gryme. Until people realize that crime affects everyone, there won't be any justice."

"Well, the police found the same type of motor oil in Sammy's warehouse club that they discovered in my father's office. Proof positive, according to them, that Nemesis was the brains behind Rudy's and Ezra's murders."

"You don't sound convinced," said Jennifer.

"Nemesis likes publicity," said Monica. "He glories in it. He loves headlines because they make it easy for his men to collect protection money. People are terrified to cross him. In the long run, I suspect Nemesis's tactics result in less mob violence than the usual gang shakedowns."

"I get it," said Jennifer. "Nemesis kills a few top crooks and grabs the front page for a few days. Because they're only crooks, the public and the cops don't get all riled up, but the deaths frighten the other crooks into paying protection without firing another shot. He's not as dumb as most people think."

"I agree one hundred percent," said Monica, finishing off her Danish. For a minute, she eyed another pastry, then shook her head. Some small measure of self-control regarding food was necessary to keep looking good. "That's why Nemesis killing Rudy and Ezra makes a lot less sense. Their murders got the wrong people angry and frightened."

"Leaving the case wide open," said Jennifer. "You have any other suspects?"

"There's talk of a new mob, some group called the Web, moving into town," said Monica. "They've been throwing around lots and lots of money. I don't see any link between them and Rudy's death, but working on crime for more than a year makes me suspicious whenever I hear about a new mob."

"The Web, huh?"

"That's what they call themselves," Monica said. "Rumor has it that they have ties to the fascists in Italy."

"Interesting," said Jennifer. "Well, I've got a scoop of

my own. Remember when the rotating restaurant on top of the Kings Tower Hotel went out of business last fall? It's been vacant ever since, even though the hotel has managed to stay in business. According to my sources, a mysterious overseas millionaire has put a substantial down payment on the restaurant. There's talk he's planning to reopen it as a fancy nightclub."

"A millionaire with cash in the Depression" said Monica. "I thought they were myths."

"This one's real," said Jennifer. "Not only is he buying the restaurant, but also the penthouse located right above it. How's that for being loaded?"

"Who do you think has that kind of money—one of the royal families? Refugees from Europe?"

"I don't know, but I plan to find out. I have a friend at the deeds office and as soon as they find out anything, I'll be first reporter to know."

"Sounds exciting." Monica pulled up her purse to her lap to take out some change, and in doing so, sent the plate holding the crumbs of her Danish skidding across the tabletop. The dish reached the table's edge, tottered on a thin metal guardrail, then dropped—right into Monica's hand. Her reflexes since she had started training in the martial arts had grown unnaturally fast.

"Wow," said Jennifer. "Pretty nifty. Soon you'll be doing magic shows in the circus."

"Very funny," said Monica. "It was just a plate. I caught it."

"Mon," said Jennifer, "it's more than just a plate. I've watched you when we're working out. After Mirimoto puts us through a workout, I'm beat to hell and you're just starting. Don't tell me it's conditioning and training.

You're a natural—more than a natural. You're gifted. Sometimes, when you're sparing with the guys in the gym, I swear I can see a gold mist form around your body. You glow when you fight, Monica."

"Strange," said Monica. "Mirimoto said something very similar. A golden glow, huh?"

"Like you're—oh, I don't know, an angel or something," said Jennifer.

"An angel? Thanks, Jen, but aren't you rushing me a bit? Life's been too interesting around here for me to want out just yet. Still, you're not the only one thinking about pushing me into the afterlife sooner rather than later."

"Someone giving you problems? You should tell the cops."

"For all I know, the cops are part of the problem. Lately, it feels like I'm being watched. Night and day—on the street, at work, in the grocery store. I thought it might be the Lombardo gang, but they're finished after the attack at the party and I still feel like I'm being watched. Nothing I can pin down. Eyes watching me, studying me, tracking me. It's a creepy sensation and it makes no sense. If anything, my life is quieter than ever. Maybe that's the problem."

Monica rose from her chair, looked to both ends of the restaurant, then bent over Jennifer for a final few words. "The money from dad's insurance policy paid off the all the newspaper's outstanding bills, so we're in the black. Business is booming. My life has never been easier. All this good luck spooks me. I don't understand the situation, Jennifer, but it makes me nervous. It makes me very nervous."

CHAPTER TWENTY-TWO

Stefan Richter looked in the mirror in his office and smiled. He was quite satisfied with what the reflection showed. He remained as handsome as ever—tall and distinguished, with the light of the devil in his eyes. Since his experiences beneath the Well of the Furies, he was stronger, smarter, and much more cunning. While that didn't show in the mirror, he knew those traits were all there. He was ten times the man he'd been before finding the Fountain of Zeus, a hundred times that man. Best of all, his body seemed to have stopped aging. He had no doubts that the massive exposure to hard radiation had extended his life indefinitely.

Knowing he was going to live for centuries upon centuries made a huge difference in Stefan's life. He was calmer, much more patient, more willing to spend time on details. The little things mattered to him now because he understood that fifteen or twenty years in the future, they might turn out to be extremely important. A wise man kept many plans spinning at the same time, with hopes that, sooner or later, one of those schemes might prove useful. Stefan considered himself a very wise man.

Only a select few in Arachnos realized exactly just how powerful Stefan had become within the organization. Fewer still knew that Stefan Richter, international pirate and soldier of fortune, and *Il Recluse*, the rarely seen leader of the Arachnos's security division, were the same man. Stefan had worked hard to shuck off his old identity as if it were nothing more than a disguise he no longer needed. And in a way, the old Stefan had been a disguise, a mask concealing his true greatness.

To live up to that greatness, Stefan would have to do more than distance himself from his past. Sooner or later, those who believed themselves Stefan's superiors in Arachnos, like the man who called himself the Weaver, would have to die. Not yet. They served a good purpose and kept the attention off him. In the meantime, he would remain in the shadows, manipulating the so-called leaders of Arachnos to his ends.

Stefan still considered himself a technocrat, but now with a slight difference. He believed more strongly than ever that science and logic should govern the world and might lift humanity to the stars. However, he had modified the tenets of the philosophy somewhat. Technocracy posited that scientists should rule mankind because they would be the wisest, most intelligent leaders. Stefan agreed that humanity needed to be led. But instead of scientists heading the new world order, he recognized now that there was a much more obvious choice for its leader. Only an immortal could properly guide mankind to its ultimate future. He should rule the world.

The glare of the office lights made him blink. He

needed to adjust the angles so they didn't shine so brightly in his eyes. Later, he'd remove some of the bulbs, turn down the power on the rest.

"Are the crime bosses here yet?" he asked, pressing a button on the intercom box on his desk.

"They await your pleasure, leader," came the voice of Sheila Gray, his secretary, from the outer office. "Should I send them in?"

"Immediately," said Stefan. He hesitated, then added, "In five minutes, summon a cleanup crew. They'll be needed."

"Yes, sir," said Sheila, with clipped precision. "Five minutes."

Twenty crime lords swaggered into Stefan's office. Proud, arrogant men, they ruled the neighborhoods of Paragon City with an iron hand. They had been promised ten thousand dollars each if they attended the meeting today. Greed was a powerful motivator. Not one of the crime lords had turned down his invitation, despite what Nemesis had done to Sammy Lombardo. Stefan liked the gangsters' attitude. Arachnos wasn't for cowards.

There were tall men smoking slim cigarettes, and short, heavyset men smoking cigars. One of the gangsters weighed at least three hundred pounds and wore white, while another was as thin as a lamppost and dressed entirely in black. Five of the crooks had tattoos and one was missing an eye. None of them believed in democracy, much less freedom, and they all worked for the love of money, not a belief in some abstract philosophy. Stefan knew that they would perform excellent work for Arachnos, as long as they were paid. With the resources of an entire fascist dictatorship backing them,

Arachnos had no problem paying them whatever they required.

"Gentlemen, please be seated," said Stefan, waving a hand in the direction of the huge conference table dominating the office. "There are chairs for everyone. Please, make yourselves comfortable."

This being a meeting of major crime bosses, men who disliked obeying orders, they sauntered to their chairs, not in any rush to sit. A few cast curious glances at Stefan, one man even sneering, as if in challenge. Stefan couldn't help but smile. His agents had delivered the real deals. These were the kind of agents he needed to control a metropolis like Paragon. Let them swagger as much as they liked—elsewhere. He would make them understand who was boss.

"Thank you for taking the time from your busy schedules to attend this meeting," said Stefan when all were seated. He remained on his feet, towering over them. No one had been allowed to enter this inner sanctum carrying a gun. Just a precaution, they had been told, to keep things orderly. Perhaps now they were starting to regret that decision. Stefan hoped so. He liked making people sweat.

"My name doesn't matter," said Stefan. "Call me Recluse if you like. I belong to an organization known as Arachnos, and our local operation is known as the Web. Since I value your time, I won't make long speeches or tell you involved stories. Instead, I'll lay my cards on the table. I want you to work for me. I want you to become strands of my web, the Web of Arachnos."

"Recluse?" said one of the bosses. He spat on the table. "What are we, kids playing hide-and-seek?"

"No, Mr. Chelli," said Stefan. He walked over to where the husky, bald-headed criminal sat, "we're not children and this is no game."

"Then what—" began Chelli, trying to rise from his chair. Before the crook could rise or even say another word, Stefan clamped his hands on his shoulders and pushed down, *hard*. Chelli's head smashed into the table. The impact crushed the gangster's face like a ripe tomato. Chelli's shoulders twitched once and then he died.

Stefan released the corpse and it slid in a bloody mess onto the floor. "Leave it there," he told the rest of the gangsters. "The cleaners will be here shortly."

Lazily, with calculated slowness, he looked around the room. "Any other interruptions? Good. I'll continue from where I left off.

"Arachnos's plan is to seize control of Paragon City with as little bloodshed as possible. More important, we plan to conquer the city without alerting the federal authorities. If this operation succeeds—and I see no reason why it should not—then similar operations will be started in major urban centers throughout the United States. Arachnos is not particularly interested in money. We leave such matters to you and your gangs. Our goal is power. The power to rule America."

"We keep the money and our individual organizations remain intact?" asked a gangster seated two chairs down from where Chelli had died. "No protection payments, nothing?"

"Nothing," said Stefan. "As I said, Arachnos isn't interested in money. Nor do we have any intention of competing with your business enterprises. We want power, nothing more, nothing less."

"What about Nemesis?" asked another crook. "He demands a twenty percent cut of all the rackets. Who's going to pay him?"

"Arachnos, with your help, plans to run this city for your benefit and ours," Stefan replied. "The mayor is in our pocket. So is the police chief. With your help, we can bring in all the aldermen. Let us end the murders. Less violence, less fear, more profit."

"Yeah, right," said another gangster, a stocky man with a piggish eyes and smashed ears. "Sounds great, but answer the original question—who pays Nemesis?"

"No one pays Nemesis," said Stefan. "He has doomed himself through his own stupidity. I happen to know that one of the world's most daring soldiers of fortune is on his way to Paragon City to hunt Nemesis down, to make him pay for killing two people very close to him."

"Hit men have gone after Nemesis before," someone sneered. "They can't even find his hideout, and he never shows himself in public. He just sends those crazy robots of his to do his dirty work."

"Watch the headlines," Stefan said calmly. "The man coming for Nemesis is far more deadly than any other assassin you've ever seen. Almost as deadly as me." Stefan's smirked unpleasantly. "Almost. All I'm asking you to do is keep about your business and watch. I can't guarantee when that fight will begin, but it will begin soon. It won't end until Nemesis has been destroyed. And then the city will be ours."

CHAPTER TWENTY-THREE

here was no ticker tape parade, no speech by the mayor, no procession down Main Street, no trumpet fanfares, no banners hanging from buildings. No crowds cheering, no horns blasting, no brass bands. Fourteen years and some months ago, Marcus Cole, with thousands of other young soldiers, had left Paragon City as part of the American expedition to save Europe from the Kaiser. They had succeeded, but the cost had been greater than any of them had ever imagined. Now, after more adventures than he could count, after several lifetimes of experience, after rebirth and regeneration, Marcus Cole had come home.

Fifteen minutes after arrival, he found himself outside the station, waiting for a taxi. Clustered around him were the three strange sisters and their two dozen pieces of luggage. Despite their bloodthirsty nature, or perhaps because of it, the trio exhibited a taste for expensive clothing.

"Ladies," he declared as they stood patiently watching for a cab, "welcome to Paragon City."

"Thank you, Marcus," said Megan. Her head slightly

tilted back, she surveyed the city's skyline. She pursed her lips, her expression thoughtful. "Do you feel it, sisters?"

"Of course," said Alexis. "Now I understand."

"The mystery is no longer a mystery," said Phoebe. "How interesting that we never suspected."

"We're getting old," said Megan. "How sad."

"Hey," said Marcus. "You three want to clue me in to what you're talking about?"

"Of course," said Phoebe. "When you and Stefan discovered the fountain, we assumed the events leading to that revelation occurred by mere chance. That fate and destiny had nothing to do with your discovery."

"So we assumed," said Alexis. "Since we had no reason to believe otherwise."

"That's changed, however, now that we've arrived in Paragon City,' said Megan. "The aura that enshrouds the city burns with activity. Paragon City is one of the focal points of this universe. Things happen here. Strange things, wonderful things, things without rational explanations— they all take place here. The city is a hub of supernatural and supernormal events. Mighty shapes move in the darkness, Marcus. What you do here affects the whole world. The fate of modern civilization is in your hands."

"How comforting," said Marcus with a laugh. "Let's try not to get carried away with things. I've returned home to find a murderer. Nothing less, but nothing more. Modern civilization will have to manage on its own."

A cab pulled up, then another. "Off you go," Marcus announced. "The hotel owner should be waiting there to show you around the restaurant and the penthouse. I'll be there a little later. First, I have a certain newspaper reporter to surprise."

Sitting in a cab heading for the Free Press Building, Marcus rubbed his eyes with his thumb and first finger. Despite their protests to the contrary, the Furies had not changed that much over the past three thousand years. They still thought that justice could only be achieved through violence, and they saw him as some sort of avenger in the making. He'd drunk the waters of the Fountain of Zeus to save his life, not to become some sort of agent of justice. He had no plans to replace the police and court system in Paragon City. Once he found the killers of his brother and stepfather, it was back to Europe for him.

Of course, that still left the problem of Stefan Richter. Marcus cursed silently. If anyone was responsible for Stefan it was him. He'd helped the man achieve his remarkable powers, and he was probably the only person on earth with the strength and knowledge to stop him. No, Stefan would have to be dealt with, too.

Solve the murders, then put Stefan out of commission. After that, Paris. . . .

The cab dropped him off at the printing plant's front entrance. An inquiry at the desk informed him that Miss Richter was out and, no, they had no idea when she would be back. She was not at home and, yes, they were certain that Mr. Cole was an old friend but Miss Richter didn't like to be disturbed when she was attending important business meetings. Oh, wait, did he say Mr. Cole—as in Ezra Cole's long lost brother, the mysterious Marcus Cole?

It turned out that everyone at the *Free Press* knew about Marcus Cole, the adventurer and thief, and Miss Monica's correspondent for the past fifteen years. The important meeting was a lunch date she had with her friend,

Miss Jennifer Nayland of the *Paragon City Times*, at the Golden Bowl restaurant. It was just down the street. Monica, who Marcus had not seen in more than a decade, was "cute as a button" according to the receptionist, while Jennifer bore more than a slight resemblance to the movie actress Jean Harlow.

Head ringing after what had been the most one-sided conversation in his life, Marcus walked the block separating the printing plant from the Golden Bowl restaurant. About to see Monica for the first time in nearly fifteen years, he suddenly wished he had gone to the hotel with the three sisters first and changed to some fresh clothing and maybe showered and shaved. For the first time in years, Marcus could feel butterflies flickering in his stomach.

The restaurant was bigger than he had guessed, but fortunately the hostess knew Monica. "Is she expecting you?" the young woman asked.

"Not in the least," said Marcus. He laughed, relaxing with that thought. "It's a surprise. Which table is it?"

"In the back," said the girl. "Third from the end, on the right. You're not just her brother or some relative or somebody like that, huh?"

"Sorry," said Marcus. "An old, old friend."

"Well," said the hostess, the slightest hint of envy in her voice, "like my mom used to tell me, the good ones are always the taken ones. See ya."

Another place, another time, Marcus would have been sure to banter a bit with the girl, but not today. He only had eyes for the third table from the end, on the right. Two young women sat there, talking animatedly while eating BLTs and potato chips. The receptionist had it right. Jennifer Nayland, dressed in white and black, with short blond hair and pale white skin, definitely resembled the notorious Jean Harlow. Monica Richter looked a lot like silent film star, Pola Negri, complete with her black bangs, wide dark eyes, button nose, and bright red lips. Dressed in a dark blue skirt and matching blue blouse with white collar and white sleeves, Monica was the picture of a bright, brash girl reporter. She was also, in Marcus's eyes, the most beautiful woman he had ever seen.

How to approach them? A loose menu provided all the inspiration necessary. Carrying it in front of his chest with both hands, he slid up to their table, a polite but distant expression on his face.

"You won't believe who's renting the restaurant on top of the Kings Tower Hotel," he heard Jennifer Nayland state in hushed tones a second before he cleared his throat.

"Ladies," he said, "how was your meal today?"

"Oh, it was swell," said Jennifer, without the least hesitation. "Nice of you to ask."

"And yours, Miss Richter?"

"It was the best," said Monica, then glanced up at Marcus. "How did you know my—?"

Monica's wide eyes sparkled like bright stars. "Oh my goodness," she murmured and, without another word, fainted.

That wasn't the reaction Marcus had been expecting, and for one of the few instances in his life, he found himself totally and utterly speechless.

"You're Marcus Cole, I bet," said Jennifer with a sly smile. "You're better looking than I was told."

"Thanks, I guess." Marcus bent down on one knee and

tried to lift Monica's head, which was slumped at a funny angle on her left shoulder. "Does she do this very often?"

"Nah," said Jennifer. Taking a glass of water from the table, she splashed the contents into Monica's face. "First time I can remember, actually."

"Who—what?" sputtered Monica. She opened her eyes and stared straight at Marcus. He didn't know what to say, so he said nothing. Just smiled.

"It's okay, folks," said Jennifer, waving her hands at the other patrons in the restaurant. Half of them had risen from their chairs to see what the commotion was all about. "Show's over. Just an amnesiac brother returning after twenty years in Tibet. Read the whole story in tomorrow's *Times*."

"Marcus Cole," said Monica, "is it really you?"

"Will you faint again if I say yes?" He pulled over a vacant chair from the next table and sat in it, a foot away from Monica. "If not, then, yes, it's me. Definitely me."

"There goes my big surprise," said Jennifer with a heavy, theatrical sigh. "I just learned this morning that the European millionaire who bought the restaurant and penthouse is your long-lost friend."

"*Lost* is the word I'd use, too," Monica said, her eyes flashing with sudden anger. "Why didn't you answer my letters for the last year?"

"The same reason you never answered mine," Marcus said. "They never got where they were supposed to go. I wrote, even though I stopped hearing from you, but someone was intercepting the notes."

"Hey, Mon, cut out the inquisition," Jennifer said. "He's here, isn't he? This is hardly the way to greet your long lost beau."

Monica turned pink. "Easy does it, Jenny," she declared. "I haven't seen Marcus since I was a little girl. We're just friends, very good friends, from a time when life was much simpler."

"Whatever you say," said Jennifer, her lips pursed together as if about to burst out laughing. "Marcus Cole, a pleasure meeting you."

"The pleasure is mine," said Marcus.

"Did Stefan come back with you?" asked Monica. She gazed around the restaurant, looking for a second man waiting to step forward.

"I'm not certain where Stefan is at the moment," said Marcus. He picked his words carefully, not wanting to lie, but knowing this was neither the time nor place for the ugly truth. "I know he's as anxious as I am to find and punish the crooks who killed Ezra and Rudy. But, for the moment at least, you'll have to settle for just me doing the investigating."

"Those are pretty dangerous odds," said Jennifer. "Especially if it turns out the police are right and the murderer is this guy called Nemesis."

"I'm much, much tougher than I look," said Marcus cryptically.

"Well," said Monica, smiling, "I'm glad that you're finally home." Reaching across the few feet that separated them, she wrapped her arms around Marcus's neck, rested her head on his shoulder, and started sobbing. She cried and cried, her body finally releasing the intense emotion she'd suppressed since Rudy's and Ezra's deaths.

Finally the tears subsided, and she looked up with bloodshot eyes at her old friend. "I'm sorry," she said, sniffling. "I think I ruined your suit."

"I can get another," said Marcus. "All finished crying?"

"For now, at least. I'm glad you're back, Marcus. I'm glad you're back."

"The journey was hell," he said softly, "but it was worth it just to hear you say that."

CHAPTER TWENTY-FOUR

Some people refuse to accept defeat gracefully. Usually, such people stumble through life unhappily, wandering from one disappointment to another. A few—a very few—fight back. Such a man was Marcus Cole.

The mayor of Paragon City, the Honorable John Gryme, was an extremely busy man, with a calendar of events scheduled months in advance. Seeing him on short notice was impossible, no matter who you were or what your reason. That's what Marcus Cole was told when he showed up at City Hall the next morning at 10:00 A.M., dressed in a spiffy new charcoal pinstripe suit and demure gray tie, and carrying a silver-capped walking stick. The mayor's secretary, Miss Anderson, was adamant in her refusal. If Mr. Cole didn't have an appointment—and she knew that was the case, since she booked all of the mayor's appointments—there was no way he was seeing him that morning. No way.

A lesser man faced with the immovable Miss Anderson would have shrugged his shoulders and walked away, leaving the mayor alone in his office with his very *private* secretary, Miss Glory Bell Johannson, and a box filled with freshly made cream donuts, but Marcus Cole was no ordinary man. He was determined to see the mayor that morning, and he was not prepared to return to his penthouse without fulfilling his mission.

So Marcus hailed a taxi in front of City Hall and directed the driver to take him to the Commerce Bank of Paragon City and wait. Five minutes later, after establishing his identity to the satisfaction of the bank's president, Marcus exited with two hundred brand new, extremely bright and crisp twenty-dollar bills. Returning to City Hall, Marcus rewarded the driver with a twenty, triple the usual fare and tip, and invited the man to stick around and watch the fun.

Twenty dollars in the midst of the Depression paid the rent for a month in most cheap hotels or fed a family of four for weeks, with change left over. Since the economy's collapse more than two years earlier, a lot of men hadn't seen a twenty, much less touched one. Marcus changed that for several of those men in the next fifteen minutes.

Standing on the street corner nearest City Hall, Marcus took fifty twenties and fanned them out in his right hand like a deck of playing cards. "Twenty dollars for twenty minutes' work," he called in a voice louder than most steamship lines' boat whistles. A voice that resonated block after block in the cement canyons of Paragon City. A voice that echoed and reechoed his offer of "Twenty dollars for twenty minutes' work."

They came in droves. Shabby men, worn men, broken men, men stone-cold sober and men so drunk they could hardly move, they all came, lashed by the promise of twenty dollars, cash money, for twenty minutes' work. They arrived willing to sledgehammer sidewalks, pull down walls, even commit robbery or murder, whatever it took to earn them that elusive twenty dollars. A hundred of them showed up in five minutes, a hundred more within ten. With enough twenties, Marcus could have started a small revolution. Twenty thousand for Paragon City, a hundred thousand for the state, several million perhaps would have gained control of the all the country east of the Mississippi River. Fortunately, all he wanted was to see the mayor.

Every crisp twenty-dollar bill bought twenty minutes of time. Twenty minutes of desperate men marching around City Hall demanding that the mayor see Marcus Cole. Twenty minutes of angry, disgruntled men crowding the office of the mayor's secretary, Miss Anderson, shouting, "Justice for Ezra Cole. Justice for Ezra Cole." Twenty minutes of purposeful loiterers blocking the street in front of City Hall, tying up traffic for the entire financial district. And they were twenty very long minutes for a mayor who disliked trouble and had no clue how to deal with civil disobedience.

At the end of those twenty minutes, a very dapper, very unconcerned Marcus Cole returned to the office of Miss Anderson and asked to see the mayor. Miss Anderson, who was in the midst of writing her resignation, assured Mr. Cole he was expected and directed him to the inner door that led to the mayor's sanctum.

Mayor Gryme, for whom the phrase "political hack" had been invented, sat prim and proper on the far side of a desk the size of a 1931 Ford. The desktop was crowded with papers—acts, ordinances, emergency relief bills, and much more. They would have impressed most visitors had they not realized that none of them were actually signed, and most weren't even dated. The mayor looked good, save for a slight yellow stain on his white shirt, the mark of a stray cream donut.

"Mr. Cole," said the mayor, rising to his feet and extending a hand in greeting as Marcus entered the room. "So glad to meet you."

Marcus shook the mayor's hand. For a politician, he had a strong grip. "The pleasure is all mine, Your Honor," said Marcus, sliding into a chair directly across from the mayor. "Thank you for adjusting your busy schedule to take a moment to see me."

"No trouble at all," said Mayor Gryme. He sat down. "My time belongs to the citizens of our fair city. Now, how can I help you? There was some mention of your brother?"

"Exactly," said Marcus. "Ezra Cole was a police department sergeant. He was shot a number of months back. You promised there would be a full investigation and a quick arrest. That hasn't happened and I'm wondering why there's been a delay."

"Ezra Cole. I remember the case. Very sad. He was one of our finest officers. A terrible loss to the entire force. And you're his brother? Wasn't there some talk about your legal, um, problems in the United States? Problems in England and Europe and all that?"

"Misunderstandings. Settled months ago. If you're worried, I suggest you call Mr. Swanson of the Commerce Bank. He'll vouch for me."

"Derek Swanson?" said the mayor. "We belong to the same club. I'm sure if you know him, then it's fine. But you don't mind if I make the call? Just to be social and all that."

"Go ahead," said Marcus, smiling.

Miss Anderson, who evidently had changed her mind

about leaving, made the connection. The mayor's conversation with Swanson was short and consisted mainly of grunts, a few "ah-hahs," and one "oh my." When he hung up, the mayor was five shades paler.

"Mr. Swanson sends his regards," he said in a subdued voice. "He confirmed that your legal misunderstandings have all been resolved and that you transferred a substantial sum from the bank's Parisian branch in the past few weeks. The sum was in the . . . *millions*?"

"Twenty million, I think it was," said Marcus, letting the amount seep into the mayor's greedy little mind. "I hope to invest at least that much in Paragon City. Perhaps more, if I find the business climate to my liking. It depends, of course, on whether my brother's murder is ever solved. I can't imagine investing that sort of money in a city that permits criminals to get away with murder."

"No, of course not," said the mayor. "I fully understand. Leave a phone number with my secretary, Mr. Cole. I'll do some checking into the investigation myself—personally, mind you—and get back to you as soon as possible. Sooner."

"Thank you, Mayor," said Marcus, standing up. "I knew I could count on you. I hope to hear from you shortly. Thanks again."

"My pleasure," said the mayor.

Marcus could already sense Gryme tallying potential campaign contributions in his head. The mayor was so transparent he would have been funny, if he hadn't been the people's representative in Paragon City. As one of the most powerful politicians in America, he was no clown. Three years ago, he had been a small-time alderman unknown outside his ward. Then, overnight, after the brutal murder of Mayor James Rabinowitz, Gryme had been swept into office by a special election. Suspicious reporters from all over the country had tried to link Gryme with Rabinowitz's death, but no solid evidence had ever been recovered.

After leaving the phone number of his penthouse with Miss Anderson, Marcus left the mayor's office. Gryme had proved to be all that Marcus had expected and more. Originally, he'd planned to visit the chief of police next, but talking to the mayor had been enough. They were part of the same corrupt machine. Now that he'd set the machine in motion, there was no need to prime it again.

Instead of police headquarters, he decided to visit the Sonoma family shipping yards. When he gave his cab driver the address, the man turned around and looked at Marcus, sizing up his suit and tie, then whistled. "You sure you got the right address, mister?"

"Absolutely."

"Your funeral," said the cabbie and off they went.

Twenty minutes later, Marcus stepped onto Steel Pier, located in the heart of Paragon's port zone. The Sonomas had run their salvage company from the pier for the past sixty years. They were a local institution, a close-knit crime family with roots in Mexico City and points south. *Family* was a catch-all phrase used to describe anyone who belonged to the crime cartel, but Marcus had attended high school one of the actual Sonoma children—Juanntanne Castillo Sonoma, grandson of Mercure Sonoma, who'd established the Paragon City operation nearly six decades earlier. Juann was scheduled to assume control of the family when his grandfather died, assuming he survived that long. Mercure, at one hundred and seven, showed no signs of slowing down.

After a complete body search, Marcus was escorted to a massive steel warehouse on the dock, where a dozen men labored on repainting a new black car deep blue. Supervising the work was Juanntanne Castillo.

"Hey, Marcus," said Juann with a huge smile. He embraced Marcus warmly. "Long time, no see. How was the war?"

"Brutal," said Marcus. "We could have used you and a few of your cousins in the trenches."

"Ah, blame the Americanos in your gringo government," said Juann. "We would have been glad to fight, to die for our adopted country, but they wouldn't take us. Said we weren't pure Americans. What hypocrites, hey? As if anyone other than the Indians were pure Americans."

Behind them, two teenagers had set up a folding table, two chairs, and a bottle of tequila with two glasses rimmed with salt. "Come, sit down," said Juann. "Tell me what you've been doing with yourself for the past fifteen years. You've come back to avenge Ezra's death, I assume?"

"And that of my stepfather," said Marcus. The tequila had a kick, especially before lunch, but anyone doing business with the Sonomas had to have a strong stomach. They ate hot peppers for snacks.

"Rudy," said Juann. "I remember him. A good man—tough, independent. Some of the papers said he died a suicide. Such deaths are a sin against the church. I'm glad to learn it was not so."

"Business is good?" asked Marcus.

"Not bad, not good. This Depression stinks. There's no money. Nothing worth stealing."

"Is the family still selling guns?" said Marcus.

"Sure," said Juann. "You need a rod?"

"Not me," said Marcus. "But a word to the wise. Crime is going to take a hit in the next few weeks. I wouldn't be surprised if there's a huge drop-off in illegal activities. A wise man might consider switching over from weapons to industrial machinery before the downturn. It would save that man millions in lost business."

"This sudden turnaround," said Juann, "what would cause it? A police crackdown? That usually doesn't amount to much."

"No. An unstoppable force is coming."

"You ran the only honest union on the dock when you lived here fifteen years ago, my friend," said Juann. "Your word was always good. I have it again on this information."

"You do."

"Then I am in your debt," said Juann. "To be honest, I could use a change. Crime doesn't pay like it once did. Turning legit will not be such a terrible thing for us."

"A very good idea," said Marcus. "The sooner the better."

"I will pass on your words to Mercure," said Juann. "And in return for your good advice, is there something I can give you?"

"Nemesis," said Marcus. "An address. A location. Some clue that would help me find his hideout."

"No one knows where he has his machine shop," said Juann. "His hideaway is a mystery. But, mysteries are made to be solved. Give me enough time and I will find out. The Sonoma family pays its debts. I will not fail."

"I know you won't," said Marcus. He raised his glass. "A toast—to old friendships renewed."

Juanntanne emptied his glass in one swallow. "And to mysteries solved."

CHAPTER TWENTY-FIVE

Marcus was able to escape the Sonoma family warehouse after four large glasses of tequila. As it was, he spent much of the cab ride back to the center of Paragon City reciting the alphabet backward and performing other mental tricks trying to sober up. Three cups of black coffee, two aspirins, and a tuna sandwich on rye at a coffee shop helped banish the fuzziness. Years of drinking wine in Europe had not prepared him for the bathtub liquor of Paragon City. He wondered if the three Furies had learned anything in their nearly four thousand years of existence about curing a hangover. It was something he'd be sure to ask.

After lunch, he spent the next two hours in the library reading editions of the *Free Press* and the *Paragon City Times* from the past five years. The news was worse than he had imagined. Paragon had once been a crown jewel of American life and culture. Lately it had fallen on hard times. A boomtown in the 1920s, the city had attracted criminals from all over the country. An outclassed police force had done its best against mobsters armed with the most advanced weapons money could buy. The cops might have won the war if it hadn't been for the tens of millions of dollars generated by illegal booze, money that fueled crime lords' reign of terror. In the end, corruption and greed had triumphed, and the few honest politicians in the system had left municipal service in disgust.

Mayor Gryme was a mob flunky—not an evil man, exactly, but a stupid, venal one without an inch of conscience. His police chief, Andrew Mooney, was as phony as a three-dollar bill. He pontificated on the perils of juvenile delinquency while averting his eyes from real crime.

Still, neither man was the true problem. They were symptoms of a much more insidious situation. The citizens of Paragon City had given up on a better life. They no longer believed in the future. They had surrendered their city to the crime bosses. Until they demanded reform, until they demanded change, the city would remain a grim and dangerous place.

Inwardly, Marcus argued that it wasn't his fault that America was in the midst of a Depression. Neither was it his fault that Paragon City was being bled dry by crime bosses. Just because he had drunk the water from the Fountain of Zeus didn't mean he had volunteered to spend the rest of his life righting such wrongs. He was no hero. At least, that was what he told himself—again and again and again.

After the dourness of the library, he needed a jolt of human warmth. The Free Press Building wasn't too far away, so he decided to walk there. The streets, he noted, were clean, with flowers growing in flowerpots on every corner. The traffic ran smoothly, the traffic lights timed for maximum flow. The citizens he saw seemed happy enough, except for the numerous panhandlers and bums who haunted the doorways of closed offices and shuttered stores. He saw no policemen. No children playing. It wasn't safe for kids in downtown Paragon City. The city was busy but static. It was a city of lost hope.

He remembered his own youth, growing up in the rough, tough dock neighborhood. Life had been a constant struggle, but there had always been a feeling of optimism in the air. People just assumed that things were going to get better. There were gangsters and crooks around, but there were also police determined to keep the peace, even in the worst sections of town. Justice was swift, mostly fair, and surprisingly honest. Gangsters didn't prowl the neighborhoods, shilling their poison in bottles. Looking around, Marcus couldn't help feeling like Ozymandias wondering how the mighty had fallen.

When Marcus reached the Free Press Building, Monica was busy on the phone, hustling up advertisers, so he sat in her office and watched as she talked with clients. She fretted between calls, worried that he was bored, but he assured her that he appreciated the quiet time after his morning tequila adventure. It also gave him a chance to study her without being terribly obvious, an opportunity, he realized, that wasn't likely to occur very often. Monica was a ball of fire. She had energy enough for two, and she rarely seemed to stand still long enough for careful observation.

Finally, she was done. Placing the receiver down, Monica slid open the top drawer of her desk and gently lowered the entire phone into the compartment. A small, decorated pillow, intended as a makeshift silencer, followed. She squeezed the drawer shut. "Sometimes that's the only way to get any peace and quiet around here," she declared, smiling at Marcus. Her cheeks, naturally rosy, lit up with color when she spoke. Looking at Monica, Marcus saw nothing in this beautiful and poised young woman of the gawky seven-year-old he remembered.

"Sorry for the interruption," said Marcus. "I didn't mean to catch you when you were so busy."

"Busy?" scoffed Monica. "This is a slow day. When things are moving, like the night before deadline, I'm never in this office. Too much to do on the floor."

"The newspaper depends on you that much?"

"Too much. But good newspapermen are hard to find. And we're on a strict budget in these dog days."

"I suppose that means there's no chance of you taking a break, then? Going on a long vacation?"

"A vacation? You're kidding, right?"

Elbows resting on the edge of Monica's desk, Marcus wrapped the fingers of his two hands into one fist. He rested his head on his fingers and stared at Monica in what he hoped was his most serious expression. "Listen, Monica, I can't lie to you. I don't want to lie to you. You deserve to know the truth, even if it hurts."

"The truth?" she asked. "About what?"

"About me. More importantly, about Stefan. He's not missing somewhere in Europe. Stefan's back in Paragon. He arrived before me, in fact. He's out there, watching, waiting, planning. But, he's not the Stefan you know, not the brother you remember. He's changed. He's become incredibly ambitious and dreams of running the city. And anyone who gets in his way, he'll destroy. Including you."

Monica nodded. She pulled out a steno pad and a pen. "Anything else I should know, since you're feeling so talkative?"

Marcus froze, stunned at Monica's reaction to his news—or, rather, her lack of reaction. "Do you understand what I'm saying?" he finally managed to ask. "Your brother has become a cold-blooded killer and his plans threaten the life and well-being of every person living in Paragon City."

"Right," said Monica. "What about the water from the Fountain of Zeus? Were you planning to tell me about that next?"

"How do you know about the fountain?" asked Marcus.

"Stefan told me," said Monica. She got up from her chair and perched herself on the front of the desk, only a few inches away from Marcus. "He visited me at home three nights ago. He stayed in the shadows so I didn't get a good look at him. I did sense his appearance has changed, and not for the better. We sat on the back porch in the semidarkness and he related your recent adventures. They sounded incredible. I'm sure they were much more dangerous than he indicated."

"He may have slanted the story a bit," said Marcus.

"Of course he did," said Monica, "but please remember I'm not seven years old anymore. I have a pretty good nose for what's true and what's not. He described finding the ancient fountain and the mysterious box. Finally, he mentioned how the two of you had a falling out and went your separate ways."

"A falling out that later resulted in him torturing and killing one of our gang," said Marcus. "Or did he forget to mention that?"

"He skipped that part," said Monica, "but I'm not surprised. The rest of his story turned darker and darker—though he swore that everything he'd done, and everything planned to do, was for the good of mankind."

"The road to Hell is paved with good intentions."

"He wants me to believe he's not some sort of monster, Marcus, and I promised I would listen to whatever he has to say. And I will. But, don't worry—I've seen the madness in his eyes. I know his path doesn't lead to salvation for Paragon City. My only hope is to save him from himself."

"Your brother plans to take over Paragon City using any means necessary," said Marcus. "I've got to be honest with you, Monica—I plan to stop him."

"Before or after you track down Nemesis and get to the bottom of the murders? I know you don't believe that he murdered Ezra and my father any more than I do, but you're assuming he knows who did, right? Have you decided yet how you're going to handle all this? Call in the First Division to back you up, maybe?"

"You're pretty flippant about all this."

"What else should I be?" Monica asked. "You think about everything I've learned in the past couple days, and you tell me how I should react."

Marcus nodded. "Point taken. To answer your earlier question, I haven't figured out yet how I'm going to accomplish everything I need to get done. But I'd like you to take a vacation. The next few weeks might get pretty rough around here, and I'd feel better if I knew you were somewhere safe."

"That's sweet," said Monica, patting him on a cheek. "But no dice. I run a newspaper and when a big story is breaking, I stay with it. I don't run from the news; I run after it."

"A reporter's answer," said Marcus. "Exactly what I expected. Oh, and just so you hear it from me first. I'm sharing the penthouse over the restaurant with three businesswomen from Greece. They're investing money in the restaurant and will run the facility when it opens. There's nothing going on between us. We're just friends."

"My, my. You are full of surprises today, aren't you?" said Monica. "Living in a lavish penthouse with three ladies. Won't the gossip columnists have a field day with that story?"

"It's entirely innocent. They're not my type. They're investors. Besides, I never mix business and pleasure."

"I don't doubt you," said Monica. "But I'm not the one you need to convince."

"I think it's time for me to head back to the penthouse and head off those gossip columnists."

"Wise idea," said Monica. Before Marcus could get to his feet, she leaned close and kissed him lightly on his forehead. "That's for not lying to me about Stefan, and for writing all those letters I never got—yes, Stefan confessed to intercepting them." In reply to Marcus's startled look, she added, "The grilling you got was nothing compared to the one I gave him. Now get going. I have work to do, too."

CHAPTER TWENTY-SIX

ollowing Monica's advice, Marcus got going. A cab ride brought him to the once-fancy Kings Tower Hotel and Social Club, and a short elevator ride took him up to the remnants of a restaurant fallen on hard times. A dozen men were working on the establishment, laboring to bring the bistro back to its 1920s glory. Depression or not, wealthy Americans liked attending fancy restaurants. Marcus planned to cater to those clients. Besides, a ritzy restaurant would draw plenty of the town's biggest crime lords and politicians. It would serve as the perfect location for gathering information on Paragon City's kings of corruption.

After checking with the crew foreman to see that everything was on schedule, Marcus climbed the private staircase leading to the penthouse. It was time to tell the three sisters what he had done so far today. He found the trio on a black leather couch, reading a copy of *Vogue*. For all their practiced calm, though, Marcus could sense their agitation. It crackled through the room like heat lightening.

"I met with the mayor," he told them. "I don't hold out any hopes there, but we can wait and see what comes of that. I didn't bother with the police chief. Both he and the mayor are figureheads, puppets being controlled by someone hiding in the shadows. Nemesis, most likely."

"And what will you do to draw Nemesis from the shadows?" asked Megan. She leaned forward, awaiting his reply with startling eagerness.

"I'm using myself for bait. The way I'm spending money, I'm sure he's already noticed me. If I keep asking questions, keep pushing the authorities for answers, he'll come after me sooner or later."

Megan slouched back on the couch, disappointed. "A weak plan, one doomed to fail. While you wait for Nemesis to rise to your bait, Stefan's power is growing."

"Someday, he will control this city," said Alexis. "And all your plans will be for naught."

"If you want justice," said Phoebe. "You must seize it by the throat. Paragon City is a haven for evil."

"This city," said Megan, "belongs to the forces of night. The stench of corruption is everywhere."

"The smell overwhelms us," said Alexis. "The voices of the innocents cry out to us for justice."

"Can't you hear the voices of your brother and father?" Phoebe hissed.

"You may ignore them, but we must respond," declared all three, their voices ringing hollow. "The city demands justice, and we must respond."

As one, the trio rose to their feet. Marcus stepped back, wondering if perhaps he had made a mistake allowing the three sisters to accompany him on this journey. As if they had given him a choice.

"The law must be served," said Megan

"The price of peace must be paid," said Alexis.

"Death and destruction," said Phoebe.

"Death and destruction," repeated the three. They linked hands, forming a small circle. Dark eyes burned with a reddish glow. The lights in the penthouse dimmed, then went out. Though it was still afternoon, the skies overhead darkened. Thunder rumbled, lightning flashed.

"Seize them," said Megan. White hands, soft and gentle, transformed into bony claws with inch-long nails like spikes.

"Smite them," said Alexis. The dark hair coiled on her head and shoulders hissed and spat as braids turned into serpents. A dozen small red snakes grew from out of the Furies' scalps, deadly poisonous snakes.

"Kill them!" cried Phoebe, as their ordinary clothes changed into jet-black robes, accentuating deathly white skin, bloodred eyes, crimson mouths, and twisted forms. No longer were the three sisters strange. They had reverted to their primal form. They were the Furies.

Staring at the horrible faces of the three sisters, Marcus realized for the first time that he had unleashed the whirlwind. "Death and destruction!" they screamed, once, twice, a third time. "Death and destruction," and then without another sound, they were gone. There was no sign of their passing. But Marcus knew they would be back.

That afternoon, a cold wind swept through the streets of Paragon City. More than a few people used the phrase "footsteps walking across my grave" to describe the sudden chill they felt. Footsteps, indeed. After nearly three thousand years, the Eumenides hunted.

They returned at midnight. Marcus sat alone in the

penthouse, on the same sofa they had used earlier in the day. He had spent the evening waiting, sipping glass after glass of their fine wine. He had sat and wondered and thought and planned, knowing whatever happened, to whomever it happened, it was ultimately his responsibility.

No wind brought them back, merely a whisper. They returned in mortal form, though their lips and the pure white skin of their fingers were painted crimson. Their eyes glowed, but the light was dimmed, their expression almost human. They returned, but they did not return alone.

Their captive was a big, heavyset man with beet-red cheeks. He had tiny pig eyes that darted, seeking an escape route. His hair was bright white, as were his eyebrows. It was the chief of police, Andrew Mooney. Clawlike fingers had ripped his uniform to shreds, and his skin was slashed in a dozen different places. A look of absolute and total terror twisted his features. A thin line of spittle dripped down his chin.

"Save me," he mumbled, kneeling on the carpet in front of Marcus. "Whoever you are, save me from these monsters."

"Enemy of the state," said Megan. "He must pay for his crimes."

"Betrayer of his trust," said Alexis. "The penalty is death."

"Traitor to the flesh," said Phoebe. "He deserves to suffer."

"He offends us. Let his blood pay the price," chanted all three in unison. Chief Mooney cowered against Marcus's legs, arms over his head, his entire body quivering. "Death and destruction."

"Enough," said Marcus, stepping between the Furies and their victim. His gaze swept across the three sisters. "What you're doing here isn't justice, it's simply revenge. The two are not the same. There must be punishment for those who have corrupted this city, but punishment tempered by justice. The law requires both, or it serves neither. You have no right to act simply because you are offended or angered or hurt."

The three sisters stood silent for a moment, not moving, red fingers clutched into fists. Then, slowly, the humanity crept back into their features. Grim, unyielding faces turned softer, more thoughtful.

"We will do as you wish," said Megan.

"We will curb our tempers," said Alexis.

"And we will not exact revenge this night," said Phoebe. "Even though you might one day wish we had. We will remain observers from now on."

"I plan on holding you to that," said Marcus darkly. "No matter what."

The three sisters nodded in unison.

"What should we do with this one?" asked Megan, pointing at Mooney. "Think carefully before you answer—his crimes are many and serious."

Marcus sighed. "Can you make him forget everything that's happened tonight?"

"He will think these events a bad dream, nothing more," said Alexis. "Those whom the gods destroy, they first make mad."

"Then return him to where you found him and let him go," Marcus said. "He'll pay for his crimes when justice catches up with him."

The four vanished as suddenly as they had arrived.

Marcus returned to the couch and emptied the last of the wine into his glass. The Furies had a lot to learn about modern justice, but they'd been right about one thing: waiting for Nemesis to come to him wasn't a very good plan. If he wanted to cripple the crime lord's network and discover who had really murdered Ezra and Rudy, he was going to have to take the fight to the Prince of Automatons.

According to everything Marcus had read about Nemesis, the Prussian was a proud, arrogant man. He possessed an ego the size of the East Coast. So the quickest way to draw the crime lord into a confrontation, short of locating his hideout, was to crowd him off the front page. And Marcus knew just how to accomplish that.

If a criminal like Nemesis who employed fantastic weapons got a lot of press, what about someone who possessed fantastic powers on his own? How much attention would a man attract if he demonstrated the power of Zeus? Marcus paused. He would have to be careful about how he displayed his might. His experience with the sisters that night had reminded him just how dangerous power could be, even in the hands of seemingly well-meaning people, when detached from the concepts of mercy and justice. If he was going to step into the public eye, to put himself forward as a super-powered hero worthy of the attention he would receive, he needed to be something special. He needed to lead by example, to show insight and imagination.

He needed to be a *statesman*.

It was a good name, he decided, for a hero.

CHAPTER TWENTY-SEVEN

Marcus Cole's plan to provoke Nemesis and confront crime started on October 5, 1931, on the corner of Bristol and Main, in the heart of Paragon's City's Steel Canyon financial district. That was the location of the Exchange Bank of Paragon City, one of the healthiest and wealthiest financial institutions in the metropolis. With the numerous jewelry exchanges and diamond merchants in the area, the Exchange Bank was home to many of the city's richest investors and real estate barons. There was little chance of it collapsing due to the poor economy. That the bank had remained unmolested by criminals was a tribute to Steel Canyon's boss, Bruce Chelli. Chelli didn't allow any poaching in his territory and he controlled the necessary muscle to back up any of his demands. But now Chelli was dead, murdered by Stefan Richter during his first meeting with the city's crime lords, which left the bank open for plunder.

At 10:05 A.M., three bold criminals—Dennis Doyle; his brother, Vince; and Wade Creegar—stepped into the front lobby of the Exchange Bank determined to make a large cash withdrawal. The men didn't have an account, but they brought something equal in power to any withdrawal slip—hand grenades and Thompson guns.

Vince Doyle, who had the loudest voice of the three, did most of the talking. This consisted mostly of him shouting at the top of his lungs, "This is a stickup! Get down on the floor and don't move!"

Most of the customers, having undergone similar ordeals at other banks over the past five years, did exactly as they were told. So did the tellers, who knew the money being stolen belonged to the bank, not them. Only one brave soul, the assistant manager, thought to activate the bank alarm. The ringing started immediately, and the noise so startled the crooks that Wade Creegar accidentally squeezed the trigger of his Tommy gun. The stream of bullets decapitated a marble statue of Lincoln in the front lobby but otherwise did no significant damage.

"Hurry up and fill those sacks," said Dennis Doyle, waving his gun around to make sure no one else tried anything stupid. "Quick. The cops will be here any minute."

Exactly one minute and thirty seconds after they had entered the bank through the front door, the Doyle mob exited the same way. Two explosions—hand grenades tossed in front of the tellers' windows to cause confusion—signaled the three crooks' departure to the street. They were headed toward their getaway car, a 1930 roadster, when a loud voice froze them in midstep.

"Stop. You three men are under arrest."

"Yeah, says who?" asked Dennis Doyle, turning to face the solitary figure standing ten feet away from him and his two associates. The man was dressed in a heavy red tunic, dark pants, high black boots, and black leather gloves. Gold stars patterned the tunic, gloves, and boots. A black domino mask circled his eyes.

"Get back to the asylum, you loon, before I blow your head off."

"Lay down your weapons before someone gets—" replied the stranger, but Doyle had already had enough. He pulled the trigger. The gun roared, dozens of rounds slamming with explosive power into the man. At that range, Doyle couldn't miss. The stranger should have been blown to hell and beyond, his body shattered and bleeding, thrown a half-block away.

Not so. Hot lead buzzed around the man in the red and black costume. Crumpled cartridges dropped to the pavement. None of them ricocheted. They smashed into the stranger, released their full energy, then fell to the earth. Somehow, the man's body absorbed the slugs' momentum.

Doyle had neither the time nor the education to consider the physics of the weird encounter. Like most crooks, he believed in the old standard—if at first you don't succeed, fire, fire again. He opened up with the Thompson. His brother and Wade Creegar opened fire, as well. They could have been throwing spitballs for all the good the bullets did.

Striding forward through the hail of gunfire, the masked man curled his right hand into a fist and swung at Vince Doyle. The stranger's hand moved with astonishing velocity over such a small distance, and when it hit Vince's jaw, bones cracked. The blow also propelled Vince backward into the outside wall of the Exchange Bank, where he collapsed in a heap.

"Dirty copper!" screamed Danny as he tried to swing the Thompson around while firing. He needn't have bothered. The man in red and black grabbed Danny's gun by the muzzle and wrenched it out of his hands. Danny Doyle was a powerfully built man, whose strength was mostly in his arms. Yet the stranger handled him with ease. A backhand slap to the chest knocked Danny to the sidewalk. A nudge from the attacker's foot sent him skidding across the cement to his brother.

Wade Creegar dropped his empty Tommy gun and snatched a huge automatic from a shoulder holster. The stranger was just turning to Wade when the crook squeezed the trigger, the muzzle only inches from the man's face. The bullet should have entered one ear and exited the other, leaving a smoking hole in its wake. It didn't. The bullet crashed into the stranger's cheek, flattened, then dropped to the sidewalk. It was impossible, unbelievable, extraordinary.

Wade swallowed, hard, and turned to run. The stranger's right hand grabbed him by the collar, wrenched, and sent Wade flying through the air and into the bank wall. He hit with enough force to knock him senseless, but not shatter his skull into mush.

When the first police car rolled up to the bank five minutes later, the officers found three stunned and bewildered criminals asking one variation or another of, "Who the hell was that?" No one knew the name of the man who had single-handedly foiled the bank heist. Neither could anyone describe his arrival or departure, except for one Italian ice vendor from a half block away, who claimed that the stranger had come from the sky. Dismissing the story as absolute hogwash, the cops wondered if the masked man was as honest as he seemed. It had been so long since anyone had helped the police they couldn't help but suspect the stranger's motive.

The masked man's second appearance lay to rest any concerns about his motives.

The Kings were one of the largest, best organized, and most vicious gangs in Paragon City. Their name came from the section of the city where their headquarters was located, Kings Row. No one challenged the Kings and survived. Not until October 5, 1931.

Home to the city's garment district, Kings Row had been especially hard hit by the Depression. Like many important businessmen, the Monroe brothers, owners of the King Garment Works, had invested most of their earnings in the stock market. When Wall Street went bust, the brothers had lost everything, including their clothing factories and warehouse facilities. Thousands found themselves jobless, with no hope of finding work. The chaos caused by the Garment Works' collapse attracted thugs and grifters, mobsters of incredible viciousness. And the gang known as the Kings was born.

The gang was spread out throughout the entire Kings Row neighborhood, but the seat of the Kings' power was the Garment Works' boarded-up main offices. The top-floor office had been converted from an executive suite into a war room, and there were enough supplies and heavy-duty armament in the building to withstand a yearlong siege.

Commander of the war room was the Kings' enforcer, a giant of a man—seven feet tall, four hundred pounds of muscle and bone, with the disposition of a wild boar—"Tank" Jones. On the streets, men whispered that Jones had killed a dozen men, maybe more, just using his hands. One eye brown, the other green, missing his two front teeth, Tank Jones looked every inch the crazed brawler. Some thought it was an act, that it was just Tank acting crazy to keep his men in line. But everyone agreed that Tank Jones was a man to avoid in a fight. Which made what happened that October afternoon all the more memorable.

The stranger came floating down from the sky, like a leaf settling in the wind. The police reports later described him as about six feet tall, well built, but not overmuscled, with handsome features that somehow seemed to blur a bit when examined too closely. He still wore his red and black costume, with its golden star trim, and the domino mask across his eyes. And he flew. There was no argument about that. Every witness agreed he had flown into the open square in front of the Kings' headquarters.

"Tank Jones," the man shouted in a voice so loud that the nearby buildings shook. "You've been accused of murder, robbery, and grand larceny. My name is Statesman and I'm cleaning up this city, starting with the Kings. Starting with you. I'm here to bring you to police headquarters to face those charges. You can either come peacefully or come in a box. The choice is entirely yours."

A minute passed. Sixty seconds without an answer. A second minute passed, then a third. A crowd had begun to gather at the edges of the square. They had heard Statesman's challenge, were waiting for Tank Jones's reply. A police car pulled up, but the two officers remained inside. Other faces, scarred and snickering visages belonging to members of the Kings, watched from windows of the fortified headquarters.

Statesman stood patiently in the middle of the square, his hands at his side. He appeared entirely at ease. Another five minutes went by. Statesman looked up to the war room, on the building's third floor. "Tank Jones," he called. "I'm still waiting."

"Talk, talk, talk," said Tank Jones from the front door of the headquarters. "I know you can shout. Let's see if you can fight."

Tank Jones walked forward into the square, flexing his muscles beneath his dirty white undershirt. He stood a foot taller than the Statesman, doubled him in width, and had a six-inch advantage in reach. More startling was the faint golden glow that surrounded him. That light, more than Tank's size or reputation, made Marcus wary. It resembled the radiance he and Stefan had released from the black box.

Jones stopped approximately three feet in front of the hero. "Man ain't supposed to fly," he sneered, looking down at Statesman. "Ain't fair in a fight."

"I'll keep my feet firmly on the ground, if you like," said Statesman. "A fair fight, all the way. I promise."

"That's all I wanted to hear, ya dope," said Jones and swung a roundhouse right at Statesman's head. There was power in that punch to crack concrete or buckle steel. It might have even rattled Statesman's teeth if it had connected. But it didn't.

Statesman moved his head back so fast that, for an instant, it seemed to be in two places at once. Jones's fist went flying over the hero's chest, connecting with nothing more than air. Undaunted, the big man jabbed with his left, aiming for Statesman's ribs. Again, the costumed fighter shifted, just enough to avoid the blow. Shaking his head in annoyance, Jones backed up a step, raising his fists in front of his face like a boxer.

"Stand still so I can hit you," he said.

"You can't hit me," said Statesman. "Not unless I let you. But, I can hit you."

Statesman flicked out his left hand and tapped Jones in the stomach. Two fingers were all he used. That was enough to send Jones staggering back, bent at the waist in terrible pain. "I guess you're not as tough as I'd heard," Statesman said.

Though obviously still in pain, Jones stomped forward, a growl of hatred rising from his chest. Hands clenched into massive fists, he lunged at Statesman, all of his strength focused in his right hand. The atmosphere popped with the force of the blow. It roared forward with the relentless drive of a freight locomotive.

Then stopped, as Statesman casually caught Jones's fist in the center of his left palm. The hero paused for a moment, to let both Jones and the crowd see what had just occurred, before he squeezed.

Tank Jones screamed. The bellow shattered windows a hundred feet away. It was a scream of such intensity that everyone hearing it understood that the suffering it expressed was not merely physical, but emotional, even spiritual. Tank Jones had believed himself untouchable, had believed himself above the law, a power unto himself in Kings Row. Now he knew better.

Statesman uncurled his fingers and released his grip on Jones's hand. With a whimper of pain, the huge crook sank to the sidewalk, clenching five broken digits.

"Anyone else?" called Statesman, but all of the faces in the windows of the Kings' headquarters were gone. "I didn't think so. But let me make this clear to all the Kings too slow to get the lesson on your own." He gestured to the crowd clustered at the edges of the square, the stunned men and women and children who had suffered under Tank's tyranny and now witnessed his defeat. "This is *their* neighborhood, not yours. If you forget that, I'll be back to remind you."

Statesman made three more appearances that day. He stopped two holdups and smashed a large counterfeiting operation.

Marcus Cole's war on crime had officially begun.

CHAPTER TWENTY-EIGHT

Three days later, after Statesman had thwarted five robberies, averted a train wreck, and delivered three notorious fugitives to the steps of police headquarters, Mayor John Gryme called a news conference. By then, he was the only politician on the East Coast who had not made some remarks about the fantastic being known as Statesman. No one was sure what the mayor would say, but based on his previous record of being against every reform measure in city history, expectations were not particularly high for a ringing endorsement.

Taking out her steno pad and a sharpened pencil, Monica wrote, *Mayor's news conference, City Hall pressroom. October 6, 1931, 9:55 A.M.* at the top of the page. Beneath it, in smaller letters, she scribbled, *Prediction: Mayor is not going to like mystery hero, Statesman.* She underlined her guess twice. She felt certain that someday she'd look back at that page and laugh, just as she did from time to time when she flipped to the page describing the mayor's speech the day after the stock market crash.

"A minor adjustment in the market," he had said that afternoon. "Nothing to worry about." She wondered how wildly off the mark the mayor would be today.

At three minutes before ten, Jennifer Nayland slid into the chair next to Monica's, hair aflutter. "I hate mornings," she whispered, trying to smooth down her skirt and pull out her steno notebook at the same time. "Did I miss anything?"

At that moment, as if in reaction to Jennifer's arrival, the mayor stepped out from behind a curtain and placed a sheet of paper on the podium. Straightening his suit lapels, he stared suspiciously out into the audience of radio reporters, newspaper columnists, and various hangers-on. Gryme hated speaking to the press. Unfortunately, his job required him to attend these nasty little circuses now and then.

"Good morning," said the mayor, nodding to Jerry Baker of the International News Syndicate, sitting in the front row. Gryme had a habit of focusing on one person in the crowd and addressing him, thus avoiding making eye contact with anyone else. Baker, who rarely opened his mouth, much less asked a question, was the mayor's usual choice. "Thanks to all of you fine folks for coming out this morning. I will make a short statement, then Chief Mooney will take the stand—uh, podium, that is— and answer any questions."

"What do you think about Statesman, Mayor?" called Hy Reiser from the *New York News*. "Is he a crook or a cop?"

"Can a man really fly?" cried Junius Long of the *Boston Globe*. "Or are the citizens of Paragon suffering some sort of mass hallucinations?"

"Please, please," said the mayor, holding up both of his

lily-white hands in protest. "No questions. Sorry, no questions. I have a statement to make. Please let me continue."

Monica flashed her notebook at Jennifer, pointing to the prediction she had underlined. Jennifer nodded, scribbled, *Gryme doesn't like anyone who makes him think. Thinking hurts his head.*

Monica giggled, earning her a nasty glare from the mayor. Straightening himself like an old ladder, he solemnly read his prepared remarks.

"Paragon City is proud of its police force and its police chief, Andrew Mooney. To imply that the police need help in controlling the criminal element in this city is not only wrong, but unpatriotic. Any man wearing a mask is most likely a criminal, otherwise why would he hide his features? A criminal, no matter what his name or the color of the clothes he wears, is still a crook. No man can take justice into his own hands. This is a city of laws, of rules and regulations. It is not a city of costumed lawbreakers. Vigilantes need not apply for work in Paragon City. We have plenty of justice here already." He cleared his throat and put on his best campaign smile. "Voters, don't forget the election is less than a month away. A vote for me is a vote for good, clean government. Since I am running unopposed, a vote for anyone else is a waste of a ballot. So remember to vote for me."

Gryme folded his paper and let the oily smile drip from his face. "And, no, I do not believe a man can fly," he said as he turned and walked back to the curtains. He disappeared, only to be replaced an instant later by red-faced Andrew Mooney, the chief of police.

Mooney walked to the podium and gripped it tightly on each side. His eyes were bloodshot and didn't seem focused. The chief appeared to be running on gin fumes. He stood quiet for a minute, staring out at the crowd of reporters, as if searching the crowd for someone or something. Finally, he spoke, in a cracked, barely audible whisper.

"I'll make a short statement, then open the floor to questions. No shouting please. I had a rough night, if you know what I mean. . . ."

The reporters couldn't help but know what the chief meant. He was a walking, talking advertisement for the ineffectiveness of Prohibition. Vaudeville comedians joked that Mooney was the only man in Paragon City who didn't have a blood type, just a proof rating.

"Vigilante justice is not allowed in Paragon City," declared Mooney in a voice so soft that he could barely be heard. "Anyone performing a citizen's arrest will be arrested. Flying without a license is strictly prohibited, so anyone caught flying in the city will be detained. Any questions?"

"So, you'll arrest Statesman if he stops another bank robbery?" asked Hy Reiser. "Is that what you're saying?"

"Nobody has the right to stop bank robbers except us police," said Mooney. "That's what we're paid to do."

"Statesman halted two robberies in progress yesterday," said Reiser, raising his voice a notch to make sure he wasn't cut off by the chief. "That's two more than the whole police force stopped in the entire month of September. Isn't that true?"

"September was a bad month," said the chief. He pointed at Monica, who had raised her hand. "Over there."

"Since Statesman can fly and the police can't," said Monica, "how do you plan on catching him?"

The chief glared at her. "It's illegal to fly in Paragon City without a license," he repeated.

"I don't think you understand my question, Chief. How do you intend to catch—"

"That's enough questions," said Mooney. He turned and half walked, half staggered off the stage.

No one else appeared, and, after a few minutes, one reporter, slightly bolder than the rest, stepped onto the podium, walked over to the drapes, and pulled them back. Nobody was there. A door leading to the back hall stood open. "They're gone," said the newsman. "Guess that means the news conference is over."

"We could try their offices," said Jennifer as she and Monica rose to their feet and prepared to exit the pressroom. "Though I'd be willing to bet Hizzoner's secretary would tell us he's out for the day."

"Right," said Monica. "And Chief Mooney's investigating a case."

"A case of beer that is," said Jennifer.

"That man's a disgrace to his profession. It's sad."

"No, that's not what's sad," said Jennifer. "What's sad is that next month there's going to be an election in Paragon City and Mayor John Gryme is running unopposed. *That's* sad."

"Sure," said Monica, a thoughtful expression on her face. "But I think Statesman's arrival is going to change Paragon City for the better."

"I'll believe it when I see it."

"Right," Monica said. "Then let's go get some proof, Jen. Let's hear what the people of Paragon City have to say about Statesman."

Five minutes later, Monica, with Jennifer close behind, walked into a Woolworth's five-and-dime. Pulling out her notebook, she marched over to the cash register in the beauty department. An attractive young woman stood behind the counter. The girl, wearing a little too much rouge and lipstick to be considered proper, looked bored.

"Miss," said Monica, "I'm a reporter from the *Free Press*. Would you mind answering a few questions for the paper's opinion column?"

"Nah, I don't mind," said the girl. "As long as it's not about history. I don't know history that well."

"Have you heard about Statesman?" asked Monica.

"Statesman?" said the girl. "Sure, I heard all about him. He's the guy who stuck it to Tank Jones, right? Woohoo! Talk about a prizefight. I woulda paid good money to see that tussle."

"So you think Statesman's on the up-and-up?"

"You betcha. Anybody who takes on the Kings is A-okay in my book."

"Thank you . . . Sally," said Monica, copying the girl's name from her staff badge. "Thanks very much."

Next up was a middle-aged man dressed in a three-piece suit, wearing thick, black-rimmed glasses and with a Vandyke beard. He was buying a pack of Camels at the cigarette counter, and, as Monica and Jennifer approached, he removed a cigarette from the pack and lit up. "First smoke of the day," he declared, taking a deep drag. "Nothing like it to get your blood flowing."

He offered the pack to Monica and Jen. "Young ladies, can I offer you a cigarette? They're good for the digestion, and they keep your lungs in order. I should know. I'm a doctor."

"Really?" asked Monica, waving aside the pack of smokes. "Would you mind being interviewed for the *Free Press*? Won't take more than a minute."

"Sure," said the man, puffing away like a smokestack. "Glad to be of assistance. Ask away."

"What do you think of Statesman? Is he an outsider meddling in city politics or a good Samaritan capturing criminals the police can't handle?"

"I don't care if he's a Democrat or Republican," said the doctor, "he's got my vote. My entire savings is locked up in the First National. If those robbers had gotten away with the loot, I'd be out of business. Flat broke. Busted."

"The mayor and the police chief both accuse Statesman of being a vigilante," said Monica. "They seem to want him arrested."

"Well, if they said that, they need to have their heads examined." The doctor dropped the butt of his cigarette on the store floor and lit up another. "Statesman's an all-American in my book. He's the best thing to hit Paragon City since—since Lucky Strike cigarettes! And I'm not a man who takes the joys of smoking lightly."

"Thank you, Doctor . . . ?

"Savage," said the doctor, with a nod. "Doctor Hart Savage at your service."

"That's two for two," said Monica as Doctor Savage exited the five-and-dime. "Are you convinced? Want to try three for three?"

"I surrender." Jennifer beat her chest twice with a closed fist in mock contrition. "*Mea culpa, mea culpa*. Statesman's a hero to the ordinary folk of Paragon City. He's the hottest thing since sliced bread. Still, he's one man and there are thousands of crooks in our fair city, not counting who-knows-how-many automatons controlled by Nemesis. Seems like the odds are stacked heavily in favor of the bad guys, despite Statesman being awfully strong and able to fly."

"Are they?" Monica asked, drawing a big question mark on an empty page of her notepad. "Now that Statesman has shown the people of Paragon City what one hero can do, maybe another will rise up and follow his example. Then another, and another, and another. . . ."

CHAPTER TWENTY-NINE

Lanny Wilcox considered being the father of a gifted child a major responsibility. Sometimes, like today, he wondered how he qualified. Or, simpler still, why he hadn't stayed single.

His son, Devon, put down the latest edition of the *Free Press*, slurped up a mouthful of cereal and milk, and then pointed to a photo on the front page. "That's what my life is going to be all about," he announced to his startled parents. "I'm going to become a crime fighter."

"Isn't that sort of dangerous?" asked his mother, Lucy, glancing down at the picture. It captured a masked man in a red and black outfit being shot at by two mobsters with machine guns. "After all, you're still only a teenager."

"I remember you telling me that you started working when you were twelve," said Devon. "Dad didn't finish high school before he got his first job on the docks."

Lanny Wilcox sighed heavily. He prided himself on never getting angry at the breakfast table, but sometimes his son made that extremely difficult. "I came from a poor family and I worked hard so that my son would be able to attend high school and maybe even college. I paid for your trip to Tibet to study with the monks. So this crazy hero stuff is out of the question."

"The monks would approve," said Devon. "They would say I was following my destiny, that the path to redemption is built from good deeds."

"Those monks," said Lucy, smiling. "It's amazing how you know exactly what they would say about the most esoteric subjects. But when we ask you to tell us a little about what they taught you, you suddenly can't remember a word."

"I'd have to hear from Pa Soong himself before I agree to you becoming a crime fighter," said Lanny. "Those crooks are firing real bullets. It's not a game out there, son. You could get hurt, even killed."

"I'd be careful," said Devon. "I promise, I'd be extremely—" Devon suddenly stopped talking. His eyes were open but stared at something far away. A blank expression washed across his features. He straightened in his chair, his hands rising to shoulder height, his fingers spread wide. The air around his body sparkled with golden light.

"*Om Mani Padme Hung*." The chant rose from Devon's lips, but the voice wasn't his. Above Devon's head a cloudy vision appeared, the face of a bald monk, projecting his thoughts from half a world away.

I see you, Lucy and Lanny Wilcox, parents of the Golden One, came a voice that spoke directly to their minds.

"We see you, Pa Soong," said Lanny Wilcox. Though

he had communicated numerous times with the leader of the Order of the Four Winds, it never ceased to amaze Lanny that such miracles could take place in their very own kitchen.

Devon's request reached me in the depths of meditation, said Pa Soong. *I came instantly. You must not refuse this entreaty. It is Devon's destiny to become the Dark Watcher.*

"His destiny?" Lanny scowled. "He's just a teenager, Pa Soong. Not much social life, quiet in school. Devon's a dreamer, an innocent soul. You'd have him fighting criminals? He could get killed."

Karma, replied the ghostly head. *Devon could walk out of your apartment and be hit by an automobile while crossing the street. Life is a series of unending gambles. Nothing is certain. The Wheel of Life spins and fate intervenes. We have no control over our own destiny much less that of others.*

"But the world is such a dangerous place," said Lucy.

Which is why Devon feels the call, said Pa Soong. *It is in him to change the world, to lessen the danger that plagues it. I understand your fears, parents of the Golden One, but you must not let your worries hold him back. He is the falcon. He is the eagle. For him to be truly alive, he must fly. He must fight evil.*

With the soft sound of temple bells, the ghostly apparition was gone. No longer being used as a psychic anchor, Devon sat perfectly still in his kitchen chair, a quizzical expression on his face. "What happened?"

"Long-distance call," said Lanny. "From Tibet."

"Rats," said Devon. "I hate when Pa Soong does that.

I'm not a phone booth." He paused, looked at both his father and mother. "So, what's the verdict? Do I have your permission?"

"I don't know," said Lanny. "After all, this Statesman character might not like working with a partner, particularly a kid. But, I guess there wouldn't be any living with you until the matter's settled. So, do your best, son."

"Really?" said Devon, totally astonished. "*Really?*"

"Yes," said Lucy. "Really. But, do be careful. Don't get hurt."

"Don't you worry about that," said Devon, jumping up from his seat at the table. "I'll be careful, Mom, Dad. I'll be really careful. There's nothing to worry about. I mean, I do have my force shield and I can teleport if necessary. Don't worry. Now, I've got to come up with a costume. If anyone sees my face, we'll have reporters camped out on the lawn and the gangsters might try to hurt you. I need a mask, a disguise to keep my identity secret. Got any ideas, Mom? You always came up with such great ideas at Halloween."

"Well, if you plan to call yourself the Dark Watcher, we need to find some dark clothing," said Lucy.

Lanny shook his head as his wife and son started hunting through closets, looking for old clothes that could be patched together into a costume. He buried himself in his paper again, though he couldn't shake the feeling he'd never look at the morning edition the same way again, not when his super-powered son was as likely as not to be battling thugs and robots on the front page.

CHAPTER THIRTY

After a three-month flurry of thwarted holdups, muggings, and thefts, the major gangs—including the Kings, the Masked Men, and the Gnarls—pulled back to lick their wounds and wait for the right time to retake their territories. Word on the street was that Statesman had come to Paragon to settle a score with Nemesis. Until that happened, no crook was safe on the street. A few independent thugs tried to take advantage of gangs' caution, but they tended to be small-time hoods the police or the gangs themselves shut down without much trouble.

Statistics published in January 1932 showed crime down seventy-two percent since the first appearance of Statesman, one of the biggest drops in the history of any major U.S. city. Even the mayor, now safely back in office for another three-year term, had to admit the costumed hero wasn't such a bad guy after all. The arrest warrant for his capture remained in place, though. The mayor wanted it clear that he stood firmly against vigilantism.

The Web remained relatively quiet, too, waging their battle with Nemesis with restraint. They kept their turf battles away from public grounds and disposed of any corpses they created discreetly. But there was no talk of compromise, of a sit-down to split the city into two territories. The Web wanted complete control of the metropolis, and its leader, the mystery man known only as Recluse, made it clear that Nemesis had only two choices: surrender or death.

Only Nemesis refused to be cowed by Statesman's heroics. The Prince of Automatons actually increased the raids and robberies conducted by his metal minions. Sometimes the heists were spectacular grabs of cash or jewels. Other times, the crimes were staged less for the loot they might net than the publicity they would generate. As Marcus had predicted, Nemesis could not seem to bear being squeezed off the front page. Marcus got good at predicting when, if not exactly where, Nemesis would strike, and he began to foil more and more of the Prussian's schemes, until the battle between them took on the semblance to a chess match. The armored car heist of January 1932 was typical of these skirmishes.

It was on the fifteenth of January, April, June, and September every year that the Department of the Treasury removed old paper currency from circulation and replaced it with crisp new bills. The system involved bank tellers going through all the bills received the month before and culling as many ripped, torn, and worn bills they could. At the end of the thirty-day period, the defective currency was packed in ten-thousand-dollar cubes and sent to the Treasury Building in Washington, where it was destroyed. New bills were issued and delivered to the participating banks the next day. An average transaction in 1930 involved around thirty million dollars. With December 1931 on record as one of the worst months ever for retail business in Paragon City, the transfer amount totaled a mere twenty million.

The worn bills were supposed to be removed from the money supply, so no record was kept of their old serial numbers. The money—singles, fives, tens, and twenties— was considered worthless paper. However, until the bills were burned, they were still legal tender. Twenty million in cash made a tempting target.

Transfer of the money was conducted by armored car with a mixed escort of local police and federal agents. The money was loaded in bags and placed into an armored car. Then, with two guards stationed inside with the money, the car's doors were double locked with steel padlocks from both the inside and outside. The truck set off on its mission from the heart of the banking district at 7:00 A.M. on the dot. A police prowl car and a car filled with Treasury agents led the convoy, and a police prowl car and a Treasury car with four agents followed. The entire force was equipped with machine guns and high-powered rifles. No attempt to rob a federal bank convoy had ever succeeded, a fact Nemesis surely considered when making this one a target.

The attack took place at exactly 7:12 A.M., while the convoy was one block away from the Orion Highway. The truck and cars were stopped at a red light right before the entrance to the highway when eight huge automatons appeared, blocking them front and rear. The machines had been delivered in large containers to a nearby warehouse the night before and the automatons had been waiting for the cáravan to arrive for hours. A few well-placed bribes had confirmed the convoy route days earlier.

The Treasury agent driving the lead car shifted the auto into first gear and sent it hurtling into an automaton's steel legs. It was a futile gesture. Nemesis had constructed his metal men so that their legs were the heaviest, most densely constructed part of their bodies. The car's impact sent the auto's motor hurtling into the front seat, crushing the driver and his two passengers. A moment later, the machine man, programmed for just such an attack, bent over and pounded the car's roof with both of its huge metal hands. The three remaining Treasury agents died instantly.

The officer in the lead prowl car slammed it into reverse. Wheels spinning, the car slid back a half dozen feet, just missing the front bumper of the armored car. Then the cop jerked the prowl car into gear, spun his steering wheel, and stomped on the gas. With a roar, the police car spun around the armored car and headed toward an alley between two warehouses. It never reached the alley. Before the car had gone twenty feet, the two robots flanking the convoy crushed it like it was made of paper, not steel.

Inside the armored car, the guards frantically called for aid on their police radios. They couldn't make contact with anyone, even the cars in the convoy. The radios emitted only static.

"It's Nemesis," said one of the guards, spitting the name out like a curse. "He must be jamming our signal."

"By the time anyone at police headquarters realizes something's gone wrong," said his partner, "we'll be dead."

"Keep trying," said the first. "It's our one chance. Our only chance."

Machine guns roared as the driver of the armored car and the lawmen in the two rear cars abandoned their vehicles. On foot, they had a small chance of survival. Remaining inside the cars was certain death. Their bullets bounced off the automatons, doing no damage, but they had to try.

One of the automatons grabbed the empty police car at the end of the convoy and, with a clunk of gears, raised the auto over its head. Metal arms straightened, hefting the car high off the ground, before the automaton launched it at the remaining officers.

Only to have it caught in midflight by a man in a red and black uniform, who came hurtling out of the sky like a meteor.

While Statesman hadn't guessed the target of Nemesis's assault that morning, he had been ready and waiting for the criminal mastermind to strike. Nemesis had been absent from the headlines for four full days, and whenever that happened, the fifth day always saw the Prussian unleash some spectacular scheme.

The car balanced over his head, Statesman hovered in midair. He took in the situation at a glance and then hurled the car back at the automaton that had first thrown it. Steel met steel with a crash that echoed for blocks. Nemesis built his robots strong, but momentum combined with acceleration was more than any automaton could stand. The metal man's head flattened with the impact and the robot crashed to the ground, destroyed.

Clenching his two hands into one massive fist, Statesman flew straight into the head of the nearest of the seven remaining robots. Near-indestructible flesh and bone smashed into solid tungsten steel. Flesh and bone won. Not even friction slowed Statesman down. He cut into the robot's head as if it were liquid, not metal, and exited the other side a tenth of a second later. The second robot came crashing down only a few feet away from the ruins of the first.

Metal clashed on metal as eight steel hands grabbed for the flying man. One hand connected, crushing Statesman between two massive fingers. Up came the machine's other hand, and its huge digits wrapped around the trapped hero like a steel shroud. Another robot's hands encircled those of the first. Together, they squeezed with enough might to turn coal into diamond.

Two of the remaining six automatons moved close to the ones holding Statesman captive, in case the hero broke free. The last two turned their attention to the armored car and the brave men guarding it. In the distance, sirens howled. The help they harbingered would never arrive in time to save the cornered officers. The cops opened fire again, doing what little they could to stave off death for a few moments more.

Then the policemen and the federal agents heard it—a strange hum audible even over the chattering din of their machine guns. The ground shook. The lawmen tumbled to the street, and the two automatons closing on them spread their arms and planted their feet to maintain their balance. All eyes—human and mechanical—turned to Statesman's robot captors.

The two automations holding the hero crushed in their grasp were the source of the quaking and the weird sound. Their huge metal bodies shook so violently that their feet were, in turn, striking the pavement like huge jackhammers. The vibrations originated in their overlapped fists—Statesman's steel prison—and raced along their entire frames. As the shivering increased, the robots' hydraulic lines snapped and their gears shattered. Pieces of armor plating dropped to the street with a clatter, not just from the two automatons holding Statesman, but the pair standing close by, guarding against the hero's escape. Even the two robots looming over the cornered policemen shivered and groaned, though they were too far away from the epicenter to be damaged more seriously.

Finally the automatons' fists flew apart and Statesman was free. His two would-be captors collapsed to the ground, nothing more than scrap metal. Grabbing the arm from one of the fallen robots, he raced toward the next pair of metal monsters. Though moving a bit more slowly than normal and missing armor plating here and there, they remained standing. But not for long. Two swings of Statesman's makeshift club and they, too, crumbled into scrap.

Six down, but still two more to go. Statesman whirled in midair and faced—nothing. The two automatons that had menaced the lawmen at the armored car were gone. An instant before, they had been standing there, anchoring themselves against the tremors, waiting to attack. Now, not even an oil slick remained. From his vantage, thirty feet off the ground, Statesman surveyed the neighborhood. Not a metal man in sight. The two machines had disappeared.

"They just vanished," said one of the federal agents when Statesman asked the obvious question. "One minute they were looming over us, the next they were gone."

"There was a strange sort of popping sound," said a second agent. "But that was it. I thought maybe you made them vanish."

"No," said Statesman. "Not me."

"Well," the agent said, "whoever did it was on our side."

"I agree," Statesman noted, even as he scanned the surrounding buildings with his heightened senses. He glimpsed a dark-clad figure on the roof of a long-abandoned bus station, a block away from the battle. "Gentleman," he said a bit hastily, "it's been a pleasure talking to you. Stay safe."

Statesman sped away into the sky, then dropped down into the maze of buildings and circled back to the bus station roof. There he found an oddly dressed teenager sitting patiently in a lotus position, apparently waiting for him. The boy wore a dark rain slicker, jeans, black boots and gloves, and a wide-brimmed slouch hat. A ski mask and goggles hid his features. "I was hoping you'd come back," he said, voice trembling only slightly. He rose to his feet. "I'm the Dark Watcher, your new assistant. I let you see me so that we might finally meet up."

"Let me see you?" Statesman asked. "Wait—new assistant?"

"I have powers," the young man said. "Like you. Not like your powers—different ones. I made those two automatons disappear."

"Uh-huh." The young man was only a few inches shorter than Statesman, but only half his weight. Marcus remembered an old saying about someone so thin they didn't cast a shadow when they turned sideways. It applied to this teenager. "Mind telling me how you managed to make the robots vanish? And where you put them?"

"It'll be easier to show you," said the Dark Watcher.

He twisted two fingers in a gesture not even Marcus could follow with his remarkable vision, and suddenly they were a hundred feet beneath the sea, surrounded by an air bubble ten feet in diameter.

"They're down there," said the Dark Watcher, pointing at the ocean bed. The two robots were lying flat on the sand, unmoving. "I sensed that they weren't waterproof so I teleported them here. We're five miles offshore, in deep waters, so I figured the wreckage wouldn't cause any trouble for passing ships. But I can move them if you know of a better place to put them. . . ."

"You teleported them five miles with a turn of your fingers?" Statesman gasped. He suddenly felt very thankful that this young man was on the side of law and order.

"Right," said the Dark Watcher. "Pretty much the same thing I just did with us. Except I made sure we were surrounded by a pocket of air."

The teenager looked down at his boots. "You're not mad at me for breaking up the fight, are you? I didn't mean to intrude. I just wanted to help."

"Feel free to help whenever you want," Statesman said. "Now, how about transporting us back to dry land."

Another wave of the teenager's fingers and they were back at the crime scene. Police reinforcements had arrived, along with a bunch of radio and newspaper reporters. Even though they stood only a dozen yards or so from the makeshift press conference taking place, no one seemed to notice them.

"We're invisible," said the Dark Watcher. "And no one can hear us unless I want them to. I usually move around like this when I'm in costume. My mom and pop want me to avoid publicity. Dad's afraid it might screw up my chances for college. He really wants me to get a good education." He slapped his forehead. "Speaking of which, school starts in twenty minutes. I've got to go—if it's okay with you, I mean."

"No, no. Your father's right. Education is important," Statesman said, trying not to laugh. "And you've done everything you can to help out here."

"Great. See you later, Statesman. It was really great helping you."

With a sudden pop, as air rushed to fill the spot where he had been standing an instant before, the Dark Watcher was gone. The reporters noticed Statesman standing nearby an instant later, and swarmed him. He took a few of their questions, but refused to speculate on the identity of the unseen hero who had made the final two automatons vanish. In keeping with the Dark Watcher's wish to avoid publicity, Marcus simply chalked up the miraculous events to the growing power of good in the city.

"Remember," Statesman concluded before he thanked the reporters and took off into the bright morning sky, "in Paragon's war against crime and injustice, all good men and women are soldiers. None of us fights alone."

CHAPTER THIRTY-ONE

Statesman, *Mysterious Ally Smash Crooked Union* proclaimed the headline on the early morning edition of the *Paragon City Post*. Beneath the huge black letters was a photo of Statesman tossing the garbagemen's union president, Jimmy "the Nose" Terrassi, into the back of a garbage truck. The caption on the picture read *Statesman continues to take out the garbage in Paragon City.*

Calmly, carefully, Stefan Richter ripped the newspaper in half, then in half again. Taking the torn pages, he crumpled them in a tight ball and tossed it away. A week ago he had moved three floors deeper below the street. His eyes had become increasingly sensitive to natural light, so he kept to underground hideouts as much as possible. As absolute ruler of a criminal empire, he rarely had to do any traveling. He had assistants for that.

Stefan rose from his desk and paced, finally settling in the darkest part of his office. When he was angry, the light hurt his eyes the most, and he preferred to stand these days. It was a natural reaction to his metamorphosis. A hump had been growing on his back—a side effect of drinking from the Fountain of Zeus, he assumed. There had been other changes, too. Soon, those changes would be complete and he'd emerge as the most powerful being ever to walk the face of the earth. Not even in the heroic age of Greece had there been a creation like him. Stefan Richter had almost vanished, and would soon be replaced forever by Lord Recluse. In the days to follow, the world would tremble beneath his feet. All that stood between him and his destiny was the defeat of his one-time friend, now his greatest foe—the man called Statesman.

Marcus Cole was proving to be no end of trouble. Stefan had assumed he would focus his energies on Nemesis, bring all his powers to bear to make the Prince of Automatons pay for the murders of Rudy and Ezra, and in doing so, would have no time to stop any other criminal activities. That hadn't turned out to be true. Marcus seemed to be attacking any and all crime in the city, keeping himself ensconced on the front page of all the local papers. His latest exploit, rounding up Jimmy the Nose, was a blow against the Web itself. Stefan's superiors in Arachnos had started to ask questions, and the Weaver himself had expressed "disappointment" in the pace at which the Web was spreading in Paragon City.

Walking back to his desk, Stefan pressed the intercom button to his secretary. "Sheila, send for Rocco Tutoro."

"Yes, leader," said Sheila. "Immediately."

Rocco arrived quickly, and entered Stefan's office with his head bowed in deference. "Lord Recluse, how can I serve you?"

"Jimmy Terrassi was arrested yesterday after Statesman provided the police with proof he was stealing from some city pension fund," said Stefan. "Why were we working with someone so obviously foolish?"

"He had the trust of the union members. When he was younger, Terrassi fought against the city on behalf of the garbagemen. He earned a reputation as a tough negotiator, dedicated to his fellow workers."

"He's a fool if he was caught like this. We should have replaced him with one of our own," said Stefan. "What about Statesman—how did Statesman discover the information on the theft?"

"As you know, Nemesis has been gathering information about our agents. It is believed he sent the information to Statesman. It was retaliation for the jewelry store heist we spoiled for him last week."

"One for one?" asked Stefan. "That doesn't sound like Nemesis."

"There will be others. Just before I was summoned, I received a call from Chief Mooney that Statesman caught Vern Kramer of the Kings shaking down a real estate broker. Because the businessman dealt in out-of-state property, the extortion was labeled a federal not local crime."

"So we won't be able to pay off the judge," said Stefan.

"Exactly," said Rocco. "Kramer is facing a twenty-to-life sentence, unless he cooperates. I've heard that the Feds are jealous of all the attention Statesman has been getting. J. Edgar Hoover of the Bureau of Investigation has been pushing his agents hard to make some headlines of their own."

"Pay Kramer's bail," said Stefan. "Do the same for Jimmy Terrassi. After they are back on the street, kill them both."

"Leader?" said Rocco. "Kill them? The other gang leaders and union officials—"

"Will learn a lesson from their deaths. They were careless enough that Nemesis could use them against us. That's the same as directly helping the Prussian in my book," Stefan snarled. "There will be no more arrests, no more mistakes by anyone associated with the Web. The penalty for violating our trust is death."

"Yes, leader," said Rocco. "Your word is law."

"Of course it is," said Stefan. "I grow weary of this fight. Nemesis betrays us, we betray him, Statesman wipes out a few more criminals. Find the location of the Prussian's hideout. It is time for the Web to take absolute control of Paragon City."

"Our men have been searching for that location for months," said Rocco. "They're doing their best."

"Their best isn't good enough," said Stefan. Reaching out with his right hand, he laid his palm on Rocco's forehead, his fingers touching his assistant's scalp. A small squeeze and he could crush Rocco's head like an eggshell. For an instant, he tightened his grip. Rocco's eyes bulged and a tear trickled from one eye. But he didn't scream. Stefan smiled. Rocco knew that screaming was a sign of weakness. "They must do better."

Stefan released his grip. Tiny rivulets of blood marked where his fingers had broken flesh.

"We will succeed, leader," Rocco said quietly. "I swear."

"Good. Now leave. I have dispatches from Italy to read. Oh, a final thought—make them suffer."

"Leader?"

"Vern Kramer and Jimmy Terrassi," said Stefan. "Before you kill them, make them suffer. Make them beg for death. Then repeat their last words to the men on our payroll. Tell them I want no more traitors."

CHAPTER THIRTY-TWO

Some men look at life and see futility and pain. Others look and see hope and opportunity. It's all a matter of perspective.

"From slave to scientist in three generations" was Raymond George Washington's motto. He loved to tell how his grandfather, Moss, had been born a slave on a plantation in Mississippi before the Civil War. How his father, the Reverend Joshua Washington, had been born free and became a minister in 1900. And finally, how he had attended the University of Chicago in 1920 and graduated with a degree in science four years later.

Meteorology was Ray's great passion and he worked as an assistant weather forecaster in the Paragon City branch of the U.S. Weather Service. It wasn't a particularly important or exciting job, but it was a job at a time during which most men, especially black men, were unemployed. More important, it was work that didn't require constant attention and thus left him time to labor away on his own projects. Like numerous meteorologists of the early 1930s, Ray wasn't satisfied with merely predicting the weather. He wanted to control it.

Weather balloons coupled with barometric readings were the lifeblood of the United States weather forecast network. Unfortunately, readings from the upper atmosphere only told weathermen what was happening at the moment, not what was going to happen in the next few days. Predicting the weather was considered by many meteorologists to be impossible. Ray thought otherwise.

Mathematics, he felt certain, was the key to predicting the movement of high and low pressure zones. In college, Ray had read about the work of British mathematical physicist, L. F. Richardson, who had tried to calculate weather patterns by using four basic equations. The equations were the conservation of mass, the conservation of momentum, the conservation of moisture, and the energy equation. Richardson mentally divided England and Europe into a huge diagram of squares. He then collected information from each square and plugged that into his equations, hoping to be able to anticipate the changes of pressure from one square to another. The calculations proved to be so difficult that forecasting the weather for the next twenty-four hours took weeks, making Richardson's idea worthless.

Ray was convinced that more accurate measurements would make for quicker calculations, which explained why, on a stormy evening in April 1932, he was standing in a field just outside the Paragon City weather station trying to guide a weather balloon into the dark clouds a half mile up. It was definitely not a safe experiment, but Ray never worried about his own safety. His only concern was science.

"Ray!" called Professor Mort Crane, standing in the

station's doorway. "Come in out of the rain before you get electrocuted!"

"In a second," Ray called. "I'm getting really great readings from the storm. Nothing to worry about!"

In retrospect, Ray realized such words were foolhardy. As he bent down to pick up the galvanometer, lightning hit the weather balloon, sending three hundred thousand volts of electricity streaming down the wire. The jolt leapt from the coil to his hands, and from there, through his entire body. The blast hurled Ray fifty feet up into the air, where, in less than a tenth of a second, he was hit by four more blasts. Fortunately, after the first shock, Ray's mind shut down and he felt nothing from the next four strikes.

Fifteen days later, Ray opened his eyes to find himself covered with bandages, immobilized in a hospital bed. It took him several minutes to recall what had happened to put him there. About the same time that his nurse arrived to check on his progress, Ray remembered.

"I was struck by lightning," he said, in a voice so scratchy that the words sounded like a bad recording. "I was hit by lightning and I'm still alive."

"You were hit *five times* by lightning and you're still alive," said the nurse, a cheerful, middle-aged blond woman by the name of Audrey Post. "If I was you, I'd spend the rest of my life in church thanking the Lord for my recovery. Never heard of such foolishness before, flying a balloon in a lightning storm. Think you're Ben Franklin or somebody?"

"No, ma'am," said Ray politely. "I'm just Raymond G. Washington, son of a minister, grandson of a slave, and damned lucky to be alive."

"At least you have the good sense to realize that," said

Nurse Post. "I'd better inform Doctor Sparling you're awake. He's going to want to take a look at your burns, see how they're healing."

"Ma'am," said Ray, as the nurse turned to leave, "why aren't I in the wing of the hospital for colored folks?"

"When you're Doctor Sparling's patient," said the nurse, "you're in the wing he wants you in. Doesn't matter what color your skin is."

The doctor, a short, bald man bubbling over with nervous energy, made it quite clear he considered Ray a bad role model for all young scientists. "Think of the example you're setting," he said as he prodded Ray's arms and legs. "Letting yourself be struck by five bolts of lightning. Not the business of an educated man, that's for sure."

"I did it in the name of science," said Ray.

"Do you think you're indestructible, young man?"

"No, sir, I don't."

"Fine, then, because you're not," said Doctor Sparling, patting Ray on the shoulder. "At least, I don't think you are. There's not a third-degree burn on your entire body. You should be fried through and through, electrified like those crooks at Sing-Sing. Despite everything that's happened to you, though, you're healthy as can be. Just a few minor burns here and there. Damned miracles make my life confusing."

"So, uh, when can I go home, Doc?" Ray asked. "This afternoon would be fine by me. Once these showers pass, it's going to be a beautiful day."

Doctor Sparling looked at the closed curtains in the room. "Did the nurse open those curtain for you, son? I told her I wanted them closed until we were certain how your eyes had reacted to the shock."

"Oh, no," Ray said. "They've been closed. I just, uh, know that we get showers quite often this time of year. It's my job. . . ."

Ray felt a little guilty for lying, but he didn't dare reveal the truth. Not unless he wanted to be escorted to the insane asylum. How could he tell a doctor—how could he tell anyone—how he knew about the rain? He hardly believed it himself.

"So, when can I go home?"

"In a few days. I want to run some tests on you. Make certain the lightning didn't blow out any tubes in the old radio, if you catch my drift. Routine stuff we do for all of our lightning survivors."

"You've treated a lot of people hit by lightning?"

"Nope," said Sparling. "You're our first—survivor that is. I thought what I said sounded better than we wanted to keep you a couple days because you're an oddity. More cheerful."

"Thanks, Doc," said Ray. "You're a real card."

"I try to keep my patients on their toes," said the doctor. "Better than letting them feel sorry for themselves. You better rest now, son. I'll check in on you tomorrow morning. If you need anything, pull the cord for Nurse Post."

Doctor Sparling departed, leaving Ray alone with his thoughts. He wondered if the five bolts of lightning hadn't, perhaps, damaged his mind. He was certain he could *sense* the movement of the clouds, the stir of moisture in the atmosphere, the rays of sunlight hitting the streets. It was very strange. He didn't need to concentrate or think about the weather. He just knew what it was doing.

Later that afternoon, the rain stopped. He knew the instant it happened. Sensed it. That night, around 3:00 A.M., hail fell for three minutes before turning to rain. He sensed that, too. The next morning not only did he feel the sunshine, but he also knew the exact temperature and from which direction the wind was blowing. The weather had no secrets from him any longer.

When Doctor Sparling removed the bandages and told Ray that he was going to carry some scars with him—a little more than someone like a boxer, but a lot less than he had any right to expect after what he'd been through. Sparling also tested his reflexes, which seemed to be better than ever. He even insisted that Ray try to read Nurse Post's mind, which was absolutely impossible—at least it was if you ignored the way she rolled her eyes at the doctor when he badgered Ray into giving it a try.

"Lightning can do strange things to people," said the doctor. "It's necessary in these cases to check every possible reaction."

"You know this from all those lightning survivors who've been through here," Ray said with a slow smile.

"Exactly!" the doctor replied. He clapped Ray on the knee. "You seem to be making a full recovery."

With a sigh of relief, Ray settled in the armchair by the side of his bed. It was his first day back on his feet in more than two weeks; he felt exhausted just sitting up straight.

"Your strength should return after a few good meals," continued Sparling. "I'll check you out tomorrow morning, though I do want you to come back to see me once a month for the next three months."

"Sounds fine to me," said Ray. "I appreciate everything you did for me. Most black people don't know what to expect when they go into a hospital. You know, race and all that."

"Race?" said Sparling. "We are all members of the *human* race, Mr. Lightning Rod. Don't let anyone tell you different."

"From your lips to God's ears," said Ray.

"Indeed," said the doctor. "And I'll bet that He's listening. So, eat a good dinner, get a good night's rest, and, tomorrow, you go home."

That night, a north wind howled, rattling the windows and keeping Ray awake. Lying there, his head on the pillow, staring at the ceiling, Ray wished the wind would calm down so he could sleep. He felt no different after the thought formed in his mind. No lightbulb exploded in his brain, no revelation swept across his soul. But no sooner had Ray *thought* the wind should settle down for the night than it did. One moment, the north wind was battering the city, the next it simply stopped.

A coincidence, Ray decided, closing his eyes. *Nothing unusual about the wind dying for a moment or two.* But as each minute passed and the night remained still, the wind calm, Ray began to suspect that this was anything but typical.

He reached out with his newfound ability to sense the weather. Ray felt the clouds and the moisture in the air and even the wind, but unlike before, when he'd been merely an observer, it was as if all those elements were looking back at him, waiting for his command.

It was then that Raymond George Washington was forced to admit that not only could he sense the weather, he could *control it*.

CHAPTER THIRTY-THREE

"That's it," said James St. John-Smythe, as he finished tightening the last screw on the power suit's receptors. "All finished."

Jimmy rolled his wheelchair back from the lab table. It was hard to believe that after nearly a year of building, calibrating, rebuilding, testing, and retesting, the Smythe-Warfield energy suit was complete. The only job left was to make sure all of the devices built inside the costume worked together properly with the control units. That was a job Jimmy couldn't handle, but would be taken care of by his partner in scientific discovery, Brandon Warfield.

"How about some champagne?" asked Brandon. He carried a chilled bottle in one hand, two glasses in the other. "Let's celebrate with a shot of the real stuff, imported from France. With our senior project complete, graduation is assured."

"Right-o," said Jimmy, taking a swallow of champagne. After four years of bathtub gin, real sparkling wine tasted like heaven. "This stuff must have cost you a fortune. How did you get it?"

"My dad knows a guy who knows a guy and so on and so on," said Brandon. "Plus, being the star football player on Paragon's championship team doesn't hurt, either."

"Indeed," said Jimmy. "Here's to American football, barbaric sport that it is."

"Gentlemen, am I interrupting?" came a voice from the door to the hallway. It was Dean Utley. Before he'd risen in the university's hierarchy to head the College of Arts and Sciences, he'd been chair of the physics department. He was known for keeping tabs on all the senior projects in what he still considered "his" department. "Word is that you've finally completed the energy suit. . . ."

"That's right, Dean. Take a look," said Brandon. "Want some champagne? It's the real stuff."

"The outfit looks terrific, James," said the dean, studying the full-length body suit, with its numerous receptors, power relays, and complex circuits. "This is a triumph for someone your age."

"Brandon helped," said Jimmy.

"Brandon is quite intelligent," said the dean, "but I know who deserves the credit. He served as your assistant and experimental subject."

"A big, dumb lab rat," Brandon grumbled. "That's me."

"Don't worry." The dean said, "you'll get credit for your help. But, we all know that without James's theory on strong energy fields in atoms, this suit would never work."

"A small accomplishment," said Jimmy. "Without Einstein's Special Theory of Relativity, I would have gone nowhere."

"You're too modest," said the dean. "Say, Southern

United Industries called me this morning, looking for recommendations. I passed your name along to them."

"Thanks, Dean," said Jimmy. "You'll be attending the demonstration tonight?"

"Of course. I wouldn't miss it for the world."

Brandon held his tongue until the dean was gone, but it was difficult. "I just don't like that man," he said. "He treats everyone like dirt—well, everyone but you. Some of the guys in the physics lab told me he picks out one or two students each year to fawn over. I guess you're it this year."

"Lucky me," Jimmy said. "Don't let him get to you, my friend. I know how important you are to this project, as does everyone but Dean Utley. Now let's get things ready for the demonstration, shall we?"

The event was staged on the football field for a select audience of professors and invited guests from the military and major research labs. The media was represented by Jennifer Nayland, from the *Paragon City Times*, along with a staff photographer. "My editor loves a good science story," she told Jimmy before the start of the event.

Fifteen minutes later, with the sky dark and everyone seated on folding chairs lined up at midfield, Jimmy wheeled himself to the front of the crowd and raised his hands for quiet.

"Ladies and gentlemen," he began, "thank you for attending this demonstration of the Smythe-Warfield energy suit. I'm James St. John-Smythe, one of the suit's creators, and my partner, Brandon Warfield, will be demonstrating its amazing abilities."

"Can you explain how the suit works, James?" The question came from Professor Hutchison, head of the engineering department. "I'm sure the non-scientists here would be interested."

"Certainly," said Jimmy. "According to Einstein, there are four basic forces in the universe: electromagnetism, gravity, the weak power of atoms, and the strong power of atoms. Weak refers to the force responsible for the decay of particles in atoms. Strong is also known as the nuclear force. It binds together the protons and neutrons that form an atom's nucleus. It is the strongest force in the universe. Our energy suit uses special receptors, developed by me, that tap into the strong force. Since our entire universe is made up of atoms, the suit never runs out of energy."

"But what does your suit actually do?" asked Jennifer.

"Why don't we show you?" said Jimmy. "Ladies and gentlemen, allow me to introduce my partner, Brandon Warfield."

Out of the darkness came a roaring missile. It streaked over Jimmy's head, then turned and proceeded to circle the field. Looking up, the crowd saw that the object was not a runaway rocket but a man dressed in a head-to-toe white diving outfit, complete with a glass facemask and a pair of miniature radio receivers covering his ears. A bright sparkle of static electricity surrounded him, a golden glow, as he looped round and round.

"The electric field surrounding Brandon is so powerful that it partially neutralizes gravity," said Jimmy. "It enables him to fly and also serves as a protective barrier against injury. He should be landing any second and we'll proceed with that part of the demonstration."

Jimmy looked up at the circling Brandon and gestured with one hand. Nothing happened. Jimmy gestured, waving his friend down. Still nothing. After a few more circuits, the crowd began to get restless.

"Sorry for the delay," said Jimmy. "I'm sure Brandon will be down in a moment."

Jimmy looked up again but Brandon showed no sign of slowing down.

"Do you have a flashlight?" asked Dean Utley, stepping next to Jimmy. "If his radio is out, maybe we can signal him that way."

"Sorry," Jimmy said sheepishly. "I don't. I, uh, don't think it's a radio problem, though. The directional control seems to be malfunctioning."

"How are you going to get him down?" the dean asked.

"How about a pistol?" muttered one of the military men. "If the thing can't do anything but circle like that, it's waste of our time."

"Now, wait a minute," said Jimmy. "This is an experimental suit. You can't expect it to work perfectly the first time it's tested."

"Maybe you—" the soldier snapped, then broke off midsentence. Brandon had stopped circling and was coming down—fast.

Brandon zoomed straight toward the gathered scholars, soldiers, and businessmen. The crowd scattered, but in the middle of the football field there was no cover. As they ran, they could hear Brandon Warfield screaming at the top of his lungs, "Jimmy, help!"

The runaway rocket man skipped across the ground for thirty yards, tearing up chunks of turf, before bouncing over the track circling the field and landing in the sand pit used for the long jump. A plume of sand and dust rose into the air. "I'm okay," Brandon shouted weakly, waving one hand in the air.

"If this is the sort of work you think is ready for public display," said of the businessmen to Jimmy, "don't bother inviting us to another demonstration. We'll just read about it in the papers from a nice safe distance—like the other side of the country."

Jimmy found Brandon, still suited up, half buried in the sand pit. Miraculously, no bones were broken.

"It should have worked," said Jimmy as he peeled the shattered power suit from his friend. "It should have worked."

"I doubt that very much, gentlemen," said Dean Utley, standing at the edge of the sand pit. "And you won't be using our labs to find out which of us is right. This little disaster cost the university a lot of grant money and damaged the physics department's reputation. You're the ones who promised me the project was ready. You're going to have to take the consequences."

"Our degrees?" asked Jimmy.

"You'll graduate," said the dean. "But you don't get another cent to work on this project. In fact, I would prefer it if you would clear out the lab you were using immediately, so it can be used for something that won't endanger the lives of our professors and trustees."

"Whatever you say, sir." Jimmy sighed.

He and Brandon sat in silence as the dean walked off and the rest of the gawkers cleared the field. "Tough luck," Jennifer Nayland said as her photographer paused to snap a shot of the defeated pair. Then they, too, were gone.

"You know, you actually had me worried there for a

second," said Jimmy quietly. "The crash landing was a little more dramatic than I was expecting."

"I was roughed up worse in the championship game,"
said Brandon. "Besides, you said you wanted to make an
impression."

"And that you did," said Jimmy with a laugh. "From
now on, when people think of the Smythe-Warfield energy suit, they'll think unmitigated disaster—just like we
want them to."

Brandon retrieved two huge suitcases and started packing them with pieces of the white diving suit. The only
parts of the costume he treated with special care were the
control units, which fit around his forearms. Jimmy called
them "vambraces" after the forearm armor worn by
medieval knights. They were the key to the suit's power. "I
do feel a bit guilty about this, I must admit," Brandon
said sadly. "Using the university's labs and their grant
money to develop the suit, and then keeping the results for
ourselves."

"I'm not so certain Dean Utley cares about anything
other than the university's coffers," Jimmy said, "and you
know as well as I do that the chaps in the physics department don't spend five minutes pondering the implications
of their research—what damage it might do, if it fell into
the wrong hands. It would be irresponsible of us to let
them have any say in what happens to the vambraces."

Brandon nodded. "Right. At least we know we'll
use them for good. There are a lot of desperate people out
there and now we can help them. . . ."

The two young men graduated with high honors from
Paragon City University a month later. No one mentioned
the energy suit disaster, but the job offers both James and

Brandon received were a lot less spectacular than they would have seen before the ill-fated experiment. Southern United Industries was James's most persistent suitor, but he, like Brandon, turned down every offer he received and simply disappeared from Paragon a few days after graduation. They retreated to the farm north of the city, where they were completing their experiments in secret.

The vambraces' most important test took place six weeks after the original "demonstration." For these experiments, only Jimmy and Brandon were present. Brandon wore a fully charged suit and waited on one end of the large barn. At the other end, Jimmy sat in his chair with a rifle specially designed with minimized recoil action. "The chaps in the physics department could make a lot of money with a gun like this," he noted as he targeted Brandon's chest. "Not that we'd ever let them have it. Ready?"

"Fire away," called Brandon.

Jimmy fired. The rifle bullet slammed to a dead stop inches away from Brandon's safety goggles, then rebounded high into the air, traveling at the same speed.

"The vambraces work with the suit to absorb the kinetic energy from any object and then transmit an equal and opposite amount in return," said Jimmy. "Thus balancing the force equation. As long as you're wearing them, you're invulnerable."

"Right," said Brandon, rising off the ground and floating halfway across the barn toward his partner. "But I'm not going to do much good fighting crime if I have to wait until the crooks run out of ammunition to fight back. Can I try out the gloves now?"

"Absolutely."

Brandon raised his arm above his head. Heavy blue

gloves covered his hands. Electricity crackled between his fingers. The smell of ozone filled the barn. The sparks from his fingers grew larger and formed a blazing fireball.

Brandon hurled the ball of energy across the barn. Fifty yards away, it crashed into a football practice dummy. With a *woosh*, the padded metal figure burst into flame.

"They seem to be working well," said Brandon.

Jimmy nodded in agreement. "One or two adjustments and everything should be ready for combat."

Brandon sighed. It had been nearly two years since they had made their pact to fight crime and corruption in Paragon City, and Jimmy still had one or two more adjustments to make. He had hoped to use a fully functioning suit before they graduated college. Some days, it seemed like he would get a chance to wear one before he retired.

Three weeks later, Brandon's dream finally came true.

"I've run out of tests," Jimmy announced, just before he turned on the radio and heard that Statesman and his mysterious ally, now being called the Dark Watcher, were battling a horde of Nemesis's automatons on the west side. They both took it as a sign that the time for action had arrived.

They broke out the final version of the suit—the all-important control units, a newly designed black costume with orange stripes running down the sides, and a face-mask that included an electronic scrambler, insuring that any camera aimed at the wearer's face would record only a blur. And under their new alias of "Vambrace," Brandon Warfield and James St. John-Smythe joined the war against crime in Paragon City.

CHAPTER THIRTY-FOUR

Monica hated wearing fancy dresses and avoided events that required formal wear whenever possible. Still, some rules were made to be broken. When Marcus Cole invited her to the opening night of the Three Sisters, his new restaurant and lounge on the top floor of the Kings Tower Hotel, there was no way in the world she could say no. Renovating the club had cost a small fortune and every major dignitary in Paragon City, and for fifty miles around, was in attendance. Several movie stars had flown in from Hollywood for the event and there was talk that the richest man in the world, John D. Rockefeller, might make an appearance later in the evening. A few newspaper reporters had even suggested that the city's most famous hero, the mysterious Statesman, might show up, though Monica felt certain they were wrong. Statesman wouldn't be there—at least not in costume.

Jack Spreadbury, the restaurant's manager, served as toastmaster, and it was his job to announce each new arrival as they made their way from the reception area into the restaurant's fabulous main dining room. Spreadbury had a superb speaking voice, having worked as a boxing announcer for years, and, dressed in a black tuxedo and tails, was the soul of fashion and good taste. The restaurant's opening was being broadcast on WNPC, the new Paragon City radio station.

Duke Ellington and his orchestra played their jazz smooth and hot. Songs in the evening's set included "The Duke Steps Out," "Black Beauty," and "The Cotton Club Stomp." The outer walls of the main dining room were entirely glass. On a clear night like tonight, it provided an incredible view of the city and surrounding suburbs. Thousands of stars twinkled in the sky, highlighting the huge spring moon.

The food served at dinner was top-notch, the handiwork of Master Chef Mattieu Rochenard, most recently head chef at New York City's famous Casino de Paree restaurant. The main meal consisted of a mosaic of salmon in black truffle butter, chicken *vol-au-vent*, and chocolate tort with vanilla ice cream. Unable to serve wine with the elegant dinner, Rochenard instead featured bottles of Perrier sparkling water at every table. Though bottled water from France had been available for several years in the United States, this was its major debut as a dinner drink. Years later, the president of Perrier credited Rochenard's famous dinner for much of the bottled water's American success.

Marcus and Monica shared their table with the restaurant's namesakes, the three sisters. Tonight, like every night Monica had seen them, the trio wore long, slinky black dresses perfectly complemented by dangling gold earrings and matching sets of white pearls. The sisters seemed not the least interested in society gossip. Their conversations with Monica centered on life in America, crime, and the latest news of super-powered heroes in the city.

Marcus spent as much time with Monica as possible. They were able to enjoy most of their meal, while discussing their happy days as children and the long years they spent apart. From time to time, a pushy reporter separated them, trying to get a scoop about Marcus's involvement with the restaurant. Oddly enough, though the sisters were easily approachable, no one tried to interview them. There was a certain air about them that kept most people at a distance. These were women not to be trifled with.

As the evening wore on, the trio proved to be good company for Monica. When Marcus went off to do a series of interviews, the three delighted in telling her the most outrageous jokes imaginable. They revealed an astonishing knowledge of politics, not only local, but also national and international. They constantly pushed Monica to reveal any secrets she might know about the mayor and the police chief. Monica, who despised Gryme and Mooney, tried to remember the worst tales regarding the pair, but as politicos, they had a fine record for burying their mistakes in places they could never be found.

"We pray for their downfall," said Alexis. She had a wicked smile. "They are enemies of the state."

"Would you care for a glass of fine wine, Monica?" said Megan. "We smuggled in a bottle from our vineyard for the celebration. I can assure you that it's like nothing on earth you've ever tasted."

"Did Marcus ever mention this wine to you?" asked Phoebe.

"No, I don't think so," said Monica. "I'm not much of a drinker."

"Try some," said Alexis. "We think you'll like it. We have a crate of the red and the white packed up as gifts for your wedding day."

Monica choked, almost spilled her drink, which would have been a crime, as the wine was the closest thing to perfection that had ever touched her taste buds. "My wedding day?"

"Of course," said Phoebe.

"You are planning to get married, aren't you?" asked Alexis.

"We've seen the way you look at Marcus," said Megan.

"Besides, we've watched the way he stares at you," said Phoebe. "It is obvious how he feels, even if he has not voiced those feelings to anyone—even you."

Monica's cheeks were burning and she knew her face must be as red as her lipstick. "How did you know all this?" she demanded. "I never said a word. Are you three some sort of fortune tellers?"

"We're not magicians, Monica," said Phoebe, managing to sound amused and insulted at the same time. "We can't tell the future. Still, we're not stupid and it's easy to see how you hang on Marcus's every word, smile at his every expression. Or observe how he acts much the same with you. The only thing keeping the two of you apart is some outdated moral code on who speaks first and when. If I'm wrong or being too forthright, tell me so and my sisters and I will never say a word about this again. Speak."

Monica couldn't think of a word to say. Instead, little tears formed at the edges of her eyes. "You're right, of course. But I don't know what to do. I realize, have realized from the moment he returned to Paragon that he had a new . . ." She let the sentence trail off.

"A new passion," said Alexis.

"Not a passion like the one he has for you," said Phoebe.

"No, quite a different sort of passion," noted Megan. "It is amusing to think you cannot recognize how Marcus feels for you when he does not hide it, yet you can see through the mask he employs to hide this other passion."

Monica stared. "You—you know? About Statesman?"

"We know many secrets," said Alexis. "More than you can imagine."

"Put aside your doubts," said Megan. "You realized he was Statesman when no one else did because your love swept aside all disguises. A love like that cannot be ignored or defeated. Marcus would be a fool not to love you in return. And we can assure you, he is no fool."

"Dry your tears," said Phoebe. "Marcus returns. Things will improve for the better. We promise. By the end of the evening, all doubts will be answered, if you can recognize the way in which those answers might best be achieved."

"I hope so," said Monica. Then, her eyes clear, she turned to Marcus. She rose from her chair and held out her hands. "How about a dance, tall, dark, and handsome?"

"My pleasure," he replied and, gathering her in his arms, swept Monica out onto the dance floor.

"Having a good time?" he asked as they danced to the gentle sounds of the Duke Ellington Orchestra. "The sisters aren't bothering you, are they?"

"Not at all," said Monica. "They're quite nice. Besides, they have a wonderful sense of humor. They're very droll."

"Live long enough," said Marcus, "and the whole word looks pretty stupid, I suppose."

"What do you mean? None of the sisters look a day over thirty."

"Looks can be deceiving," said Marcus, and after that, would not say another word about the sisters.

Monica debated telling Marcus about her glass of wine, then decided it was better kept a secret. Besides, the sisters had said that after tonight, all her problems would be solved, all her questions answered. For some reason she couldn't quite explain, she trusted them.

The dance ended and they slowly returned to their seats. Marcus held her hand, and as far as Monica was concerned, the world was a wonderful place. Here she was at the society event of the year, surrounded by the most important people in Paragon City, and dancing with the most handsome bachelor on the East Coast. A man she knew was the mysterious crime fighter called Statesman.

Despite his masked face and incredible powers, the first time Monica saw Statesman she instantly recognized the boy she'd grown up idolizing. But, since those days, her feelings had changed. Since Marcus had returned from Europe, Monica had gotten to know him and understood that he was a caring, compassionate man who was wise beyond his years. He believed in justice but he also believed in fairness. He was unswerving in his dedication to the unfortunate, as he had experienced firsthand the crushing burden of poverty. Yet he still was able to laugh.

As the sisters had sensed, Monica was in love with Marcus. Her feelings hadn't blossomed suddenly, but had grown over a period of months. Unfortunately, she believed that Marcus's secret identity, his war against crime, would keep them apart. Knowing Marcus as she did, she suspected he would never marry, for fear of putting his wife in danger. They had both read too many newspaper stories about gangsters taking revenge upon their enemies' loved ones.

"Time for the big floor show," said Marcus as the lights dimmed. Jack Spreadbury, a huge grin on his face, bounded up onto the raised stage directly in front of a huge picture window. "Good evening, folks," said Spreadbury into a radio microphone. "We're glad you could make it here tonight, for the grand opening of the Three Sisters Club. Here we are, high above Paragon City. Isn't it a beautiful night? I can lean right against these huge windows and look out over this great metropolis. But don't be worried, Mr. and Mrs. America—the windows here are laced with carbon steel filaments and are so strong that not even a bullet can penetrate them. Stand as close to the edge as you like and you're still as safe as can be."

"Oh no you ain't," came a loud, ferocious snarl from the rear of the room. All heads turned to see what the commotion was about. Six men dressed as maintenance workers stood near the doors to the kitchen. Each man held a Thompson submachine gun in his arms and wore a yellow bandana over half his face. "Try anything foolish," said the gang's leader, "and you rich snobs will discover the one thing money can't buy—a new life."

"This is outrageous," bellowed Mayor Gryme, rising from his seat at the table he shared with the police commissioner, the city park director, and three stunning young women. "Do you have any idea who I am?"

"Yeah," said the man and casually pointed his Tommy gun a few feet above the mayor's head. The crook squeezed the trigger, sending a stream of hot lead into the ceiling. Dust and plaster rained down on the city officials.

"Be thankful I'm not feeling dangerous tonight," said the gangster. "Or you'd be filled with more holes than the ceiling."

The crook turned and faced the crowd, his Tommy gun still exhaling smoke. "If you folks have any doubts as to my serious intentions, don't. The next person who makes me angry, man or woman, gets tossed off the roof. That's a pretty steep plunge. You'd end up flat as a pancake. Maybe flatter. So, stay calm and nobody has to die."

Another man wielding a machine gun joined the first man on the stage.

"We're all ready," announced the gang leader. "My men will bring a cloth sack around to every table, and you'll donate your rings, necklaces, watches, and any other expensive baubles you might have. Don't be stingy. If my men find anything you've forgotten to contribute, they have my permission to shoot you."

The four men started their rounds.

"We're still on the air, right?" the ringleader asked the broadcast team from WNPC. When they nodded, he smiled broadly. "Good."

He grabbed the microphone from Jack Spreadbury and held it close to his lips. "Good evening, everyone in radio land. This is Calvin Casanova, speaking to you from the top of the Kings Tower Hotel. Me and my gang are robbing the swell crowd here, and that's a fact. We cut the elevator cables and blocked the stairway, so there's no way in or out of the building. If Statesman or any of his buddies are thinking of flying in from the roof, we can see for miles in every direction from this height and as soon as we spot a hero soaring toward this building, we'll start shooting our hostages. So, I'd advise him to keep his distance. That's it for now. Calvin Casanova, world's greatest crook, over and out."

"This is a—a—" the mayor stuttered.

"Yeah, yeah. An outrage," said Casanova. "I think we've heard that line before. Repeat it one more time and we'll see how many times you bounce if we push you off the roof."

"You thug," said the mayor. "I hope Statesman knocks your head clean off your shoulders."

Monica could feel Marcus's fingers tighten around hers. She knew he wanted to act but chances were extremely slim anyone—even Statesman—could knock out all the men before someone squeezed a trigger. A burst of bullets into the densely packed restaurant crowd would kill dozens. For now, it was better to wait and hope the crooks made some sort of mistake. Until then, the most powerful man in Paragon City was helpless. Monica squeezed Marcus's hand in return. She understood his frustration. More than anything, she wanted to fight this injustice.

Suddenly, in the clear night sky, thunder crashed and lightning flashed. It was a deafening, blinding display that caught everyone by surprise. Out of nowhere came a ferocious blast of wind—not against the window, but inside the restaurant. Chairs flew, tables overturned, and everyone but the three sisters was sent sprawling. The quartet of crooks carrying sacks crashed to the floor, their guns flying from their hands, the contents of their bags pouring out at their feet. They soon found themselves at the mercy of some very irate guests.

Calvin Casanova and his lieutenant didn't even have

time to shout in surprise before the blast of wind reached the stage. They were tossed about by the wind like deadfall leaves and deposited fifty feet across the room against the heavy plate-glass window. The impact sent thin cracks up and down the glass, while leaving the two men battered and unconscious. Gone were their machine guns, pulled from their grasp by two tiny whirlwinds.

Hovering in midair outside the restaurant, outlined in ball lightning, flew another super-powered hero, a black man clad in a bright blue uniform, decorated on the front with a silver storm emblem. "Sorry for the disturbance, friends," he said in a voice that rolled like thunder. "The police are on their way up the emergency steps, with medics close behind. Enjoy the rest of your evening!" He sped away in what appeared to be a miniature tornado.

Monica couldn't help but smile at the astonished look on Marcus Cole's face. He'd been as surprised as everyone else. It was nice to know that even he could be caught off guard.

Monica realized then that the sisters had been right. She could resolve all her doubts tonight, and she knew precisely how to do it. If she caught him totally by surprise, he wouldn't have time to shield his feelings from her. Quite casually, she leaned over and, shocking everyone at the nearby tables, kissed Marcus firmly on the lips.

"What was that for?" he asked a few seconds later.

"I needed to know," she replied, curling both her arms around his neck, "if you loved me as much as I love you."

His embrace was all the answer she required.

CHAPTER THIRTY-FIVE

tefan Richter sat alone in a dark office reading reports. A single low-watt lightbulb cast a dim glow on the desktop. His eyes had been getting progressively worse, and he found the bright glow of daylight impossible to bear. In his office and his apartment he had all but one light disconnected. The glare from too many lights at once made him dizzy. He preferred the darkness. He had become a being of the night. Even his own men were afraid of him. Stefan found their fear amusing. He required neither love nor friendship, only respect.

The reports on his desk all dealt with the same subject— the attempted robbery at the Three Sisters Club the evening before. Of the hundreds of guests, nearly half of them worked for Stefan in one capacity or another. The thieves' plan was clever enough. It might have succeeded if it hadn't been for the latest super-powered hero, the man the newspapers were calling Elementar. Of course, if they had gotten away from the police, the Web would have closed around them. Then they would have wished the authorities had caught them, for the price Stefan extracted from those who attempted any criminal activity without his permission was steep.

Stefan pressed the top button on his intercom. "I want to see the mayor and the police chief this morning," he said. "Tell them to arrive before noon or there will be *tragic* consequences. I don't care what appointments they have to cancel, what meetings they won't be able to make."

"Yes, sir," said Sheila Gray. "I'll make the calls right now."

"After them, have Rocco, Viktor, and Luigi come to my office. Tell them that I have important news for the three of them."

Slightly more than an hour later, Mayor Gryme stood in front of Stefan's desk. The mayor was dressed for a morning round of golf, his most frequent activity during his years in public office. "This morning I was to be part of a golf foursome that included two of the city's wealthiest men," he noted, his voice trembling with fear. "I was planning to hit them up for money to build a new public arena and outdoor theater, exactly as you requested. The money from that project would have been incredible. The bribes from the unions, the cement companies, and the builders would have been in the millions. All filtered through the Web. Now I'll have to start all over again making my case."

"Do that," said Stefan and, with a wave of one hand, dismissed the mayor's concerns. "The arena project will be approved. Don't make the mistake of thinking I care about the cash. Money means nothing to the Web. Our organization controls billions of dollars, Mayor. *Billions*.

These petty projects and swindles are about control, control of the city, not loot."

"But money makes the world go round," said Gryme.

"Nonsense," answered Stefan. "Money is means to an end. That end is power. It's simple as that. The Web hungers for power. Paragon City is nearly in our grasp, under our control, except for two problems: Nemesis and the heroes led by Statesman."

"But what do you want me to do?" asked the mayor. "Nemesis can't be found. We've been searching for him for well over a year without any luck. And Statesman has become an idol to Paragon's citizens. If we arrested him, we'd have a riot on our hands."

"Do I care about your problems?" said Stefan. "I'm tired of these crime fighters. They're interfering with the Web. I want them gone, and I want them gone for good."

"But, the people—"

"The people don't matter!" said Stefan. "The people belong to the state, and I am the state. Remember that, Mayor Gryme. Whatever I want becomes law."

"Yes, Lord Recluse," said the mayor. "What do you wish me to do?"

"Pass a law that outlaws vigilantes in the city," said Stefan. "Make it clear that anyone caught taking the law into his own hands will be punished with a long prison term, maybe even death. Remember, this is the United States, land of the free, home of the brave. We can't have mob rule. Brand Statesman and anyone who follows him an outlaw and an enemy of the people."

"The voters will crucify me in the next election if I do that."

"If you don't, I'll crucify you now," said Stefan. "The next election isn't for another two years. The public will have long forgotten these crime busters by then. People are stupid, Mayor. Let Babe Ruth hit a bunch of home runs and no one will remember Statesman's name."

"I won't fail you, Lord Recluse," said the mayor, sweat trickling down his pale face. "I'm a loyal member of the Web. Everything will be done according to your orders."

"Statesman will be dust under my feet," said Stefan. "When the time is right, I'll destroy him with my own hands."

"When will the time be right?"

"Soon," said Stefan. "Very soon. Now leave me. Our meeting is over."

Fifteen minutes after the mayor departed, Chief Mooney arrived. He was the picture of a man suffering a killer hangover—face crimson, eyes bloodshot, white shirt a mass of wrinkles, tie askew. Mooney collapsed into the nearest chair and stared at Stefan with eyes that barely focused. "Sorry I'm late. It's not been one of my better days."

"You don't have better days," said Stefan. "You drink too much and too often. Someday the booze will kill you."

"I'm trying to cut back," said the chief. "I am. I swear I am. It's difficult to lay off the juice when I'm under so much pressure. I need a jolt now and then just to keep up my courage. But you know I do everything the Web requires. Always."

"If you didn't, you'd be dead."

"I understand," said the chief. "I knew what I was getting into when I joined your organization, Recluse. You bought me body and soul. I never promised I'd stay sober."

"You've never failed me," said Stefan. "I'll give you that."

The chief's bravery came from a bottle. He was a drunkard, but he never disobeyed an order and knew how to get things done in the police department. A nudge in the right direction was all that was needed to get results. "What can you tell me about the men who attacked the big party last night? Your report indicated none of them came from Paragon City. They're all outsiders. Were they working for Nemesis?"

"No," answered Mooney, straightening up and adjusting his tie. When he talked police affairs, he was all business. "My men questioned the six separately, trying to flip one of them on the rest. No such luck. These guys are pros—from Chicago or Detroit, I'm thinking. If that new crime fighter hadn't stopped them, they would have made a clean getaway."

"I don't like it when a new gang tries to establish themselves here," said Stefan. "We need to make it clear to outsiders that Paragon City is off limits. The message we send must be short and to the point. Do you understand, Chief?"

"A message—short and to the point," said Mooney. "I understand. What do you want me to do?"

"Arrange for the murders of the six robbers," said Stefan.

"Right," said the chief. He didn't sound surprised. "Killing six men while they're in police custody isn't going to be easy. These guys are big news."

"I have complete confidence in your abilities. And I

guarantee you'll be protected. No matter what happens, the mayor will never ask for your resignation and any investigation will end with you cleared. The usual sound and fury, signifying nothing. Blame the crime on the criminals."

"They're locked in separate cells in the city prison, awaiting bail hearings."

"We'll use poison," said Stefan. "My subordinates will contact you and arrange everything. If a few other crooks have to die to hide the real targets from the public, no matter. Their lives are worthless. What's important is that we send a warning to anyone else thinking of robbing our city."

"Murdered in a jail cell," said the chief, smirking. He was a man with no conscience. "That's better than sending a telegram, for sure."

"Death speaks," said Stefan, "and everyone listens. I knew you'd find the plan appealing, Chief. You have an excellent taste for irony. Now, leave. I have other business to attend to."

Fifteen minutes later, Sheila ushered Rocco, Viktor, and Luigi into Stefan's office. All three of these men had been selected personally by the Weaver to accompany Stefan on his trip to America. They were the best that Arachnos had to offer.

"Sit," said Stefan, pointing to three chairs arranged in a row in front of his desk. Once the men were comfortable, he rose to his feet. The hump on his back shifted as if it were a living thing. He paid the motion no attention. His aides remained silent.

"Do you have a report on the proto-metal experiments, Viktor?"

"It is turning out to be everything you said it would, leader. The lab is having trouble forging it into the shapes you requested, because of its strange properties, but they will succeed eventually."

Stefan nodded. "Excellent. And the teleportation gateway tests?"

"On schedule," Luigi replied.

"Fine." Stefan paced for a moment, then said, "Recently, there have been whispers among the men about my handling of the Web. These critics say that I've spent too much time pursuing these experiments and too little time consolidating my power base among the city's politicians. Such comments are harmful to morale and have a habit of making their way back to Rome. I can understand such doubts being voiced by the lower ranks, who cannot understand the potential of the technology we are developing, but by the Web's top officers. . . ."

"Surely, leader," said Rocco. "You're not suggesting—"

"That all three of you are spreading such allegations? Of course not. You would already be dead."

Stefan took three steps back from his desk. Shrouded in darkness, he continued. "One of you was secretly recruited by the Weaver to make certain my mission in Paragon City ends in failure. The Weaver fears my abilities, my intelligence, and most of all, my ambition. He is scheming to undermine my position in Arachnos by sabotaging the Web."

Stefan laughed. "I knew his agent had to be one of you three. That's why Viktor and Luigi were assigned work inside our headquarters. Under tight watch, you could manage very little against me. I kept Rocco at my side. None of you were able to sabotage my mission, though you tried and tried. Perhaps if the Weaver had trusted you enough to mention the other traitor he planted in this operation, you might have succeeded. But your master in Italy is an egomaniac and he is so predictable."

Rocco rose from his chair. "I'm no traitor. You know that. It's one of these other two."

"Not me," said Viktor, also on his feet. "I'm loyal."

"I would never betray you," declared Luigi, the last one standing. "I know the penalty for treachery."

"Unfortunately," said Stefan, moving to block the only exit from the room, "I have been unable to determine which of you three was the Weaver's pawn. So I devised this simple test. I am going to leave this office. The next man who exits will continue to serve me. The other two will be dead."

"But the traitor might win," said Rocco.

"Whoever survives will know not to cross me in the future," said Stefan. "That's really all that matters."

Without another word, he opened the door and stepped into the outer office. An instant later, hell erupted inside his office.

"Did you send for the cleanup crew I requested?" Stefan asked Sheila. He ignored the shouts coming from the inner office.

"Yes, leader. They will be here in a few minutes."

"Just enough time, I think," said Stefan. "You told them to bring three body bags?"

"As you commanded," said Sheila. "But I heard you say only two of the men in your office would die."

"Correct. The third bag is for you."

Sheila shrugged, seemingly unimpressed. "So you finally realized I was working for the Weaver. Congratulations.

Here's another surprise. I've packed my desk with enough explosives to blow this base to atoms. Touch me and you're a dead man."

Stefan laughed. His right hand lashed out and caught Sheila by the neck. Her eyes bulged in sudden fear. The fear turned to panic then horror as Stefan's fingers contracted.

"I disconnected the detonator before you came to work today," said Stefan. He chuckled. "I hate surprises."

CHAPTER THIRTY-SIX

The doorbell to the penthouse suite rang. And rang. And rang.

Grumbling to himself about lazy goddesses, Marcus Cole staggered to the door. It had been a late night, a very late night, and he'd celebrated his engagement to the most wonderful young woman in the world with a few too many glasses of wine. Despite being made from grapes grown on slopes irrigated by nectar and ambrosia, the Furies' wine still packed a tremendous wallop. Even gifted mortals suffered from hangovers, and this morning, Marcus suffered like never before.

Marcus threw the door open. Standing there, looking quite astonished to see Marcus in his pajamas, was Juanntanne Castillo Sonoma. "Did I catch you at a bad time, *amigo*?"

"Somehow, I suspect any time would be a bad time today," said Marcus, waving his old friend inside. "Would you care for a cup of coffee?"

"Of course," said Juann. "Black, with a twist of lemon."

"Ugh," said Marcus, starting the water boiling. "Congratulate me. I got engaged last night."

"Hey, that's great news. Don't tell me—you're marrying the little girl who followed you around in high school. Stefan's sister, right?"

"You have a good memory." Marcus poured them both cups of hot coffee. "That was fifteen years ago."

"A Sonoma never forgets," said Juann as he gulped down the steaming coffee in two swallows. "Mercure sends his regards. Your information proved quite valuable. Since the arrival of Statesman, every loco criminal in the city wants a Tommy gun instead of a pistol. Some are even asking for Maxim guns. Crazy fellows. We are happy to take their money. After we sell them guns, we leak their names to the police. For a small gratuity, of course. The streets are a lot safer than they used to be."

"You're not worried the crooks will catch on to your scam?"

"Nobody challenges the honor of the Sonoma family," said Juann. "Besides, most of the crazies who buy the machine guns end up dead pretty quick."

"It's a rough business," said Marcus. "How's the family doing?"

"All of the money we are making is being put into legitimate enterprises," said Juann. "Real estate, housing, maybe even a bank for our people. Mercure saw real quick that Statesman is invincible. We have no argument with him, and we hope he has no argument with us."

"I'm sure Statesman appreciates your efforts to turn legitimate," said Marcus. "I can't imagine him causing you any trouble."

"Wonderful, my friend. That's very fine news. Now, I

made you a promise and I am here to keep it. I've located Nemesis. At least, as best he can be located. My pull with the dockworkers union paid off. A big shipment of steel machine parts came in from Europe last week. The stuff was supposed to be shipped by truck to Rochester, New York. There were the usual bribes, money passed under the table so no one would look inside the containers. My cousin Santana grew suspicious. Thought there might be guns and ammunition in the boxes. So he sneaked a look. No guns, but lots of gears and arms and heads. Pieces of mechanical men, waiting to be assembled."

"They never went to Rochester, I'd imagine."

"We kept a careful eye on those trucks," said Juann. "Their contents were loaded onto flatcars and wheeled into an unused subway tunnel. A couple of my best men, trackers from the badlands, they followed the trains into the darkness. It's a maze down there. Took them hours of searching, but they finally found the drop-off point for the steel. There were lots of machines working there, but no people."

"Nemesis's headquarters?"

"We think so. It looked like an abandoned storage area for the subway. My friends were not certain of the exact location—they are not used to tracking underground—but it's safe to say it was somewhere beneath Steel Canyon. The place isn't marked on any regular subway map. If you find the old subway blueprint, I'm sure it lists the spot."

"Excellent," said Marcus. "I'll make sure this information gets to the right people. If I were you, I'd keep away from that section of town for a while."

"A word to the wise is sufficient, my friend," said Juann. Rising out of his chair, he headed for the door. "I must return to the shipyards. Take care of yourself. A raw egg with some Tabasco sauce will cure your hangover, Marcus. And congratulations again on your engagement. Mercure will surely want to send a present. *Adios.*"

"Go with God," responded Marcus and headed back to his bedroom to get dressed. Now that he knew approximately where Nemesis was located, it was time for Statesman to take the fight to the Prince of Automatons.

First, however, he needed to gather his forces, rally his allies. Last night, in the wee hours before dawn, Monica had whispered something about bringing together all the costumed crime fighters in Paragon City and forming a company of soldiers who would fight together against their common enemies. Nemesis certainly qualified as an enemy to them all.

The first meeting of the crime fighters of Paragon City took place on July 4, 1932. Of the six people in attendance, only Marcus Cole knew the significance of that particular day to the nascent age of heroes—though he suspected that if each of the others searched his memory, he would be able to identify the exact moment the golden light had been released from the mysterious black box on Praxidae. These gifted few had all benefitted somehow from the strange events on the Isle of Vengeance. In a sense, these heroes were the creations of Marcus Cole. And Stefan Richter.

"Friends, friends," began Marcus, rapping his knuckles on the top of the cement table in the underground bunker. The sound of unbreakable bones digging into unyielding concrete was painful and caught the attention of everyone present. "I invited you here today in hopes of forming a league for our mutual protection and aide."

A young man dressed in dark clothing and a slouch hat stepped forward. "I've never been part of a team, but if Statesman says it's a good idea, I'm willing to join. You can count on the Dark Watcher."

"Sounds like a fine idea to me." Since his appearance at the attempted robbery of the Three Sisters Club, the black man in the blue costume with the silver storm emblem had come to be known as Elementar, Master of the Weather. His storm powers made him a formidable addition to the team. "I'd be glad to join this new organization. Some sort of league, perhaps. I'd suggest the League of Gentlemen, but since we have a lady present, that won't do. How about the League of American Justice?"

"Not a bad name," said one of the two people not in a costume, a wheelchair-bound young man with a British accent. "Except that we're not all Americans."

Statesman nodded. "Welcome to our group, James. Thanks for coming. Together, Mr. St. John-Smythe and his friend in the suit there, Mr. Warfield, make up the team called Vambrace. They made an unexpected appearance in our battle with Nemesis's automatons last week. Vambrace's power bolts fried the robots' control systems and proved to be the difference between victory and defeat."

"Glad to be of assistance," said Brandon.

"Well, I think it's pretty much settled that an alliance would be in everyone's best interest," said the one woman present. Though she wasn't a movie star or radio singer, Monica Richter was well known in Paragon City as the editor and publisher of the sole independent newspaper. No one had a problem with her presence at the meeting, despite her press connections. Monica exuded trust. She belonged here.

"There's strength in numbers," said Elementar. "On our own, we're good. Fighting together, we'd be invincible."

"That reminds me of the old Greek and Roman soldiers," said James St. John-Smythe. "When they hooked shields and advanced on their enemies, they couldn't be defeated. They were more than just soldiers, they were a moving formation, an indestructible wall. They called that formation a *phalanx*."

"That's what we need to be," said Brandon, "an unbreakable, unstoppable unit fighting for justice and liberty. How about we call ourselves the Freedom Phalanx?"

"It sounds fine to me," said Statesman. "Any objections? If not, then we are named the Freedom Phalanx."

"For our first official act," said Monica, "I suggest those of the team who are masked reveal their true identities to everyone. A costume's a good method of keeping our names out of the papers, to protect our friends and families, but among ourselves we should know who we are."

"Raymond George Washington's my name," declared the man with the silver storm emblem on the front of his uniform. "When I'm not controlling the weather, I'm forecasting it. I work at the weather station here in Paragon City."

"I'm Devon Wilcox," said the Dark Watcher, taking off his hat, ski mask, and goggles. "I'm going to be a junior in high school this fall when classes begin. I'm able to teleport from place to place, make people face their worst fears, and travel to other dimensions."

"Just in case someone doesn't recognize me," said Monica, "I'm Monica Richter, the editor and publisher of the *Free Press*."

"Hey, I thought you looked familiar," said Devon. "My dad reads your paper every week. He thinks it's great. Not a rag like the *Paragon City Times*."

Monica beamed. "Why, thank you. We try our best."

"I'm Statesman," said Marcus, removing his domino mask. "My real identity is Marcus Cole. I've been gone from Paragon City for fifteen years. But, now I'm back. I'm hoping to find justice for my murdered brother and stepfather—no matter how long it takes to complete the job."

"Marcus Cole?" said Jimmy the Smith. "I read about your exploits in the London newspapers."

"Those were tales of my wild youth," said Marcus, smiling. "I've settled down since I've returned to Paragon City." He laughed and grabbed hold of one of Monica's hands. "Nothing tames a man faster than the love of a good woman."

Monica blushed. "We're going to be married soon."

"After we put Lord Recluse and Nemesis behind bars," said Marcus. "And speaking of the Prince of Automatons, I received some interesting information about him this morning. A trusted friend told me that Nemesis is working from an underground hideout in the Steel Canyon district. It was probably an abandoned subway storage area at one time."

"All the construction going on in Steel Canyon at street level would hide whatever racket his robots made," Raymond noted. "Why, Southern United Industries alone is doubling the size of its corporate offices."

"SUI?" both Jimmy and Brandon said in unison. They laughed, then Jimmy explained: "We've been investigating some disappearances among the SUI staff—engineers and scientists who seem to have vanished. The company claims they've been reassigned to a top secret project, but their families are getting concerned."

"Yeah," Brandon said. "We went to school with one of the guys who's gone missing. In fact, all the missing staff were top students at Paragon City University."

"Do you think, uh, the two might be connected?" Devon said. "Nemesis's hideout and the disappearances, I mean. He'd need smart guys like that to work on his robots, right? And the offices are near his hideout. . . ."

"SUI started working in robotics not too long ago," Monica said. "We ran a story on it in the paper. They were designing mechanical devices to replace factory workers. They'd have the perfect staff for him to raid."

"I think you're right about the connection, Devon," Marcus said, and the boy's smile lit up the room. "Either Southern United is being forced to cover up for the disappearances or they're working with Nemesis willingly. Either way, we need to look into this."

"Dean Utley at the university seems to be the one directing the best and brightest science graduates to SUI," said Brandon. "He even tried to recruit my pal Jimmy here. Vambrace will go have a chat with him, I think."

"I can look into the public records," said Monica. "I should be able to compare the old subway maps with the blueprints and the building permits for SUI's corporate office, to see how closely together the two are situated."

"And I can look for clues inside SUI's offices with no one being the wiser," said the Dark Watcher. He slowly faded from view until all that remained was his voice. "Nobody sees me unless I want them to."

"I'll turn on the rain over the city for the next few

days," said Elementar. "Nothing serious, just steady showers, maybe a little lightning. Nemesis never pulls any jobs when it's raining. His automatons don't work as well in water."

"Sounds like a good plan to me," said Marcus. "Let criminals beware. The Freedom Phalanx is on the march."

CHAPTER THIRTY-SEVEN

The Paragon City records depository reminded Monica of the main library's newspaper morgue, but it was even less cheerful. The library at least had Jasper Johnston. There was one clerk working in the records depository and in past two years of searching there for information, Monica had never met him. Like everything old in the city, the records were located in a basement, in this case, the subbasement of City Hall. They were stacked in light brown document boxes, one piled on another, six feet high, arranged in ten long rows running from the building's front to the back. It was a distance of approximately one hundred yards. Each row was arranged five feet from the next, and the stacks were broken every ten yards by narrow alleyways. In total, there were a hundred piles of boxes, each about thirty feet long. It was enough paper to drive a file clerk mad.

"Hello, is anyone here?" she called when she entered the gigantic underground repository. The subbasement was twenty-five feet beneath street level but the lighting was better than in most city buildings. Monica could actually see where she was going without using a flashlight.

"Hello?" she called, knowing that most likely, no one would answer. The clerk never seemed to be around. It seemed at times as if he avoided human contact as much as possible. Still, she had to at least make herself known.

It didn't matter if the place was empty. Monica knew exactly where to go. According to the card catalog reference file at the entrance, records relating to the abandoned subway lines could be found in location A-3. That meant the first row from the west wall, and the third stack of boxes. There were numbers painted on the cement floor, but innumerable footsteps over the years had worn them into vague shadows. Still, she soon located the records for the Steel Canyon area and noted what information existed about the abandoned storage area Marcus had mentioned.

Then she returned to the card catalogue to look up the location of the Southern United Building blueprints. When she found the card, she was surprised to see it secured in the file cabinet by a wire. A similar one had held the card for the subway files in place, but that was the only other card affixed in the same way. Monica dismissed the coincidence and removed the card from the cabinet, placing it atop the subway records card in the little box atop the cabinet, so the clerk could track what records had been researched. Then she went in search of the box holding the original blueprints for the Southern United Industries Building. Those were located in C-7, about seventy feet from the front of the room.

Monica was able to find the proper boxes fairly quickly. The only problem was that they rested right in the middle of a ten-foot-high stack. Getting to the correct box from the stack was going to take time.

Cautiously Monica grasped one of the Southern United records boxes by the edge and tried pulling it from the stack. Someday, she hoped, it would turn out that all the boxes above the one she needed were empty and the box would slide right out. Unfortunately, today was not that day. With a sigh, she walked farther down the aisle searching for one of the sliding ladders used in the stacks. An hour or so of shifting boxes should uncover the proper files.

She was ten feet down the aisle when she heard an odd grinding noise from the far corner. It sounded like a panel sliding aside in the wall or a little-used door being opened. Monica paused and listened. No sooner had the grinding stopped than it was replaced by a whirring and several sharp taps, like metal canes rapping the floor. The strange sounds were moving toward her.

Since she had come down here to investigate Nemesis, that sound immediately caused Monica to think of robots. She had a terrible feeling that a robot was loose in the depository. Images of the carnage she'd witnessed at the bank came flooding back. Monica had no illusions about stopping such a killer on her own. It was time to get out of there as fast as possible. The blueprints could wait.

But the tap of unseen metal feet moved quickly along one of the aisles parallel to Monica, cutting her off from the exit. Then a second whirring sounded from the far corner. There were two of them now. She felt a scream of panic well in her throat, but refused to give it voice. Instead, Monica slipped off her shoes and dropped them. She moved faster without heels and made less noise.

The metallic thing that scuttled into the aisle before her stood a little over three feet tall. It balanced on six legs and held two thin, brutally clawed arms raised toward the ceiling. The appendages were attached to wide silver saucer, giving the robot the appearance of a mechanical crab. Around the outer edge of the disc-shaped body, parallel to the ground, rotated a saw with serrated teeth. The thing was a walking buzz saw. If Monica let the automaton get too close, it would cut her in half.

Four white eyes on eyestalks attached to the inner disc stared straight at her. Gears whirring, the robot started toward her. With each step the thing took, the outer disc rotated faster. The crab-machine walked slowly, but it blocked the entire aisle. There was no way Monica could get around it.

Five feet ahead of her was a break in the aisle. She hurried forward. Retreat was out of the question. If she let the robot trap her in the rear of the room, she was finished. She raced ahead and ducked out of the aisle, but in doing so came face-to-face with the other automaton she had heard.

Monica hesitated for an instant, then turned around and ran to the ninth and final row. Quickly she scanned the path in both directions. In the far corner she could see an ancient service elevator, its door forced open. From the gaping blackness of the elevator shaft another automaton emerged, and another. Monica suspected her search of the card catalog had set off an alarm in Nemesis's headquarters; that would explain the purpose of the wires on those particular cards. And the robots traveled from a staging ground or even his underground headquarters through some sort of access tunnel. Monica gasped. What if Nemesis had burrowed similar access routes into other important buildings?

She rushed down the aisle toward the exit.

Monica was less than ten feet from the stairs when the boxes in front of her exploded into gouts of confetti. She skidded to a stop as a robot, its outer blade spinning so fast it was nearly invisible, emerged from the paper storm. Gasping in surprise, Monica turned to flee, only to find more robots less than a dozen feet away. The things moved faster than she thought, and they were closing in on her.

Unable to go forward or back, Monica did the only thing possible: She went up. She climbed to the top of a pile of boxes. Beneath her, the two crab-machines made a noise that resembled a human grumble. Then the stack on which she was standing started to shake. The robots were attacking the boxes with their buzz saws. Monica looked around. She couldn't move toward the exit, so she scampered to the end of the row, using her arms to balance as she moved.

Behind her, the boxes upon which she had been standing a few seconds before crashed to the floor. The entire row shook, as if shuddering in sympathy for the part of it that had been torn apart. Monica knew she couldn't stay balanced here. She could hear the buzz of a dozen robots, perhaps more. The subbasement was crawling with them and somehow she had to escape.

Leaping across the five-foot gap between stacks of boxes without causing them to topple would have been impossible for a man the size of Statesman. For Monica, the feat proved no special challenge. Her martial arts training and superb sense of balance served her well. She made the jump without trouble—as well as the next, and the next.

After her fourth jump, Monica landed in a catlike crouch for better balance, but her luck had run out. The clicking of dozens of metal claws below her made it clear that she was surrounded. The crablike robots closed in, attacking not only the column of boxes upon which Monica rested, but all the others around her. There was now no place for her to jump. In just a second, the automatons would bring down the stack and she'd be at their mercy.

"Like hell I will," swore Monica and, catching the robots by surprise, jumped off the boxes right onto the back of her nearest attacker. Her weight drove the machine to the cement, but it pushed itself up and reached up its clawed arms for an attack. Monica had already moved on. She leapt from robot to robot, padding from one silver platter to another, and the automatons were unable to stop her. Their spinning blades were useless against something moving atop them, and Monica easily dodged their arms. If the waving limbs came too close, she snapped the thin stalks supporting the claws with a powerful kick. With almost a childlike glee, she stomped her way across the automatons toward the exit.

Monica made it to the stone stairway leading out of the subbasement and took the steps four at a time. She met the long-lost clerk and a security guard heading down to find out what all the racket was about, but convinced them to turn around and follow her up to the first floor, where they barricaded the door against the automatons. Fortunately, the stairwell was so narrow that only a single robot could attack the door at any one time, and the heavy metal cabinets with which Monica and the others shored up the barricade proved sturdy enough to keep the things at bay until the riot squad arrived.

"You saved a lot of lives today," a records room clerk told Monica, after promising never to be on break again when she came looking for files. "If those things had gotten up here into the main floor offices. . . . Well, I don't even like to think about it."

The security guard chimed in with, "Not even Statesman could have done a better job. All you need is a costume and a name, and you could give him a run for his money!"

By the time Monica had finished giving her statement to the police, she'd decided that the security guard was right. The costume might take her a while, but the name was easy. At moments like this she could still hear her father encouraging her, cheering her to fight for the causes he'd held so dear. To be his brave "maiden of justice."

And that, Monica Richter decided, was just who she would become.

CHAPTER THIRTY-EIGHT

Leading a group of costumed crime fighters involved more than fighting beside them, Marcus soon discovered. Reports from Vambrace, the Dark Watcher, and Maiden Justice, as Monica was now known, established the fact that Nemesis controlled Southern Union Industries. The Prussian's headquarters were located in an abandoned subway parts warehouse directly beneath the corporation's main office building in the Steel Canyon district. He did not have tunnels burrowed to all the city's most important buildings, as Monica had feared, but only a few, like City Hall, and even those routes were found sabotaged after the attack in the records depository. The Prince of Automatons knew that the heroes were on his trail and was doing his best to complicate their search. Dean Utley vanished from campus a few hours after admitting to Vambrace that he and Southern United Industries were working together to provide Nemesis with researchers, and using SUI facilities to help improve the automatons. Statesman doubted that they would ever see the dean again—not alive at least. Like the unfortunate SUI scientists who had discovered the connection of their work to Nemesis's schemes, he would meet a grim end. Through his invisible prowling, the Dark Watcher had uncovered more than enough evidence to lead police to the missing men's graves.

Proof positive that the mad Prussian was aware of their investigation came on Friday, when Nemesis interrupted all live radio shows being broadcast in Paragon City with a message sent from his own transmitter, hidden somewhere in the financial district:

"Citizens of Paragon City, this is Nemesis, Prince of Automatons," the radio address began. The man speaking sounded old, but his voice was firm and his words echoed clear in the city streets. "I am broadcasting live from the very heart of Paragon City. I do this to demonstrate my power. For years I have raided your banks, defied your police force, and battled your so-called champions. But, my patience is not endless and I grow weary of such play. It is time for me to seize my destiny and embrace it. Steel Canyon is mine. Paragon City is mine. Today, I declare myself absolute ruler of this city, which will be renamed New Prussia. All citizens are welcome to remain and live peacefully under my fair and benevolent rule. There will be no taxes, no Prohibition, and most important, no crime. New Prussia will be a utopia, the first country in the world run by robots. But, not, I assure you, the last.

"You have until Monday, noon, to make up your minds. At that time, I expect Mayor Grime to deliver to Blyde Square a document handing over full control of Paragon City to me. Resistance in any form will not be tolerated. Disobey my commands, and my robots will cause casualties beyond counting."

The speech ended on that grim note.

Everyone agreed that Nemesis had to be stopped. The mayor grew frantic when his entreaties to Lord Recluse received no replies; if the Web was planning to intercede, they were not going to do so through the local authorities. Or perhaps, Mayor Gryme decided, the Web had given up on Paragon City and had already left. He would have to look for help elsewhere.

To this end, the mayor flooded the airwaves with pleas to the Freedom Phalanx. He also had crews post hundreds of billboards throughout the city, begging Statesman for assistance. He promised full immunity from the laws against vigilantism he had pushed through the city council months before. The mayor need not have worried. The Freedom Phalanx was already busy on the case.

Following an entire week of clouds and steady rain, the citizens of Paragon City welcomed clear blue skies and hot sun on Monday, July 11, 1932. Temperatures rose all through the morning and, by noon, the official reading taken at Atlas Park was 94°. It was the hottest day of the year so far, according to the weather service, but few complained about the temperature after a week of chilly, rain-swept days.

The Freedom Phalanx assembled at ten minutes before twelve that afternoon. Noon was the time selected by Nemesis for the mayor's surrender, and most offices in the Steel Canyon district had let their employees off early, so no one could blame the companies for injuries resulting from any possible confrontation. Blyde Square was mostly empty, and the streets were quieter than anyone could remember. The governor had promised to send the National Guard to help keep the peace, but had been forced to deploy the men elsewhere in the state that morning to battle a series of mysterious wildfires. A few police officers in riot gear milled at the other end of the park, but much of the force, including Chief Mooney, had called in sick. It was not the department's finest hour.

First to arrive in Steel Canyon was Statesman. He hurtled out of the sky and landed in the middle of Blyde Square. The park—a square filled with grassy knolls and low hills—attracted all the goofballs in town. It was a favorite location for Reds, Socialists, and assorted other fanatics to yell out their complaints about America. They mainly screamed at each other. Today, even they were wise enough to find other venues for their ranting. The park was empty, though some incautious onlookers still gawked at the scene from the offices and storefronts facing it.

Next to arrive, with the sound of a speeding electric train, was Vambrace. He zipped back and forth in the air, making sudden stops and reversals, before slowly sinking to a position at Statesman's right.

Third to arrive, only seconds after Vambrace, was Elementar. A clap of thunder announced his presence. He also could fly, but instead of circling Statesman, he flew straight as an arrow at the heroes, pulling away at the last second to land at Statesman's left.

The fourth and fifth members of the team materialized from thin air in front of Statesman. The Dark Watcher wore his usual overcoat, slouch hat, ski mask, and goggles. Standing next to him, holding tightly to one of his hands, was the beautiful young crime fighter known as Maiden Justice. She wore a red and blue costume with high white boots and a domino mask much like Statesman's.

"Nemesis," called Statesman. "The city rejects your offer. Surrender or be destroyed. The choice is yours."

"Nonsense," answered an amplified voice that was so loud it hurt the ears of anyone close to the square. "You are the ones who will be destroyed!"

The sidewalk shook. Streetlamps swayed. A large window in a storefront facing the park shattered, and screams of panic rang out. The Dark Watcher vanished for a second, then reappeared. "Two dead," he declared, his voice shaking. "The jewelry shop window fell on them."

"Elementar," said Statesman. "We need to clear the people away from the buildings facing the park. Now."

Fast as lightning, Elementar flew to the middle of the boulevard. "Get off the streets and away from the windows," he cried. With a dramatic flick of a wrist, he directed a gust of wind to gently push the few remaining onlookers down the street. "Clear the area!" The onlookers did as they were told.

"It's not an earthquake," Maiden Justice told Statesman, back in the park. "This rumble is the sound of automatons on the move."

She pointed to the Southern United Building, half a block away. The pavement in front of the skyscraper was crumbling. Huge chunks of earth and cement burst outward from a widening pit. The road collapsed as a huge claw ripped open the street from one side to the other. Burst mains spewed water high into the air. Immense forms appeared in the water and dust rising from the pit.

"I think Nemesis has opened his bag of tricks," Statesman said.

The automatons emerged from the dust cloud in rows of three. They moved without trouble through the deluge, demonstrating already that Nemesis had learned from his previous battles with the heroes. Their robots' metallic shells were twenty feet in diameter, and edged with a rotating blade like the smaller models Monica had faced in the records office. These hulking brutes stood a little more than four feet off the ground and balanced on six thick, black metallic legs that marched in perfect harmony. A dozen metal stalks rose above each machine's inner rim. Four held mechanical eyes, shielded with armor and shatterproof glass, while the rest carried weapons. In the first trio of automatons, these were flame throwers.

"The robots from the records depository must have been prototypes!" Maiden Justice had to yell to be heard over the din. "These are the real things!"

Marching with mechanical precision, a second row of robots followed the first from the pit. These carried machine guns on their backs instead of flame throwers, and they sprayed bullets in all directions. The windows and facades of the department stores and office buildings facing Blyde Square were quickly reduced to ruins.

"Maiden Justice, I want you and the Dark Watcher to go into the buildings lining Blyde Square and make certain there's no one trapped inside. If you find people, get them out of the buildings or at least to a safe spot in the basement. Vambrace, Elementar, and I will take out these mechanical monsters."

"On our way," said the Dark Watcher. With a whoosh

of air rushing into the place where they had just been, he and Maiden Justice vanished.

"Three of us against all those robots?" said Elementar. "Those aren't very good odds."

"But we aren't alone," said Vambrace. He pointed to a squad of police officers in riot gear. They had raced from the other side of the park to form a line in front of the advancing automatons. They positioned their cars as a makeshift barrier across the street. The roar of their rifles was deafening. But when the smoke cleared, the robots were unharmed. The bullets hadn't even dented their armor.

The missile that struck the robots next, however, did far more damage.

An abandoned car held high over his head, Vambrace dropped from the sky through a barrage of bullets and sizzling gouts of flame. With an ear-splitting crash, the car struck the lead automaton. The thing's legs buckled and it collapsed sideways. As it fell, its spinning blade bit into the legs of the automaton next to it. The second robot teetered, but seemed ready to right itself—until a miniature tornado slammed into it, flipping it all the way over. As the thing struggled on its back, the tornado touched down again, this time slipping into a gap in the armor left by one of the broken legs. The helpless robot bucked and shuddered as the wind tore it apart from the inside.

A figure raced forward, past the line of steadfast policemen in riot gear. He held his arms at his side, his body bent nearly in half. His head was down, but his eyes remained focused on the ground ahead of him. Marcus Cole had learned how to navigate across a battlefield during some of the worst conflicts of the war; it wasn't a skill you ever forgot, and it served him well now. Moving with more-than-human speed, he made it underneath the last of the three lead automatons. Crouching, he tensed his shoulders, then burst upward. Steel screeched and groaned as Statesman slammed into the robot. The impact lifted it high off the ground, and it landed with a metallic shriek atop an automaton in the second wave.

Nemesis had made a major tactical blunder sending his robots out in a dense formation. Stopping a few halted the entire operation. And once they had been stalled, the machines made easy targets for Vambrace's power blasts, Elementar's miniature tornadoes, and Statesman's fists.

Only two civilians died in the initial wave of attacks, thanks to the efforts of the Dark Watcher and Maiden Justice. But the day was far from won. The second act of the battle that would come to be known as Brass Monday was about to begin. There were no overblown threats from Nemesis this time. He had no need to speak. The clacking and whirring of thousands of gears suddenly rang out in Steel Canyon, and that sound promised death and destruction in his stead.

This was a battle Nemesis did not intend to lose.

Neither did the Freedom Phalanx.

CHAPTER THIRTY-NINE

Perhaps the most astonishing law passed in the twentieth century was proposed, seconded, received a unanimous vote from the Paragon City aldermen, and was ratified into action on July 18, 1932. The bill, in simplest form, declared that the words *robot* and *horde* could not be used together in the same sentence. The measure was only aimed at books, magazines, newspapers, and billboards published or exhibited in Paragon City, though it soon became famous throughout the United States. It was repealed several years later, after being found unconstitutional by the Supreme Court. Several of the justices, however, did express sympathy with the bill's purpose. They understood that no one, from the mayor to the most ordinary citizen, wanted to be reminded of the events of Brass Monday.

Exactly how many thirty-foot-tall robots emerged from Nemesis's underground base in the abandoned subway station beneath Steel Canyon was never known. Estimates ranged from seven hundred machines to a high of just over

a thousand. Whatever the number, the second wave of automatons unleashed upon Paragon City that day dwarfed
any threat ever before faced by an American metropolis.

Nemesis's automatons were built for one thing—
destruction—and they excelled at that. Unlike the first robots sent against Paragon's defenders, the second wave
consisted of humanoid creations. They walked slowly,
weighted down by extremely heavy feet that crushed anything in their path. They possessed two arms, each ending
in a three-fingered hand. A modified flame thrower atop
their heads spit fireballs. The purpose of the second muzzle, directly beneath the robot's eyes, remained unclear
until the fight was well under way.

As soon as they emerged onto the streets, the machines
began overturning cars, smashing ambulances, and attacking everyone in sight. A dozen policemen died in the
first moments of the fight, as they tried once more to
stand their ground. That the death toll wasn't five times
worse was a direct result of the incredible efforts of the
Freedom Phalanx.

The team couldn't be everywhere at once, but they
tried. The Dark Watcher teleported from one hot spot to
the other, grabbing cops by their gun belts and whisking
them to safety inside the huge Bloomburg's department
store before they had even realized what was happening.

Vambrace, using the full power of his amazing energy
suit, hurled three robots into office buildings just as they
were about to crush a group of cornered policemen.
"Thanks for the help, but you need to leave now," he
shouted to the cops as he hovered over their heads. "Find
someplace safe and stay there."

Elementar conjured up a thunderstorm high above

Steel Canyon's skyscrapers and called down its lightning. Nemesis's robots were too well insulated to be short circuited, but the weather master directed the bolts at the buildings, and each strike sent brick and cement hurtling down on the robots in deadly avalanches. Crushing them wasn't as satisfactory as ripping them apart with a tornado, but it did the job faster.

Statesman fought the humanoid robots on the ground, using tactics similar to those that worked on the first wave machines. Every time a robot drew near, he grabbed it by one foot and heaved upward with all his strength. Unable to maintain its balance on one leg, the mechanical man toppled onto its back. A few well-placed punches to the robot's head put it out of commission.

The first two machines Statesman battled went down without a fight, but the third proved to be a much more challenging opponent. The confrontation took place directly in front of the Southern United Building. As Statesman closed on the automaton, it launched a twelve-foot span of black chain from the muzzle beneath its eyes. The chain wrapped itself around Statesman. The metal, covered with a mixture of heavy oil and a powerful acid, sizzled like a steam iron against his flesh. Shocked by the sudden pain, he staggered back, struggling to free himself from the metal links. With a roar of sheer determination, Statesman flexed his arms and shattered the chain.

No sooner had Statesman freed himself than he was crushed into the earth by a robot's massive foot. There was a pause, a deathly silence in which, had the automaton been capable of emotions, it might have cheered its seeming victory over the leader of the Freedom Phalanx. That celebration would have been short, though, as a moment later Statesman drove his fists up through the robot's legs and the metal man burst apart.

"Freedom Phalanx," Statesman called in a voice that rose above the tumult, "to me!"

They assembled in less than a minute. The Dark Watcher, his coat stained and tattered, appeared out of nowhere. Elementar came howling down the street, surrounded by a miniature tornado. Vambrace, his energy suit humming with power, dropped out of the sky. And Maiden Justice, carrying a leather-covered book filled with old blueprints, rushed out of the entrance to the building right behind him.

All four alive, all unhurt. Statesman breathed a sigh of relief.

"The black chains," he said quickly. "They're coated with acid. Deadly stuff made by Nemesis."

"I got hit with a chain," said the Dark Watcher, "but I teleported away before the acid could do any real damage. It just ate into my coat."

"That's why I'm inside a tornado," said Elementar. "I use the winds to send the chains flying back at the robots that launch them."

"Those chains aren't our only problem," said Vambrace. "I flew over the pit in the street. There are hundreds of robots marching up the ramps from below. We can't stop a machine army. They'll overrun the entire city. Tens of thousands of people will die."

"Any ideas?" Statesman asked. "Anyone notice if the robots exhibited a particular weakness?"

Precious seconds ticked by as the five members of the Freedom Phalanx tried to think of some detail that would give them the edge in the fight. The answer they sought came from an unexpected source.

"Jimmy's in touch with me on our private radio band-width," said Vambrace. "He says the robots move so slowly because they're too heavily weighted on the bottom."

"I noticed that," said the Dark Watcher. "They hardly lift their feet when they move."

"Jimmy thinks Nemesis made the robots too tall. They're hobbled by the square cubed law," said Vambrace. "They weigh so much it's impossible for them to climb over obstacles."

"The buildings in this part of town are a hundred feet or higher," said Statesman. "That makes them impassable. If we can seal off some of the streets quickly, the majority of the robots will be trapped in Steel Canyon. That would give us plenty of time to smash them to pieces, one after another."

"That sounds like a plan of action," said the Dark Watcher. "But how can we close off the streets?"

"Don't worry, we'll do it," said Statesman. He turned to Maiden Justice. "Did you find the records?"

She held up the blueprint book. "Right here," she said. "They're more complete than the ones at City Hall. I think I can find my way down through the basement to Nemesis's lair. Maybe I can find a way to disable all the robots at once down there."

"Be careful," said Statesman as Maiden Justice turned back toward the Southern United offices. "That goes for all of us."

The battle of Steel Canyon was a death struggle that every man, woman, and child in Paragon City followed on the radio, listening to live broadcasts telecast by all of the great city's news networks. Two newscasters, trying to get close to the action, died during the fight, bringing home the intensity of the battle. Their stories made it clear that, should the robots succeed in battling past the crime fighters, no one in the entire metropolis would be safe. Thousands in the city fled, most by automobile, but many others by foot. The major streets leading out of Paragon were choked with traffic, and at least fifty accidents were blamed on the panic. Fortunately, because of the huge traffic snarls on the roads, most cars were traveling under twenty miles an hour when the collisions took place and there were no fatalities.

Back in Steel Canyon, each hero set to work constructing barriers to prevent the automatons from spreading beyond the maze of tall buildings. The Dark Watcher applied one-time heavyweight champion Bob Fitzsimmon's famous remark, "The bigger they are, the farther they have to fall," in creating his wall. Selecting the two nearest robots—a pair being the most he could teleport with any accuracy—Watcher sent the machines three hundred feet above the spot he wanted to create his barrier and let them drop. They crashed with enough impact to smash every circuit, joint, and vacuum tube in their bodies and once they hit the street, they remained in place. The street was narrow enough that the robots behind the blockage had trouble turning around, making them easy targets. After ten minutes of smashing the metal monsters one atop another, the Dark Watcher had constructed a steel barrier fifty feet high and impossible to displace. He then set to work on the next street over, and the next, and the next.

Vambrace gathered up cars and other easily moveable debris, then piled it high and pounded it into a solid mass using his powerful punch. He quickly discovered that bricks and concrete tended to explode when struck this way, so he focused his attention on metal objects. Once the automatons had been slowed by the initial barricade, Vambrace added more than one of their ruined shells to the walls he built, just as the Dark Watcher had done elsewhere in Steel Canyon.

Elementar let the weather do his talking. The weather master called up a tornado that spread from one side of the street to the other, then directed it toward the oncoming robot army. Any machine that got within fifteen feet of the vortex was ripped to pieces. Elementar then commanded the tornado to deposit the wreckage as barricades. Working on his own, the weather master destroyed nearly half the automatons and blocked many of the streets by which the others might have escaped.

Statesman flew to the Southern United construction site. Using his flying speed and his indestructible body, he drilled a hundred holes through concrete, brick, and steel, causing the building's unfinished upper floors to collapse onto the street two hundred feet below. Those few robots that had already made it past the landslide, Statesman smashed into scrap with a girder.

The destruction was vast, but the value of lives saved by the heroes' quick actions was incalculable. The robots were trapped. Hundreds of steel giants marched back and forth searching for a way out of the prison the heroes had created, but there was no escape. Slowly but relentlessly, the four most powerful members of the Freedom Phalanx destroyed every one of Nemesis's automatons. Not one was spared, though the heads of several were saved so they could be examined and studied by scientists throughout the United States.

As the battle raged in the street, Maiden Justice made

good use of her time. The book she had recovered from the SUI skyscraper contained the building's blueprints. From those she located a tunnel in the basement that connected the structure with an underground subway parts warehouse two hundred yards north. According to the records she'd seen at City Hall before the robots attacked, the storage area had originally been planned as a staging ground to bring fresh food and drink into Steel Canyon without having to navigate the aboveground traffic. Similar tunnels had worked wonders for sections of New York and Chicago. Unfortunately, a minor earthquake in 1914 convinced the city planners to shut down that section of the subway and the old station had been converted into a warehouse for used train parts. Maiden Justice felt quite certain that the area housed something far more sinister these days.

Cautiously Maiden Justice inched her way down the old tunnel. The passageway was remarkably well maintained for a route closed twenty years ago. There were even electric lights in the walls, and the bulbs, all on, appeared new. Step by step, she descended, trying to remain as quiet as humanly possible.

She didn't have to worry. The tunnel ended in an underground train yard. The place stank of machine oil, and two huge steel ramps led from the station up to the surface. Marching two at a time up those ramps were dozens of robots. They were the last of Nemesis's army and this place was obviously his base.

Across the yard huddled a dilapidated wooden shack. A dim yellow light glowed in the window. Maiden Justice crept closer. As she did, she heard two voices arguing.

"You forgot to take into account the square cubed law," one voice shrieked. "You were so concerned about making them so tall they'd frighten everyone into surrendering you ignored basic engineering principles."

Another voice answered, but his words were nearly incomprehensible. Maiden Justice moved to an ill-made door hanging on cheap metal hinges on the cabin's near side. She pressed one eye to a crack in the wood.

The cabin consisted of a single room, eight feet long by eight feet wide by eight feet high. There was a large glass window in the front, a door on this side, and another door on the opposite side. The room was filled with machinery. On the floor were heaped a hundred different tools, from small calibrators to sledgehammers. There were drawing instruments, T-squares, a stock market ticker, and an abacus, everything scattered without any sense of rhyme or reason. Pinned on the rear wall were diagrams of the giant automatons and the specifications for the crablike robots she'd battled at City Hall.

As interesting as the room was, its inhabitants were even more bizarre. The man who had been yelling at the top of his voice stood a little over five feet tall. He was totally bald, with crystal-blue eyes and a white beard that hung down to cover most of his chest. He had short stumpy legs and short stumpy arms, but his fingers were incredibly long. The man was dressed in a white shirt and black tuxedo pants, neither of which fit him very well. He was the oldest, oddest-looking man Maiden Justice had ever seen.

Facing him was a robot. Its body was the size of an oil drum, four feet high and two feet in diameter. Two black steel legs extended from the bottom of the drum to six five-inch-long metal bars, each sixty degrees apart from the previous. Two chains served as the thing's fingers. It had ten digits total, each one of them ending in a tool. Its head was a circular piece of glass with two bulbs for eyes and a small speaker from which its voice emerged.

"Those heroes are making a mess of our troops," said the white-haired man to the machine. "Should we order a retreat?"

"A retreat?" screeched the machine's sound box. "Never! We didn't spend twenty-five years building to this day to run away!"

"Better that than be captured," said the white-haired man. "We should act while we still have a choice."

It was at that moment Maiden Justice kicked open the door to the cabin. "Too late for that," she said. "You're under arrest."

The robot's eye stalks swiveled around and focused on Maiden Justice. They quivered as if shocked beyond measure.

"Don't blame the stupid machine," howled the robot and smashed its metal body into the door on the opposite wall. The wood gave way, and the automaton vanished into the subway tunnel. Maiden Justice let it go; there was no way she could catch the robot and keep the man in the cabin prisoner.

"Hands up," she commanded.

"Why should I?" the old man said. "You don't even have a gun."

"I don't need a gun," she replied with a wicked smile. "Don't believe me?"

Maiden Justice lashed out at a nearby metal pole. Her empty-handed strike folded it nearly in half. Without another word, the old man slowly raised his hands.

Thirty minutes later, as the rest of the Freedom Phalanx

mopped up the last of the automatons, Maiden Justice walked up the ramp leading from the abandoned substation to the edge of Blyde Square. Following close behind, bound with knots that would have troubled a master contortionist, was the white-haired old man, who Maiden Justice introduced as Gerhardt Eisenstadt, better known to the people of Paragon City as Nemesis.

CHAPTER FORTY

As midnight approached and Brass Monday crept toward its much-welcomed close, Marcus stood on the open-air patio of his penthouse. After the last of the robots had been destroyed, he had spent the next several hours alongside the police and federal agents interrogating Nemesis. The old man had seemed happy to reveal what he knew of crime in the city—those he'd committed and those committed by his rivals. He was particularly pleased to spill the details of the Web's schemes. The murders he attributed to the Stefan's minion made for a long list and included several familiar names, including Ezra Cole and Rudy Richter. It was possible he was lying about everything, even his identity. No recent pictures existed of the Prussian Prince of Automatons, and the doctor the police had examine the old man cast doubt on his actual age, though he also admitted he'd never seen anyone who'd reached one hundred and twenty before. Only time would tell how much of what the prisoner told them was true. Still, Marcus believed what the old man had revealed about the Web, and he was glad to finally have someone confirm his suspicions about the murders. Now he had to decide what to do with the information.

There was, as the old saying went, no rest for the weary.

He considered calling Monica at the Free Press Building. The police had allowed only Statesman to witness the interrogation, so she'd left Steel Canyon by early evening to make certain the paper had all the angles of the story covered. Marcus was glad that she'd not heard Nemesis cursing the Web and its leader—her brother—for trying to frame him for the assassinations. He, at least, could deliver the grim news as gently as possible.

Marcus had just decided to take a cab over to the Free Press Building when the phone in the living room rang. He slipped through the open patio doors, not bothering to turn on the lights. He wondered if it might not be Monica calling him for news. "Hello?"

"Hello, old friend. I believe I have something of yours."

"I'm done playing games with you, Stefan."

"No, you're not. We have one last game to play. Listen to this. . . ."

The next voice on the phone was Monica's. "Don't do what he asks, Marcus. I love you. Don't—" Someone clapped a hand over her mouth, cutting her off.

"Enough of that," Stefan sneered. "If you ever want to see Monica alive again, meet me at our castle site in Perez Park. You remember where that was, I'm sure. And come alone, Marcus. Don't bring any cops, or super-powered pals, or stylishly dressed Greek demigods. If anyone else is with you, Monica dies. I'll see you in, let's say, *one hour*?"

Before Marcus could say another word, Stefan hung up.

"You will need our help," said a familiar voice from the darkness.

Marcus switched on a table lamp to find the three sisters standing there. They were dressed in pure white togas, their hair tied in a knot atop their heads, three dabs of crimson on their cheeks and foreheads. Phoebe held a wine bottle and a single wineglass.

"You will need something to drink," she said, setting the wine bottle and glass on the coffee table in front of Marcus. "This bottle comes from our finest harvest, over a thousand years ago. It will cure you of your exhaustion. You will need all your strength to finally confront the murderer of your brother and stepfather."

Marcus poured himself a glass and drank. Though it was perhaps the finest wine ever produced in the world, he hardly tasted it. "You knew," said Marcus. "The three of you knew the truth about the murders all along."

"Of course we did," said Phoebe. "We are the Erinyes, the Angry Ones. We are the protectors of the state, of the natural order. Our sacred duty is to pursue the murderers of fathers and brothers." For an instant, her face was a white mask of unimaginable horror, her hair a nest of hissing bloodred snakes. Then, her features returned to the typical beauty.

"On Kythria, you and Stefan ate our food, drank our wine," Alexis said. "That act bound you to us. When Stefan ordered the killings of Ezra and Rudy, he violated our trust and we felt it."

"Did he actually kill them himself?" Marcus asked.

"No," said Megan. "It was Chief Mooney who carried out Stefan's orders and committed the crimes. But he is already dead, a suicide."

"That night when you brought Mooney here—you told me I might one day wish you had exacted revenge."

"And do you wish that?" Phoebe asked.

"Do you regret turning aside our anger?" said Megan.

"Will you put aside justice for vengeance?" said Alexis.

Marcus paused before answering. He felt the anger burning within him, heard its siren call for destruction. With the power he now possessed, no one could stop him from having, at long last, his revenge. And that, he knew, was precisely the reason he should not seek it.

"I haven't changed my mind," he said after a time. "I want justice, not retribution."

"Then you are, at last, a true agent of Order, Marcus Cole," the sisters said in unison.

Alexis stepped close to him and, with a bloody fingertip, painted a red mark on his right cheek. "You fight for family."

"You fight for honor," said Phoebe, marking a red spot on his left cheek.

"Most of all," said Megan, dragging her bloody thumb across his forehead, "you fight for justice. You will not fail."

Marcus nodded. "Summon the Dark Watcher, but stay hidden. Once the fight begins, have him teleport Monica to safety. I'll do the rest."

The three Furies vanished. A second later, so did Marcus Cole.

Statesman stood atop a small hill near the center of Perez Park. When he and Stefan were kids, they used to build snow castles there in the winter and defend them from all comers. Over the course of three years, their castles had never been overrun. It was a record that children in Paragon City were still trying to break. Marcus could almost hear the laughter he shared with Stefan as he called into the summer night, "I'm here. Stop hiding behind your sister's skirt and show yourself."

Stefan stepped out of the trees that surrounded the clearing. In the bright moonlight, he was a portrait of sheer malevolence. His entire body seemed to have expanded. His arms, his legs, his torso had grown larger, much more powerful. His muscles rippled with tremendous power. Beneath his flowing black cape something shifted on his back. He wore a black mask that covered the top half of his face, but his eyes glared with a blood-red hatred.

"An appropriate place for our last meeting, don't you think? Our friendship began in Paragon City, and now it ends in Paragon City."

"Where's Monica?"

"My assistant, Rocco, who you might remember from Paris, has her safe a short distance from here. She's alive, as I promised. But not for long. Once I'm done with you, I'm going to watch Rocco break every bone in her body. He's very through at those sorts of tasks."

Statesman leapt forward, hands clenched into fists, and attacked Stefan with all the power he'd gained from the fountain and the box.

Over the years, the two friends had boxed hundreds of matches, but always for fun or for training. This fight was to the finish. Marcus lead with a right to the stomach, then followed with a left to the jaw, a right to the head, and another right to the stomach. Crowding in close, he pounded Stefan with one fist after another. The big man retreated, trying to bring his massive arms and fists into play, but Statesman stayed too close. He wouldn't let Stefan step far enough away to defend himself or strike back.

Marcus smashed Stefan in the abdomen with three hard punches in a row, causing the big man to stagger. A right shoulder to Stefan's chest, a punch to the stomach. Stefan pounded Statesman's back and shoulders, but did little damage. The hero lashed out with one foot, catching Stefan in the ankle and causing him to stumble. A rain of fists followed, pounding into the big man's chest, until he finally crashed to the ground. Stefan raised his arms, protecting his face. "Stop it, Marcus. I'll have her killed, if you don't."

Statesman stepped back.

Stefan pushed himself up by his elbows into a half-seated position. His clothes were ripped to pieces, his face battered and bruised. Stefan chuckled. "You still need work focusing your anger. You expend all that energy to no good purpose. Besides, I was just taunting you about Monica."

Stefan waved a hand at a dark jumble of trees and underbrush thirty feet away. A flashlight beam flickered, spotlighting Monica. She was chained to a massive oak tree, a gag stuffed in her mouth. Rocco held a gun to her temple. "He's seen enough," said Stefan and the flashlight clicked off.

"I'd never kill her without first making her watch you die," said Stefan, rising to his feet. "Think of it as a small payback for the way she betrayed me by siding with you. I actually felt slightly sorry about having Ezra and my father killed. But their deaths were necessary to lure you back to America to fight Nemesis. I dared not risk fighting that lunatic on my own. I appreciate you bringing him to justice. With his capture, my web is complete."

"Not yours," said Statesman. "The web of *Arachnos*. You're just a flunky for those fascist megalomaniacs."

"They think so," said Stefan. "But they're wrong, just as you were wrong when you assumed I would remain your stooge forever. Given time, Arachnos will be mine. First we'll control Italy, then the rest of Europe, then America. Crime, corruption, and greed make powerful weapons. With them I can rule the world."

"Not for as long as I'm alive."

"My thoughts exactly," said Stefan as he slowly raised his arms into the air. Then raised another pair, and another, and another.

"The water from the Fountain of Zeus gave you power greater than any man," said Stefan. "Those same waters transformed me, too. But I controlled that change. My thoughts harnessed that power, wielded it, and ultimately used it to reshape my body into a living weapon. I made myself into a being greater than any god, a being of supreme power. Stefan Richter is no more! I am *Lord Recluse*!"

Statesman retreated a step in shock. The horror beneath the cloak was finally revealed. Stefan had evolved into a monstrous hybrid of man and spider—a brute with eight gigantic arachnid legs that emerged from his back. The limbs were sheathed with curved, razor-edged blades that narrowed at the ends to stiletto points.

"Let's get down to business, shall we?" said Lord Recluse, taking a step toward Marcus.

Statesman swung a punch at Stefan's face, only to have his fist blocked by two spider legs. At the same instant, another pair of limbs lashed at his chest, one missing, but the other connecting with incredible force. Astoundingly, the blade drew blood.

"Proto-metal," Stefan crowed. "It can cut even your skin, hero."

A pair of spider legs slashed Statesman's left arm, even as Stefan's human hands pummeled him with blow after blow.

Marcus felt as if he were fighting four men, with all four able to strike at the same moment and coordinate each blow. It was an impossible matchup and one that Statesman was doomed to lose.

In a desperate bid to end to the fight, the hero invested all his power into a single blow. Two spider limbs intercepted the strike, the flats of their blades forming a shield. Marcus felt the impact of his fist on the strange metal shudder up his arm. In that instant, Stefan clamped his hands down on Marcus's shoulders and raised all eight of his spider limbs to strike.

"My moment of triumph," Lord Recluse declared—and then shrieked in fury. Statesman had vanished.

Stefan scanned the clearing and found Statesman standing a dozen yards away, surrounded now by the rest of the Freedom Phalanx. Nearby, the three sisters were freeing Monica from the chains. There was no sign of Rocco.

"Thanks, Watcher," Marcus said.

"No problem," the dark-garbed figure said. "We're a team, right? Want me to send him off to join his friend in jail?"

"Feel free to try," Lord Recluse sneered. "But I control my own fate."

The Dark Watcher concentrated. "I—I can't seem to teleport him. Something is shielding him from my powers."

Stefan rolled back the heavy sleeve from his right wrist,

revealing a thick bracelet dotted with dials and blinking lights. "You sort always underestimate the power of technology," he said, then pushed a button on the gadget.

Statesman and Vambrace raced forward, but by the time they reached Stefan, he was nothing but a ghostly image, a transparent outline. "The field is yours, Marcus," he said, his voice distant and hollow. "For now."

A brilliant flash of light pulsed through the night, and Lord Recluse was gone.

"That bracelet gadget is my first target next time I see him," Elementar said. "If he's foolish enough to show himself in Paragon again, that is."

"He'll be back," Statesman said. "But we have a lot of work to do, even if he stays away."

"The Web's agents are all over the city," Monica said. "It could take years to uncover them all."

"Not at all," said Marcus. "Nemesis told the police that he's been using listening devices planted all over the city to compile a list of everyone working for Lord Recluse. He's going to turn over everything to the authorities. With that information in hand, it shouldn't take very long at all to break up the Web."

"How ironic," said Phoebe.

"Stefan and Nemesis were each responsible for the destruction of the other's organization," said Alexis.

"Sometimes justice works in mysterious ways," concluded Megan.

And the members of the Freedom Phalanx had to admit she was right.

CHAPTER FORTY-ONE

Though the Freedom Phalanx hunted for Stefan Richter for months after the battle in Perez Park, they could find no trace of him anywhere. But while Lord Recluse was gone, his minions and agents remained spread across the city. The city and the federal government cooperated on a series of raids, which netted hundreds of criminals. The Bureau of Investigation prosecuted the cases and used the publicity to push for tighter laws against foreign spies in the United States. A number of bills were drafted, but they languished in the House of Representatives for months. The most repeated question asked of those proposals by the isolationists in Congress was "why bother?" The answer came on December 7, 1941 at Pearl Harbor.

Still, with Nemesis in jail and Recluse in hiding, Marcus and Monica saw no reason to delay their wedding plans. They set a date in August and sent out invitations. Then things got busy.

There was a meal to plan, a cake to order, and criminal gangs to fight. With the Web no longer in charge of criminal activities, the various crime lords of Paragon City regained their positions of power. After months of relative quiet on the streets, violence returned as new gangs and old waged turf wars for control of the city's most prized neighborhoods. The Freedom Phalanx, who had thought they'd earned a break, discovered the first law of criminal enterprise: crime never sleeps. Less than a month after the fall of Nemesis and the Web, the heroes were back to battling crime on street corners and dark alleys.

On August 7, 1932, Statesman made a speech on the steps of City Hall. His hopeful words about the city's future became a rallying cry that the newspapers and radio stations played up for months afterward. Many people regarded Statesman's speech that day as the beginning of the reform movement that would, within the next few years, sweep the city clean of corrupt politicians for the first time in five decades.

Speaking to a much smaller audience the next day, a tearful Monica Richter told her future husband that unless drastic measures were taken immediately to get the wedding plans moving, the ceremony was not going to take place on the date announced. Demonstrating the same organizational skills that had made him so useful on the battlefield, Marcus did what every intelligent leader since the time of Julius Caesar had done—delegate authority.

Marcus called upon everyone he knew in the city to help arrange the wedding, and gave them whatever funds they needed to make things happen. Money might not buy happiness, but it worked miracles for staging weddings.

While Marcus and the Freedom Phalanx battled the Kings in one brutal battle after another during the first weeks of August, Jennifer Nayland and Lucy Wilcox fought equally tough skirmishes with floral arrangers, musicians, and dress designers. The day Statesmen punched Albert "the Alligator" Quade halfway across Atlas Park, Jack Spreadbury signed Monica's favorite orchestra, the Benny Carter All Star Swing Band, to play at the wedding. And, the day the Dark Watcher broke up a riot at Independence Port by conjuring up a vision of a giant sea kraken, Chef Mattieu Rochenard agreed to create the finest dinner of his entire life for the celebration. One way or another, things got done. Life went on.

Monica Richter and Marcus Cole were married in a simple ceremony conducted by a justice of the peace on August 29, 1932, at the rooftop restaurant known as the Three Sisters, high above Paragon City. Serving as maid of honor for the bride was her best friend and rival newspaper reporter, Jennifer Nayland. The best man was an army buddy of the groom by the name of Alan Gleason, who had come all the way from Europe with a few other old friends to attend the service. The weather, which only the night before had been forecast as cloudy with thunderstorms, was perfect. A group of about a hundred people celebrated the wonderful occasion with dinner and dancing at the Three Sisters after the service. Though the food was magnificent, one of the best meals ever served in Paragon City, hardly anyone commented on its fine quality. The wine got everyone's attention. Even Chef Rochenard, usually the biggest booster of his fine creations, found himself engaged in a long conversation with the strange sisters on how he might obtain some more bot-tles. Since the success of the restaurant depended on the quality of food served there, the sisters were willing to import a reasonable amount to the States for Rochenard's private use.

The debate, which continued most of the night, focused primarily on the definition of the word *reasonable*.

Jennifer caught Monica's bridal bouquet, but she was surrounded by so many handsome young men she found herself totally confused about which one to dance with first. Marcus's three friends from Europe—Alan Gleason, Sid Sawyer, and Riley Shaw—were fascinating figures in their own right. Gleason was somewhat darker, a more dangerous figure, while Sawyer was a wit with a dry sense of humor, and Shaw was a man who got things done and didn't let anything stand in his path. Three dream dates, and Jennifer only had time to spend with one. And that said nothing about the somewhat younger, but quite handsome fellow, Brandon Warfield, whose name she vaguely remembered from a story she'd covered some time back. What was a single girl to do?

Separated from his bride for a few minutes while she talked to her newspaper staff, Marcus wandered through the restaurant making sure everyone was having a good time. He wasn't the least surprised to see that the surviving members of the Cole gang fitting right in with the Freedom Phalanx. In so many ways, these men were so similar. And yet so different.

Gleason, Sawyer, and the rest were good men, but they were focused on themselves, not the world around them. They had been criminals because it was the easiest and quickest way for them to get what they wanted. It was a philosophy that Marcus had once embraced, but had long since abandoned. All men were created equal and all men deserved equal opportunities. Anything else would be criminal. Which was why Marcus was glad to see his old friends, but also glad to know they were returning to Europe in a few days. Old habits died hard and Marcus

Cole knew for a fact that Statesman had no desire to arrest any members of the once-famous Cole gang.

The most memorable moment of the evening, other than the exchange of vows, came at its end, when all the guests had departed and Monica and Marcus were relaxing at the head table, discussing matters of the heart. As was oft their style, the three sisters appeared suddenly before them, Phoebe, the eldest, carrying a gift.

"As is the custom in this new land, as it was the tradition in our home, we bring a gift for the bride on this happy day," said the trio in unison. Phoebe presented the small, neatly wrapped package to Monica, and the three strange sisters smiled.

"I thought you said you were only going to observe what I did and never interfere?" said Marcus, not entirely sure he wanted Monica to unwrap the Furies' present.

"That's true," said Alexis.

"But we said that only about you," said Megan.

"Not your bride," said Phoebe. "The gift is for the bride, not the groom."

"I'm sure it's nothing to worry about," said Monica, laughing. She pulled off the wrapping paper to reveal a slender leather belt, with decorations of woven silver and gold. "How beautiful! It's stunning."

"The Girdle of Hera," said Megan. "Wearing it gives the user the powers of the goddess."

"May you use it wisely," said Phoebe.

"And pass it on to those who will use it equally so," said Alexis. "For one day you will be so blessed."

"I always wanted a girl," said Monica. "How perfect." Marcus actually blushed.

The three Furies said nothing. They merely smiled.

EPILOGUE

After the last of the wedding guests departed, Marcus and Monica stood alone on the penthouse balcony, watching the sunrise. Tomorrow afternoon they were off on a short honeymoon to Niagara Falls. Not too far away to return to Paragon City if some new terrifying criminal mastermind threatened, but far enough that they might also escape some of the less exotic demands on their attention.

As they sat on the terrace, looking out on the cityscape, comfortable and supremely happy in each other's presence, Monica spoke.

"When I put the front page of the newspaper together on Wednesday night, I noticed something. A lot of the news around Paragon is actually good these days."

"Of course," began Marcus. "Because—"

"Shhhh," said Monica, putting a finger on his lips. "Let me say it."

Her eyes glowed as she continued to speak. "Things are getting better because attitudes are changing. The people of Paragon City have heroes again. They've learned that there are good, honest, heroic people out there willing to fight for what's right. They've seen what one determined person can do to change the world for the better and they're getting excited."

Monica rose to her feet. "Did you know that a new political party has formed in the city? They're calling themselves the Reform Ticket. They're going to run a full slate of candidates in the next election. The people of Paragon City will have a chance to rise up and take back their city. It's a miracle, and you made it happen."

Marcus was standing now, too, and he took Monica in his arms. "Not me alone, but you and Vambrace and Elementar and the Dark Watcher. And those police officers who stood with us in Steel Canyon. Working together, we all made it happen. For too long, this was a city of lost dreams, a city of crime. Now, it has the chance to be something marvelous, something never seen before in history. Paragon City might one day become a city of heroes."

a sample from the
upcoming *City of Heroes*™
novel

THE FREEDOM
PHALANX

by Robin D. Laws

in bookstores April 2006

Ray and Steve stepped across crumbling curbs on their way to the rendezvous point.

"I dunno, man," said Steven Berry. "I zoomed down there this morning to take another look at the guy. I think you might wanna go with Plan B. You know—the one where you're encased in armor?" He'd adopted his usual look of slapped-together, ageless cool: suede jacket, plain red T-shirt, clean sneakers, and a crisply fitting pair of comfortably aged jeans. Nothing about him—especially not his skull-hugging, chestnut hair—said it was 1986. It was classic all the way for Steve. The style of not having a style. His fashion goal was to never have to cringe when he saw himself in an old photo. Okay, that was goal number two. Second only to impressing the ladies.

His best bud, Doctor Raymond Keyes, was the same age as him: twenty-seven. They'd grown up together. Been roommates in college. Shared a house together even now, right down the block at 266 Rhine Street, right in the heart of Fultonhurst.

Ray was one heck of a brilliant guy, but in some areas—outward presentation, for example—he still required remedial assistance. Steve's project for the year was bringing him up to code in that department. Ray was trying but hadn't entirely mastered the big picture. He had a T-shirt on, stain-free and everything. It showed off the benefits, physique-wise, of all the working out he'd been doing in the months since the craziness went down. But that computer company logo bannered across the chest—that cost him major coolness points. Then there were the plaid, pleated pants, which were a couple years out of date and had, in Steve's opinion, been goofy even when they were current. Ray's athletic shoes were way past their prime, worn down to the nubs. He kept promising to pick up some new stuff, but the lab always beckoned. It was like he was determined to remain a lousy wingman. Which was a shame, because there was a good-looking guy mere inches beneath the surface. With a little scrubbing and a tad more attention to detail, the good doctor could be a chick magnet second only to Steve himself.

Today, though, it was not Ray's entirely correctable deficiencies in the romance department that had Steve worried. The dude was about to get his jaw busted open.

"Humor me," Steve said, "and explain to me one more time why you want to do this without the armor. . . ."

"Look at this street. This used to be quite a beautiful neighborhood."

Steve knew this stretch of Rhine Street like he'd been raised here, but he followed Ray's pointing finger anyhow.

A mailbox lay like a mugging victim in the middle of the westbound lane. Newspapers took grudging flight in a gust of wind and rattled along the pavement. Corner boys sulked on the stoop of a condemned brownstone. Poor old Ricky Nakano did the junkie shuffle past shuttered retail shops, his skin spotted with the abscesses and blemishes of his habit. He held out a jittering palm to panhandle from nonexistent passersby. The bang of nail on wood echoed through the morning air; across the street, Mr. Ho was boarding up the windows of his bodega.

Ray answered the question. "It's a risk-reward thing. Okay, so this way I'm personally in a little more danger. The upside of that is, if it works, folks can look out the window and see people like themselves standing up to the punks who've ruined their neighborhood. It's possible that one tiny incident is all we need to kick start an honest-to-gosh grassroots movement to take back the city."

"Yeah, but is it probable?"

"Don't you think it's preferable if the change comes from the bottom up?"

"I think it's preferable, Ray, if your skull stays unbroken."

"If my hypothesis turns out to be wrong, don't worry about me. Just make sure nobody else gets hurt."

"Then what?"

"Then we lick our wounds and move on to the next theory. That's the scientific method, Steve. You keep getting it wrong until finally you get it right. C'mon," he said, charting a diagonal course straight for Ricky Nakano. He reached into his pocket for the fold of dollar bills he kept on hand as his charity slush fund.

Steve was undecided on whether his friend's kindness was really helping anybody. He zipped up his jacket as a gust of cold October air rolled in from Paragon Bay.

Ricky's dull eyes brightened when he saw Ray coming. He slapped Ray happily on the shoulder.

"You beefing up, bro," Ricky told Ray.

Steve hung back. His sense of heroism did not extend to braving the smell of a streeter like Nakano.

"I'm on a regimen," Ray replied. Ricky's gaze was glued to the bills in Ray's hand, but Ray was withholding them. Before the donation would come the brief sermon. "Taking better care of myself lately. You should be, too."

Ricky's attitude took a hairpin turn toward the mournful. "Ain't that the truth. But there's no getting around the temptations of the day, Doctor Ray. The temptations of the day. And the terrors of the night."

"Have you been going to your meetings?" Ray gently interrogated.

Ricky hopped guiltily in place. "I have not. I have not been going to meetings. I understand I should, but you know there's sometimes that gap between understanding and doing."

"You know the advantage of those meetings, right? It's being part of a group. Pooling your willpower."

Ricky showed his agreement with a vigorous round of nodding. "Truer words weren't never spoke."

"So let me make you a deal, okay?"

Ricky followed the money in Ray's hand like a cat checking the progress of a toy on a string. "I'm always ready to make a deal," said Ricky.

"I give you some cash for tonight, and you do what you feel you gotta. But tomorrow, Ricky, you promise me you'll spend at least five minutes thinking—seriously thinking—about getting back to that meeting. Rejoin the community."

Ricky's open palm trembled for the dollar bills. "I promise, Doctor Ray. You are so right. Pooling group willpower."

Ray dropped a few dollars into Ricky's hand and closed his fingers over them. Ricky turned to bow out his gratitude even as he scampered up to the stoop to transact with the corner boys.

Steve shook his head. "He's not going to any meeting."

"Five minutes ago, there was no chance. Now, there's a non-zero chance."

To make up the lost minutes, they walked briskly past Rhine Street's closed shops and diners. Together the stores showed a history of the neighborhood, and of the city. For over a hundred years, Fultonhurst had served as the first point of arrival for Paragon City's immigrants. Each community that came here left traces that lingered, even after they grew prosperous and moved elsewhere, out to the 'burbs or into the condos of the Skyway district. Every group that left was replaced by another, but a store or two stayed behind, like a marker. Over one threshold Hebrew letters announced the former location of a dairy. Next door, the remains of an Italian produce shop. Across the way, a Portuguese restaurant, shut just three months ago. Beside it, a Chinese takeout, then a Jamaican patty shop, then an empanada counter. Then you came to the tree-rings of the neighborhood's doomed stab at gentrification: a brief row of chichi bistros, their once-enticing menu cards fading under glass.

Steve paused longingly before the list of entrees from

the Giorni Grill. A plywood sheet took the place of the restaurant's shattered front window. "Man, I remember that bucatini."

"You remember having that bucatini with Andrea Asher," said Ray.

"That I do. I never shoulda lost touch with her."

"Didn't she send you a wedding invite last year?"

"Yeah, what I said."

Up ahead, Mr. Ho hammered the final nail into the hoarding around his bodega. He stood back to assess his work.

"I have to say it's a letdown to see you're leaving," said Ray.

Mr. Ho jumped; for an instant, till he recognized Ray, he brandished his hammer at him. He was a portly man. Only a last few vestiges of hair clung to his wide and squarish head. He'd wrapped an apron around his cable-knit sweater and black slacks. "Oh," he said. "You."

"I thought you hadn't made a final decision," said Ray.

"One of Steamroller's punks help me decide," Mr. Ho said. "This morning. He come in, he just take. Fill his arms up with six-packs. I tell him to pay, he shake head and laugh. He say I complain, Steamroller come pay me till I black and blue. Not worth it, Raymond. Not worth it no more."

"Come with us. A whole bunch of us are going. Together."

"You have good heart, but you are extremely crazy." He looked to Steve. "You, Steve, you got more sense. You talk him out of it. And any other poor idiot he drag along with him."

Steve shrugged. "I've been trying, Mr. Ho. Telling him to use this other trick we have up our sleeves."

"You tell him better, because this one, he like my oldest son, Walter. He so smart, he stupid."

"There you go," said Steve. "That's the phrase I was groping for."

"Come on, Mr. Ho," said Ray. "Just wait a week, and you'll see the difference. All of us working together, we can turn this block around. And one little change like that, that's all you need sometimes to catalyze a wider transformation. We can get the whole city back the way it used to be, not so long ago."

"I don't need this, Raymond."

"But Rhine Street needs a bodega. It especially needs you, Mr. Ho. All of Fultonhurst needs people like you."

"My daughter July, she ask me why I stay down here, risking my neck, when I got enough to retire on. When I can move in with her in monster housing development. And even though her husband Young-Min is someone I can't stand, I do it. I get out of here."

They said goodbye to Mr. Ho and hiked glumly down the block.

"You can't expect him to be a hero, Ray."

"I don't. It sucks, though, doesn't it, that just to run a shop in this neighborhood you've got to be a hero?"

"Sure."

"It won't turn around without a catalyst."

"You'll get yourself knocked silly."

"Someone has to put his chin out there."

"What if you get somebody else hurt? How will you feel then?"

"This will work."

"And what's the scientific reasoning behind that one?"

"Because it has to."

They turned the corner onto Sedgwick Avenue and picked up the pace till they reached the hoops court. They strolled through the gate in the chain-link fence, waving to the neighbors gathered on the court's last remaining set of bleachers. Ray hid his disappointment: so far, the turnout was less than a dozen. Something crunched under his foot. He lifted his sneaker's rubberized sole to see the broken glass remnants of a crack vial stuck to it.

Greg Stites, the watch's most vocal member aside from Ray, stepped down from the stands, holding out an open bag of hard candies. Greg, a lean African-American man in his early fifties, served as the super over at the Wareham Building, on nearby Dock Street. He spoke in a preacher's cadence, which he said he'd caught from his father. The lilt elevated even his most ordinary statements: "Care for a humbug, boys?"

Before Ray or Steve could decline, Alvaro Luis, a tool and die man from farther south on Rhine, reached over to intercept a handful of candies. He popped the lot of them into his mouth like pills and let them roll around together.

"Where's Travis?" Ray asked.

Greg shrugged.

"How about Chuck? Or Mr. McElwraith?"

"Seems like it's only us, Doctor Keyes."

No matter how many times he asked, Ray could not get Greg to use his first name, even though the man was old enough to be his dad. He'd given up trying.

"Well then, if someone else shows up, he shows up. Meantime, we go over the approach. All right?"

The men on the bleachers nodded gravely. The bag of candy got passed around.

"First of all, this is a confrontation, but a peaceful one. Last thing we need is to give Steamroller a reason to lay charges on any of us. We keep our shoulders straight, we stay proud, and we speak politely. We demand our neighborhood back. He's a bully. That equals coward."

"He's got one of them super-powered hero names," Alvaro said, his voice slurred by humbugs.

"Super-powered *villain* names," corrected Nathan Schultz. Unlike the mostly older men who made up the watch, he was about the same age as Ray and Steve. A slight man with a high mop of slick, curly hair, Nathan didn't even live in the neighborhood. He was an investor who'd bought into the area during its brief gentrification boom and was prepared to intervene personally on behalf of his real estate portfolio. He was dressed like he'd just come from the office, in a shiny suit jacket, a white-collared pink shirt, and a blue silk power tie. Nathan tugged uncomfortably at the collar, to make like he was one of the guys.

"I'm just sayin'," said Alvaro, "if he's one of them capes, maybe he isn't a coward. Maybe he can back it up." He sucked nervously on his mouthful of candy. "I'm not sayin' we shouldn't go ahead. Maybe after more looking into it, that would be better. Because if he's one of them mutants or androids or whatever, could be he's connected. Part of one of them hero groups."

"*Villain* groups."

"That's what I'm sayin', Nathan. You know, when I was coming up, the good freaks outnumbered the bad freaks. Now it ain't like that."

"There's still Statesman."

Statesman was the city's greatest hero, and had been for nearly fifty years.

Alvaro did not acknowledge Nathan's correction. "I'm not saying we shouldn't be acting like men, or solving our own problems. If it goes wrong, though, it ain't like there's a Freedom Phalanx no more, to fly to our rescue."

The name needed no explanation. The Freedom Phalanx had been the city's preeminent hero organization. It had fizzled out over a decade ago, as most of its founders gradually retired or disappeared. There were other super-powered teams in Paragon City, but no one had ever matched the Phalanx.

Alvaro's clacking candies reached a crescendo. "You know what I heard somebody saying the other week at that Irish joint over on State Street? They say the Phalanx quit and covered up the real reason—which is, they got bought off by the gangs."

Ray jumped in. "That's nothing but conspiracy theory nonsense, Alvaro. Statesman led that group. He'd never sell out. It shows the sad state we've gotten ourselves into around here when a stand-up citizen like you could believe that for a millisecond. So let's not allow our nerves to derail us, okay?"

"What this city needs," interrupted Greg, "is for a man like Statesman to take over. These fools running for mayor now—what's either of them going to do for us? Let Statesman toss them both in the river and start over. Scrub the place clean. String up anyone who's asking for it. I mean it. And don't have no more elections till it's safe again to sleep in our homes without fear of being burgled or having our throats slit in the night."

"Or our kids having to dodge dope slingers every morning on the way to school," agreed Alvaro.

"Wait, wait, wait," said Ray. "A: That's so wrong I don't even know where to start. And, B: This isn't another gab session. Tonight's when we act. Right?"

"Yeah, right."

"Whatever you say, Doctor Keyes."

"So, I'll take point. All of you are my backup. You stand there, strong and silent, like you've been pushed far enough and from here on in, we're back in charge. Don't look like you want to start anything. Just look like if *they* start it, we finish it. Exactly how we went over it the other night."

Nathan decided it was a good time to remove his tie entirely. He stuffed it in his jacket pocket. "You're sure they won't have guns?"

"They probably do but they're not going to use them. Shoot down twelve solid citizens right on their own doorstep? Won't happen, I assure you. That'd bring the entire police department down on them forever. Remember, our fear makes it possible for these lowlifes to exist. We withdraw that from them, and they'll close up shop. It's Criminal Psychology 101."

Ray repeated the main points of his pep talk as the group made its way out of the ball court. They marched onto Sedgwick, then south on Rhine. Gunfire popped in the distance; judging from the volume, it was a small-caliber pistol, at least ten blocks away.

A beat-up Gremlin idled in front of a vacant lot. A young runner sidled up to its open passenger-side window to hand off a clutch of vials in a wrinkled paper bag. The twelve-year-old trafficker was the only kid on the street.

Loud music beckoned from their destination. It was hair metal, cranked to the max. Piercing notes climbed screechingly up the fretwork of a recorded guitar.

"Bad enough our neighborhood is ruined," said the youngest of the watch members, an honor roll student named Omar. "But we got to have white trash gangbangers? That's adding insult to injury."

Steamroller's boys lounged on appropriated furniture in front of a three-story multi-apartment structure. Boards blocked its glassless windows. The place had been condemned since 1982. Before the downturn hit, it had been slated for demolition and replacement by mixed-use condos and retail. Old bullet hits pitted its stone façade. Skateboarders had eroded the steps of its sprawling concrete stoop. Cracked cement slabs covered the small court area inside a low fence of brick and wrought iron. Open bags of trash were heaped against the building wall, their plastic fluttering and snapping in the wind. A burn barrel, blackened and rusted, lay on its side; it housed a haphazardly stacked armory of baseball bats and two-by-fours.

The gangbangers marshaled their vibe of nonchalant menace as the neighborhood watch came near. Eyes swept to the weapons in the burn barrel. Omar's complaint to the contrary, this was a mixed-race crew: black, white, Latino, even Asian. They wore biker gear, with handstitched steamrollers sewn to the backs of their armless denim jackets. If these guys had bikes to match their clothes, they weren't parked anywhere anybody knew about. There were only five of them present. Ray's band of activists outnumbered them by a margin of more than two to one.

A long-limbed hood with iguana tattoos crawling up

his ropy arms appointed himself spokesman. He leaned back in his stolen lawn chair and flashed an array of nicotine-stained teeth. "You is in the wrong location," he drawled.

Ray stepped up. Steve stuck to his right shoulder; the men of the watch formed a V behind him. Ray was stirred by their straight shoulders and proud chins. "We're here to talk to Steamroller."

Iguana Arms widened his grin. "Too bad for you that office hours are not in progress."

Ray leaned over the gate and stuck out his arm, inviting a handshake. "I'm Ray Keyes. What's your name?"

The hood shifted forward, letting the front legs of his lawn chair drop down onto the cement. "Never you mind that."

"Well, Mr. Nevermind, we respectfully request a conversation with your friend Mr. Steamroller. Would one of you like to call him for us, or do we have to be rude and shout?"

The hood's lips moved as he paused to read the writing on Ray's T-shirt. "You can shout all you want, Computer Boy, but I ain't doin' jack—"

A whiskey-snarled voice cut him off. "Hey now, Marco, the boy asked politely."

A fat-bellied man with a fox-colored beard ambled coolly from the building. It was Steamroller. He had a cape name, but he didn't look like a cape. Instead, he was decked out like a roadie for ZZ Top, from his leather jacket to his biker boots, all the way up to the forest of split ends cascading from his chin. He spit a wad of phlegm into the air; most of it came back at him, fouling his beard. His face wrinkled and turned red. He patted down his dampened facial frizz and bounded down the steps. At no more than five-six, Steamroller was surprisingly short. He put himself nose to nose with Ray. "All right, boy. You got something to say to me, say it. Then get your sorry carcasses outta my face."

"My name's Ray. What should I call you, other than Steamroller?"

"You ain't got the right to call me anything, far as I can see."

"I'll get right to it, then. We represent the people of this neighborhood. This is our home. Where we look after our old folks and raise our kids. This used to be a great place, not too long ago."

"Thanks for the history lesson."

"It was bad enough when you guys used the neighborhood as a party zone. Keeping everyone up all night with the non-stop music. When you turned this building into a reeking trash heap, we let that slide, too. That was foolish of us, wasn't it?"

"Never foolish to mind your own damn business, I don't think."

"Well, it looks to us like every inch we give you, you're going to take another. The parties and the vandalism were just the start. Now you're acting as muscle for drug slingers. You've scared away every shopkeeper on the block. You've taken advantage of us, and we let you. We were afraid to call the cops."

Steamroller chortled, inviting a round of guffaws from his buddies. "The cops are afraid to come."

"Maybe we'll have to see about that. We've let you and your friends here run wild. So it's only fair to warn you that we've gotten together, and we're looking for things to change. You want to be good neighbors, take away our reasons to complain—we're fine with that. Otherwise, you'd better move quietly along, the sooner the better. We're serving notice. Every inch we've given you, we're taking back. Rhine Street belongs to us again."

Steamroller huffed tobacco-rancid breath into Ray's face. "And if we pack up and move two blocks over, to that abandoned factory over on Whitham Street?"

"Then I go over to Whitham Street and build up the neighborhood watch over there."

The portly biker performed a mocking gesture, blinking and lovingly stroking his beard, as if caught in a lengthy philosophical rumination. "You know what?"

"No, tell me."

"This is what, Computer Boy." Steamroller's body twitched and jerked. His face bulged. Veins popped along the flabby flesh of his arms. His jeans ripped at the seams. He grew taller. The man's skin, previously pale and flecked with rosaceous, broken capillaries, took on a metallic sheen. His fingers cracked, swelled, and finally fused into flat, hammerlike appendages.

Steamroller swung one of them at Ray. He ducked, but the first was a feint, to position him for a left-hand uppercut. Ray felt himself lifted off the pavement and hurled into the air. He went blind for a moment before he landed on his hands and skidded to the middle of the street.

The men of the neighborhood watch had fled, running to the north and south, whichever seemed closer. Steve had vanished.

Steamroller and his boys strode toward Ray like a lynch mob in a spaghetti Western. Ray tried to stand but his legs refused to cooperate. A crimson slash of a smile opened up inside Steamroller's beard as he raised his gleaming, mutant fist, ready to hammer a final blow down on Ray's head. "You love Rhine Street, don't you?" he asked. "You love it so much, you're about to marry it."

A streak of red and blue came rocketing at Steamroller. It zigzagged right and left, seeming to pick up energy as it flashed down the length of Rhine Street. The air crackled with the sound of sparking electrical energy. A sharp smell suffused the air.

Steamroller barely had time to turn his head in the direction of the red-blue blur before a lightning bolt struck his upraised, metallic fist. A swirling yellow halo wrapped itself around the hammerlike appendage. It whirled around him, leaping from one fist to the other. Steamroller convulsed. Tendrils of smoke wafted from his beard. His head fell backward. His knees bent. He toppled.

Ray rolled, trying feebly to get out of the way before the mutant biker fell on him. The red-blue streak zipped over and slammed into Steamroller's barely conscious frame, altering the trajectory of his fall, bouncing him into the air. The gang leader landed on the wrought iron fence, crumpling it. He slumped there, his features slack, shrinking. He seemed to deflate like a party balloon, his body losing its preternatural mass. The steel hammers on the ends of his arms withered into pink, stubby fingers, their tips and nails stained by nicotine.

Steamroller's crew routed; their breakneck flight made the retreat of the neighborhood watch seem orderly by comparison.

Only the hood with the iguana tattoos was dumb enough to stay and fight. He lunged for the burn barrel full of baseball bats. The streak shot at him, clipping his legs, sending him headfirst into the rusted-out container. The blur of motion darted away, then back. An electrical bolt burst from it, hitting the metal barrel. The barrel shot into the air and, with Iguana Arms still inside, rolled clatteringly down the street.

The streak slowed. It turned in circles, looping around parked cars, skidding diagonally across the roadway. It coalesced into a figure. A lithe, fit man clad in a skintight outfit of red and blue, a silver lattice design across the chest, stood before Ray, one hand outstretched. His chin and mouth were visible; a headpiece dominated by iridescent one-piece shades obscured his face.

A slight smirk pulled at his mouth. "Care for a hand, citizen?" He was doing a voice—a takeoff on the deep, sincere boom of Statesman from the early seventies cartoon.

Ray grabbed Steve's hand and wobbled upright. "Smartass."

Greg, Alvaro, Nathan, Omar, and the other members of the watch emerged from their hiding places behind trashed cars or within the entrances to basement apartments. They whooped and applauded.